DEBRA DIER
LINDA JONES
RUTH RYAN LANGAN
LINDA MADL

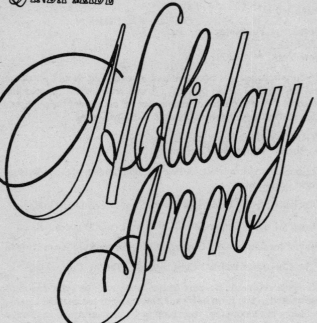

Holiday Inn

LEISURE BOOKS NEW YORK CITY

Grateful acknowledgment is made to Ruth Ryan Langan for her contribution of the background concept for this anthology.

A LEISURE BOOK®

November 1996

Published by

Dorchester Publishing Co., Inc.
276 Fifth Avenue
New York, NY 10001

Printed in the United States of America.

Love's Light

LINDA JONES

For Joanna and Jenny and Chris, three people who do so much to make what I do a pleasure as well as an obsession.

Chapter One

Port Wentworth, New Hampshire—1781

"How does it look?" Alex asked, his voice more anxious than he would have liked. The creaking of the wheels on the bridge sang a different tune from the drone he had become accustomed to. Hour after hour, day after day, the wagon had crept along rutted dirt paths and lately, as they'd neared the coast, the occasional shell road.

"Good," Josh said softly, and Alex could hear the satisfaction in his brother's voice. "Needs a coat of paint, but it's home."

Home. Josh could've been here weeks ago, if he'd ridden a decent horse that could manage narrow and overgrown paths the wagon didn't dare attempt. But he'd insisted on escorting Alex personally.

Alex gripped the seat with one hand, grounding himself. It was the one aspect of blindness that still surprised him, that feeling of always being off balance. That and the lack of darkness. He'd always imagined that the blind lived in the dark, as if they were lost in a cave or shut up in a windowless room, but that wasn't true. At least, not for him. Not since Yorktown.

The wagon left the bridge with a small lurch, and Alex was glad of his grip against the solid wood. Five years they'd been gone, since the winter of '76. He'd thought of home often, of the tavern and the farm, of his mother and father, of little Caroline—who would be fifteen now. Not so little. He'd thought about home so hard sometimes he could almost sympathize with the deserters. Almost.

He'd never expected to come home like this.

The first sound he heard was his mother's squeal, unmistakable in its shrillness. It was a familiar sound, one he and Josh had heard often in their younger years. Happiness, surprise, a touch of sadness. He could hear all that and more in his mother's greeting.

"My babies," she said, her voice softening as the wagon halted.

Alex didn't move, but waited silently as Josh leapt from the wagon and was welcomed by their mother. The reunion only lasted a moment, but as the seconds passed, Alex felt increasingly isolated, utterly alone.

"Here you go," Josh said lightly, taking Alex's hand and helping him from the wagon in a ritual they had mastered during their journey.

"Alexander." He felt his mother's hand, faltering, soft against his face. Her uncertainty didn't last long, and she threw her arms around his waist to hold him as only a mother would dare. Alex could even smile. The top of Sarah Stark's head didn't even come close to his chin, and she was as amply built as she'd been five years ago.

They'd been expected, of course, though the date of their arrival had been indefinite. The physician who'd cared for Alex after Yorktown had tried unsuccessfully to convince him to remain in bed for a few more weeks, to rest his battered skull in the unlikely prospect that his sight would return. It was a hope Alex still held on to, even though that same physician had been skeptical.

"You received my letter?" Alex asked as his mother drew away.

"Yes."

It had been a difficult letter to write, informing the family of his blindness. He hadn't told them that the physician held out a slim hope that his sight, some or all, would return. Offering that false hope to his family seemed too cruel, even as he grasped it himself. But the letter had been necessary. There were some things he couldn't face.

"You told Meghan Campbell I couldn't marry her?"

"I did." Disapproval was clear in her voice. Sarah Stark had never been one to keep her opinions to herself. "But you shouldn't be so hasty—"

"Is she still in Port Wentworth?" A long moment of silence followed Alex's question, a moment when he could hear the roar of the ocean so near.

"The Campbells sailed three weeks ago for Savannah. Jane has family there."

"Will Campbell?"

"Dead these past two years. Jane and the girls tried to run the farm themselves, but it was just too hard."

Alex raised his hand slowly and laid it on his mother's arm. Jane Campbell had been her good friend, a sweet woman who would never be strong enough to run that farm without a man's help. And the girls . . .

Meghan had been seventeen when he'd left, and the other seven Campbell girls were all younger than she.

"Did she sell the farm to Pa?"

"Yes." Her answer was joyless.

"Then there's really no need for me to marry Meghan Campbell after all, is there?"

Silence was his answer, an answer that spoke Sarah Stark's disapproval as surely as another piercing shriek would have. Finally she whispered, "I know you had reservations about the match your father and Will Campbell arranged, but . . . Meghan waited for you all these years."

"And I should reward her vigilance by making her marry a blind man who is useless. An invalid she can attend to for the rest of her life."

"Alexander," his mother admonished lightly, "you can't think that way. Josh's letter said there was a chance—"

"A very small one." He sighed. "I wish he hadn't told you. I don't want—"

They were interrupted by another burst of shouted greetings: Elias Stark's bellow followed by a squeal much like Alex's mother's. Little Caroline, no doubt.

Alex, allowing himself to be caught up in their excitement, gave in to the chaos that surrounded him. Since his injury, order had become his way of life, the only way he could survive. Simple. Quiet. Isolated. It was the only kind of life he could lead, the only way he could have any control.

But for now, he let the chaos wash over him in a wave as strong as the breakers he heard in the distance.

She didn't want to intrude on the homecoming, so she remained seated in the back of the room, in a rather comfortably padded chair placed near the foot of the stairs, her hands clasped in her lap.

Sarah looked as if she might burst, with excitement, with love. There was a son at either elbow, and Sarah held on tight, as if they might try to leave her again. Five years was a very long time.

Caroline all but twittered, jumping around like a cricket, in her own way as excited as her mother. What did Caroline remember of her older brothers? Laughing boys perhaps. Likely not the solemn men who stepped into the tavern and removed their battered cocked hats with near reverence.

Their clothing had seen better days, but it was far from the rags so many soldiers had returned in. Both men wore linen shirts and dark knee breeches and frock coats. There were even silver buckles on their shoes.

Introductions would come soon, she imagined, and the prospect frightened her more than she'd expected it would.

Josh looked around the main room of the tavern, deserted at this time of day, a bright smile creeping across his face, while Alex stood stock-still, as if he were afraid to move, even to breathe. There was tension in his stance, in his stiffened spine, his face and his neck. She could even see the strain in hands he clenched tightly.

"There's someone I'd like you boys to meet," Sarah said, leading Alexander and Joshua Stark to the back of the room, where their visitor waited in the shadows. "Medora Hayden," she said, stopping as Medora stood. "She's been staying with us here at the tavern for several weeks now and expects to remain until after the New Year."

Josh squinted at Medora, opened his mouth, but was silenced by a glare and a pinch from his mother.

"I've heard so much about you both." Oddly

enough, Medora's voice was calm. "Your mother is delighted to have you home at last."

Josh gave her a half grin and a curt bow, but Alex ignored her.

His black hair was pulled into a queue with a plain black ribbon; a strand had escaped and fallen across his cheek. His eyes . . . they were beautiful, even though they stared unseeing past her, through her. So dark a brown they were almost black, they were fringed with long lashes that would have been too feminine on most men. On Alex Stark they were perfect.

"Miss Hayden," Josh said, taking her hand. "What a pleasure to meet you."

Josh had an appeal all his own, but next to Alex he paled. His light brown hair was lackluster, his brown eyes ordinary. His charm annoyingly boyish.

"Welcome home," she said sincerely as she withdrew her hand from Josh's.

She could see the mild confusion on Alex's face. What was he thinking? That an outsider had no business intruding on his homecoming? That the last thing in the world he needed was a strange woman underfoot?

"Welcome home," Medora said again, reaching forward and taking Alex's hand in her own. Her boldness surprised him. His hand jerked just once when she touched it, but then he relaxed and allowed his long fingers to fold over hers.

"Thank you, Miss—"

"Medora," she said softly. "Please. Your family has been so kind to me. And your mother has told me so many wonderful stories, I feel as if I already know you."

Reluctantly, she pulled her hand away from his. She knew Alex had no reason to smile, but perversely she wished he would. A crooked grin like Josh's even or a softening of those perfect lips to hint at a smile. But his face was hard, fixed, remote. What would it take to make Alex Stark smile again? To release the real man from behind the mask?

"I think I'll go to my room," she said, taking a single step backward.

"No," Sarah said quickly. "We'd like you to stay."

"This is a special time for your family, Sarah. Welcome your sons home. I'll be down for dinner," Medora promised, backing up the stairs. "Besides, I need a short nap before dinner. I didn't sleep well last night."

She turned and ran up the stairs before Sarah could protest again.

Alex hated meals most of all. It had been bad enough during the long journey home, with no one but Josh to watch his fumbling, but here just the prospect was torture. His first meal at a table, and the entire family was present to watch him make a fool of himself. The entire family and Medora Hayden.

She was quiet, but he'd been aware of her since she'd entered the private family dining room and taken her seat across from him. He'd listened carefully to the rustle of her gown, eavesdropped as she'd whispered a soft word of greeting to Caroline, who sat beside her. Medora Hayden had a sweet, almost melodious voice that was more intriguing than it should have been.

A plate was set before him, and Josh leaned close. "Corn pudding at the top," Josh said in a low voice. "Sliced beef on your left, a hunk of bread overlapping, and peas to your right."

Peas. Damnation.

"This looks just wonderful." Medora Hayden's

voice was clear, light as a summer breeze. She sounded lovely, if that were possible. Her hand in his as she'd welcomed him home had been soft and small, smooth and warm. "I love peas and corn pudding. When I was a little girl, my mother made them often, and I always mixed them together." Her fork scraped loudly against her plate. "I hope no one minds if I make a mess and stir my peas into the corn pudding. It looks a muddled mash, I know, but it's very tasty."

He guessed what she was doing, but how could she know? How could she understand that he was terrified of lifting a fork to his mouth and finding it empty? Of sprinkling the table and the floor and Josh with tiny round peas he couldn't see? Did she somehow know, or was he just overly anxious?

"I think I'll try it," Caroline said, touching her own fork noisily against her plate.

Soon all he could hear was the scrape of utensils across tin plates, as everyone mixed vegetables together. Even Josh, at his right side.

A week ago, Josh would have had to reach over and stir the peas into the corn pudding for Alex. A month ago, Alex was still being fed like a helpless infant. But he'd been practicing a task that had once been mindlessly easy so he wouldn't come home and humiliate himself.

He mixed the stubborn peas into the corn pudding, careful, grateful, disgraced because he was still certain that this was all, somehow, for his benefit.

The talk turned to the war, to Cornwallis's surrender at Yorktown. Alex let Josh do all the talking. His little brother had always been better at carrying on a conversation than he had anyway, and now Alex was much more comfortable keeping his mouth shut. Since he couldn't see what was going on around him, couldn't tell who had a mouthful of the tough beef, he was cautious about opening his mouth. What if he spoke to his father, only to find that Elias Stark had just quietly left the room? What if he asked Caroline a question and she all but choked on a mouthful of beef in order to answer him?

There had been countless evenings much like this one around the long table. Arguments, heated discussions, laughter. Josh always gestured wildly with his hands when he spoke, punctuating each statement with a wave of his hand or defiantly pointed fingers, and Alex found that he missed the sight of his brother's vehemence more than he'd expected.

Medora said little, but laughed lightly on occasion. The comments she made were soft, asides to Caroline, who responded in kind. Why was he listening so closely for the voice of a woman he didn't know, would never know?

"Alex, what do you think the township should be renamed?" Medora asked, her voice strong and soft.

Alex set his fork aside. Why was he so angry? He recognized the fact that she was speaking to him only out of pity, because he was so terribly isolated even with his family around him. "I didn't know that had been proposed."

"Well, Wentworth *was* New Hampshire's royal governor, and it makes little sense to keep the name. There's a town meeting coming up shortly to discuss it. Your father has said that he might rename the tavern as well."

"Really." It had been Wentworth Tavern for years, since Elias and Sarah Stark had opened their large family home for business. "It's just a name. I don't see that it makes any difference."

"But it does—"

"Let me make myself clear. It doesn't make any difference to *me*."

The silence that followed his statement was complete. Perhaps his answer had been harsh, but, dammit, he didn't need or want some woman with soft hands and a musical voice pitying him, trying to draw him into the conversation out of charity.

"I just thought—" she began again.

"Don't," he interrupted. "I don't care where your thoughts might wander any more than I care if or what they rename this town."

Caroline gasped almost silently. The only other sound in the warm room was the soft clatter of pewter forks being placed against tin plates. No one challenged Alex or defended him.

"Pardon me," Medora finally said, and he was surprised to hear real animosity there as she pushed back her chair and stood. Her gown rustled loudly. "How silly of me to think that a man who would make such sacrifices for his country would have an interest in the changes he helped to facilitate."

She left the room, and Josh immediately tried to make light of the incident.

"Alex, old boy, we're going to have to work on your way with women. If you send them running from the room every time you open your mouth—"

"There's nothing amusing about sending a very sweet woman from the family table in tears," his mother snapped.

He'd heard that bite in her voice many times over the years. Disapproval. Disappointment. Alex could almost feel chagrined. Tears? Had he been that harsh?

"I didn't intend to lambaste the woman," Alex said. "I only want to be left alone."

"Don't be trying that with me, Alexander Stark." His

mother's strong hand was at his shoulder, her voice low but certain.

"Trying what?"

"You'll not be using your injury as an excuse for rudeness, not in this house. I didn't raise you that way, Alexander."

"You're right, of course," he conceded. "I'm sorry."

"Don't apologize to me," she snapped. "Apologize to Medora."

Chapter Two

Alex occupied the stuffed chair at the bottom of the stairs, sitting so still it was as if he were afraid to move. His face was expressionless, his hands steady on the arms of the chair.

Medora wondered if she could really help Alex or if she was simply wasting her time. She'd been so certain before she'd actually had to face him. The blindness she could handle. It was the anger that frightened her.

He'd been home for three days, and she hadn't seen that anger fade. Somehow, he drew into himself, isolated himself even when he was surrounded by his family.

She'd tried, on occasion, to speak to him in passing. A warm greeting, a remark on the weather. Safe comments that required no response but perhaps a nod of the head. Twice he had done just that, nodded briefly and coldly in her direction.

Safe. Perhaps too safe, too guarded. They could go on like this forever, strangers living under the same roof, exchanging nothing more than an occasional safe greeting.

"Good morning, Alex," she said, knowing it was unfair to stand there and watch him without letting him know that she was in the room.

His head turned instinctively in her direction, and he returned her greeting with little enthusiasm. It would have been so easy to leave him there, to allow him to separate himself from the world.

"It's a beautiful day," she said. "Cold, of course, but the sun is shining."

Alex's face was blank, dark and remote. She might have been talking to the chair. It would have been so easy to turn away, to leave him with his misery and wish in her heart for the best. Medora didn't have any faith in even the most heartfelt wishes.

"Would you care to walk with me?" she offered hesitantly. "Just to the beach and back, for a glimpse of the ocean."

"No, thank you. I wouldn't care for a *glimpse* of the ocean this morning."

She took a deep breath and forced herself to stand her ground. "Bad choice of words," she admitted.

He was resolute. His pride was going to keep him in that chair. Medora bit her bottom lip. Maybe pride would get him out of it.

"Of course, if you can't manage . . ." She allowed the sentence to trail off, allowed him to imagine that she thought him incapable of even the smallest tasks.

Alex was hesitant, his silence long enough for her to turn away and disappear. "All right," he finally conceded, standing slowly. Medora's heart skipped a beat. What if she couldn't help him at all? What if her interference only made matters worse?

She helped Alex into his coat and slipped hers on before she opened the door and allowed a blast of cold air into the room.

"I don't recall taking many seaside walks in December even when I could see where I was going," Alex said darkly as Medora took his arm and led him into the sunshine.

She decided to ignore his cheerless remark. "I don't mind the cold, unless it's wet." It was a short walk to the flat rock that looked out over the Atlantic, and Medora held onto Alex's arm as they made the short hike. He turned his face toward the ocean he couldn't see and took a deep breath.

"Shall we sit here?" she suggested, still holding Alex's arm.

"I thought you wanted to walk."

"I'd rather sit and listen to the waves and smell the sea air until I just can't stand the cold any longer."

Alex lowered himself to the flat rock, and Medora sat beside him. As close as she dared.

The waves crashed, savage, as angry as Alex, and the wind that came off the water was like ice. It made sense to settle herself near to her reluctant companion.

"It's all right, you know," he said, his voice not as austere as it had been before.

"What?"

"You can have your glimpse of the ocean, watch the waves even if I cannot."

A cold breeze lifted strands of black hair and blew them across his face. After a long moment, Medora reached up and brushed them away. He turned toward her, toward the uninvited touch.

"I'm told I owe you an apology, for my rude behavior on the evening of my homecoming."

"Don't apologize because your mother asks it of

you. You're entitled to your anger for now."

"For now?"

Medora leaned closer to Alex so that her face was protected from the wind. "You can't live with that kind of anger. Not for long. It will eat away at you, from the inside out. So save your apology until you mean it."

"What are you doing here?"

There were many possible meanings to that simple question. Medora chose to answer safely. "After the first of the year I'll be sailing out of Port Wentworth. I needed a place to stay until then, and your mother offered me a very reasonable rate."

His response was a cynical growl, but he didn't ask her what she was doing sitting so close to him, seeking him out, dragging him from his comfortable chair near the fire.

"What will you do now?" she asked, and he turned away from her so that the cold wind caught him full in the face. She thought for a moment that he wouldn't answer, that he had withdrawn from her completely.

"Josh and I had planned to build a sawmill on the west edge of the property. There will be a real need for lumber in the years to come."

"I'm sure it will be successful," Medora said softly.

Alex turned back to her, and she could see a brief look of pain on his face that quickly faded into hard resolve. His way of protecting himself. "Josh will have to go it alone."

"Why?" she whispered.

This time there was no yielding of his grave expression. "Are you cruel or just stupid?"

"Neither," she answered without hesitation. "I'm . . . I'm an optimist."

"I'm a realist. Josh is my brother and a good man.

He would, without a word of complaint, allow me to spend the rest of my life getting in his way, making his own life difficult. I refuse to do that to him. He's done enough. He deserves better."

"You deserve better," Medora said quickly. "You talk as though your life is over."

"It is."

"No." Medora placed a hand over his forearm, rested it there as if it belonged. "Your life isn't over. It's just . . . changed."

Alex didn't readily accept what she said, nor did he reject it. There was a long span of silence, a passing of minutes when all she could hear was the pounding of the ocean.

When Alex did speak, he managed to surprise her. "What do you look like?"

"Just . . . like any ordinary woman."

"You don't sound ordinary."

Medora smiled softly at the resignation in Alex's voice.

"What color is your hair?" he asked.

Medora took a deep breath. "Brown."

He waited for more, and when she didn't elaborate he asked insistently, "Light? Dark? Curly? Straight?" She could hear his frustration.

"Dark," she said. "Not dark like your black hair, but more of a reddish brown. It's not really curly or straight. When it's down it waves a little, around my face, and tries to turn up at the ends."

"Your eyes."

"Green," Medora answered simply.

Her face was almost frozen with the cold wind that buffeted it, but she didn't mind. Alex's features had softened slightly, and he appeared years younger. Almost smug. His lips relaxed, and the frown lines she'd seen etched on his forehead seemed less severe.

"Dammit, Medora," he swore softly. "Light? Dark? Blue-green? Brownish green?"

"Just an ordinary mossy green with flecks of brown around the outer edge."

It was small, but for the first time since his return, Medora saw Alex smile. It wasn't much, but she wanted more. Needed more.

She took his hand, warmed it for a moment between her own, then placed it against her cheek. After hesitating for a long minute, he lifted his other hand to the opposite cheek. His fingers trailed over her jaw, meeting at her chin and then rose to lightly trace her lips.

"You're cold," he said after his careful and soft examination.

"It's the wind," she answered, whispering against his fingers.

His hands rested against her face, warming her cheeks, protecting her from the cold gusts. He held her, and strong fingers fluttered across her skin. After a few moments, Alex drew his hands away from her almost reluctantly and turned his face toward the ocean again.

"I'm sorry," he said quietly, not turning to her, but lifting his face to the wind. "For treating you badly. For accusing you of cruelty or stupidity. I don't suppose optimism is a character fault or a crime."

Medora leaned in close so that Alex's body blocked most of the chilling wind. "Apology accepted," she whispered.

He heard the commotion—low voices, the whisper of skirts, an occasional thump—just seconds before Medora spoke.

"It's your mother and Caroline," she said softly, naturally, "loading the wagon in rather a hurry."

Alex was at first grateful, and then the frustration he felt so often rose to the surface. There was a beautiful, warm woman on his arm, and she was forced to lead him around, to tell him what was happening around them.

"There you are." His mother's voice was quick, and he could tell that she was anxious about something. What he didn't know was whom she addressed. Him or Medora? "I just got word from Mary Mayfield's boy that she's not doing well. Goodness," she snapped in a more normal, biting tongue. "Since she's having a baby at her age, I suppose problems are to be expected. I told her I'd be there to lend a hand, but she didn't expect the child to arrive until after the New Year."

"We'll take care of things here," Medora said calmly. "You know I will be happy to help if Elias needs me."

"Oh, Alexander," his mother said in a softer tone of voice, a voice that grew closer quickly. She laid a hand on his arm. "I'm sorry to leave now, so soon after your return, but you're in good hands. Caroline and I will be back in time for Christmas, I hope. Goodness, that's little more than a week away. We'll have a feast, just like in the old days. All your favorites."

Whose good hands did she mean? His father's? Josh's? He had a strong notion that his mother spoke of Medora, and that idea set off a warning he couldn't ignore.

Medora had been too eager, too quick to offer comfort. In the past days she'd always been close, taunting him with those gentle movements, that soft voice. Always there. She had known that he needed to touch her face, to feel the smooth skin beneath his fingers. The picture of herself that she had painted at his request had been perfect, providing him a clear image. As if she'd known exactly what he needed. Her knowing what he needed was too easy.

Alex reassured his mother as best he could, sent her on her way with a forced smile and listened to the wagon pull away from the tavern.

"Tell me something, Medora," he said as she led him to the entrance. "Why are you really here?"

"I told you—"

"You gave me a very vague and almost believable explanation for your presence here, and I very nearly fell for it."

Medora was silent, and when they stood inside the tavern, away from the cold wind, she tried to release his arm. He reached out and grabbed her, catching the sleeve of her coat, using that reference to guide his other hand to her wrist. She didn't struggle or attempt to pull away from him.

"Did my mother employ you to be my caretaker?" Alex asked.

"Alex, please, don't be—"

"Are you here to take care of me, Medora?" he whispered.

She didn't answer immediately, but sighed deeply. Resigned. Abandoning her weak protest. "And if I am?"

He turned away from her and took a single step before he banged his thigh against the edge of a table. He swore, loud and long, vile curses no lady should ever hear. When he was silent once again, Medora spoke softly.

"When the letter arrived, your mother cried. Hard and long and loud, the way a mother cries for her child when he's hurt. But you know Sarah. When those tears were gone there were no more."

He heard her movements behind him, the whisper

of every motion as she removed her coat, as she stepped softly across the floor until she stood directly behind him.

"Every night, she prays for you. She prays for a miracle to restore your sight. But Sarah is much too practical to place all her trust in miracles."

"And that's where you come in?" he said, placing both hands on the table before him, fixing himself solidly against the haze that threatened to overcome him.

"If you'll allow it."

"And if I don't?"

"Then after the New Year I shall sail away from Port Wentworth, just as I said I would." She laid a hand on his shoulder, warm and soft.

"How very clever of you," he said darkly, "to pretend to befriend me rather than stating your purpose outright."

"I didn't pretend," she whispered.

Alex turned, easily found Medora and placed his hands on her shoulders. Then he slipped those hands across her back. "How far did you plan to take this scheme?"

"It's no—"

"How far, Medora?" he pressed. "How far were you willing to take this?"

She didn't try to draw away from him. Instead she leaned in closer and lifted her hand to his face as if she were blind herself. "It's not a scheme, Alex." Her body shifted beneath his hands. "I promise you that."

Her whispered breath touched his lips; then she kissed him. Light, sweet, tentative, the kiss was little more than a brush of her lips against his, and it didn't last nearly long enough. Medora stepped out of his arms quietly, and his hands trailed over her back and across her shoulders until they fell away.

Alex hardened himself against the hopes her caress provoked. "You're very dedicated," he said in a low voice. "But you're wasting your time and talents. I don't want or need a nursemaid."

"I'm not a nursemaid, Alex," Medora said, and he heard the rise of anger in her voice. He'd sparked that temper on his first night at home, and she'd left the table in tears, his mother had informed him.

"If you'll show me to my room," he offered, "you'll be free to pack your things. I'm sure there are ships sailing before the New Year."

He waited for Medora to take his arm, to lead him to the small parlor off the main room that his mother had converted into a bedchamber so he wouldn't be forced to attempt the stairs. But she didn't approach.

"The room is arranged quite simply," she said softly. "If you turn to your right, you'll be in the widest space in the room. It continues uninterrupted to the stairs. There are two long tables, benches at both. If you follow the length of this first table, guiding yourself either with your leg against the bench or your hand brushing the table, and turn right again, you'll have but a few steps to your room. I would guess, with the length of your step, five paces will take you to your door."

Her voice remained soft, but the information was delivered in a no-nonsense manner. He had no choice but to follow her instructions.

He turned, his hand against the table, his leg brushing the bench. After a moment he felt sound enough, his feet sure and his hands guiding him safely. At the end of the table he turned, took five steps and found himself at his door.

"Alex?" Medora called as he laid his fingers on the handle.

"Yes?" He didn't turn. He saw no reason to since he

couldn't see her face. God help him, he would never see her face.

"I won't be packing."

Medora closed her eyes when Alex slammed the door; then she reached up to sweep away the damp tears. It was not as if she wept easily. Her tears usually came, unbidden, when her temper got the best of her. Alex could rouse that temper so easily. With a word or two, with a look of resignation, he stirred the anger and frustration she so rarely felt.

She should have known that Alex would question her presence there, would suspect her closeness with the family as well as her interest in him. Perhaps she had hoped that he wouldn't challenge her until later, when she'd already had some time.

The kiss had been a mistake, but she hadn't been able to help herself any more than she'd been able to keep from leading his hands to her face. Deep down, she'd been afraid as she'd pressed her mouth to his. Alex resented her, already, perhaps even hated her. But he'd been so close, and his lips had been so tempting. Had she really thought that he would welcome her touch?

How far are you willing to go? he'd asked. Medora touched one finger to her lips, there where she still tasted him. It was a question she had not yet asked herself, but the answer was clear, immediate. She would go as far as she needed to in order to help Alex.

Chapter Three

Alex lay on the soft bed, his hands behind his head as he listened to the sounds of the activity just outside his door. Laughter, shouts, low voices. Earlier in the evening, Josh had tried to cajole him into making an appearance at the town meeting, into greeting old friends and new ones over New England rum. He wasn't ready for that. There were moments when he was certain he never would be.

He'd spent the last two days since his encounter with Medora in this room. Eating alone at the small table in the corner. Sleeping too long. Battling the headaches and the barrage of stars that teased him, shooting bright beneath his eyelids.

He'd half expected Medora to appear, to try to coax him from his hideaway. To insist that he walk to the ocean or that he learn to feel his way around the large main room of the tavern. Perhaps that wasn't an impossibility. In the past two days he'd become comfortable in this room. He knew where everything was, and he could walk from his bed to the table without tripping, without feeling so completely disoriented that he wanted to fall to his knees.

Could it be the same with the rest of the large house? And perhaps even beyond the comfort and safety of Wentworth Tavern?

Several times since his self-imposed seclusion had begun, he'd found himself listening for Medora's soft step in the main room on the other side of his door. Longing silently, reluctantly, for the sweet sound of her voice. How quickly he had become addicted to the soft and silvery tones.

The crowd was suddenly quiet, the loud voices falling silent, the laughter dying away. A voice, Josh's if Alex were correct, addressed the room, and a murmur followed. So many of the town meetings had been held outside this door. Arguments, an occasional fight, plans for the township's future. Alliances, sometimes easy and often shaky, were formed over mugs of rum and ale.

It had been in that room that Alex had first heard and listened to whispers of rebellion. At twenty, he had effortlessly embraced a cause so right and pure. And now, five years later, he knew too well that anything worth fighting for came at a price. A price that was higher for some than for others.

Had he really fought for a nation's independence only to lose his own? Did he have no strength left within him? Was that why Medora was here—to teach him how to fight again?

A woman like Medora was worth fighting for. Already he knew that she was strong, sweet tempered, brave, soft. Another kiss was worth fighting for. A kiss like hers was enough to make a man forget, for a few precious moments, that his life was over.

Alex sat up slowly and combed his hair back with his fingers as he stood. Then he checked his clothing with his hands as he walked to the door, assuring himself that his shirt was straight, the collar smooth.

One comment Medora had made stuck in his mind, even though in the past two days he'd done his best to forget it. He hadn't been able to, any more than he'd been able to forget the feel of her face in his hands, of her lips against his.

Your life isn't over. It's just changed.

She, more than anyone, seemed to realize just how much his life had changed.

Taking a deep breath, Alex opened the door.

Her trunk was open and half of her belongings were neatly folded and stored. She didn't have much. Several plain gowns, one good one, a nightdress. Twice today she'd begun to pack, changed her mind and emptied the small trunk, and now she had begun again.

She was a fool, had been a fool all along to believe that Alex would allow her to give comfort and aid. A nursemaid, he had called her before he'd ordered her to pack and be on her way.

He hadn't left his room in two days. Josh or Elias had delivered meals, anxious to do whatever Alex asked. She couldn't convince them, as she would have been able to convince Sarah, that Alex didn't need to be coddled. They saw only a blind man, a helpless man. Alex wasn't helpless. She refused to allow it. Just as he refused to allow her into his life.

The room below had become quiet, and Medora was startled when a great shout went up. Someone called Alex's name loudly, and in spite of her heartache she smiled.

Opening the door quietly, Medora crept to the top

of the stairs, standing to the side and in the shadows where she wouldn't be seen. Alex was stepping cautiously into the crowd, one hand lightly brushing a table. He was surrounded by smiling faces, shouted and spoken greetings.

Alex even smiled himself when he was welcomed home by an old friend. Someone pulled out a chair, and with just a brief moment of assistance, Alex was seated among the crowd. Medora smiled when the meeting continued as if it had never been interrupted, Alex at the center of it all, where he belonged.

In the middle of his speech Josh lifted his head, saw Medora there and acknowledged her with a nod so small no one else seemed to notice. Medora backed away and went to her room to finish unpacking.

Medora placed the coin on the table, just a few inches from Alex's hand. "Pick it up," she ordered softly.

"What?" He didn't move at all. Even his face remained stoic, impassive.

"Pick up the coin I just placed on the table."

The main room was deserted this time of morning, except for the two of them. A roaring fire heated the large room, and in the noon hour it would be filled with townspeople seeking that warmth. But for now, she and Alex were alone.

Reluctantly, Alex spread his fingers and slid his hand forward, feeling for the silver coin she had placed there.

"No." Medora picked up the coin. "Listen this time."

She dropped the coin on the table again, in much the same spot as before, and Alex reached out. His fingers came close, and with a minimum of searching he lifted the coin. After just a few tries, his efforts were unerring.

"Very good," Medora said as she put the silver coin aside.

"Yes," Alex said wryly. "Clever Alex."

"You have to learn to use your ears," she said, ignoring his comment. "To locate things and people. It's the only way you'll be able to properly orient yourself. This tavern should be easy. You were raised here, and once you learn to fix yourself in any given room, you will be able to visualize the space around you."

Alex obviously didn't enjoy the morning, grumbling and scowling as Medora passed him object after object and made him identify each. All the while, she walked around the room, making noises, snapping her fingers.

But her strategy worked. He became sharper, his movements more confident. When she spoke he turned his face to her, as if he were watching her. The same stubbornness that had made him try to send her away would make him accept her help—grudgingly—because there would be no worse sentence for Alex Stark than to be helpless.

"Let's take a moment," she suggested, moving to sit across the long table from Alex, "before we continue."

The next step would be more difficult. Actually moving around the room, learning to maneuver between the tables without fault, to find his way to the front entrance or the kitchen door as unerringly as he could now place a soft sigh or the click of a heel against the wooden floor.

"Would you like to tell me what happened? How you were hurt?" The explanation of Alex's injury and the resulting blindness had been brief—a blow to the head during the battle at Yorktown—but Medora wanted to know more. She wanted to know everything.

"Is this part of the treatment?" Alex asked.

"No."

He hesitated, frowning, and Medora regretted the impulsive question. "I don't remember much," he admitted quietly, as if his inability to remember were a fault. "Evidently, my horse was shot out from under me. He went down and threw me quite a distance. I landed on my head."

"What happened after that?" Medora pressed when she realized that Alex intended to tell nothing more.

"It was days before I woke," he said. "Josh had taken me to a nearby house, where a family agreed to put us up until I could travel, and he engaged a physician who had seen this sort of injury before."

"The physician who said there was a chance your sight would return?"

Alex smiled, but his grin was bitter and cold. "I don't anticipate any improvement, nor should anyone else. The odds are small, and the physician made it clear that, with every day that passes with no improvement, I'm less likely to recover even a portion of my sight."

Alex rested one hand on the table, and one finger tapped nervously. Medora had an impulse to reach out and cover his hand with her own, but she didn't. It wasn't time for that, not yet.

"Is it . . . painful?" Medora asked.

"Can we talk about something else?"

Alex waited, perhaps expecting her to apologize for being so impertinent. She had no right to pry, to delve into his mind, but she wanted to know everything. She wanted to be able to fix everything for him.

"Sarah tells me that before the accident you were engaged to be married."

"I have headaches," Alex said without hesitation, obviously preferring the previous unpleasant subject to the new one she introduced.

Medora said nothing, and the silence hung between them like a cloud. A barrier. Did he feel it, too? His face told her nothing. If he would smile, or scowl, she would at least have a clue.

"Her name was Meghan Campbell," he said in a low voice. "She was a very sweet little girl, and the marriage was arranged by our fathers. It was all very medieval, an arrangement to join the Stark property and the Campbell farm."

"So you . . . didn't care for her?"

"I didn't *know* her. Not really. The families threw us together on occasion, but—"

"Was she as antagonistic about the arrangement as you?"

Alex shrugged his shoulders and lifted his hand from the table in a gesture of surrender. "I don't have any idea. Meghan was a quiet girl. I don't know that she ever said more than three words in my presence. I would guess that she was as distressed as I was about the obligation."

"Distressed?"

"No one likes to be told what to do, especially regarding such an important matter. The choice of a wife or a husband should be just that. A choice, not a mandate."

Medora had no answer for that, but her stomach knotted unpleasantly.

"And what about you?" Alex asked, his voice changing, taking on a lighter note as he left the disagreeable discussion of his betrothal behind. "Are you married? Promised? I can't see you, but I know you're beautiful because I've touched your face. Your skin's smooth, and your lips are full." He paused, waiting. "I've shared with you all my secrets, Medora. What are yours?"

"I was engaged once," she said softly. "But the war

changed everything." Her voice quavered, and it was Alex who reached forward, found her hand without groping for it and wrapped his fingers around hers.

"I'm sorry," he said sincerely. "I didn't mean to upset you."

Medora didn't answer, but clasped his hand tightly and closed her eyes.

"Medora?" he said, and she heard a hint of alarm in his voice. "Say something, dammit. I hate the silence."

"Would you like a cup of coffee?" Her voice was calmer, but still not as strong as it should have been. "The next lesson is going to be tough. You'll likely come away this afternoon with a few bruises."

"In a minute," he said softly. He held her hand as if he needed that touch as much as she did. More. He rocked his thumb across the palm of her hand. "I didn't make you cry, did I? Mother will have my hide if I make a habit of upsetting you."

Medora smiled. Alex actually sounded contrite. "No, I'm not crying." She stood and leaned over the rough-hewn table. "See for yourself."

He reached up with his free hand, not even bothering to chastise her for her choice of words. Touching her jaw with the tips of his fingers, he brushed his thumb across her cheek, not once but three times. Even when he was still, his fingers resting against her cheek, he didn't move his hand away from her face immediately.

"Good," he said as his hand dropped away. "I think I'll have that coffee now to fortify myself against your planned torment for the rest of the day."

"I only torment you because—" Medora silenced herself quickly. *Because I love you.* That confession would betray her, and she wasn't ready for that. Not yet. "Because your mother is providing free room and board," she said as she released his hand.

He growled as she left the room, but there was a touch of humor in his irascibility. In the safety of the kitchen, Medora closed her eyes and took a deep breath. She'd been so sure she could do this. Heaven help her, she had no choice.

She filled two tin cups with lukewarm coffee, taking care not to fill them too full. Elias's coffee was strong, bitter, best taken in small doses in any case.

When Josh pushed through the door, she jumped. Until now, she'd managed to avoid being alone with Alex's little brother.

"Alex said you were warming the coffee," he said, and she turned to face a wicked grin.

"There's plenty," she whispered.

Josh leaned against the door, blocking her exit, sighing dramatically. "I've been waiting for an opportunity to speak privately with you . . . Medora." Her name rolled off his tongue. "Or may I call you Meghan when Alex is not around?"

"Hush," she ordered. "He might hear you."

Josh shrugged as if he didn't care. And he probably didn't.

"Medora is my second name," she whispered.

"Meghan Medora Campbell," he answered in a low voice. "What the hell are you doing to my brother?"

"I'm trying to help him."

"Why?" he shot quickly.

"Because I care for him," she answered just as quickly. "I've always cared for Alex, you know that."

The stern expression on his face softened. "Are you going to tell him the truth? Don't you think it's cruel to deceive him this way?"

"I don't have a choice," she whispered.

Josh stepped forward and gripped her arm. Medora

winced at the clasp against her tender skin, and Josh's eyes narrowed.

"What is it?" he asked, taking the mugs of coffee from her and placing them on the table. He returned his hands to her quickly and pushed up the loose sleeves of her gown. The bruises he revealed were not as black as they had been, but a mixture of blue and yellow.

"My God," he whispered. "What happened to you?"

Medora pulled away from him. "It's nothing."

"Nothing?" His lips hardened. "Shall I examine your legs for bruises as well?"

She knew Josh well enough to realize that he did not make idle threats. While the bruises on her legs were healing nicely, they would still be noticeable on close inspection.

"I fell down the stairs," she said.

Josh's eyebrows lifted, and he wagged a finger in her face. "Down the stairs? You could have been killed."

"Well, I wasn't."

"Meghan Medora Campbell," he whispered, a warning in his voice as he demanded more.

Medora sighed, giving in, giving up. "I didn't know what else to do when the letter came telling us what had happened to Alex, demanding that the engagement be broken. It didn't take me long to decide that I wouldn't run away from this, but I didn't know what to do. How could I expect to help Alex if I didn't understand what he was going through?"

"What are you saying?"

"I wore a blindfold for a little more than a week. It didn't come off, not night or day. That's why I knew the peas would be torture, why I knew that Alex would have to stay on the ground floor, at least until he learned to make his way around safely. I learned to move freely around the tavern with only sound and smell and touch to guide me, and I'm not leaving here until Alex can do the same. Until he knows that his life isn't over."

"If you could learn on your own—" Josh began.

Medora passed him and picked up the two mugs of coffee. "The difference is that I knew the blindfold would be coming off, that if I really needed to all I had to do was whisk the cloth away. Alex doesn't have that option."

An uncommonly silent Josh stared after her as she left the kitchen.

Chapter Four

He hadn't thought he'd ever feel this content again. Almost happy. The kitchen was filled with familiar odors: spices and coffee, baking fruit. Fragrant steam filled the room, surrounded him comfortingly. He followed Medora, mentally cataloging her movements as she stirred a sweet-scented batter in his mother's best and biggest earthenware bowl, as she tsked at the gingerbread she pulled from the brick oven that was built into the fireplace.

"Sarah is a much better cook than I am," Medora declared, the anxiety clear in her tired voice.

"She's had more practice than you have."

"Well, I hope she gets home before Christmas. If I have to cook a holiday meal everyone will be disappointed. The girls your mother hired to keep the kitchen running won't work that day, and I'm most certain Elias and Josh can't cook." Her voice grew progressively faster, almost excited.

"Come sit down for a minute." He kicked the chair next to him out just slightly, and after a moment's protest he heard Medora lower herself into the seat with a dejected sigh.

"I burned the gingerbread," she breathed.

"Just a little," he assured her. "If it was truly burnt I think the smell would not be so pleasant."

"But it's not like your mother's," Medora insisted. "Sarah wants this Christmas to be perfect, but if Mary's baby doesn't come, or if she feels she can't leave, she and Caroline won't be here."

"Perhaps you'll have to teach me to cook," Alex said with a smile.

"Are you suggesting that even *you* could cook better than I?" He heard the levity return to her voice. "Now I really am insulted."

"Try me."

She moved, but didn't leave her chair. "What's this?" she said, laying a smooth object in his hand. He closed his fingers around it.

"An egg."

Something heavy slid across the table, and he reached out to touch the rim of a small bowl.

"You know what to do," Medora said calmly.

Alex cracked the egg on the edge of the heavy bowl and carefully broke it open. When he had laid the shell aside, he checked the sides of the bowl to see if he'd spilled anything.

"Perfect," Medora said, as if she expected nothing less from him. "Give me your hand."

He offered her his hand, palm upward, and she deposited something very small, very lightweight in the center. Touching the object with a single finger, feeling the texture, he identified it easily.

"A raisin."

"No," Medora answered quickly, that wonderful

touch of merriment in her voice. "Try again."

Alex lifted his palm near to his face and took a deep breath. "It's a raisin."

Medora leaned close to him and placed a soft hand on his knee. "No. Wrong again. What you're holding in your hand is Alexander Stark's heart."

Alex reached up slowly until he cupped Medora's chin in one hand. "In that case, there's only one fitting end for the tiny, shriveled thing."

He placed the raisin between her lips. She didn't laugh or back away.

"How is it?" he asked. He placed one finger against her mouth, reluctant to pull away.

"Tough. Bitter."

"And what of Medora's heart?"

She hesitated for a moment. Then, rather than answering, she took the hand he'd fed her with in her own and placed it solidly beneath her breast so he could feel the beat of her heart in his hand.

He drew her forward, cupped her chin and guided her slowly until her mouth was against his. Her lips were soft, and they trembled against his. Not with uncertainty, but with restrained longing. He recognized that reaction easily, because he felt the same need, the same doubt.

But Medora didn't pull back, and he didn't push her away. He couldn't bear to draw away from Medora's lips, even though he knew it was wrong to allow her or anyone else to get this close. But it felt so damn good, and it was just a kiss . . . just a single stolen kiss.

He parted her lips with his tongue, and Medora uttered a small sigh, of surprise, of pleasure. Then she closed the small space that remained between them to sit on his thigh, never once taking her lips from his. Her arms snaked around his neck, and she tasted him as he had tasted her, probing gently with her tongue.

Alex held her tight, drowning in the vivid sensations that grew with every passing second. Lost in the warmth and passion of Medora's mouth, of the body she pressed against his until he ached to bury himself in her. He wanted to make love to Medora, to claim her as his own. That could never happen, but he couldn't force himself to pull away. He didn't want to leave behind this moment of such pure and wondrous perfection.

One hand crept upward until he was able to slide his fingers into her silky hair. It was piled atop her head, but soft tendrils had fallen to brush her neck and her back. It was easy work to slip out the pins that held it firm until the heavy tresses fell. He buried his hands in Medora's hair, deepening the kiss until it became a kind of delicious torture where he touched and tasted and inhaled what he wanted most.

Medora's earlier hesitation was gone, melted away, and her lips moved against his tenderly, naturally. She pulled her lips from his just long enough to whisper his name hoarsely. It was such a soft whisper, little more than a breath of air, but it was enough to break the spell that allowed him to believe that he could have this woman, that she could want him. He had no right to love her, and he certainly had no right to ask her to love him.

He took his mouth from hers, trailed his mouth along the soft column of her throat. "I like this lesson," he whispered against her warm skin, his voice hoarse, drunken. "What comes next?"

Medora backed away from him, and he could feel the tightening of her muscles, hear the sharp intake of breath. Surprise. Embarrassment perhaps.

"Tell me," he said stridently as Medora left his lap. "How many patients have you had? Exactly how many blind men have you guided into the land of the living by way of your bed?"

He heard her move, but he didn't expect the weak slap that followed. "Not fair," he protested calmly.

"You deserved it." Her voice shook.

"For the kiss? You seemed to enjoy it well enough."

"For the suggestion that I . . . that I—"

"How quickly you change from adept teacher to stammering maid."

She left the kitchen without another word, and when she was gone Alex dropped his head into one hand. Another damn headache coming on. Another of the bad ones that pounded his skull and teased him with lights that flashed beneath his eyelids. But the headache wasn't what made him feel so ill.

Why had Medora done this to him? Why had she touched his hand or his arm or his face with such tenderness? Why had she kissed him that day he'd tried to send her away? Why had she kissed him so ardently and made him question everything he knew to be true? Pity? Sorrow? Was it part of her *job?*

Her motivations didn't matter. It would be too easy to fall in love with a woman like Medora, to let her heal all the wounds he'd brought home with him. He wouldn't do that to her.

Medora knew what he was doing, but that didn't mean Alex's words didn't hurt. Medora sat on the rock that faced the ocean, hugged her knees to her chest and hid in the folds of her long coat. A hood covered her head, but strands of hair, the strands Alex had freed as they'd kissed, whipped across her face.

How long had she dreamed of a kiss like that? All her life? She remembered with frightening clarity the moment she'd realized her love for Alex, a moment as clear as the minutes that had just passed. Well, it had been love as an innocent fourteen-year-old perceives it.

The occasion had been a town social, and Alex had danced with her, just once, at the insistence of his mother. All evening she'd watched him dance with a succession of girls prettier than she, girls who wore brightly colored dresses with ribbons and flowers in their hair, girls who could laugh and talk and dance with ease.

She'd always been so tongue-tied around boys, and with Alex in particular. Josh was closer to her age, just a year older, and she had exchanged a word or two with him on occasion. But Alex . . . so dark and tall and wonderfully assured . . . when he looked her way it was as if her mouth ceased to function.

During their all-too-brief dance, he'd smiled at her. A brilliant smile that had stolen her heart completely. And he'd gazed at her so hard, really looked at *her,* with those eyes so dark they were endless.

She'd fallen in love with him in that moment. Because he was perfect. Because he was handsome. Because for a few flawless minutes he had danced with her and looked at her as if she were the only woman in the world.

When the betrothal had been announced little more than a year later, she'd been so happy she thought she might burst. It hadn't taken long to realize that Alex didn't share her happiness.

Those days were gone. She wasn't a naive girl any longer. Alex wasn't perfect. They might never dance again, and he would surely never look at her the way he had that night. And still, she loved him.

He was trying to push her away, trying to separate himself from her and from everyone else. If he knew the truth, what would he say? The prospect of Alex discovering her true identity frightened her, because she knew him well enough to know what his reaction would be.

More than anything, she wanted the slim chance of recovery the physician in Yorktown had offered to become reality for Alex. Wanted him to be able to see again. But if his mother's prayers were answered . . . if Alex recovered his sight . . . he would surely send her away.

There was normally little afternoon activity in the Wentworth Tavern once the noontime crowd had cleared. Travelers usually rose early, ate a hearty breakfast and continued their journey. The evening activities—new arrivals, locals who stopped in for a drink, meetings around the long tables—rarely started before dark.

But this afternoon there was a new guest, a sailor who had, to hear him tell it, been serving with a privateer and would soon be heading home. He was loud, and he demanded his rum with coarse shouts directed at Medora. Elias and Josh were absent, and the girls who had been hired to do the cooking and serving had not yet arrived.

Alex had been wondering if there was a way to apologize to Medora without encouraging this impossible relationship. She'd been so silent since he'd heard her return to the tavern. What else could he expect from her? And he could think of no way to defend his words without giving away more than he dared. So he sat in the main room not far from the door to his bedchamber, listened to the unrefined sailor demand more rum and followed intently Medora's movements and her softly spoken responses to the sailor's questions.

"Ye work here?" the sailor asked, the changing tone in his voice alerting Alex.

"On occasion," Medora answered. "I'm a friend of the Stark family."

"Yer a purty one," the sailor cooed. "Would you like to earn a coin or two on the sly? I been asea two month an' without the company of a woman."

Alex stood slowly.

"Don't turn your back on me like that, wench." A bench scraped against the floor, and Alex knew that the sailor had stood and that he was somehow threatening Medora.

"I'm not the kind of woman you're looking for," Medora said, her voice calm. Still, Alex could hear the hint of fear there.

"I think ye are."

It was a sharp intake of breath, not a scream, but it sent Alex toward the muffled sounds of movement.

"Release my arm," Medora said, and now she did sound frightened.

"Just a kiss then," the sailor demanded. "A welcome home from the sea for a lonely salt."

Alex followed the echoes of the coarse voice, reached out and grasped the back of the man's collar. With a jerk and a surprised shout, the sailor came backward. Alex spun the man around and pressed his face against the table.

"We don't want or need your business here," Alex said blandly. "Get out."

With that, he shoved the sailor aside and released him so that the man stumbled and fell to the floor with a thud.

"Ye can't treat me like this!"

The man rose quickly, and the blow that followed caught Alex by surprise, but it was a weak clip that glanced off of his jaw.

"Stop it!" Medora shouted. Alex ignored her, reached forward and gripped the sailor by the throat.

"Out." Alex squeezed, and took a step forward with the offensive man in his grasp. "And don't come back."

"What's wrong with you?" the sailor asked, his voice straining from the pressure at his throat. "Bloody hell, yer blind." Alex could feel the air in front of his face stir, and it almost seemed that the gray he saw changed, darkened.

Instinctively, he reached out and grasped the man's wrist, stilled the hand the sailor had been waving in front of his face.

"Yes," he said, continuing toward the front entrance. "But that won't stop me from beating you to within an inch of your life if you dare to show your face here again. Wouldn't that be embarrassing?" he added as they reached the door and he pushed the ill-mannered man onto the ground.

The man muttered to himself, but slunk away. Alex stood in the doorway until he was sure the man was gone.

"What a foolish performance," Medora snapped. "What if he'd had a knife or a pistol? Heavens, Alex, you could have been hurt."

"I couldn't let him maul you," he answered.

Medora didn't respond. Did she think he was reserving that right for himself?

"Besides, he stunk to high heaven."

Medora sighed, resigning her anger. "It was a foolish stunt," she muttered as she reached past him to close the door.

It could have been a trick of the lights that danced behind Alex's eyelids, but as Medora crossed between him and the open door, the grays shifted again. A shadow, a shifting of the light perhaps.

She closed the door, and it was gone, whatever it had been. Had he really had a glimpse of Medora? Had it been her shape blocking the bright light that his eyes sensed? Was it possible that his vision was returning? This could be just the beginning.

No one could know. Not unless it happened again and then again. He wouldn't tell anyone, not unless he saw a real, true improvement. There was nothing crueler than false hope.

If he regained his sight, if he became whole again, what of Medora? He could offer her a life, a good life. He could love her easily.

"Medora?" He reached toward her, locating her face effortlessly, tracing her jaw with his fingers. "I'm sorry. I must apologize to you yet again. I don't want you to think that I'm like that seaman."

"I don't," she answered softly. "You needn't apologize to me, Alex."

"I know," he said, his voice low. "I'm entitled to my anger for now. It does make me do . . . foolish things."

"We all do foolish things."

He could almost believe, listening to her soft voice, that she had truly forgiven him. But she didn't take his hand and draw it to her lips, didn't reach out to touch his face as she so often had. Just as he'd planned, he had succeeded in isolating himself from Medora. That was best for now.

For now.

Chapter Five

"Are you sure you won't come with us?" Josh asked again, but Alex only shook his head. "It's to be an event," Josh added in a hushed voice, gesturing dramatically even though Alex couldn't see his brother's antics. "Music, dancing in the street—"

"Cold wind, drunken soldiers, boring speeches," Alex interrupted. "I suppose one of those boring speeches will be yours?"

"It won't be boring," Josh said indignantly. "This is a momentous occasion."

Medora watched, silent, afraid to encourage or discourage. Alex didn't want to leave his haven, at least not yet. He was comfortable here after several days of practice. But to leave the tavern, to step into an unfamiliar street where he was likely to be jostled, disoriented—it was too much to ask.

But he couldn't hide here forever. She didn't really think he would. Since the afternoon he'd tossed out that rude sailor, he'd been more confident. More daring.

"What about you, Medora?" Josh asked, turning to face her. If Alex decided to attend the celebratory renaming of the town, she would have no choice but to stay away. Too many townspeople knew her only as Meghan. A single shouted greeting would give her away.

But if Alex didn't go, he'd be left alone in the tavern. She couldn't stand the thought of him sitting in the main room all alone with nothing but silence. He hated the silence.

"I don't think so," she said softly. "I haven't been feeling well today. And besides, if a guest should arrive someone should be here, and I know Elias wants to attend the ceremony."

She didn't fool Josh, not for a second. He stared at her just a moment too long and lifted his dark eyebrows dubiously before he surrendered and turned away.

"Never mind that this night will not come again," Josh said, obviously nettled. "Hide here like two mice if you must while the rest of the town rejoices."

He waited to see if his words were going to have an effect and sighed grandly when he saw that he was wasting his time. When Josh left, he slammed the door solidly behind him, leaving Medora alone with Alex.

For a long moment neither of them moved. The main room suddenly seemed huge, cavernous, the space that separated her from Alex an impassable one.

"Would you like a tankard of wine?" she asked, moving to the plank bar Elias usually manned during the evening.

"If you'll join me," Alex agreed.

She didn't fool herself that Alex cared for her company. He just didn't want to be left alone.

Medora filled two tankards half full, and sat across from Alex as she placed his wine before him.

"Port Freedom," she said, making conversation. "It's a good name."

"Yes," Alex agreed as he lifted the tankard to his mouth.

"Elias wants to rename this place as well. Freedom Tavern. He's having two new placards made—one to hang over the front entrance and one for the wall behind the bar. John Salisbury is making them both, and they're to be carved and painted quite lavishly, to hear your father tell it."

"Yes, I know. He's told me all about it," Alex said quietly. "I was rather surprised when he sat down with me this morning and began to speak. Since my return he has, for the most part, avoided me. I fear I make him uncomfortable."

"I don't think that's—"

"You don't have to try to make me feel better. I understand why he's uneasy, and I believe that with time it will pass."

"Poor Elias," Medora breathed. "It seems he doesn't know whether to ignore your blindness or treat you like a total invalid. Whether to be angry or sad."

"You, Medora, are the only individual in this household who accepts me as a whole person. Who laughs and lambastes me when I need it. Who is, at least on occasion, at ease in my presence. Why is that?"

Because I love you. She certainly couldn't tell him that. "You're not giving your family the credit they deserve," she suggested instead. "They care very much for you."

"And yet I make them anxious." Alex drank his wine, his dark eyes focused above Medora's head.

"Give them time. . . ." Medora began, leaning forward. Her elbow brushed her tankard, and wine spilled across the table, soaking into the wood as Medora stood to keep the dark liquid from streaming over the edge and onto her skirt.

"Clumsy," she breathed as she lifted her head.

Alex was staring at her. Not off to the side or over her head, but directly *at* her. Guided by her voice? Was it all in her imagination? She stepped to the side, quietly, and—impossibly—those black eyes followed her.

"Alex," she whispered. "Can you—" How could she ask such a question? It would undoubtedly sound cruel.

He smiled, as close to a mischievous grin as she'd seen from him since his return, bright and carefree. "Can I see you? Is that the question you're afraid to ask?"

"Yes."

Alex stood and reached his hand across the table. His movements were not completely confident, but they weren't blind either. "Shadows," he whispered, "and light. For the past two days. I can't *see* you, not as I would like, but I can discern your movements. Shadows and light, Medora."

"Why didn't you say anything?" she asked, her voice rising gradually.

"What if this is the only improvement? Granted, it's better than nothing, but I don't want to raise anyone's hopes prematurely. Not Josh's or my father's. Not yours."

"What about your own?" Medora whispered.

Alex didn't answer, but she knew that he was as afraid of raising those hopes for himself and then perhaps having to face disappointment.

"This is wonderful," she said, trying not to sound too optimistic.

"Perhaps."

"Perhaps?" Medora stepped around the end of the long table, and Alex's eyes followed her. "Don't ask me not to expect the best for you."

Medora stopped when she stood before Alex. If he recovered his sight and recognized her, he would be furious. And with good reason. She'd lied, stayed in his home after he'd asked her to leave, pretended to be someone else just so she could stay close to him. His recovery would mean an end to her dream. And still she rejoiced for him. He might be skeptical, but she was confident that his recovery would continue.

"You're so quiet," Alex said, lifting his hand hesitantly to her face. He fumbled, just a little, so that she knew his sight hadn't come back completely. Shadows and light, he'd said.

"I don't know what to say." She covered the large hand that brushed her jaw.

"I do." Alex said gruffly. "Since my return, I've treated you terribly at times."

"Don't apologize—"

"Let me finish. You believed in me when I didn't believe in myself. Helped me when I refused to help myself." His thumb rocked gently against her cheek. "If . . . if the improvement continues, if I get my sight back, I want you to stay. We just met, but I can't think of anyone I'd rather spend the rest of my life with than you, Medora."

"And if you don't regain your sight?"

"I won't do that to you," he said gruffly. "You deserve better."

Medora took a deep breath, strengthening her resolve. "It doesn't matter to me if you never see anything more than shadows and light. I love you."

"You can't—"

"I fell in love with you the first time I saw you smile," she confessed.

"I can't ask you to stay, not like this." He raised an impatient hand to his eyes, then dropped it quickly.

"Do you think me so fickle that I can fall in and out of love easily? Isn't it enough that your blindness doesn't matter to me? I want your recovery, Alex, but I want it for *you,* not for myself."

Alex dropped his hand from her face, but Medora stepped forward, closing the short distance between them. "I love you, Alex," she whispered. "I've never loved another man. I never will love another man. No matter what happens, I want you to remember that."

"What of the man you were betrothed to?"

Medora touched his face lightly, almost fearfully. "I did think that I knew what love was, but I was a child. What I felt was nothing like this."

He kissed her, a soft and restrained kiss unlike their last caress. Tears burned Medora's eyes. She couldn't win. If Alex's sight didn't return, he wouldn't have her. If it did, he would despise her for her lies.

In the distance, a shout went up, and Alex pulled his mouth from hers.

"You should have gone to the ceremony," he whispered, trailing his fingers over her cheek and down her throat.

Medora took that hand, lifted a silver candlestick from the end of the table and led Alex toward the stairway. "Are you ready to try the stairs?" she asked with a small smile. "All the way to the third floor."

"For what?"

"One of those small rooms looks over the square. I'll give you a detailed account of the activities."

Alex clasped her hand and followed her lead, their way lit by the single burning candle in Medora's hand. With one hand in hers and the other on the rail, Alex made his way slowly to the second-story landing. There they turned, and continued up to the third floor.

Caroline's room was there, and Josh's as well. Medora had used one of the rooms herself for a while, but when Alex returned, Sarah had insisted on moving Medora to the second floor, where the guest rooms were located. It was her old room that looked over the square.

The rooms on the third floor were smaller than the guest rooms, but very nice just the same. Medora had never had a room of her own until she'd come to live with the Starks. The Campbells' farmhouse was small, and Medora had felt crowded all her life.

She placed the candlestick on a square table near the door and led Alex across the sparsely furnished room. There, she lowered herself to the floor by the window, and Alex cautiously sat beside her.

"Goodness," she said as she looked out on the scene below. "It looks as if we're the only two people in New Hampshire not in attendance. Children, soldiers in uniform, women—everyone's there. There are torches all around the square, and a stage built in the center of it all. Josh is speaking," she said with a smile. "Waving his arms dramatically, as he likes to do, giving much of his attention to a group of young ladies who stare up at him in apparent awe."

"Some things never change," Alex said wryly.

"Elias is standing close to the front of the stage, his face lifted to watch Josh."

Alex laid his hand on her shoulder, and after a few silent minutes, Medora turned from the scene below to face him. "Can you see me now?" she whispered.

"No."

Was it a blessing or a curse that Alex couldn't see

her face, that he didn't know that she was a liar? The silence that surrounded them was complete, but there was comfort in it. For now, Alex was beside her.

She turned back to the window and placed her palm against the cold glass. "Josh is still talking, still waving his arms. Your father is looking around the crowd, nodding to a few friends." Medora laughed lightly. "Even the young ladies seem to be losing their patience. It seems Josh's speech has gone on too long."

"Imagine that," Alex drawled. He wrapped a long arm around Medora's waist and drew her onto his lap so that they sat, gently entwined, on the floor beneath the window.

"Medora?" he whispered, and she settled herself against his chest. "Did you mean what you said?"

"About loving you?"

"And about not caring about this . . . this—"

"Blindness," she said bluntly, and he flinched just a little. "Of course I meant it." Her voice softened, and she stroked the arm that surrounded her so gently.

A shout went up from the crowd below, but Medora didn't move. Alex's arms would be her haven, her sanctuary, for as long as he allowed it.

Alex thought for a moment that Medora was asleep. Asleep in his arms with her head resting against his shoulder. And then her fingers trailed across his forearm, lazy, airy, the touch of an angel.

It was impossible that she could love him; yet he believed it was true. Perhaps he could accept her avowal because he had fallen in love with her so quickly, so completely.

"I love you, Medora," he whispered, and she stirred in his arms, lifted her mouth to his for a brief, warm kiss that made him crave more.

"You've just made me very happy," she whispered, her breath against his lips. "I've wanted to hear that . . . more than you know. More than you'll ever know."

Her lips came back to his, burning and searching, ardent and hungry and *right.* As if Medora belonged here in his arms, as if his place in the world was with her, no matter what happened in the days to come.

He lifted a hand to her hair, then released it so that the heavy strands fell over his hands and down her back. He loved the silky and luxurious feel of Medora's hair in his hands, loved the warmth and the texture, the clean smell, the stroke of those strands as he threaded his fingers through the mass of soft locks.

There had been moments . . . hours . . . days in the past several weeks when he'd questioned his very life. Wondered bitterly why he hadn't died in Yorktown. Why Josh hadn't left him on the battlefield and allowed him to die a soldier's death.

And now, with Medora in his arms, he knew this was the best, the finest moment of his life. A moment he would gladly give his sight to gain. Because he belonged here with Medora, with her mouth against his. Nothing else mattered, nothing but this. Warmth, passion, love.

Medora shifted, then turned in his arms until she faced him fully. As her breasts pressed against him, she wrapped her arms around his neck, slipped her fingers through the hair at the back of his head, moaned softly into his mouth. When she pulled her mouth from his, he protested, drawing her back with gentle hands, thrusting his tongue into her mouth possessively. But she drew away again, slowly, insistently.

Leaning forward, Medora rested her head against his shoulder, but she didn't lessen her grip. She held on tight, stroked his hair and his neck. Melted into his arms. Her breathing was hard and deep, matching his own.

"Alex," she whispered breathlessly, her normally musical voice hoarse.

"Yes, my love?"

She didn't speak, but lay very still against his chest. Her hands rested against his back, soothing, warm. Her breath penetrated the linen of his shirt and teased him. When Medora finally lifted her head, she placed her warm lips against his throat, tasted him with a slow working of her mouth against his skin.

Alex placed his fingers against the swell of Medora's breast, and she moved forward, pressing her softness against his hand, catching her breath in surprise. And Alex knew that, no matter what happened when tomorrow came, Medora belonged with him, to him, tonight.

Chapter Six

It might be her only chance. That was the thought that spurred Medora on, that gave her the strength to go on as she boldly pressed herself against Alex's hand.

She had dreamed of this, but the sensations were more powerful, more wonderful than she had imagined they could be. Shadows and light dancing through her body, new and wondrous energy in Alex's hands and mouth igniting a bright light within her.

Alex unfastened the tiny buttons at her bodice, the gentle movement of his mouth against hers never faltering as his hands loosened her gown and exposed the lace of her chemise. His tongue flickered lightly against hers, then drove deeply, taking her breath away.

His fingers swayed against her skin, teased the swell of her breasts before continuing the downward journey. Alex's hands never faltered as he undressed her, feeling his way confidently around the buttons and ties, leisurely discarding all but her thin chemise.

She should have been chilled so close to the window, but she felt heated. Warmed by a heat as gentle and as strong as the summer sun. Alex touched her sensitive skin everywhere, his fingers caressing her tenderly and fanning the flames within her.

Longing to feel his skin in her hands, Medora tugged at the long shirt that was tucked into his breeches. Then she loosened the linen one inch at a time until she could slip her hands beneath the fabric to touch his flesh. Alex's skin was as warm as her own, his chest hard but silken. She brushed her fingers across his chest, around to his back, reveling in the feel of his body in her hands as she took her mouth from his and lifted the shirt quickly and tossed it aside. Their lips came together quickly, hungrily, and Medora laid her hands against Alex's bare skin, trailing her fingers across hard, warm flesh.

When Alex slipped his hand between her legs and touched her, Medora was startled by a new and incredible pleasure. He stroked her lightly, and the pleasure changed. She wanted more. She wanted everything.

Alex pulled his mouth from hers and whipped the chemise, her last piece of clothing, over her head. He touched her breasts, the hard nipples that were so very responsive, as she straddled him, her naked body pressed against his, his every touch making her ache for more.

It was Alex who drew away slightly, who slowed the frenzy that threatened to overtake them. He stood, his arms still around her, his hand dropping to brush her bare bottom almost lazily.

The candle by the door flickered, and the soft light illuminated Alex's face for her. She could read so much on his face. Desire, happiness, even love. If only he could see her face, could see that she felt all those emotions and more. She drew his hand to her face as she stepped backward and to the bed. After kissing the palm of his hand, she moved her head slowly so that his fingers touched her cheeks and her nose, then brushed lightly over her eyes.

"Do you see that I love you?" she whispered.

"Yes."

He placed her on the wide bed, stood at her side and shed his last pieces of clothing while she watched. Everything about Alex was magnificent. The smile she'd fallen in love with, that handsome face. Those strong arms that held her so well, the strength of his chest. The muscles in his legs were just as impressive, smooth and hard, and the hardened arousal he revealed as he shucked his knee breeches away astounded her. The sight should have frightened her, but she wanted him too much to be afraid.

She took his hand and guided him to her. Alex towered above her for a moment, then lowered his mouth to hers. He kissed her deeply, perfectly, aroused within her passions she'd never expected. Craving in a way she'd never known before. As he kissed her, he touched her again, explored the delicate folds of flesh with stroking fingers.

When Alex lowered his mouth to her breast and suckled gently, Medora's hips lifted, arched upward to meet his probing fingers, to still the demand for more. He lingered over her breasts, kissing one and then the other, drawing a nipple deep into his mouth before teasing it lightly.

When he lifted his face to hers and pressed his manhood against her warmth, she met him with ardor in her mouth and in the hips she lifted to accept him. Alex thrust deep, past the barrier of her maidenhead to fill her completely.

He made love to her, giving and taking, joining them in a way that went much farther than the union of their bodies. Alex was not simply inside her—he was a part of her.

She whispered his name, an involuntary appeal, as the vivid sensations changed and grew, as Alex held her and she came apart in his hands.

His thrust changed then, and he filled her harder, faster. She felt the spasms that coursed through his body, the tightening of every fiber of his being as he whispered her name.

"Medora," he whispered again, softly, gently as he covered her mouth and kissed her with lazy, lingering lips.

Medora returned his kiss, blissfully spent, unable to move, unwilling to move. She heard the faint echoes of inexpertly played music from the streets below, the shouts and laughter of the residents of Port Freedom that had probably been going on for quite some time. She hadn't heard it until now. She'd heard only Alex.

"I love you so much," she whispered. "With all my heart. Promise me you will remember that always, no matter what."

He traced her jaw with his thumb. "Would you really willingly marry a man who could not see? Who could never tell you how beautiful you are? Who could never see his own children?"

"Yes, if that man is you. And remember, you did tell me once that I was beautiful. You saw me with your hands, with those fingers. You can see our children just as you see me, with your hands and your ears. Isn't that enough for you?" She lost her fingers in the strands of black hair that fell forward to hide Alex's face from her. Then she pushed those strands away to reveal strong features and dark eyes. "It's enough for me, Alex."

"Medora Hayden will you marry me?" he asked quickly, as if he were afraid one of them would have a change of heart.

"Yes," she whispered. "But I have to tell you . . ." *The truth.* How could she marry him and not tell him who she really was? She couldn't tell him now, not while he was still joined with her, while she was still flushed from loving him. "I'm a terrible cook."

"I don't care," he said with a laugh and a brush of his lips against hers.

They lay there, the faint sounds of revelry beneath the window, finding warmth in one another's arms.

"You had not been with a man before tonight," Alex said thoughtfully. "You saved your virtue."

"For you, Alex," she whispered. "Only for you."

She carried Alex's warmth with her, it seemed, throughout the morning, but there was one cold spot deep within her heart that warmth couldn't touch: her lie, the knowledge that soon he would discover her deception.

"Good morning, my love," Alex whispered, sneaking up behind her to wrap his arms around her waist and plant a kiss on her neck.

She had not moved, had not spoken, yet he had located her.

"Good morning," she whispered, twisting in his arms to kiss him lightly before she stepped away. Alex reached out and snagged her wrist.

"Where are you going?" he asked as he drew her back into the refuge of his arms.

"Josh and your father are in the kitchen. They might step into the room at any moment."

"And if they do?" He reached up and brushed away

a strand of hair that fell over her cheek.

"You can see me," she whispered. "Can't you?"

He gave her a smile so bright it took her breath away. "A little." Alex held her tightly and pulled her gently into the sunlight that shone brightly though the front window.

Her heart stopped as Alex fingered the collar of her plain dress, as he traced her jaw with a single assured finger. "Not well enough," he whispered. "Not nearly well enough."

"Soon." Her response was nothing more than a breath.

Soon. Too soon. How could she tell Alex what she'd done? He wouldn't forgive her, not this.

Medora reached up and placed her palm against his face. All that mattered was that he was healing, that he would soon be well. He would be the old Alex Stark, perfect once again. He certainly wouldn't need her, definitely wouldn't want her in his life.

"Kiss me quickly," she said in a soft voice. "Before Elias returns, before Josh steps into the room and ruins this opportunity."

Alex did kiss her, wholly, completely, unreservedly. With all his heart and soul. She felt that purity, drank it in as she wondered if he could feel the icy block in her heart. If he could sense the lie that would, in the end, destroy her.

Alex watched the activity in the newly renamed Freedom Tavern, trying to focus on the bleary images that swam before his eyes. Shapes: a large man, a long table, a tankard lifted into the air near his face. These things took shape before his eyes.

He was ecstatic, and horribly frustrated. He still couldn't *see.* More than anything, he wanted to see Medora's face.

Medora wasn't present on this evening; she had pleaded a headache and retired early. He tried to convince himself that it was that simple, that a headache had made her distant throughout the day. It didn't ring true. Did she regret agreeing to marry him, giving herself to him? He didn't doubt, in spite of her new reticence, that she loved him. But was it enough?

It was Christmas Eve, and the crowd of regulars had cleared out early to be with their families. Elias wiped down the bar, and Josh was sweeping the room when the front door burst open and Sarah Stark swept in with Caroline a single step behind her.

"I told you I'd be home by Christmas," she declared brightly. "Mary had twins," she said as she placed her bag on the floor. "Two tiny little girls. They're all doing well, so Caroline and I left the lot of them in the care of the family."

Alex stood and faced the door, and his mother started walking toward him. He lifted a hand to stop her, and the shadowy shape he followed with his eyes came to a halt in the center of the tavern. He stepped away from the table, around the end, heading straight for his mother.

"Alexander," she breathed. "Can you see me?"

He grinned and stopped just short of his mother to place his hands on her shoulders. "Just a little. It's coming back, more every day."

She threw her arms around him, hugging him tight before she gathered herself and backed away. "I knew it would happen," she said pragmatically. "I never doubted for a moment."

"You could have told me," Josh said, his feelings obviously hurt. "How long has this been going on?"

"A few days. I didn't say anything because I was afraid . . . I was afraid the improvement would stop while everything was still a blur."

Everyone spoke at once, his father briefly but loudly, Caroline with a shrill squeal, Josh and their mother vying for dominance.

Alex didn't know how long Medora had been there, but he turned his blurry gaze to the stairs and she was there. Little more than a silhouette, a mass of dark hair around her shoulders, a full gray skirt billowing around her, she was silent, motionless.

"I have more good tidings," he said, lifting a hand to Medora. She floated down the stairs to him and laid her hand in his. The family was silent, even Josh and Sarah. "I've asked Medora to marry me, and she has said yes."

Caroline chirped, but everyone else was silent for a long moment.

"That's wonderful," Sarah said, laying her hands over theirs. "When is this to take place?"

"Call the magistrate and he can marry us tonight," Alex suggested with a grin.

"No." Medora's voice was soft, but insistent. "We'll wait until Alex can see my face. Then, if he still wants to call the magistrate, we'll be married here."

It was an odd statement for Medora to make, and she sounded so somber. Was she afraid he wouldn't like her appearance? She'd felt beautiful beneath his fingers, and he knew that no matter how her features were arranged, she'd always be fair to him.

"Soon," he said, lifting her hand to his mouth, brushing his lips over the knuckles. But she slipped her hand from his and backed away slowly.

"We'll start cooking early in the morning," Sarah said with artificial brightness. "Tomorrow will be a Christmas to remember. My sons home after so many years, and a new and wonderful daughter to welcome to the family."

The silence that followed his mother's statement

was awkward. Alex knew they all loved Medora, would love her even more as time passed. There should be shouts and laughter to accompany their announcement.

"Good night," Medora said, her voice low. "I'll see you all early in the morning."

Alex watched her retreating form, heard her footsteps as she hurried up the stairs, listened even more carefully as she stepped down the hallway and opened a door.

There was little resembling holiday spirit in the room as one by one his family bid one another good night and retired. Elias was last, bolting the front entrance as he did every night, clearing his throat frequently as if he had something to say but was unsure. Watching the hulking and silent shadow of his father, Alex followed Elias's movements as the old man readied the tavern for the night and finally came to stand before Alex.

"Congratulations, son," Elias said in a coarse voice. "Medora is an uncommon woman. You're right lucky that she'll have you."

It was his father's way. Gruff. Brief. To the point. Alex didn't even have time to agree with his father's assessment of Medora before the older man turned away with a curt good night.

There was a single candle left burning, and Alex lifted it as he turned to the stairs. Holding the flame so close to his face made it harder to see distinctly, but he was glad of the light. He'd believed for a time that he'd live the rest of his life without it.

He had no trouble making his way to the stairway. Once there, he gripped the railing in one hand and the candleholder in the other as he placed his foot on the bottom step.

He climbed the stairs slowly, carefully, the indistinctness of his vision disorienting even now. When he stepped into the hallway, he closed his eyes, remembering the sounds of Medora's footsteps against the floorboards, following her path.

Or so he hoped. It would be embarrassing if he entered the room of that Puritan woman who was staying in one of these second-floor rooms or of the privateer captain who had sworn to sleep through Christmas and possibly clear to the New Year.

When he opened his eyes he was standing in front of a door. He had to know what was wrong, why Medora was so subdued.

She listened to his footsteps, so sure and steady. Held her breath as he laid his hand against the handle of her door so that it rattled slightly.

When he stepped into the room, his candle held high so that the soft light bathed his face, Medora's heart stopped. She'd loved Alex all her life, it seemed, but in the past days that love had grown to something stronger, more powerful than she could have imagined.

"Medora?" he breathed hesitantly.

She sat taller in the bed. "Yes," she whispered.

He smiled softly. "I was afraid for a moment I had the wrong room."

Alex took long strides to the side of the bed, and Medora took the burning candle from him, lowering it to her bedside table, dousing the flame with a quick breath to leave them in darkness.

"For a moment I could almost see you," he said as he sat on the edge of the bed. "Why are you afraid? Do you regret last night?"

"No," Medora said quickly, reaching out to take Alex's hand. "I swear to you, I have no regrets. My love for you is only stronger."

"Then why—" He threaded his fingers through hers. "Why do you insist that we wait until I can see you before we marry? One minute you swear it makes no difference and the next—"

"I only want you to see who you're binding yourself to before you speak the vows."

"Medora." Alex leaned forward and kissed her lightly. "If you wish it, we'll wait. But I promise there's nothing that will change my love for you." He raised a hand to her cheek. "It won't be a long delay."

Medora knew that was true, that his sight was returning at an alarming rate. She leaned into Alex and buried her head against his shoulder. If he asked her to leave again it would destroy her. This was where she belonged, by his side, in his arms. But when he learned the truth he would despise her for her lies.

"Stay with me tonight," she whispered. "Love me again and sleep beside me so that my first sight on Christmas morning is of your face."

Alex lifted her face with gentle fingers, then gave her his answer with a deep kiss that eased her fears. In the darkened room they were equal, guided only by touch and sound and instinct. For a while, Medora forgot that this perfection wouldn't last forever.

Chapter Seven

It was the light that woke him, sunlight streaming through the window and touching Medora's hair. His face was resting against that luxurious hair, and her back was pressed against his chest, her bare skin warming his.

She had described her hair well, dark brown with red highlights the sun revealed. Not quite straight, but not curly either. Alex lifted a handful, careful not to disturb Medora, and rubbed his fingers against the silky wealth. He could see the strands in the bright sunlight, could see the warm flesh pressed against him. His vision was not flawless, but he could see Medora.

Alex didn't want to wake her, not yet. Instead, he marveled at the contrast of her creaminess against his darker skin, at the richness of her hair, the curve of her hip beneath his hand.

She would have everything she'd ever dreamed of.

He planned to see to it. To make her dreams come true, to watch her smile again and again.

Her face was turned into the white pillow, her hair spilling over her cheek and rippling in dark waves across the pure softness. With unhurried fingers, he brushed aside the dark strands to reveal a smooth cheek that was flushed pink with sleep. He ran a single finger along her jaw, remembering the first time he'd seen her that way, the first time she'd drawn his hands to her face.

He slipped that hand onto the warmth of the pillow beneath her head and turned her face to his. The sunlight made her squeeze her eyes tighter, and she frowned slightly against the brightness that threatened to intrude upon her sleep. He could see that much as the fog that dimmed his vision came and went.

Medora turned away from the light and buried her face against his chest, but not before he caught a second's clear glimpse of her. With a frown, Alex tipped her face forward so that the sun fell softly across her cheeks, illuminating every feature for his perusal.

She was beautiful, as she had always been. In her description of herself, she had omitted the light sprinkling of freckles across her nose. Had she thought that revelation would give her away? When she was fourteen those freckles had been prominent. Now, they were almost gone, a pleasing imperfection on an otherwise flawless face.

She opened her eyes and smiled. Green eyes, as she'd described, with flecks of brown. He hadn't remembered that detail, hadn't remembered those eyes being so bright, so deep.

"Good morning," she whispered, lifting an indolent hand to his jaw, rubbing lightly at the morning stubble there. "Merry Christmas."

"Merry Christmas, Meghan Campbell."

She stiffened, went cold in his arms and allowed her hand to fall away from his face. "You can see me that clearly?"

Alex rolled from the bed and began to dress with his back to her. "Was it entertaining, Meghan? Or should I continue to call you Medora?"

"Medora is my second name," she said softly.

He wanted to ask *why,* wanted an explanation. It had all been false from his first day at home. There was no *real* Medora. She was a fabrication, a contrivance, a game. At least she had the good sense not to try to explain away her lie. She was silent as he dressed in the clothing he had so hastily and happily discarded in the dark.

He didn't turn to look at her when he was finished dressing, but made his way to the door without laying his eyes on her again.

As he threw the door open, his pain grew, a pain deeper and more excruciating than anything he'd ever experienced. He'd fallen deeply in love with a woman who didn't exist. He had cherished every moment, every touch . . . and none of it had been real.

"Get out," he said as he stepped into the hall and slammed the door shut.

Medora dressed methodically, slipping on her best chemise and the blue wool. It would keep her warm enough as she traveled. She laid out her heavy cloak, tossing it across the bed that was still warm from Alex's body.

She had known this would happen. That Alex would see her face and hate her for what she'd done. She had known his rejection would hurt, but she hadn't expected it to hurt so badly, hadn't known that the physical pain would well deep in her chest and make her ache. It didn't paralyze her though, didn't stop her from tossing everything she owned into her small trunk.

That done, she stood in the center of her room for several minutes. She couldn't face Sarah and Elias, Josh and Caroline. Couldn't bear to say good-bye, as she should. She wouldn't leave Alex in tears, and if she had to face his family she would.

The hallway was deserted, silent but for Medora's own footfall as she made her way to the room next to hers. She knocked quietly, got no response, and knocked again. More insistently, this time.

The door swung open and she found herself face-to-face with a pirate. Long blond hair, piercing blue eyes, two days' of pale stubble on his face, gold loops in his earlobes. He had hastily pulled on his knee breeches, but his broad chest was bare.

"What the hell do you want? I left instructions that I was not to be disturbed!"

Medora didn't back away from his angry shout, but stood her ground, eyes straight ahead and on his bare chest, which was crossed with a number of faint scars. "You have a ship," she said softly. "And I must leave here. Would you take me? Savannah. I have family there."

"Not for gold nor silver nor useless notes of one sort or another."

"I have no money," Medora said softly.

The seaman crossed his arms across his chest and leaned insolently against the doorjamb. "Do I look like a bloody saint? A Christmas angel? A knight who rescues damsels in distress for sport?"

She lifted her eyes to his, then stared defiantly into the cold blue depths. This had been a foolish impulse. He would not assist her. No one would. "No," she finally whispered, "you do not."

Medora turned away from the captain. What now? Could she find another family in Port Freedom to take her in until she could earn her passage to Savannah? A quick hand caught her arm, and she was spun around to face the captain.

His face had softened, but not much. "You're in a bit of trouble, eh?"

Medora nodded, unable to speak for the knot in her throat.

"No money?"

When she shook her head, the captain crooked a finger under her chin and lifted her face to study it closely. "You're a comely lass," he conceded with a half smile. "Would you consent to share my cabin for the duration of the voyage?"

"I have to get away from here. Today. This morning."

"Would you consent?" he asked again.

Medora took a deep breath, fighting her revulsion. "Anything. It doesn't matter."

"I'll take that as a yes," the captain said, offering his hand. "Captain Nathan Morse."

"Medora—" She hesitated. "Meghan Campbell." She ignored the offered hand.

Captain Morse reached down and took her hand anyway in a move gentler than she would have expected from him. "Whatever foolish man has broken your heart, Miss Campbell, I'll make you forget him. For a few, gloriously happy days at least."

Instinctively, Medora shook her head slightly.

"I'll dress you in silk," he promised. "Red and sapphire blue and shining gold, and I'll wrap diamonds and emeralds and pearls around your pretty neck. I like pretty things around me." The captain, who resembled a pirate of old, lowered his voice. "And if you are as delectable as you look, we'll go to Savannah by way of Liverpool."

Alex waited until he had gathered his senses. In his ground floor room he'd shaved and bathed and changed into a fresh linen shirt and dark knee breeches. He didn't want to go storming into the kitchen while he still felt as if he were spinning out of control. It had taken him longer than he'd expected to get past the blinding anger.

His mother was bustling about, attending the brick stove and the pots that swung above the fire or rested on a grate close to the flames. The room was warm, fragrant, full of laughter and bright voices. None of that changed when he stepped into the room, as he felt it should have. He was cold deep inside, and while he felt more in control than he had when he'd seen Meghan's face, he was still full of rage. They had all lied to him.

"Merry Christmas, Alexander." His mother gave him a quick and hearty hug, which he could not return, but she was too busy to notice his restraint. "It's about time you showed yourself, sleepyhead. That leaves only Medora. She should have joined us by now. Goodness, she never sleeps this late. Caroline, go give a soft knock—"

"Leave Meghan alone," Alex said in a low voice that silenced the room. There was no sound but the sizzle of a portion of their Christmas feast on the fire.

"We thought it was for the best, Alexander—"

"You thought it was best to lie to me when I was blind and could not see Meghan's face. To carry on an elaborate charade I had no way of seeing through. It was a cruel trick."

"It was no trick," Sarah insisted.

"What do you call it?" Alex asked, the anger he was

trying to control rising to the surface.

They had no answer for that. Caroline hung her head, and Elias did much the same, giving his attention to a tin cup of coffee steaming in his hands. Sarah and Josh at least had the nerve to face him, to look him square in the face.

"And you, Josh," Alex said accusingly. He felt his brother's betrayal most of all. After all they had been through. His brother's face swam momentarily, a haze flitting across Alex's vision and blurring everything again. "Why didn't you tell me?"

There were no answers from the silent conspirators who surrounded him. They were his *family,* and yet at the moment he felt they were his enemies. They had lied, and they had taken Medora's side in this gentle battle he had no chance of winning.

"Tell him about the stairs," Josh said, speaking to Sarah, but keeping his eyes on Alex. "Tell him about the bruises."

"I gave my solemn oath to Medora—"

"Meghan!" Alex shouted. Medora didn't exist.

"Tell him!" Josh shouted just as loudly, stepping forward. "Or I will!"

She hugged the cloak tightly, trying unsuccessfully to block the cold wind that whipped in from the sea. Captain Morse was making the last of his arrangements, rounding up his crew, paying his debts. Next, he would load the trunk at her feet onto his ship, placing it in his cabin, and she would be on her journey away from this place.

The cost would be high, but she couldn't wait. Not another day, not another hour. She was so numb it didn't matter to her. Not really. Nothing mattered.

"Medora?"

She turned toward the hesitant voice and faced

Alex more bravely than she'd thought she could. He squinted against the harsh light and the cold wind, and a single strand of black hair that had come loose from his queue lashed across his face.

"I've made preparations to leave," she assured him. "You needn't worry."

"Why?" he asked, stepping forward until he was within arm's reach. "I don't understand why you lied to me."

He was no longer furious, but the frustration was still there. It edged his voice, lined his face.

"When your letter arrived, I could think of only three paths. I could leave as you asked, I could stay and beg you to have me or I could lie. I lied to keep you, Alex, and it worked for a while." She turned her back to him, unable to look at his face, into his accusing eyes. He was right, of course. She had deceived him, and love wasn't enough to make him forget that truth.

He didn't say anything for a while, but she knew he hadn't moved from his spot near the flat rock.

"Josh told me about the blindfold," he said, puzzlement in his voice. "About your fall. Why?"

"It was all I could think of to help you, those days in the dark. I wanted to try to feel what you felt, to discover what you'd need in the days to come. I knew tears wouldn't help, hiding wouldn't help, leaving would have accomplished *nothing.*"

"You're leaving now," he said softly.

"You told me to. And besides, you don't need me anymore. You're going to be all right, Alex."

He laid his hand on her shoulder and she felt it, like a sharp current, even through her heavy cloak.

"What about you? Will you be all right?"

"Yes," she lied.

Gently but insistently, Alex forced her to turn to face him. "I think you're wrong," he said as he reached down to touch her cheek as he had when he hadn't been able to see her at all. "I think I do need you."

She shook her head, but he stopped that motion with a steady hand on each side of her face.

"Tell me this," he whispered. "If I had never recovered my sight, if I had never been able to see your face . . . would you have stayed with me?"

"Yes."

"Would you ever have told me who you really were?"

"I don't know." The tears welled up in her eyes, and she hated her weakness, hated more for Alex to see it. "I think . . . I think, perhaps, no. Deep down, I'm a coward. Would I risk losing you? Risk seeing the hatred I saw in your eyes this morning? No. I don't think so."

"Why?" He rocked his thumb against the side of her face.

"Why? Why? There's one answer to all your whys, Alex. I've always loved you. Don't ask me why, because I can't explain it. Love just *is*. It grew even when you rejected me, even when you hated me—"

"I never hated you," he swore.

She wanted to believe that, but she couldn't.

"I never hated you," he said again. "I only wanted the freedom to choose for myself."

"You have that now, don't you?" Medora said, trying to turn away from Alex's black stare, preferring the whip of cold wind against her face.

"I do," he whispered, holding her tenderly in place.

"Let me go." Her voice was too soft, lost in the howl of icy wind that surrounded them.

"Not yet."

His hands warmed her face, large, tender hands she would dream about for the rest of her life.

"Meghan Medora Campbell." Alex leaned forward, blocking the wind. "Will you marry me?"

For a moment, she thought the wind and Alex's soft voice were playing a trick on her. But his smile convinced her. A warm, bright smile. The smile she had fallen in love with.

"Alex—"

"You're not going to say no, are you?" His smile faded.

"Are you certain? I did deceive you. I lied, and given the same circumstances I'd do the same again."

His smile crept back.

"Why?" she pressed. "Why do you want me as your wife?"

"There's one answer to all your whys, Medora. I love you."

Medora threw herself into Alex's arms. This was all she'd ever wanted. Everything she'd ever dreamed of.

He held her for a long time, against the wind, against his angry words. Alex whispered into her ear, told her again and again that he was sorry he'd told her to leave, that he would never let her go.

Medora didn't apologize for her lies, because she didn't regret them.

"Do you think the magistrate will consent to marry us on Christmas Day?" Alex asked as he led her back to the tavern.

"Perhaps," she said, leaning into his side. "If your mother promises to feed him I'm sure he will."

They had just stepped into the tavern when Captain Morse handed a coin to Elias and turned to the door.

"Are you ready, Miss Campbell?" he asked with a

bright grin. "All's arranged." The captain's bright smile faded as he observed Medora's arm through Alex's. "We're not going anywhere, are we?"

Medora shook her head, and the captain turned back to Elias. "Can I reengage my room, by chance? Once I inform my crew that we're not sailing after all, I want to sleep for a week. *Undisturbed,* if you please."

Morse gazed at Medora, grumbled loudly, shook his head, and passed by her and Alex as they entered the dimly lit room and he left it.

"So she'll be staying?" Elias asked coolly.

"Yes," Alex answered quickly.

"I'd best tell your mother so she'll quit ranting," he said, stoic as always.

Elias left them alone, and Medora turned her face to Alex's. He blinked hard, then closed his eyes for a second.

"What is it?"

"My sight's not completely restored. Sometimes it's as if a cloud passes between my eyes and the world around me. It may never get any better, Medora. Are you sure—"

Medora silenced Alex with a finger over his lips. He took her hand and kissed it. "Of course I'm sure," she answered. "Are you?"

"Yes," he answered without hesitation. "As long as I have you beside me, my world will never be dark. You're my light, Meghan Medora Campbell. My sunlight, my candle, my daybreak after a dark, cold night."

Sarah came bursting from the kitchen, arms wide to embrace them both. Caroline and Josh were right behind her, and Elias followed quietly with a satisfied grin on his face.

Medora's fears were gone. They had vanished with

Alex's words. She hadn't had an opportunity to tell him that he was the light of her world, that she needed him to guide her as much as he'd ever needed her. There would be time for that confession. Later.

The Christmas Pearls

LINDA MADL

To my father, who was a loving husband, a caring dad, and always the spirit of Christmas in our house.

Prologue

Amsterdam—1813

Soft Dutch daylight poured through the shop window, making the fortune of diamonds spilled on dark cloth sparkle and wink up at Captain Eli Whittaker. Each gem was larger than the tip of his little finger and each was of the highest quality and expert cut. Yet none of them pleased him.

"These won't do." Eli frowned and shook his head. "This gift I want must be truly special."

The old diamond merchant squinted at him with sharp, discerning eyes. Eli stared back. Undoubtedly the old man had sized up many a prospective customer during his years in the diamond trade. The merchant sighed, bent over the diamonds on the table between them and began replacing them one by one in a black velvet bag.

Eli studied the wispy white hair fringing the old

man's pink pate. The merchant had come highly recommended. Though this was not Eli's first trip to Amsterdam, it was his first trip with prize ship money in his pocket. He'd come prepared to spend it all if he found what he wanted. Surely the wily old merchant had divined that, but so far he hadn't shown Eli a single gem worth haggling over.

"Perhaps rubies or emeralds would suit the lady better," the old man offered without looking up.

"No, I don't think so." Eli had given this gift and the lady who was to receive it a lot of thought. "Emeralds are too hard and cold. Rubies are too ordinary."

The diamonds continued to disappear into the old merchant's velvet bag. "This gift you want—is it for the woman you love?"

"Yes, for my bride."

"Is she dark or fair?"

"I'm not certain," Eli admitted, sitting back in his chair. "I have not met her yet. I thought, after hostilities have ceased, I'll be able to find her."

The wizened merchant blinked. Then his eyes narrowed to a reassessing squint as if he were seeing Eli anew.

"Whether she is dark or fair is of no consequence," Eli explained. "It's her character that is important."

The old man nodded. "Tell me what you know of her character."

"My bride will have a generous and courageous soul. Her heart will be loving and loyal, and she will be a lady who knows her own mind."

A slow smile spread across the merchant's face. "You're a brave man to take on such a woman and a patient one if you seek a bride with so many virtues." The merchant drew the string on the bag of diamonds, slipped it into his waistcoat pocket and shook his head. "And what do you wish this wedding gift to tell the woman worthy of you heart?"

"That I pledge to cherish and honor and care for her," Eli said, realizing he was expressing something that he'd always known, but had never put into words before. "I want her to know she is the woman to whom I will be faithful. With whom I will have children and share the rest of my life."

"Then you are correct. Diamonds are not for your bride." The merchant shook his head.

"What then?" Eli wondered cynically what the shrewd old merchant had decided to foist off on him. "What do you suggest?"

"A gem from the sea," the old man announced as if there could be no other answer. "That is what a sea captain should give the lady he loves."

"What gem of the sea?" Eli asked, growing impatient. The only stone he could think of was coral, and that was not precious enough for *his* bride.

The old merchant rose from the table and held up a finger, a silent request for patience. Then he shuffled behind the black curtain that separated the front from the back of the shop.

Eli waited. He heard the voices of children playing outside along the canal. From the floor above drifted the aroma of boiling cabbage. He wondered again why he was wasting his time in this little out-of-the-way shop. He almost got up to leave, yet a certain curiosity kept him in his chair. Gem of the sea?

When the old man swept aside the black curtain again, he carried a blue velvet bag cupped in one hand. Once more he sat down across from Eli. Tenderly the merchant loosened the silk drawstrings and with a flourish spilled the contents of the bag onto the cloth. Pearls flowed forth, a long glowing rope, rich with softness and shiny smooth as ivory. Entranced by their beauty, Eli leaned over the table to peer at them more closely.

"I have had these for some months," the merchant confided. "They are of the finest quality from India and they come with a fascinating story."

When the merchant paused, Eli took his eyes off the pearls for the first time since the old man had poured them out on the cloth. "What story?"

"These were originally part of a raja's many-stranded belt," the merchant said, apparently satisfied that he had captured Eli's interest at last. "He wore it around his middle like a great sash and it ended in a tassel of tiny seed pearls and rubies. He married a princess whom he loved very much and she loved him in return. When enemies invaded the raja's kingdom and he prepared to go off to war, his bride asked him for a token of his love that she could wear always. So he gave her this strand of pearls from his belt, and she wore it till the day she died.

"Did the raja survive the war?"

"Yes, but he was gravely wounded and held prisoner for many years," the merchant said. "His beloved rani protected their kingdom while he was gone and welcomed him home when he returned at last. The tale goes that they had twelve children after his return."

Eli liked the story. It was full of love and loyalty, and it held no hint of darkness. But he didn't want to look too eager to the merchant.

"I've shown them to only one other patron," the merchant continued. "Not everyone understands pearls. They don't flash. They don't sparkle. Only a few people are perceptive enough to appreciate the virtue of their astonishing beauty."

Speechless, Eli nodded. He'd never thought of pearls as gems of the sea. He'd certainly never seen any pearls as beautiful and perfect as these. "I do like these better than the diamonds."

"Diamonds stand for eternity," the merchant admitted. "A nice thought. But pearls—ah, pearls, Neptune's gems, are smooth and round, almost ripe with life and luster."

When Eli continued to bait the merchant with silence, the old man leaned across the counter to confide something more. "The best part is the old belief that of all the gems in the world only pearls represent perfect love and beauty."

The merchant repeated the virtues slowly for Eli: "Perfect love and beauty. What better gift could a sea captain give the woman he loves?"

Eli bought the pearls without haggling.

Chapter One

Port Freedom, New Hampshire—1815

The moment Sara Larkfield set eyes on the infamous privateer, Captain Eli Whittaker, standing by the hearth, she was disappointed—and a little frightened.

He looked nothing like her idea of a pirate, nothing like Blackbeard. He was tall enough and broad enough and he even had a beard, yet she'd expected something more. She wanted to see a crazed pirate who wore a ragged, smelly beard, dressed in a grimy naval officer's coat and flourished a bloodied saber.

This man looked perfectly respectable. Sara's stomach did an icy flip-flop. She glanced swiftly around the Freedom Tavern parlor, searching the shadowy corners for the true privateer.

At her side, Abby smiled. "How nice to see you again, Captain Whittaker."

Without hesitation, Sara's little sister walked

straight across the room and offered her hand to her future husband. He was stunningly handsome in a blue wool cutaway coat, a wine-colored striped waistcoat and a stylish ruffled shirt. His snowy-white stock was tied in a soft bow beneath his dark neatly trimmed beard. His black boots gleamed in the light of the fire. Accepting Abby's hand, the dark-haired man smiled a devilishly handsome smile and dropped a possessive, yet properly brief kiss on her mouth.

Sara gaped. Abby's vague description of her intended had given Sara's imagination little to work with. Knowing that Captain Eli Whittaker had been a privateer during the war, she had allowed her mind's eye to conjure up an ignoble pirate. But this gentleman—except for the beard—was as presentable as any society bridegroom should be. No wonder her papa had been so easily swayed by him. Try as she might, Sara could find nothing uncouth or unsuitable enough to declare on first sight that he would never do as a husband for her little sister.

"You had a safe, comfortable trip, I trust," the gentleman inquired, smiling down into Abby's face.

"Yes, we had a pleasant journey. Thank you." Blushing from the kiss, Abby backed away and turned to Sara. "Please let me introduce my half sister, Mrs. Sara Larkfield. This is Captain Whittaker."

Sara forced herself to nod politely. "I've heard much about you, Captain."

"All good I hope, Mrs. Larkfield." He smiled coolly at Sara. She could feel his keen brown eyes taking her in, noting the widow's black of her gown and calculating her experience and age. She prayed that he saw a woman who would not be flimflammed as her father had been.

"Your success at sea is very nearly legendary." Sara moved into the room, thankful that the carpet muffled the tapping of her walking stick.

Unhurriedly, the captain pulled a chair out from the table and held it for her. "Please sit, Mrs. Larkfield, and warm yourself by the fire."

"Thank you, sir." Sara sat down. "Papa regrets that he cannot be here. Only pressing business would keep him away for Abigail's wedding. I have come in his stead."

"Rest assured I understand," the captain said. Sara glimpsed a frown of annoyance flash across his face. "I hope you find the accommodations here at the Freedom Tavern satisfactory. It's a convenient meeting place between Boston and Brunswick. Besides that, Thanksgiving and Christmas are my favorite time of year. The tavern is well-known for its gay festivities and good food during this season."

"Indeed, I find the accommodations acceptable, Captain Whittaker," Sara admitted without so much as a glance to admire the room, which was decorated with pine-bough garlands. Inwardly she had to admit the captain had known exactly what he was doing when he'd chosen the tavern for the site of this meeting. What better setting than a hospitable New England inn to pursue a romance intended to end in a wedding?

The captain turned to his bride-to-be. "And you, Abigail. Does Freedom Tavern suit you?"

"She finds it acceptable also," Sara replied before Abby could open her mouth.

A scowl flickered across the captain's features when he glanced in Sara's direction. With deliberation, he turned to Abby again. "Please tell me that is so, Abigail."

Sara bridled, but said nothing. Abby looked uneasily toward her sister before replying. "It is a lovely place, Captain. I like it very much."

"I'm glad you like it. I've ordered tea be served as soon as you arrived."

"Very thoughtful, Captain," Sara said, satisfied with the observance of the social amenities. "Papa explained to me that the marriage agreement is signed and duly registered. I appreciate—Abigail and I appreciate the thoughtful plans you have made for a Christmas wedding. However . . ."

Sara paused, and Abby stared at her hands. Sara regretted embarrassing her sister like this, yet the subject could not be avoided. She eyed the captain narrowly. "Frankly, sir, my father assured me that should I have any doubts, or should Abigail have any second thoughts, we are under no obligation to go forward with these plans."

Once more something flickered in the captain's eyes, then disappeared. Sara knew he did not like her interference, but he said, "I understand completely. Our meeting in Boston was brief—was it not, Abigail? We're not living in the dark ages. This is 1815, soon to be 1816, and young ladies aren't forced to marry strangers any longer."

"No, sir," Abigail said, offering him an uncertain smile. The captain smiled back, clearly captivated with her beauty and sweetness.

"Indeed, we are not living in the dark ages." Sara sat up a little straighter. "Abby, dear, would you help Mrs. Stark with our tea tray."

Abigail glanced at her sister in surprise, then rose obediently. "Yes, of course, Sara. May I get something special for you, Captain Whittaker?"

The captain rose from his chair. "Please. You must remember to call me Eli. Tea will do fine, thank you."

"Yes, Eli." Abigail bobbed a curtsy and left the small parlor that the captain had hired for the next week.

Sara squared her shoulders as he sat down across from her again. "Let's be perfectly clear about things, Captain."

"By all means," he said.

Sara frowned at the smile of amusement that threatened his lips. "Perhaps you and Papa think a few dances at a ball, a few hours over dinner and four days at Freedom Tavern is the stuff a marriage is built on. I do not."

"I was quite taken with your sister from the moment I saw her at the ball," he said. "I suppose you believe in love. Doesn't that come later?"

"I am a widow and too old for such nonsense," she assured him with a sniff, "but Abigail does believe in it. However, that is not my point. A lady's family must think of her future, and I have grave concerns about Abigail finding happiness with an infamous privateer."

The amusement instantly vanished from the captain's lips and his brown eyes smoldered with anger. Sara shrank back in her chair. Captain Eli Whittaker did not like being disparaged for being a privateer.

"That seems an easy judgment for you to make after sailors like my men and I defended your rights to free trade and safe travel on the high seas."

"That may be so—"

"The war has been over for several months now, Mrs. Larkfield," the captain reminded her, his careful control evident in the harsh lines of his face and the deadly quiet of his deep voice. "Congress fully commissioned my activities. May I also remind you that, after some discussion, your father is satisfied with the legitimacy of my business."

"As you say, Captain. There are, however, those who took unfair advantage of their commissions." Unwilling to give way, Sara gripped the arms of her chair and said what she wanted to say. "Few will ever forget the questionable tactics of the privateers. Memories are long in these parts, Captain. Even marrying into the respectable Conway family is unlikely to restore your reputation."

The captain frowned. "I disagree with you, ma'am. Alliance with your prestigious family can only add respectability to the Whittaker name and shipping business. More importantly, I'm certain my money can enable your father to rescue your family mercantile from certain financial disaster."

Sara felt the color rise in her cheeks. She turned away to contemplate the fire, hoping her embarrassment wasn't too evident.

"The sum of it is, Mrs. Larkfield," the captain continued, speaking softly as he leaned across the table toward her, "we both need this marriage to happen. Since your papa is not here, you and I and Abigail have these four days until Christmas to make certain we're all satisfied with this bargain. Since we are being frank, will you be working with me or against me, ma'am?"

She turned back to him, unable to hide her fierce determination. "Let there be no doubt, sir. I will be working for Abigail's happiness, wherever that lies."

"Fair enough." The captain sat back in his chair as if he were satisfied that they had each laid their cards on the table. He gave a slight shrug. "From my point of view, that simply means I have two women to win over instead of just one. Believe me, I've faced greater odds."

Sara glared at him. His arrogance was exactly what she had expected from a pirate. Fortunately, Abigail returned then with Mrs. Stark, who was carrying the tea tray.

It troubled Sara little that she and the captain had

crossed swords within moments of their first meeting. Captain Whittaker's cold-blooded assessment of her family's financial situation might be painfully accurate, but she did not like him for taking advantage of it. Abigail deserved better than an opportunist. A man did not have to be Blackbeard to be a pirate of another kind.

"Why don't you pour, dear," Sara suggested as Abigail resumed her chair. Her half sister was the perfect hostess, pouring the tea and leading the conversation with ease and grace. As Abby performed the tea ritual, Sara nibbled a tea sandwich and sipped from her cup, observing Captain Whittaker over the rim.

Sara watched him lean close to Abigail, charming her with a humorous tale of his travels. Abigail listened intently, her eyes bright with fascination. Yet the sadness was still there, lurking in the depths of those big blue eyes. Strange how that sorrow drew men to Abigail's side like flies to honey. Sara didn't think they understood what was so appealing about her little half sister. Abigail's beauty was obvious. Her vulnerability was less evident. No doubt some men sensed it and yielded to a desire to protect. The captain had been honest about his attraction to Abby: the Conway family name.

Across the table, Abby laughed at something witty the captain had said. Sara gave herself a mental shake. What on earth had ever made her think all pirates would look like Blackbeard? Why couldn't they be handsome, charming, and seductive as the devil himself—as Captain Eli Whittaker himself. Sara's sudden realization of her helplessness against such an attractive, worldly man turned the tasty bite of sandwich in her mouth to sawdust.

"Oh, Eli, I would love to see the ship you sailed

here," Abby declared, clapping her hands in delight. "Wouldn't you, Sara?"

"Wouldn't I what, dear?"

"Captain—Eli has asked us to visit his ship tomorrow," Abby explained. "He sailed from Brunswick, Maine, you know. Just imagine: no muddy, bumpy carriage ride for a sea captain. And his ship is docked here at Port Freedom. He's inviting us aboard. May we go see it?"

"Well, I don't know," Sara said, astonished by Abigail's enthusiasm. The girl had grown up in Boston and seen many a ship anchored in the harbor without expressing a bit of interest.

"Oh, please, Sara," Abby pleaded. "What did you say its name is, Captain?"

"She. A ship is always a lady, despite what a crew may call her from time to time," the captain said. "Her name is *Victoire.* You are welcome to accompany us, of course, Mrs. Larkfield."

"Your invitation is very kind, captain," Sara said, knowing he had to invite her because she was Abby's chaperon.

"Oh, good. I can hardly wait to see her," Abby said. "This will be my first tour of a frigate."

"Then I'll make the arrangements." The captain smiled smugly over the top of Abby's head as she poured him more tea. Sara grimaced at the gleam of success that glowed in his dark eyes.

Chapter Two

"Good morning, Cap—Eli," Abigail greeted, beaming a sweet smile up at Eli.

The sight of her angelic face framed by fair curls and the green velvet brim of her fur-trimmed bonnet stirred Eli's admiration. Returning her smile he took her gloved hand and helped her into the carriage that awaited them at the inn door.

"It's a beautiful day for the tour of your ship," she said.

"Indeed, I couldn't have arranged for a better morning myself," he agreed, turning to find Mrs. Larkfield glaring at him, her sea-green eyes cool and narrow.

"Good morning to you, ma'am," he said, inclining his head respectfully and trying to rid himself of the feeling he'd just had a bucket of cold water thrown on him. "I'm glad you're joining us," he lied.

"You know why I'm here," Mrs. Larkfield snapped,

brushing passed him and climbing into the carriage without his assistance.

Undaunted, Eli joined the ladies in the carriage and ordered the driver to take them to the docks. He'd made his decision in the early hours of the morning. He was going to see this marriage agreement through, though he'd seriously considered calling the whole thing off, especially since Jacob Conway hadn't deigned to make an appearance himself.

Eli found it offensive that the man had sent his daughters off to deal with marriage and a near stranger alone. He wasn't insulted so much for himself as he was for Abigail. Sweet Abigail, who sat next to him. She deserved better than this indifference from her papa.

As Abigail chatted on enthusiastically about the coming shipboard tour, Eli glanced at Mrs. Larkfield sitting across from him, her back as straight as a mizzenmast. Abigail's older half sister was the other reason he'd almost called this marriage agreement off. Certainly he'd expected to deal with a chaperon; that was only right and proper and in Abigail's best interest. However, he'd never anticipated being burdened with a dour woman in widow's weeds.

On the other hand, he'd invested too much time and energy to foolishly toss aside his efforts now. He was too close to beginning the New Year and a new life with a beautiful, respectable bride to let his pride get in the way.

"Will we be sailing today?" Abigail asked, her expectant smile reminding Eli that he was supposed to be entertaining his intended bride.

He smiled at her sweet enthusiasm. "No, not today. I've given the crew a few days' liberty."

Across from them, Mrs. Larkfield sat in silence, a

soft frown unfurled on her lips. Eli rubbed his bearded chin thoughtfully. He didn't recall ever meeting a woman who truly disliked him, not that he considered himself a lady's man. The fact that he'd reached the age of thirty-two without taking a wife was his choice, not for lack of opportunity. He was a little dismayed that his new suit of clothes, the height of fashion according to the Portsmouth tailor, had failed to make a favorable impression. Maybe he should have shaved his beard after all, he thought. At any rate, Sara Larkfield's animosity posed a new challenge.

He eyed her more closely. The widow's black of her wool coat and velvet bonnet betrayed the smooth creaminess of her skin and enhanced the sea-green depths of her eyes. She had a straight yet delicate nose, a high smooth brow and a full-lipped mouth. Eli noted with a bit of surprise that she was really quite pretty in her own right.

"And will this be your first tour of a frigate, Mrs. Larkfield?" Eli asked politely, wondering what she expected to see aboard the *Victoire.*

"Yes, sir," she replied, rubbing the silver knob of her walking stick.

"Oh, Sara has never even set foot on anything afloat," Abigail supplied for her sister. "Not even a punt on the Charles River."

"You'll like the *Victoire* better than any punt," Eli promised, understanding exactly why Sara Larkfield had remained a landlubber. "There's the *Victoire*'s mast right there, the tallest one flying the Stars and Stripes."

As soon as the carriage pulled up at the dock, Eli alighted and helped Abigail climb nimbly from the carriage. Ignoring the snow and ice on the dock, she ran ahead of them to the foot of the ship's gangway.

Eli waited to help Sara Larkfield down from the vehicle. When he offered his hand, she clasped her walking stick with both hands and frowned as if his assistance were unwelcome and dangerous. "Thank you, sir, but I really am quite able to get around on my own."

"I have little doubt of that, ma'am," Eli said, taking her arm and helping her from the carriage despite her objections. He tucked her free hand under his arm with a firmness that prevented her from withdrawing from his grasp. "Why should you march along on your own when I'm here?"

"What did you say her name is?" Abigail called, gazing up at the frigate's masts thrusting up against the gray sky.

"The *Victoire,*" Eli said as they reached the foot of the gangway.

"The *Victoire,*" Abigail repeated slowly. Then, without waiting for him to assist her, Abigail darted up the narrow gangway. At the top, a courteous sailor handed her down to the deck and gave her a snappy salute. She laughed with delight and saluted back. The surprised sailor blushed.

Sara Larkfield pulled away from Eli again and insisted, "I really can manage. See to Abby."

He released her, satisfied that the ropes along the gangway would steady her if she needed assistance. But as she had said, she managed very well.

The sailor saluted them also. "Welcome aboard, ladies," Eli said.

"Thank you, Captain." Mrs. Larkfield looked over the ship critically.

Even though the day was mild, the sea was unusually heavy. The deck heaved beneath them, yet the uncertain cant seemed to give her no more difficulty than navigating a steady floor.

Eli allowed her to look around on her own for a few moments. He was proud of his growing fleet of sailing vessels, of which the *Victoire* was the flagship. Everywhere, the brass fittings gleamed mirror bright. The deck was scrubbed clean and the gunwales glowed pristine white. Nary a cleat nor a spar bore a speck of rust. Every rope was stowed and every sail neatly furled. And her eyes noted each detail.

Eli couldn't resist leaning close and speaking in a low voice. "We scrubbed away the blood and guts just for your visit."

She pressed her lips together, plainly swallowing an outraged gasp. "You mock me, Captain."

He grinned, enjoying her pique and the color that stained her cheeks. "Never, Mrs. Larkfield. However, I'm glad to know that you have enough humor to accuse me of such a deed."

Chagrin softened her tight expression a bit. Eli decided to play his advantage. "The fact is, I have the greatest respect for your concern for Abigail's future. She is young and you have every right to be concerned about the man who is going to take her from the security of her home."

That seemed to appease her a bit. "I'm glad you appreciate my purpose, sir."

"I wish you'd call me Eli as Abby does."

"I'm quite comfortable calling you Captain."

"As you will, ma'am." Eli inclined his head. So that was how it was going to be. "I just want you to know that Abigail's happiness is as important to me as it is to you."

She rounded on him. "How can I believe you're being honest with me, Captain? You hardly know her. You can't possibly love Abby enough to put her happiness first. If you did, you would not have drawn up this agreement with Papa."

"The agreement was drawn up with every thought for Abigail's happiness," Eli assured her, a bit taken aback by the depth of her feeling. "You must know that."

"I do not." Fire of outrage flashed in her eyes. "Arranged marriages are drawn up for someone's convenience."

"Oh, Sara, look at the cannons," Abigail called from across the deck. She had bent low to peer along the barrel of one the shiny cannons. "Did you fire them, Eli? The cannons I mean."

"Now and again." Eli crossed the deck to Abigail's side. "Usually only a few volleys are necessary."

"Will you take us below deck, Cap—Eli?"

"Is that where you'd like to begin the tour?" he asked, aware his pride in the ship probably showed in his smile. He turned to offer his help to Sara Larkfield once again; she waved him away. The outrage that he'd glimpsed in her eyes had disappeared.

"See to your intended," Sara said, and he took Abigail's arm and led the way below deck.

The efficiency and compactness of the officers' cabins and mess seemed to amuse the ladies. They peered into the hold, deep, black, and stinking of bilge water. Abigail's chatter subsided and she turned slightly pale. Eli led her away toward fresh air.

They climbed to the forecastle to examine the wheel at the helm. Mrs. Larkfield expressed an interest in navigation and Eli patiently described the principles of the sextant, surprised to find she actually seemed to comprehend what he told her. Abigail had become silent and added little to the conversation.

They clambered astern, where they looked out over the gunwale into the harbor. The sea pitched gently beneath them. Sara Larkfield began to quiz him about how the rudder and the wheel at the helm were connected. Eli wondered what any of this had to do with his suitability as a bridegroom, but he did his best to answer her question. Far be it from him to discourage the lady's interest.

Only as he finished his explanation did he realize Mrs. Larkfield wasn't listening to him. She was staring at Abigail. When he followed her gaze, he saw that Abby's complexion had turned from white to green—nearly as green as her fur-trimmed bonnet.

"Abby, are you feeling all right?" Mrs. Larkfield asked.

"Yes, oh, yes," Abigail murmured, without meeting her sister's eyes or looking in the direction of the captain. "It's just the excitement of seeing this beautiful ship."

Eli caught Sara Larkfield's gaze. He knew she understood as well as he did what troubled her younger sister. His heart sank. Though the *Victoire* had never even left the dock, Abigail was pea green with seasickness.

"I think it's time we went ashore," Mrs. Larkfield suggested, hurriedly taking Abigail's arm.

"Of course," Eli agreed. Immediately, he escorted the ladies off the *Victoire* and to the dock.

"Take deep breaths," he overheard Sara Larkfield whisper into Abigail's ear. "That's good. Keep it up. Your head should clear and your stomach settle in a few moments."

"Yes, I hope so," Abigail muttered. "Oh, I'm so embarrassed. Oh, Eli, please don't be disappointed with me."

"I'm certain the captain is not the least disappointed in you," Sara Larkfield said, glancing over Abigail's shoulder at him.

"Of course not," Eli said, doing his best to cover his dismay.

"I think we'd better get her back to the inn and put her to bed," Sara Larkfield said, avoiding Eli's gaze.

Yet as he swung his bride-to-be up in his arms and turned to carry Abigail to the carriage, he glimpsed a gleam in Mrs. Larkfield's eyes that troubled him.

Sara followed the captain along the dock to the carriage, glad that he could not see her face. She was sorry that Abby wasn't feeling well, but the seasickness was a godsend. With it, inspiration had struck Sara like a bolt of lightning. While Eli Whittaker was no fool, he was a man. There was no mistake about that. And it was the little inconveniences that came with having a woman around that a man could not tolerate. Even if Abby's seasickness alone did not deter the captain from marriage, Sara knew *now* what would.

Eli put a rush to the fire in the parlor hearth; and when it caught a flame, he put it to his pipe and drew on it until he tasted the rich flavor of the tobacco. He had only a few moments to enjoy his pipe before the ladies came down dressed for the evening's dance.

To his relief, Abigail had recovered from her illness overnight, and after spending a day together, he was feeling content and confident. Their courtship was moving along very well, very well indeed, despite the unfortunate episode aboard the *Victoire*.

That morning he and Abigail had explored Port Freedom's few shops—in Mrs. Larkfield's watchful company, of course. Abigail proved to be a delightful companion: talkative, undemanding, and excited with each new sight and sound the walk through the town brought. If he hadn't been mistaken, he'd seen admiration in her eyes when she looked up at him.

That afternoon they had gone for a sleigh ride through the snow-covered countryside. Eli had tucked the bear-rug throw carefully around Abigail's feet, and he would have taken more pleasure in their closeness if Mrs. Larkfield hadn't been sitting equally close on the other side of him.

At first only the jingling sleigh bells and the hiss of the runners through the snow filled the quiet as they drove along. Eli feared the sleigh ride was going to be as disastrous as the shipboard tour until Abigail began to sing a child's song. Eli joined in. When that was finished, they moved on to a Christmas carol. Finally Mrs. Larkfield relented and joined them. They spent the rest of the drive reminding each other of childhood rhymes and singing at the top of their lungs. He thought the afternoon had been a great success; at least he had enjoyed himself.

Eli drew thoughtfully on his pipe once more. Beyond the parlor door Alex and Medora Stark were clearing the rooms for the dance and welcoming inn guests and Port Freedom citizens. Eli could hear the musicians tuning up their instruments in the large parlor next door. Furniture scraped across the floor as it was moved.

Eli's mind drifted back to the sleigh ride. Even Sara Larkfield had been smiling a lovely tantalizing half smile by the time they had returned to the stable. He couldn't help wondering what might have happened if she had been at dinner at the Conway Beacon Hill mansion when he'd met Abigail for the second time.

He could almost imagine her sitting across the table contemplating him with that daunting lift of her brow. A cautious, skeptical tilt to her chin. Would the outcome of the marriage agreement have been different if she had been there?

He didn't think so. He was too pleased with Abigail and the prospect of making her his bride to be fazed by Sara Larkfield. Abigail was modest—despite her beauty—soft-spoken and demure. Being a Conway made her the perfect candidate for his bride. He would have her.

He would hardly be the first sea captain with a wife who hated sailing. But he'd hoped to take Abigail along on the safer voyages. Still, he supposed her seasickness was an inconvenience he would learn to tolerate.

The tap of Sara Larkfield's walking stick alerted Eli to the arrival of the ladies. He had hardly moved away from the parlor hearth when Mrs. Larkfield entered the room, obscuring her halting gait with her regal carriage.

"Have I interrupted your smoking?" she asked, none too cordially.

"Not at all, ma'am," he said, laying his pipe on the mantel. "Won't you sit and enjoy the fire with me?"

"I will. Thank you. Abigail is on her way."

Sara Larkfield wore a high-waisted, plum-colored mourning gown, a party frock, sedately decorated with black velvet ribbons and a white lace shawl collar. The afternoon outdoors had pinkened her cheeks, giving her a vibrant glow. In the parlor candlelight, Eli noted for the first time the rich gold highlights in her carefully arranged brown curls.

Abigail appeared in the doorway behind her sister, wearing a blue gown with puff sleeves and a rucked silk hem. She blushed and looked away under Eli's scrutiny.

"Delightful," Eli said, admiring Abigail's gown also. "May I say, both of you ladies look lovely this evening. The fresh air seems to have agreed with you both."

With a charming smile, Abigail bobbed a curtsy. "Why, thank you, sir."

Mrs. Larkfield arched one brow at him as if to acknowledge an obligatory compliment. Her obvious refusal to take Eli's praise seriously annoyed him. Surely she must realize how really lovely she was. It wasn't the same ethereal beauty as Abigail's, yet she possessed a kind of comfortable loveliness that a man would find pleasing to wake to each morning.

For the first time, Eli wondered about the woman's husband. Had he been proud to have this lady on his arm? Had he had enough sense to tell her so?

When the musicians suddenly struck up the first tune of the evening, Eli said, "I believe the dancing is about to begin."

"Yes, I can hear the musicians," Abigail agreed.

A boy of about sixteen stopped in the doorway. "Excuse me, Captain. We need to clear the parlor for the dancing."

"Of course," Eli said. "Are the ladies and I in the way?"

"No, sir, it just takes a moment."

The boy disappeared. A moment later the wood-paneled walls of the room began to fold back from the corner beam. Alex Stark's son appeared again, carefully sliding the panels toward the wall until the smaller parlor opened up into the large one. Alex came in and began to move the table and chairs back toward the walls while the boy rolled up the rug and the Stark girls brought in candle shades to soften the glare. Then the musicians—a violinist, a clarinetist, and a pianist—began a lively country dance.

"I hope you are feeling sprightly, Captain," Sara Larkfield warned, with a soft smile that revealed an unexpected dimple in her left cheek. She seated herself in a chair near the fire. "Abigail loves to dance."

When Eli turned to Abigail, he found her ominously tapping her foot to the music.

Chapter Three

Pleased with the prospect of dancing with his future bride, Eli held out his hand for Abigail's. "Shall we begin?"

"Yes, let's do." Abigail seized his hand and led him onto the dance floor.

The crowd in the inn had already grown from some thirty guests and townspeople—sailors, captains, merchants and tradesmen—to over sixty, all laughing and good-naturedly jostling each other on and off the dance floor. Children ducked in and out of the rooms, enjoying their own games. Even the innkeeper and his family occasionally joined in the festivities as they went about serving drinks and offering food.

Eli discovered that Abigail was an indefatigable dancer, just as Mrs. Larkfield had warned. They danced the jig, the reel, circle dances and several quadrilles. Perspiration soon dampened the hair on Eli's forehead and at the collar of his shirt. He gratefully gave over his place as Abigail's partner to an eager young man whose lady had deserted him. Abigail laughed, clearly delighted to remain on the dance floor. She waved to Eli as he went in search of Sara Larkfield.

He found her still in the chair by the fire, where he'd left her watching the dancers with lively interest. When she spotted him approaching her, she gave him a knowing smile of welcome.

"I see what you mean about Abigail's energy on the dance floor," he conceded before she could utter any kind of 'I told you so.'

"There is no end to her endurance when it comes to dancing," she observed.

A youngster arrived with a tray of punch and grog. Mrs. Larkfield took a cup of punch and Eli helped himself to the grog. When the boy had moved on, she leaned closer to Eli as if to confide in him over the music and laughter.

"She really is very young, you know." Sara Larkfield sipped her punch. The shaded candlelight limned the gold highlights of her hair and rendered her eyes dark and mysterious.

"I'm not insensitive to that," Eli said, wondering what the lady was leading up to.

"No, indeed, you have not been," she agreed. "I did not mean to imply that, Captain. It's just that with youth comes a certain curiosity and wide-eyed wonder that most of us have left behind and that we sometimes find trying after we've matured."

"Like dancing all evening?"

"That and dancing every evening possible," Mrs. Larkfield continued, then added with a shrug, "Abigail never turned down an invitation in Boston. The frolics of youth."

"It was difficult to miss her popularity even at the

one ball I attended," Eli admitted. "But you can hardly expect a man to select a wife who retires to the corner amid festivities."

Eli regretted the words the instant they were out of his mouth. Because of Sara Larkfield's infirmity, she had undoubtedly always been consigned to the corner of the ballroom. "Perhaps that makes me a bit of a fool. For I would miss the company of other charming ladies such as yourself."

She eyed him without the hint of a frown—or a smile. "You are almost as nimble of mind, Captain, as you are of foot."

"Ah, but not nimble enough it would seem," he admitted.

She offered Eli that beguiling half smile that intrigued him so. He decided to ask what he'd longed to know since he'd first met her in the parlor. "How did it happen, the injury to your leg? It was an injury, wasn't it?"

A frown creased her brow. He knew her crippled leg was not a subject she liked to discuss, but he did not withdraw the question or apologize for it.

"An injury," she admitted so quietly that he could barely hear her over the noisy dancers. "When I was ten."

"What happened?"

Her frown deepened. "It's not a very interesting tale. Abigail and I were playing in the carriage house, and we had crawled under the buggy. The groom didn't know I was there. When he pulled the buggy out to ready it for my stepmother, a wheel ran over my leg."

"Abigail was not hurt?"

"Thank heavens, she was out of the way."

Eli suspected that had been more than a stroke of good fortune for Abigail. Sara Larkfield would have seen to it that her sister was out of the way.

"As I was about to say, Abigail is the youngest. My father's favorite."

"So your father told me."

"I must confess, her family has indulged and spoiled her and she has received little preparation for duties of marriage."

"What are you trying to say, Mrs. Larkfield?"

"Oh, don't misunderstand me, Captain," she hurried to say. Eli looked down at the imploring hand she put on his sleeve. The gesture seemed unlike her. Her touch was light, and the warmth of her fingers soaked through his sleeve and seeped into his bones. He stared down at her slender fingers, almost losing track of what she was saying.

"I do not mean to disparage my sister in any way. Abigail is sweet and vital and so very beautiful. I simply mean to beg your patience with her when you find that your new bride has much to learn about running a household and performing the—uh—the various other duties of a wife."

Stunned by his reaction to her touch, Eli said nothing. After Mrs. Larkfield withdrew her hand and turned back to watch the dancers, his body longed to feel the heat of her hand on his arm again. His gut was telling him to listen to her carefully.

"Then there is Abby's penchant for costly gowns. However, I'm sure that a fatherly word from you will make her restrain herself."

"Fatherly?"

"I'm so sorry." Chagrin crossed her face. "A difference of almost fourteen years is of little importance here. Perhaps husbandly is a better word."

"I prefer husbandly," Eli muttered, becoming uncomfortable with the trend of the conversation. "What else should I know?"

"Oh, there's nothing else." Sara Larkfield paused, an additional thought seeming to come to mind. "I hope you love dogs. She adores keeping the house full of mutts—the little fuzzy, lap sort."

"I don't remember any dogs at the house when I dined there."

"Oh, I'm sure Papa had them shut away," she said, waving her hand as if she were shooing the dogs away. "Ordinarily, they make for a very lively homecoming."

Every ship had a cat or two to control the rat population in the hold. That was the extent of Eli's experience with pets. He did not relish the thought of coming home to his bride and have his ankles attacked by yapping, four-footed dust mops.

"Let us talk of something else," she said, with a flutter of her hands. "You have time to get to know Abby yourself in the next few days."

Eli studied Sara Larkfield closely. "While we're talking about your sister, perhaps you can tell me why there is such sadness in her eyes sometimes."

She blinked, then opened her mouth and closed it.

"Come now. You've been so honest with me about her credits and her debits. You must answer this for me."

She looked at him again. Eli could feel her stretching a mental measuring string around him. Was she concerned about his trustworthiness or about how he would react to her answer?

She sipped from her punch cup and took a deep breath. "I must have your promise to keep this matter in confidence."

"Of course," Eli said. "I'm practically family, am I not?"

Mrs. Larkfield seemed to cast a guilty glance in the

direction of her sister. "Well, you see, Abigail is sometimes troubled by—moodiness."

Eli waited for her to explain, and she said, "The malady doesn't trouble her often, and when it does, it's very mild. If it were more than that I'm sure Papa would have felt compelled to explain it to you. There you have it. Simple moodiness. She even weeps sometimes. Nothing to fret about. She simply needs a bit of comforting."

Moodiness? Eli stared across the dance floor at Abigail, who was laughing as she and her dance partner ducked under the clasped arms of the other dancers. Her cheeks glowed with the exertion of the dance and her silvery curls bounced in time with the music as she executed the dance steps.

"Captain, it's truly nothing to be concerned about." She touched his arm again.

Eli turned and held her gaze. He was not an intuitive man. He liked facts and prided himself on his accurate, unemotional perceptions, but he sensed something was wrong with her explanation. Sara Larkfield was not being completely honest with him. She looked away and busied herself with sipping from her punch cup.

When the dance ended, Eli watched as Abigail's partner escorted her to his side and she thanked the young man for partnering her. Eli admired her pretty manners and failed to find any hint of sadness in her eyes at the moment.

"Are you having a good time, Abby?" Her sister asked.

"Indeed, quite delightful," Abigail said, still breathless from the dancing.

Eli rose from his chair. "I believe supper is being served in the dining room, ladies. Please allow me to escort you."

To his dismay, Abigail's laughter faded. As she took his arm, he saw the sadness return to her eyes. "Of course, sir. Please be our escort."

Sara Larkfield rose. Steadying herself with her walking stick, she leaned toward Eli's shoulder and whispered up into his ear, "Nothing to worry about. Rest assured."

Later that night the truth of what Sara Larkfield was doing hit Eli with such force that it brought him up out of a sound sleep. Wide-awake, he sat up in the dark, completely aware of what the gleam in Mrs. Larkfield's eye had been all about. Despite her lip service to Abigail's happiness, she simply did not want him to marry her sister. She had made no secret of how she felt, and she was willing to tell any tale to prevent his marriage to Abigail.

Eli settled back in bed, slipped his hands flat behind his head and contemplated the problem. Was Sara Larkfield jealous of her sister, unwilling to allow Abigail to find happiness when she had none? The lady was clearly not happy. Or did she love Abigail enough to lie to save her from a man she considered unworthy? Was he unworthy because he'd been a privateer? Did Sara Larkfield truly see him as a ruthless pirate who could never make Abigail happy?

At first, the revelation stung. Then as the sting faded, Eli smiled to himself in the darkness. Mrs. Larkfield was not jealous. Her ready admission, without a hint of rancor, that Abigail was her father's favorite child proved that. It also told him that Abigail was a favorite of her sister's, too. If that were true, then she would fight like a tigress to protect Abigail.

Abigail moody? He chuckled to himself. He recalled the nervous flutter of Sara Larkfield's hands as she'd used the word. She'd been lying about Abigail's moodiness. There was another explanation for Abigail's sadness. He was certain of it. She was only a child. He would discover the source and remedy the problem in no time. What else had Sara Larkfield lied about?

As for Abigail's inexperience in running a house—if that weren't another of her sister's fabrications—he had lived under all sorts of make-do circumstances. He could survive most any kind of household until Abby gained the experience she needed. And as for her dancing . . .

He could deal with Abigail's youthful shortcomings. It was her sister, Sara, who posed the real problem for him. And when had he started thinking of her as Sara? At any rate, he knew exactly what to do about her perception of him as a ruthless sea captain, he thought as he drifted off to sleep. He knew exactly what to do to reassure Sara Larkfield.

Sleepless, Sara lay on her back, listening to the faint crash of waves against the rocky shore. Next to her, Abby slept peacefully.

Heavens, she hated fibbing, even to a privateer who had probably done far more devious things, but doing so seemed necessary. The lies about Abigail's youthful frivolity had rolled off her tongue easily. What was she to say to him when he asked about the sadness in Abby's eyes? There was no denying it. Even after the passage of three months, the memories of Abby's disappointment still plagued the girl. When it did, the sadness always surfaced in her lovely blue eyes.

Papa could pretend he had no role in it, but the grief in Abby's eyes troubled Sara. Of all the young men who had been drawn to the sorrow in those blue eyes, only the captain had asked about it.

He'd spoken up and cut straight to the core of the

matter as though he really cared. Sara had to admire him for that, much as she didn't want to. She was beginning to think he might be a truly caring man. It was even possible he might not be a bad husband. Sara could accept that, provided Abby chose him of her own free will.

Sara had studied the marriage agreement her father had signed with Captain Whittaker. One point had been clear: If Abigail called off the wedding, the captain would cover all the expenses, but the Conways received nothing. However, if the captain changed his mind, if he defaulted for any reason, he would still pay the expenses and the Conways would receive a portion of Whittaker's promised investment in the family business—only a portion.

In the business sense, it was a fair agreement. Still, Sara's father needed the whole sum to rescue him from his debts. She knew that. Abby knew it too and undoubtedly felt compelled to agree to the marriage for Papa's sake.

Long ago, Sara had accepted a marriage for the good of the family. It had been a match no better than a young woman with a bad leg could expect.

But Abby was beautiful, sweet and perfect. She deserved better than a marriage of convenience to benefit the Conways. Sara was determined that her younger sister have that choice. Privateer Eli Whittaker would just have to look to his own welfare—and so would Papa.

Chapter Four

A fresh snow fell during the night, whitening the grimy streets, blanketing the gray shake roofs and frosting the bare tree branches. It sparkled even in the pale rays of the dawning winter sun. In the bay, just beyond the inn, the ocean glittered sea green and foamy white.

Eli rose early and ordered hot water; when it arrived, he shaved off his beard. To satisfy himself that he'd done the right thing, he examined his jaw closely in the mirror. He'd not spent many days in the sun since winter had set in, so his face had a uniform coloring. If it were summer, he'd have had a tanned forehead and nose and white jaws and chin. He rubbed his bare chin. He looked good, he decided. He hoped the ladies would think so, too.

The process must have taken longer than he had expected. When he went downstairs to the dining room, he found that Abigail and Sara had eaten already and left.

"Downed their tea, gobbled their sausage and doughnuts and hurried outside," Medora Stark told him as she cleared the table where the sisters had breakfasted.

"Outside?"

"Indeed," she said, shaking her head. "They said to tell you they'd be back directly. You might catch them if you hurry. They just ran around the corner of the building. Mrs. Larkfield doesn't allow that bad leg of hers to keep her from doing much, does she?"

"No, she doesn't," Eli agreed as he headed out of the dining room to find his own coat and hat.

Outside he followed the girls' trail in the snow around the inn, back toward the kitchen door. They had stopped at the corner and thrown snowballs at each other. He saw the evidence of their frolicking in the blemished snow.

He wondered where they were now. The only sound disturbing the crisp air was the breaking of the waves on the rocky shore in front of the inn. From the lake behind the inn came the cries and laughter of morning ice-skaters.

When he rounded the corner near the kitchen, he glimpsed Sara—Mrs. Larkfield—wearing a black coat and bonnet as usual. She was working diligently on a snowman with cranberry eyes.

"There you are," he said, smiling at the sight of stern Sara Larkfield placing a pinecone nose on the snowman's face. "Mrs. Stark said you and Abigail were outside already. Good morning."

She stared at him. When she continued to stare, Eli looked over his shoulder, wondering if someone or something else had appeared on the scene without his knowledge. "Is something wrong?"

"Oh, no," she said. "I'm sorry. You—you shaved off your beard."

Eli rubbed his denuded chin. "I thought it might please . . . Abigail."

"Well, yes, I'm sure it will," she said. "Clean shaven is fashionable these days. But—"

"But?"

Shyly, she cast him that enigmatic half smile. "I rather liked your beard. Trimmed and all."

"Oh?" Eli did not understand why it pleased him that she had liked his beard, but he suddenly regretted shaving it off. "Uh, where is Abigail?"

"She went into the kitchen to ask for some hot maple syrup."

"For what? Didn't she have breakfast with you?"

"To make candy," she said, apparently astonished that he needed to ask the reason. "You know, syrup-and-snow candy. You remember making that when you were a boy, don't you?"

"I went to sea when I was ten years old," Eli said. "I don't remember anything about snow candy."

"You went to sea when you were ten?"

"Not to be a privateer, of course," Eli explained. "My father was a fisherman and he needed all the help he could get. So my brother and I were signed on as soon as we could haul a net over the gunwales."

"Oh, well, then you're in for a treat." She gazed up at him with curiosity in her eyes. "So you began your career as a fisherman?"

"A fine honest trade," Eli said, giving the snowman a tree-branch arm. "My fall from grace came later in life."

"You mean the privateering?" she asked, picking up a small branch to give the snowman his other arm.

"If you knew it was a fall, why did you become a privateer?"

"It did not take me and my brother long to discover that there are more lucrative professions practiced on the high seas than fishing." When Sara said no more, Eli added, "My younger brother and I were about to get our shipping business off the ground when the war started. The opportunity to make some quick money was too good to pass up. So we applied for a commission."

"That sounds very opportunistic, Captain."

"I have found that successful business is often a matter of opportunism, Sa—Mrs. Larkfield. By the way, I invited my brother to the wedding, but he had to remain in Brunswick for business reasons. He sends his regrets."

She frowned, but said nothing. Eli wondered if the frown was over his brother or mention of the wedding.

The kitchen door opened and Abigail scurried out, carrying a steaming tin pitcher of maple syrup in one hand and a flat wooden spatula in the other. The rich scent of maple and vanilla filled the crisp morning air. "Good morning, Captain. Have you joined us for syrup-and-snow candy?"

"So it seems. Your sister assures me it is quite a treat."

"And so it is," Abigail agreed. "Where do you think is the best place, Sara? Where is the best snow?"

"I think over here," Sara Larkfield said, leading the way across the yard, her walking stick piercing the snow ahead of her and her hem brushing aside the fresh dry flakes. She stopped near a small drift of pristine crystals.

"This looks perfect," Abigail agreed.

She held the pitcher out away from her skirts and

poured the fragrant whiskey-colored syrup into the snow. The icy flakes melted where the syrup first hit the snow and vapor steamed into the air. The syrup crystallized instantly as ropes of rich maple color spiraled across the snow. Abigail stopped pouring; then she and Sara peered at the brown spot in silence.

"We have to wait for it to harden," Abigail explained in a whisper as if speaking aloud would hamper the process.

Eli watched the ladies study the snow, waiting for a magic moment only they seemed to understand. Suddenly Sara pulled off her mitten, took the spatula from Abigail and scooped it into the snow. She came up with a brown sugary lump of dripping-wet candy.

"Try it first," she said to Abigail. "We want to be sure it's right for the captain."

Obediently, Abigail pinched off a piece and popped it into her mouth. Closing her eyes, she tasted the candy. Then her delicate brows came together in a delightful furrow of concentration.

Eli waited in patient silence until Abigail opened her eyes and said, "Yes, it's right. Just right. Here, try this piece, Captain."

Abigail plucked another piece from the candy lump and held it up for the captain to take in his mouth. Before he could eat from Abigail's bare fingers, her sister snatched the piece of candy and thrust the candy-laden spatula between Abigail and Eli. "Here, take a big piece from the whole, Captain."

Eli hesitated only a moment. It would have pleased him to take the candy from Abigail. Receiving food from a lady's hand was a seemingly innocent yet intimate gesture that stirred him.

But Sara Larkfield was the chaperon. He should respect her wishes, he reminded himself. Dutiful he pinched off a sticky piece of hardened syrup-and-snow candy for himself and put it into his mouth.

At first he tried to chew it, but it stuck to every tooth in his mouth. Then he decided to let it melt on his tongue, cold and flavorful.

Sara watched his face as the rich sweet golden maple flavor suffused throughout his mouth and tickled his senses—and his sweet tooth. Apparently satisfied that he was developing an appropriate appreciation for snow candy, she took a piece for herself.

"More?" She offered the spatula.

Abigail suddenly began to giggle. She covered her full mouth with her hand and danced in mysterious and uncontrollable mirth. Mystified, Eli and Sara stared at her.

At last she gulped down her candy and pointed at Eli. "I just noticed. You shaved off your beard."

"Yes. What do you think?" Eli asked, already annoyed with her laughter.

"It's very nice," she said, nodding her head in appreciation. "Truly, it makes you look younger."

"Younger?" Eli caught a glimpse of amusement spreading across Sara's face just before she turned away.

"I mean," Abigail stammered, laughter still in her voice, her pretty mouth working in and out of a bow shape as she fought to control her hilarity. "It makes you look more like a man of your youthful years. It's very handsome. Truly, I think so. Sara, give him more candy."

When Sara turned and offered him the candy again, Eli could see she was biting her lip, choking back laughter that he understood sprang from a source entirely different from her sister's. "I thank you, ma'am," he said, hearing the stiffness in his own voice. "I think you should take another bite."

Eli swiftly pinched the last of the candy from the spatula and put it to Sara's lips. He pressed it so closely to her mouth that she could hardly refuse it. Laughing aloud, she accepted it. As she did, he felt her warm lips brush against the sensitive pad of his bare thumb. Her warmth seared through his body and her softness aroused him.

Forgetting that Abigail was standing right there, he suddenly longed to draw his thumb along Sara's lips, touching her moistness and soaking up her warmth. Then he wanted to kiss her, soundly, sharing the heavenly maple sweetness and shivering chill of the candy. He wanted to put his hands on her body and feel her move beneath them, alive and responsive to his touch.

Her gaze met his briefly, her eyes widening in surprise—and understanding. Had their unexpected contact excited her as much as it had him? He ached to think so.

"We need to make more." Abigail was already pouring more syrup into the snow.

"More?" Eli repeated, totally confused.

"Oh, no, I think I've had quite enough." Sara thrust the spatula into her sister's hand and turned toward the kitchen. "I'm going in. It's much too cold for me out here."

"Sara, you're missing something special," Abigail teased.

Eli watched Sara go, well aware that he should be glad to be left alone with his bride-to-be. What bridegroom didn't treasure the moments when a sharp-eyed chaperon turned her back? But he really longed to go inside and sit by the fire with Sara. He turned, unable to resist watching Sara walk toward the inn, her black skirts brushing through the fresh snow. Abigail was already scooping candy from the snow.

"The syrup-and-snow candy is ready," she cried with youthful glee. "Here, try this."

Eli heard the door close behind Sara as he took the piece of candy Abigail offered and put it in his mouth. He smiled faintly at Abigail, but he found the candy's sweetness was gone.

Eli and Abigail whiled away the rest of the morning with a walk through the woods. Abigail chatted about plays and books Eli had vaguely heard of. He was pleased with the extent of her education and surprised by the range and depth of her reading. A business man, a shipper, needed a well-informed wife. He wondered if Sara was also so well-read.

Upon their return, they enjoyed a hot lunch alone in the small parlor. Sara sent her regrets by way of Medora Stark. She had a headache and wished to rest, Medora reported; then the hostess invited Eli and Abigail to join her and some Portsmouth couples for an apple-paring bee.

Eli and Abigail agreed the frolic sounded like fun. When they entered the kitchen, they found it full of courting couples laughing and talking and ready to begin the bee. Medora introduced them around.

Eli seated Abigail at the kitchen table, where she immediately joined the conversation, laughter, and nonsensical shuffling of the wooden bowls and switching of chairs. Eli smiled at their youthful foolishness all the while wondering how Sara's headache was and hoping she might be feeling better soon.

"Most of my cooking may still be terrible, but my apple pies are the best in New Hampshire," Medora told the young people when she'd gained their attention. Cheers of agreement came from the youths seated in her kitchen. "I know it's because I always have the best parers in the state."

After more cheers, she said, "In this basket of apples by the door is one apple dyed cherry red—only one. Whoever finds the red apple may claim a kiss from whomever he or she favors. Now no digging through to find the dyed apple. You must pare them as they come. Understand?"

The group laughed. Sanctioned kisses were a rare commodity in a New England town, and Eli knew each young man around the table would be eager to find the apple. He wondered how many of them would heed the rules to get it. He didn't intend to.

"Begin," Medora challenged.

Eli slipped the blade of his knife just beneath the wrinkled skin of the dried apple and began spiraling the peel away. The fruit was from the fall harvest and had already become too shriveled to eat out of hand, yet the maturity made the fruit excellent for baking. There was something to be said for being seasoned and mellowed, Eli thought. Beside him, Abigail began to peel also.

"I bet I can peel more than you," she whispered to him.

"Don't be too sure," Eli warned, caught up in Abigail's zeal. He had every intention of claiming the kiss.

The apple parers worked steadily, but laughed and teased as each filled his or her wooden bowl with apples ready for baking in Medora Stark's pies.

Soon Eli was surprised to see that Abigail's bowl was filled with apples. So were many others, but no one had found the dyed apple yet. Eli finished the last apple at his elbow and left his seat to get more from the basket by the door. He dug through the fruit, searching for the right piece, the red one he needed.

On his first trip to the basket he didn't find the apple and had to give up his search when Medora Stark turned a stern eye on him. Another boy went to the basket next and returned without it, too. Finally Medora turned her attention to helping one of her grandsons and Eli headed for the basket. Quickly he delved through the layers of apples. There it was on the very bottom. Mrs. Stark would know he had dug through the fruit to find it, but Eli didn't care. It was time to kiss Abigail.

"I found it." He held up the cherry-red fruit.

"And so you have, Captain," Medora said, smiling knowingly at Eli. "And I'm not surprised either."

"You must allow him to claim a kiss, Abigail," a girl cried from across the table.

Smiling, Eli advanced on Abigail. The crowd laughed and applauded. She rose from her chair, a look of consternation on her face, which Eli attributed to surprise and inexperience. When she allowed him to put his finger under her chin and to lift her face to his, everyone in the kitchen fell expectantly silent.

"So we share a kiss, at last," he murmured, then bent to press his lips against hers.

He brushed her mouth lightly. She remained frozen in place. Then he pressed his lips more firmly against hers, aware that they had a kitchen full of witnesses. No time for passion, but definitely the moment to display enthusiasm for the benefit of the audience—and his intended. To his surprise, he felt neither.

When Eli pulled away and looked down into Abigail's face, her expression stunned him. A huge tear rolled down her cheek. He stepped back, bewildered.

"Excuse me," she nearly sobbed and dashed from the room.

Baffled, Eli turned to the others, and Medora Stark explained, "Bridal nerves."

"Yes, I fear so." He left the room desperately trying to believe that himself.

Chapter Five

The small parlor was empty, except for the healthy fire burning in the grate. The candles in the wall sconces had been lit, and the pewter and china laid out on the supper table gleamed in the flickering light.

Sara sighed with relief and entered the room. Though her headache had disappeared, she wasn't quite ready to face the captain yet. Selecting the large upright chair next to the hearth, she settled into it and leaned her walking stick between the arm of her chair and her skirt.

Abigail followed her in, wringing her hands and looking guiltily around the parlor. "What do you think he means when he says he wants to talk about my marriage portion?"

"I have no idea." Sara said. The captain had sent a message to the girls' room requesting their presence before supper to discuss the marriage portion. "I believed Papa and Captain Whittaker had settled all those details."

"So did I." Abigail perched on a chair across from Sara. "Do you think he's going to hold my lack of a portion and what happened this afternoon against me?"

"I don't know, Abby," Sara said, careful not to betray her concern to her younger sister. Between sobs Abby had confessed all about the kiss and the tearful scene in the kitchen. "However, I am certain a man does not feel very flattered to have the young woman he has just kissed burst out in tears—especially when the young woman is his promised bride and she weeps in front of a roomful of people."

"It's not because I don't like him," Abby wailed softly. "He's really very nice. He's handsome and polite. And if I must marry a man who *father* chooses—"

"I know, dear," Sara said, hoping to calm Abby. "We still have time to stop this marriage if you want. However, the captain seems a reasonable man. I think he might forgive you if that's what you want."

"I don't know," Abby confessed. "I just don't know."

"Then calm yourself and do be agreeable this evening."

"I'll try."

Medora Stark appeared in the doorway, wiping her hands on her apron. "May we bring the chests in now, Mrs. Larkfield?"

"Chests?" Puzzled, Sara looked to Abby, who shrugged.

"Yes, ma'am. The captain said you ladies would be wanting to go through the chests this evening."

"Well, of course, if it's something the captain wants. Yes, bring them in."

Soon a strapping lad Sara had seen in the stables

the day she had arrived staggered through the doorway carrying an enormous wooden chest on his back. Another lad followed with a second chest and even a third boy trudged into the parlor bearing another. They lined the chests up on the floor beneath the window, made a courteous bow to the ladies and left the room, huffing and puffing. Sara and Abigail stared at the huge wooden boxes, then at each other.

"Do you think there's some mistake?" Abigail whispered.

"No mistake, Miss Conway. That's the last of the boxes the captain ordered delivered to you," Medora Stark said from the doorway. "You must be excited by all this. It's so romantic the way the captain has arranged for your courtship and wedding. You know, Mr. Stark and I had an arranged marriage."

"Truly?" Abigail asked, clearly astonished. "Who arranged your match?"

"Our parents." Medora continued nostalgically. "But I knew Alex was something special from the time we were very young. Oh, there were some ups and downs. Some unexpected obstacles"—she paused with a small smile—"indeed there were. But we were married on Christmas Day, too, just as you are to be. Thirty-four years ago it will be this Christmas Day. I haven't regretted a minute of our life together."

"You and Mr. Stark seem very happy," Sara said, touched by Medora Stark's smile of contentment and by her effort to comfort Abigail.

"Indeed we are," Medora said. "The heart only grows fonder with time. Don't let the newness and strangeness of your marriage frighten you, Abigail. The captain is a fine man. Everything will work out just fine—as long as you truly love each other."

"Thank you, Mrs. Stark," Abigail said.

"You're entirely welcome," Medora said, turning to

leave the parlor. "Just let me know if you need anything else."

Sara and Abby stared at the boxes again. Then Abby giggled and asked, "What do you think is in them? Maybe treasure? Maybe chains of gold, jeweled sabers and pieces of eight."

"Abigail, contain your fantasies," Sara cautioned, though she entertained similar thoughts. "He wouldn't bring such a thing as his booty here. Not in front of us. The Starks obviously run a respectable place."

They both started at the sound of booted feet outside the door and looked around as the captain strode into the room.

"Good evening, ladies." Tonight he wore a brown velvet coat, the fabric as rich and dark as his eyes, with a waistcoat the color of burnt sienna and a ruffled white shirt. Clean shaven, well dressed and smiling, he looked anything but an infamous privateer or a rough ship's captain. He was so incredibly handsome that Sara could hardly take her eyes off him.

Her insides warmed at his smile and the light in his keen eyes made her heart flutter just a bit. The spot on her lip where his thumb had touched her that morning began to ache.

"Did Mr. Stark bring—" he began, then halted in the middle of the room. "Ah, there they are—the chests I asked for. In fact, they are a gift for you, Abigail."

"The chests are for me?" Abby had been staring at him, too. An unfamiliar, unexpected stab of envy lanced through Sara, leaving her longing for the first time in her life to be in her sister's place.

"Yes. Here, let's get them open." The captain turned and called out the door. "Mr. Stark, a crowbar if you will. We have shipping boxes to open."

Once the crowbar arrived, the captain began to pry nails from the lids. "I hope you will not think me presumptuous."

"Oh, Captain—Eli, we would never think such a thing," Abby said.

The lid of the first chest popped off. The captain leaned it against the box and parted the packing materials to reveal a chest full of bolts of silks, calicoes, linen and sturdy broadcloth.

"When your father told me that there would not be enough for you to bring a marriage portion to the altar, I thought it regrettable that a bride should be without her portion on her wedding day."

Sara and Abby stared at the box in breathless silence.

"There are goods here for towels and bed linens," the captain explained as if he found the awestruck silence awkward. "There is ticking and—You will need to cut and hem the items yourself . . . or we can have them made if you wish. Won't you come see what is here for yourself?"

"Oh, Captain," Abby gasped at last and scurried across the room to kneel before the chest and caress the treasures inside. "You don't know how I've longed to sew my own linens as a bride and wife is meant to do."

The captain smiled down at the top of Abigail's head, then glanced across at Sara.

"So many dress goods," Abby cried. "Cambric and chintz, too."

Sara cleared her throat. "Very generous, sir."

His thoughtfulness and generosity genuinely touched her. By rights, her papa should have made certain Abby had these things to bring to her marriage. Most brides expected to present these household items to their new husband. If for some reason they were unable to, most men would have simply given their new wives permission to make the necessary purchases after the wedding. Few gave their brides' family pride in their marriage portions little more thought.

Eli's smile broadened; then he moved quickly to the next chest and pried it open. "Let's see what's in here. Kettles, skillets, pots, pewter and china."

Even before he pried off the last lid, Sara could smell the spices. As soon as Eli laid the lid aside, Abigail stooped over the box to examine the contents as excited as a child on Christmas morning. The scents of sandalwood and more filled the room.

"Oh, look, Sara!" Abby cried. "Nutmeg, cinnamon, tea, molasses, indigo and brandy. Everything is here. Everything a household could possibly need. Oh, and look at this: the best needles and embroidery silks and—"

Smiling, the captain laid the crowbar aside and joined Sara in front of the fire while Abby continued to paw through the goods. He stopped before Sara and pulled a long narrow box from his coat pocket.

"And for you, Sara." He offered the box to her.

The sound of her Christian name spoken in his deep voice made Sara tingle with awareness. She blushed. "A gift is not necessary, sir."

"I want you to have something," he said with a droll smile and a slight, mocking bow. "For your many kindnesses."

Sara smiled at him, amused by his teasing, yet touched by the gesture of a gift. She opened the box to find an intricately carved sandalwood fan. "It's lovely, Eli. Thank you."

Together they watched as Abby dug through the chests discovering more treasures. Then Sara looked up at him, feeling suddenly shy. "I don't know how to thank you, Captain. Every bride wishes to bring her own household goods to a marriage. The lack of a marriage portion has troubled Abby."

"I only wish for my bride to be happy," the captain said. He turned suddenly on Sara as if some new thought had occurred to him. "I hope you had a portion to bring to your marriage?"

The intimacy of the question surprised and embarrassed her. She blushed again and flipped the fan open as though to examine it more closely. "As a matter of fact, I did. It was a modest one, but Papa had not yet fallen upon such hard times. And taking a woman like me to wife, my husband wasn't expecting much."

Sara suddenly wished she hadn't revealed so much.

Eli frowned and leaned against the mantel, but his gaze remained on Abby. "I'm sure your husband was pleased with your contribution to the household."

"Amos Larkfield was an older man who'd been widowed twice," Sara stated simply, surprised by the sudden resentment she felt rising inside. "He was not much interested in my marriage portion. His household was already established and well supplied."

"An older man like myself?"

Sara glanced up at Eli to see that he was teasing her. "Oh, much, much older!" she assured him, quick to mend any offense. "Mr. Larkfield was nearly Papa's age and had lost his tolerance for youthful frolics."

Distant memories of her own wedding six years before suddenly unfolded before her. It had been a significant day in her life, yet not one she would have counted among the happiest. Her bridegroom had taken little pleasure in their wedding festivities. For Amos Larkfield, their union was a practical arrangement: He was a man with bad lungs looking for a good nurse and wife. Papa had been very pleased with the match.

"He died some time ago, did he not?" the captain asked. "You must mourn his passing greatly, to be still wearing black."

"Mr. Larkfield was an old family friend."

"And you must miss him."

"We were content enough," Sara felt obliged to add.

"Then you should have no concern about the fourteen years that separate Abigail and me."

"My marriage to Mr. Larkfield is not the standard I choose to measure Abigail's future against," Sara said, suddenly impatient with conversation and the captain. "My situation was nothing like Abigail's. She is young and lovely and full of life. She deserves more than I had with Mr. Larkfield."

Eli turned from the mantel and regarded her, the teasing light in his eyes replaced by some emotion dark and strange to Sara. "Are you saying that for some reason you didn't deserve to be happy?"

"Nonsense, I'm merely saying that Abigail has many more choices than I had and I'm here to be certain that she makes the most of them."

"Oh? Pray explain," he implored.

Sara knew he was baiting her. "I need not explain myself to you, sir. My arranged marriage was a very good match for a young woman with—for me. And I was content in it. Abigail's future is another matter."

The captain grew restless, turning back to the hearth and kicking at a hot coal that had rolled from the fire. "I see no reason a lady of your quality should have settled for anything less than the happiness you desire."

Sara stared at him, surprised by his words and even more surprised by the way he'd raised his voice almost as if he were angry about something she'd said.

"Eli? Sara?"

"Yes, Abigail." The captain turned to Abby.

"Look what I've found." Abby brandished a pair of intricately wrought silver candlesticks.

To Sara's relief the captain left the fireside and joined Abby beside the chest.

"Aren't they the most beautiful candlesticks you've ever seen? Oh, Captain, thank you."

"You are welcome. Did you see that the pewter and the silver are all prepared for monogramming with our initials?"

"Indeed, you've thought of everything." Abby swung the candlesticks wide, bounced up on her tiptoes and spontaneously planted a kiss on his cheek.

For a moment, Sara thought the captain was going to kiss Abby in return. But he did not. Instead, a smile spread across his handsome face and he laughed.

"That's much more promising than our experience this afternoon."

Abby blushed. "You've been very kind and patient with me, sir—Eli." Abigail turned and grinned at Sara. "Isn't he wonderful?"

Sara nodded, afraid to speak. Afraid a quaver in her voice would betray her fear that the captain had at last won Abby's heart.

Chapter Six

Eli's gift of the marriage portion banished the sorrow from Abby's eyes. Sara watched for it, but no sadness returned that evening or the next morning as they all sat down to breakfast together. She wondered that Abigail's unhappiness could be so easily dismissed, but the light of excitement in her little sister's eyes reassured her. Abby's pleasure bubbled over in her voice and her smiles and her energy.

"Do you ice-skate, Eli?" Abby asked. "I'd love to go ice-skating. I heard the girls at the paring bee say the ice on the lake behind the inn is excellent."

The captain cast a questioning glance at Sara. "I skated some as a boy."

"Mrs. Stark told me that there are all kinds of ice skates in the warming shed," Abby said. "Something for everyone."

"Then you must go, you two," Sara said, afraid that the captain was hesitating on her account. With false enthusiasm, she added, "Abby is an excellent skater. I'm sure, Eli, that the skill will come back to you as soon as you are on the ice. I'll enjoy some reading."

"No, you must come," he insisted with some mysterious purpose in his dark eyes.

"You're very kind, Captain, to want to include me—" Sara glanced at Abby for help.

"Sara really doesn't mind sitting by herself, Eli," Abby said.

"But I *would* like for you to come," he insisted, his eyes on Sara. "Let's go see what they have in the warming shed that we can use to amuse ourselves on the ice."

"That might be fun, Sara." Abby had never been one to exclude her from anything. "Why not come?"

"Oh, why not," Sara relented, feeling outnumbered. Once they were out on the ice and involved in their games she could always take her leave. "If I'm going to sit watching you, I'll change into something warmer."

"Good." The captain grinned, amazingly pleased with her acquiescence.

The lake lay behind Freedom Tavern, an icy-blue expanse filling a valley between the wooded hills. Bare maples, oaks and chestnuts stood straight and black against the white snow. A clear sunlit sky stretched overhead. Fragrant green pines sang softly every time the breeze gusted in from the sea.

Inn guests had already worn a path between the outbuildings to the warming shed and the lake beyond. Another trail branched off to the Starks' lumber mill on the other side of the hill. It had been shut down for the coldest part of the winter. The threesome trudged along the path, their insides warmed with a breakfast of hot tea, grilled fish and buttered toast.

When they reached the warming shed by the lake, the captain shoved open the door. "First, we get a fire started in the stove."

While he raked ashes aside in the iron stove and laid in fresh wood for a fire, Abby began to examine the variety of skates hanging from the wall. Benches lined one side of the narrow shed opposite the wall on which hung skating blades. Sara settled herself on the bench. At a quick glance, she saw nothing on the wall that could be of use to her.

Using the tinderbox left on a shelf above the woodbox, the captain lit the fire in the stove. Turning to Sara, he said, "We'll have this place warm soon."

Abby pulled a pair of blades from the collection on the wall. "I think these will work for me."

"Good. What else is here?" he asked, joining Abby in her perusal of the blades.

Feeling a little forlorn and annoyed with herself for it, Sara looked about the shed. She wondered about how many skaters had sat on the benches, strapping on their skates, laughing in anticipation, then returned later with numb toes, red noses and stiff fingers. A New England winter's tradition. She really shouldn't have come.

"Ho, Sara, look here," the captain called from the far corner behind the stove.

Sara could hear him rummaging around in a stack of discarded furniture and baskets. A moment later he came from around the stove carrying a straight-backed armchair with short sled runners fastened on the legs. To the back were attached two grips much like plow handles, one on each side for pushing the contraption.

"And would this suit you, Sara?"

"Well, I've never seen such a contrivance," Sara said, staring at it with wonder and curiosity.

"The product of Yankee ingenuity, no doubt," the captain said. "I asked Alex Stark about something like this while you were putting on your heavier clothes. He assured me it is sound and used often."

Sara stared at the chair, trying to decide if the idea of being pushed across the ice in such an apparatus delighted her fancy or insulted her infirmity. What would happen if the driver lost control?

"Well—" she began.

"I think it's a wonderful thing!" Abby cried. "Let's try it. *I* want to ride in it, even if you don't."

"I think you should put skates on, too," the captain said, retreating to the wall to select blades before Sara could object.

"Skates?" Sara stared at him, convinced he'd lost his mind. She still wasn't certain about riding in the chair. And what earthly good would skates be to her? "I don't think—"

"You'll see," he said, turning to eye the tips of her boots that peeked from beneath her skirts. He reached for a set of skates hanging from the wall. "These will do."

"Captain, I don't think—"

"You'll see." He knelt before Sara and reached for her left leg, but she pulled her bad foot away from him. Catching her eye, he promised, "It'll be all right, Sara. Will you trust me in this?"

Beside them, Abigail sat down and began to put on her skates. Panic caught at Sara's heart. Even with only a small audience of Abby and the captain, she had no desire to make a fool of herself on the ice.

Yet she found herself gazing into Eli's dark eyes, longing to trust him. She was about to let Abby marry him. She wanted to believe that, whatever he might be at sea, with her and Abby he was a gentleman who wouldn't betray them.

"Will you?" he prompted, holding out his hand for her foot.

Her heart in her throat, Sara allowed him to strap the blades to her feet. His hands worked deftly, impersonally, giving no more offense than a cobbler fitting a last. Then he sat down on the other side of Sara and began to strap on his blades, fastening the buckles around his ankles and across the toes of his boots.

"Let's go," Abby said, already at the door. The captain followed, picking up the chair in one hand and pulling Sara to her feet with the other. Sara stood, resisting his tug on her hand. She wanted to test her steadiness before she allowed him to lead her out of the shed. She felt no pain, yet her ankles wobbled.

"Everyone is a little shaky at first," he assured her. "Come on."

Sara took one step, then another. She turned to reach for her walking stick.

"No, leave it," Eli said. "You'll have my arm or the chair. Let's go. Abby is already on the ice."

Reluctantly, Sara did as he asked. She took his arm and decided for a little while at least she'd have to trust him. They made their way down to the ice, as awkward on their skates in the snow as ducks waddling on dry land.

Abby was halfway across the pond. She set out at a swift pace across the lake, skating in a wide graceful arc that almost made Sara jealous.

"It's wonderful," she called back, "solid as rock and smooth as glass."

The captain followed Sara's gaze, then turned back to her. Swiftly he set the strange chair down on the ice and motioned for Sara. "Let's go. We can catch up with her. I know we can."

"You mean you want to race her?" Sara asked, never having seriously thought of such a thing. She'd given up racing long ago.

Eli motioned to the chair again. "Let's go."

Finding herself just a little giddy at the thought of a race, Sara took a deep breath. "Why not. Let's go."

With a helping hand from him, she navigated over the edge of the slippery ice and seated herself in the chair.

"Hang on," he warned and shoved off across the ice.

The freezing breeze numbed Sara's nose and stung her cheeks, but she laughed at the smooth ease with which they covered the distance to the center of the lake, following Abby around in her skating antics. The chair blades sang along the cold hard surface, music in Sara's ears.

"This is wonderful!" Sara laughed, heady with the speed and the freedom. She longed to thank Eli for making her come with them, but there wasn't time. "Eli! Abby is getting away from us."

"No, she's not."

The chair surged ahead, gaining on Abby, who laughed and called back to them, "Now follow the leader. Here we go."

Follow her they did, around the lake, then back along a narrow channel where woods arched over the frozen water creating a tree cave. Finally, they glided out into the open and back to the center, even completing a wide figure eight.

Sara laughed, catching the wind in her breath and returning it to the air in a cloud of mist. Tireless, the captain raced them around the lake again, leaving Abby skating in their wake. She called after them, but Sara couldn't understand her sister's words. She could only hear her bonnet ribbons fluttering in the breeze and her own giggles accompanied by the captain's baritone laughter.

"Whoa," Abby cried again, grabbing on to the arm of Sara's chair to slow them down. "It's my turn. I want to ride."

Sara turned and looked up at the captain. "I don't want to give it up."

"I suppose we must give Abigail a turn," the captain said.

"Yes, I want a turn," Abby pleaded. It occurred to Sara the pair sounded more like parent and child than future man and wife.

"You do the pushing this time, Sara," the captain suggested. "Here, take my arm and hold on to the chair. You are going to push your sister—you'll see."

"Wait. I don't think I can do this," Sara said, terrified at the thought of finding herself languishing on the ice as helpless as a turtle turned on its back.

"You can do it." Eli pulled her from the chair while Abby steadied it. "Remember, you're trusting me."

Once on her feet, Sara was surprised at the balance she achieved with Eli's help.

"Take the arm of the chair," he directed.

She did, following each of his instructions, startled at how easy and natural each action was. Once she was behind the chair, both handles in her hands, Abby sat down on it. Abby grabbed the arms of the chair and giggled in anticipation. "I'm ready."

Sara glanced uncertainly at Eli.

Releasing the chair, he stepped aside. "You're at the helm, Sara. Go."

Sara gave a tentative push with her bad leg. The chair moved slightly.

"Let's go," Abby urged.

"You're all right," Eli assured Sara. "Go on. You can

do this. You can ice-skate."

Sara pushed again, with more effort this time, and off the chair went ahead of her. For an instant, she thought she'd never catch up with it. With another quick push of her injured leg, she regained her balance and control.

"That's it," Abby cried.

Sara pushed again. It wasn't that hard. She couldn't push the chair with the speed that Eli had, but they were gliding across the lake with ease. Eli skated along beside them, grinning.

Sara's heart was pounding with the excitement and the thrill of the freedom. She was ice-skating with the help of a chair, but she was skating on her own feet when she had never dreamed she could. Glancing across the ice at Eli, a second surge of gratitude made her long to express her appreciation.

If only she could throw her arms around his neck and kiss him, just as Abby had done the night before. He had given her a gift so precious and priceless. He'd made her feel that there was no reason for her to ever be consigned to the fringes of any activity again. With a little thought and patience, she could tackle most anything.

Yet she didn't think Eli even began to understand what it meant to her—how wonderful it was to be out on the ice with them. To be part of the fun, not just sitting to the side and looking on.

When they skated out into the center again, Abby said, "That's enough. Stop. I've ridden enough. Now it's Eli's turn."

Sara stopped. Her good leg was tired, but she wasn't ready to give up yet. "I think you're right. It's only fair that Eli have a turn."

"Wait," he began.

"And why not?" Sara said. "You'll make me think

you don't trust my ability to pilot this chair."

"She's right you know," Abby joined in. "Have a seat."

"Perhaps a short ride," Eli agreed, finally settling himself in the chair. "I want to do figure eights in the middle of the lake."

"What?" Sara exclaimed. "How boring."

"That's what I want," Eli said, speaking over his shoulder to Sara. "The passenger gets his choice. Right? That's what we've been doing."

"You didn't ask me what I wanted," Sara pointed out. "We just did what you wanted. I'm captain now and—"

They bantered back and forth good-naturedly for several minutes. When Sara sniffed, suddenly conscious her nose was runny, she frantically searched the sleeve of her coat for her handkerchief.

Abby, who had grown silent and wide-eyed during Eli and Sara's playful exchange, searched her sleeves also. "I've lost mine, too."

With a gallant flourish from the chair, Eli offered his large, masculine handkerchief. Sara accepted it with a flippant curtsey and a laugh. At the moment neither of them realized that Abby's watchfulness had turned into mute sorrow.

Still giggling, Sara dabbed at her nose and Eli chuckled.

Abby suddenly wailed. "Oh, I can't stand to see you two—"

"Abby—" Sara began, dismayed with the reappearance of the sadness in her sister's eyes.

"What is it?" Eli jumped from the chair, nearly upsetting it and Sara. But she managed to recover her balance.

Big glistening tears rolled down Abby's cheeks. She wiped them away with the back of her gloved hands.

"It's nothing." Abby sobbed and turned away. Sara knew it was more than nothing.

"She's overly tired," Sara hurried to explain, "or perhaps the cold is too much for her."

Eli regarded each of them with a skeptical frown. "Let's go in. We can warm up in the shed, then walk back to the inn."

"No, no," Abby managed to stammer through her tears. "You stay. I'm fine, really. I don't want to spoil your fun. Stay, please." With that, she turned and left the ice.

"What should we do?" Eli asked, still watching Abby make her way onto the snowy lakeshore.

"I'm not sure," Sara said, knowing perfectly well there was nothing she or Eli could do to cure the reason for her sister's tears.

On the lakeshore, Abby hastily pulled off her skates and waved to Eli and Sara. "Promise me you'll stay and enjoy yourselves," she called across the expanse of ice.

Only when Eli and Sara returned her wave did she turn and hurry along the path toward Freedom Tavern.

Sara wondered how long the memory of Jerome Bascom was going to haunt Abby's life.

Chapter Seven

Eli turned to Sara, clearly bewildered. "We've agreed to be frank, have we not? Did I say something wrong?"

Sara shook her head. "If Abby says she will be all right, then she will be. After all, she is facing a lot of changes in her life. I think she just wants some time alone."

Eli nodded.

"Do you still want your ride?" Sara asked, feeling a little selfish, yet eager to dispel the pall that Abby's tears had cast over their fun. Part of what she told Eli was true: Abby would be all right after some time to herself.

Eli smiled at her, obviously eager to go on with their game. "Sure, I'll ride in the chair. Figure eights, just as I said."

Sara waited for him to sit down in the chair, then pushed off, skating as fast as she could. "Some figure eights for you, then whatever else I want for me."

Eli laughed. Then they skated for some time more, Sara becoming quite good at the figure eights before she skated off faster than ever to the tree cave. Eli clutched the chair arms and shouted in mock terror that she was skating too fast. When they emerged, they were laughing and arguing over the quality of her growing skill.

The cold had numbed her toes, her nose and her fingers, but she didn't care. She was having a wonderful time. Then a stinging gust of wind pricked tears from her eyes.

"Oh, not you, too!" Eli said, studying her over his shoulder. "I'm beginning to lose faith in my charm with ladies."

"Oh, no," Sara said, sniffling and hurriedly wiping away the tears, lest he think she was also weeping like her sister. "It's just the cold."

"Then let's go warm up." He led the way off the ice and into the warming shed.

The fire in the potbellied stove had warmed the shelter, but not enough to melt the frost on the panes of the window. Sara sucked in the warmth. After over an hour on the ice, she welcomed any amount of warmth. She made her way to the bench nearest to the stove, sat down and leaned her head back against the wooden wall. She took the moment to let the heat tingle into her cheeks and nose and to catch her breath.

When Eli peered into her face, she assured him, "I'm all right. Really I am."

Only then did he peel his gloves off and begin to replenish the fire with new wood. Fresh flames flared and the fire roared in the little iron stove.

Eli sat down beside Sara and began to unstrap his skates. "We shouldn't have stayed out so long."

"But it was fun," Sara said, closing her eyes and remembering her freedom on the ice. "So much fun. I'm glad you talked me into it."

She opened her eyes and saw that Eli already had removed his skates. She pulled off her mittens and reached for her skates, then realized her fingers were still too stiff to manage.

"Let me," Eli offered, dropping to his knees in front of her and beginning to work on the frozen leather straps. "Your boots are so thin your feet must be frozen."

He looked up into her face. "Good Lord, Sara, your lips are purple. I should have never let you stay out so long. Let the heat from the stove help."

He reached up, pulling loose the ribbon of her bonnet, then attacking the buttons of her coat and opening it wide.

"Oh, no, I'm all right," Sara said, still too thrilled with having skated on her own to be concerned about a man tugging at her clothes. "We were so active I didn't have chance to get cold. Really I didn't—until that one gust of wind."

He cast aside her skates and seized her cold, reddened hands, rubbing them between his own and blowing on them. His touch and his breath sent heat flooding throughout Sara, but not the kind that could be recorded on a thermometer. Still she could not bring herself to pull away.

When he looked up at her, rubbing her hands between his, she lost herself in the depths of his dark eyes and savored the firm smoothness of his jaw. She almost reached out to touch it.

"May I ask you something personal?"

He chuckled and bent to blow on her finger tips again.

"Do you miss your beard?"

He looked up at her again, plainly startled, yet amused. "Do I miss my beard?"

"Why do men grow beards anyway, unless it's to keep warm?"

"Because wearing a beard is simpler than shaving," Eli said. "Have you ever thought of wielding a razor aboard a ship at sea? Then there's the issue of water. However, to answer your question, yes, I miss it. It warmed my face."

"Oh," Sara said, staring at his smooth-shaven face now ruddy with windburn, still longing to touch him. He had been so good to her and so patient when another man would have looked through her or blustered. It wasn't that other men had been unkind to her. It was just that they thought her lacking and ignored her. She had come to think that was all she could expect.

Then as if he'd read her mind, he took her hands and pressed them to his cheeks and grinned. "If I had a beard, I couldn't warm your hands like this."

Beneath her fingers his skin was amazingly smooth and warm. He smelled spicy like sandalwood and citrus. Additional heat coursed through Sara, overwhelming her shock at the intimate gesture. The physical contact made her bold.

She took a deep breath. He was watching her intently. "The days are passing and tomorrow is Christmas Eve already—"

"Yes, the time has gone quickly."

"In the event I don't have another opportunity, I want to thank you for your generosity to me and to my sister. I appreciate all that you have done—like finding that unique chair and strapping the ice skates on my feet. I would never have attempted skating if you hadn't insisted."

Then she leaned over, intending to kiss him on the

cheek, but he turned his face and caught her mouth with his. His nose was cold when she brushed against it, yet his lips were warm. The smell of him—of tobacco and soap and just the hint of spice—filled her senses. Inhaling his scent deeply, she gave herself up to the firmness of his lips pressed against her own and the warmth of his cheek so near hers. The sensation of his tongue along her lower lip seemed perfectly natural and right. All the coldness inside her began to melt.

He seized her by the waist, his grip so sudden and unexpected that Sara almost cried out in surprise. She was instantly ashamed that she was taking such exquisite pleasure in this kiss. She struggled briefly to be free of his embrace, but his hands remained firm inside her coat, the touch of his fingers almost burning through the wool of her gown.

"It's all right," he whispered reassuringly, his voice soft and husky.

Breathless and confused, she peered into his face, wanting with all her heart to believe him.

Without releasing her, he climbed onto the bench beside her and took up the kiss again, pulling her closer this time. Sara couldn't help slipping her arms around his neck and leaning into him, pressing herself against his solid strength. Opening her mouth to the demands of his tongue.

She'd never been kissed like this, with lips and tongue and the gentle nip of teeth at the corner of her mouth. It made her heart sing with delight and her body burn with desire. Divine and wanton all at once. It was passion. Though the emotion was unique in her experience, she recognized it with a woman's instinct. She knew she didn't want it to ever end.

He was kissing her face, her eyes, her brow, then breathing into her hair. His hands stroked her back, firm and compelling, drawing her closer, telling her of the passion he felt, too. The flat of his palm skimmed pleasantly along her ribs and brushed tantalizingly against the side of her breasts. They grew heavy and began to ache—for more of his touch.

Breathless, Sara clung to him, her face pressed against his chest. She could hear the pounding of his heart and the raggedness of his breathing. She leaned back to see his face, wondering if she would find the intense need she felt mirrored there.

His dark eyes were hooded and he shook his head, putting his finger to her lips. "Not yet, Sara. I don't want it to be over yet."

He bent to kiss her again. Lifting her face to his eagerly, Sara surrendered herself to him and slipped her hands beneath his waistcoat to indulge her desire to stroke the cords of his back. All the while she relished the feel of his hand cupped over her breast, kneading gently until he found her sensitive nipple. Sara moaned. He teased the turgid bud with his thumb until she was forced to break free of the kiss to gasp in pleasure. He trailed kisses down her neck while his thumb worked relentless magic on her.

"Oh, Eli," Sara said, the moans of pleasure still rising in her throat. She knew she should push his hand away, but she didn't want to.

"Sara," he whispered into her ear. "Sweet Sara, don't you know you deserve so much more than you have."

As he buried his face against Sara's neck, she glimpsed something white lying on the dirt floor. Not far from the shed door lay a pristine white wad of cloth with a blue letter A delicately embroidered in the corner. It was Abby's lost handkerchief.

Sara felt as if she'd been slapped with a cold rag. She fought the resistance of her senses, the aching in her breasts and the sweet seduction of Eli's hands. With great effort and sudden anger, she shoved Eli away. How could he kiss her like this when he was promised to her sister.

Astonishment on his face, Eli released her.

"What are we doing?" Sara pushed herself even farther away from him. Guilt washed over her anger. "What about Abby?"

Eli passed his hand over his face. "Abby."

Sara stared at him, realizing she was the one who had tried to kiss him first. "I'm sorry. I started something I shouldn't. It's just that you've been so kind—"

"I don't think those were kisses of kindness," Eli said, passing his hand over his face.

"We'd better get back," Sara said, hurriedly buttoning up her coat, then tying the ribbons of her bonnet. She jumped to her feet and headed for the door, where she stopped and turned to him. "I can't imagine why I—anyway, there's no need to say anything about this to Abby. I don't want her to be hurt any more than she has been already."

Eli looked up at her. "What do you mean?"

The slip made Sara's heart thump harder. She'd promised Papa she would say nothing about Abby's secret. "I mean this arranged marriage is difficult for her. This, between you and me, this was just some kind of foolish mistake. We, you and I, should not—"

Uncertain of what more she wanted to say, Sara decided to leave. She grabbed her walking stick and left, banging the warming-shed door behind her.

Behind an outbuilding at the head of the path, she stopped to catch her breath and to compose herself. While smoothing the front of her coat and straightening her bonnet, she wondered if there was any evidence of Eli's kiss on her lips. She'd never heard of kisses leaving marks; still, Eli's kisses had left her feeling branded. The last thing she needed was to walk into the inn to face the Starks and Abby with the imprint of Eli's lips on her mouth.

She couldn't believe that what had promised to be the most wonderful day of her life was quickly becoming the worst. It had all begun as innocent fun on the ice. Then she'd practically thrown herself into Eli's arms, willing to submit to any intimate touch he desired to bestow. She choked on the mortification of her actions. If she'd been told the day she'd met him she would come to love Captain Eli Whittaker, she would have laughed in scorn at the idea. Much as she wanted to deny it, she'd fallen in love with her sister's bridegroom.

In another day she would have to stand by and watch him smile down at her sister and speak his marriage vows. She would say nothing, because she knew that he would be good to Abigail. Maybe he wasn't exactly who Abigail would have chosen for herself, but he would be a good husband.

Clamping a hand over her mouth, Sara stifled a sob. If she didn't stifle this first cry of pain, she'd never be able to stop the wails of sorrow and regret.

She scooped up handfuls of snow and pressed them against her cheeks, letting the snow chill away the heat of her tears. The cold soothed her and numbed the emotions churning inside her.

After a few more minutes, Sara felt sufficiently composed to return to the inn. Brushing melted snow from her face and straightening her bonnet one more time, she marched on along the path.

Chapter Eight

Eli let his head thump back against the shed wall and groaned. What had he done? When he'd invited Sara to come along on the skating party, the idea had been to spend a few enjoyable hours with Abigail and to let Sara try something she'd never done. He knew he'd won Abigail over with the marriage portion.

Even Sara had been softened by the gift. He'd seen it in her eyes. Still, she was the more discerning of the two girls and more difficult to please. He'd thought ice-skating and showing her how much more she could do would please her and secure her blessing for certain.

Sweet heaven, he'd never been prepared for how her pleasure would effect him. Something about the sound of Sara laughing with joy and the glow of happiness shining in her eyes as she skated had drawn him to her. Holding Sara, kissing her, hearing her sighs had been so sweet, so incredibly arousing that he still ached.

Eli knew she'd been as powerless as he to resist the pleasures of sharing and touching. She'd never surrendered herself like that to anyone, not even her husband. He was certain of that. He wondered if she'd even known she was capable of such ardor. He wondered if she knew how close she'd come to making love on a bench in the warming shed.

"Oh, Sara, how I'd love to be the man who gives you your first real taste of happiness, who brings you the pleasure and passion you deserve," Eli whispered aloud. The words inspired the vision of her in his bed, naked, breathless and oh so willing, just as she'd been a few moments ago. The ache in his loins increased rather than eased. He squeezed his eyes closed and mentally shut out the vision of Sara in his arms.

Abby was his promised bride. Abby was the one he was about to pledge his life to. He'd been delighted with her on first sight. He squeezed his eyes shut once more. Yet concentrate as he might, he could not envision Abigail in his bed, passionate beneath his caresses. All he could see in his mind's eye was Abby's face with tears rolling down her cheeks—on her wedding night.

Silently he cursed the mess he was in. His bride-to-be had burst into tears when he kissed her, and her chaperon had melted at his touch. Abby was bright and sweet and full of life, but Sara—ah, Sara knew something of the world and would be there when a man needed her. Was it possible that despite all his efforts, he'd only succeeded in pushing himself farther from his goal rather than closer? His wedding was only a day away.

Eli uttered an oath of frustration and rose to bank the fire in the stove before he left the warming shed.

* * *

"A gentleman has called to see you, Captain," Mr. Stark said when Eli returned to the inn.

"Is it a well-wisher?" Eli wondered if some acquaintance had heard he was at Freedom Tavern and had stopped by to say hello. "Did he give his name?"

"No," Stark said. Eli read anxiety in the innkeeper's face as he took Eli's coat and cap. "He was rather mysterious and just said he'd come to call and he wasn't ready to speak to Mrs. Larkfield or Miss Conway as yet. I asked him to wait in the small parlor."

"I see," Eli muttered. What kind of complication was he about to run into? He'd hardly had time to make sense of what had just happened between himself and Sara. Yet he didn't believe in putting off problems. Without any more delay, Eli went into the parlor to meet his caller.

As he stepped inside, the thin young man standing at the window drew himself up to his full height, which was a few inches shorter than Eli's six feet. The young man's hair was mussed from where his beaver top hat had set and his cravat was twisted askew. However, his brown wool frock coat and green velvet waistcoat looked new, if not expensive. "Do I have the privilege of addressing Captain Eli Whittaker?"

"I'm Captain Whittaker," Eli said. "Who might you be?"

"I'm Jerome Bascom come from Albany, lately from Boston." The young man spoke a bit louder than necessary, his prominent chin lifted a fraction of an inch in defiance. "I've come to ask your intentions toward Miss Abigail Conway."

Surprised to find himself unwilling to declare that he and Abigail were to be wed on the morrow, Eli stared at the young man.

"My intentions?" Eli repeated, searching for an

honest but evasive answer. Memories of Sara still lingered too sharp and clear in his head and weighed too heavy on his conscience.

"I believe wedding arrangements are made for you and Miss Abigail?"

"That is so." Eli crossed the room to warm his hands at the fire in the hearth. "Arrangements have been made."

"Well, then, I am here to inform you that Abigail is pledged to me."

Eli's heart skipped a beat. A strange, unexpected pang of hope lanced through him. Slowly he turned to face the earnest young man still standing at the window. "You are here to inform me of what?"

"Yes, well, I'm quite sure she has not spoken of me," Bascom said. "Her father probably forbade her. Abigail is a gentle and an obedient daughter. But we—she and I—have been pledged to one another for almost a year."

Eli forgot about warming his hands at the fire. When he'd settled the marriage agreement with Abigail's father, there had been no hint of another suitor. When she'd laughed at his jests and smiled at him so charmingly across the dinner table, he'd assumed his way was clear.

"Her father assured me she was free to marry," Eli said.

"I am sure he did. Her father did not approve of a match between us." Bascom raked his hand through his sandy-brown hair, mussing it even more. "I realize this must come as a shock to you."

Eli's initial surprise sparked into irritation. His next unspoken thought was to wonder how much did Sara know about this. "Miss Abigail is a fine young woman and I find it difficult to believe that she would have agreed to marry me if she was promised to another."

"Abigail does not know that I am here," Bascom admitted. "I wanted to speak with you first so that we can settle this man to man. And I'm prepared to offer you money, Captain. Or we can settle this another way."

Bascom marched to the parlor table and threw open the ebony box to reveal a pair of dueling pistols nestled inside. The scent of gun oil filled the air; the sleek barrels gleamed in the winter sunlight.

Eli's grip on the mantel tightened as he grappled for control of his temper. He resented the fact that people assumed he'd rather fight than settle things sensibly. He'd brought more than one ship to surrender with well-placed cannonballs through its rigging. Negotiations always followed, resulting in the loss of cargo, not life—unless someone was foolish like this arrogant young pup. "Just what is your calling, Mr. Bascom?"

"I'm a schoolmaster, sir."

Eli turned his deepest frown on the young schoolmaster and shook his head. "Don't you know a seaman prefers to fight at close quarters? My weapon of choice is a cutlass."

Bascom paled and his gulp of distress was audible, but he held his ground. "If that is your—your choice, sir, then we'll fight with cutlasses."

Eli studied Abigail's erstwhile suitor. He was an honest young man and sincere, if perhaps a little naive.

"I love her, Captain," Bascom declared, filling the painful silence Eli had purposely allowed to spin out between them. "I'll do whatever I must to make her my bride."

Eli realized that he couldn't honestly say he was

willing to do the same for Abigail. As much as he admired her beauty, her virtues and her accomplishments, he knew he did not love her. He'd told himself, of course, that would change once they were married, but what if Abigail had indeed already given her heart to another? Could he make her love him? Would he be satisfied with a woman who had taken him only as second choice? "I think we should decided this another way."

Bascom's eyes widened in further alarm. "How then?"

"I think Abigail should tell us where her heart lies. You see," Eli went on, "this is not necessarily a thing to be decided between men. Ask Mrs. Stark to send Abigail to the parlor."

Bascom's color returned a bit, and he looked as if he were about to protest about being ordered around. Then he seemed to think better of it and went to the door to find Mrs. Stark.

Abigail soon arrived, followed by Sara. When Sara entered the parlor, her gaze fell on Eli first; then she turned away to close the door. Eli wondered if she had told Abigail of the kiss they had shared in the warming shed.

"Abigail, we have a caller who says he knows you." Eli gestured toward the young man standing by the windows.

"Jerome!" Abigail gasped. A flush flooded into her cheeks. She took a step in the schoolmaster's direction. Then, with an uncertain glance at Sara, she remained where she was.

Sara was frowning at the box of dueling pistols. When she looked to Eli, the fear he saw in her eyes gratified him. Maybe she hadn't told him all that she knew about Abigail and Jerome; still, she was at least concerned for his safety.

"What's going on here?" Sara demanded.

"You do know Mr. Bascom?" Eli baited.

"Of course, we know Mr. Bascom," Sara said, turning to speak in the young man's direction. Her lips pursed in aggravation and disapproval. "He left Boston some months ago and we had no idea where he went."

"Where have you been, Jerome?" Abigail pleaded so softly Eli could barely hear her over the hiss of the fire.

"In Albany, seeking a teaching position," Bascom said, taking a hesitant step toward her. "Didn't you get my letters?"

"No, I've received nothing. Papa said—"

"Well, even if my letters never got through," Jerome went on in a defiant tone, "when I heard that you were to marry Captain Whittaker, I came to tell him the truth about you and me."

"Abby, I think perhaps you should go ahead and explain to Captain Whittaker about you and Jerome," Sara said at last. "And tell the truth please."

"How can I do that when there is still Papa to think of?"

"I'd like to hear the truth," Eli said, already annoyed with the betrayal that was already becoming evident. "We'll talk about your papa later."

Abigail looked from Jerome to Eli, then down at her hands before she spoke. "Jerome and I did pledge our hearts to each other over a year ago. Sara knows. I told her. Then Jerome asked Papa for my hand in marriage, but Papa—" Abigail's pretty face crumbled into sobbing and she covered her face with her hands.

"Mr. Conway nearly threw me out," Bascom finished for her, barely restraining his desire to go to her. "He said I had nothing to offer his daughter."

"Papa had set his sights higher than an unemployed

schoolmaster," Sara said to Eli as if he needed that explanation.

"And he was willing to wed his youngest daughter to a rich privateer." Eli had known all along that Conway wanted to save his business by wedding his daughter to someone with money. He'd willingly taken advantage of the old man's aspirations. With uncomfortable clarity, Eli realized he only had himself to blame for this scene.

Sara turned to Jerome. "What did you expect Papa to do? You had no position, Jerome, no prospects to offer."

"I do now," Bascom protested. "That's why I've come. I want to offer for Abigail again. I came to tell Mr. Conway that I have secured a good position at a school in Albany. The income is modest, but a house comes with the job."

Jerome turned to Abigail. "Oh, Abby, it's not a large house, but it has a small garden and a big kitchen. I know we could be so happy there."

"Jerome, that sounds wonderful." Abigail's joy shone through her tears.

Eli's heart tripped a beat. There was no denying she had indeed given her heart to Jerome Bascom. Jacob Conway had signed over something that wasn't his to give. And Sara had known all along.

For the first time since they had confronted each other at the Freedom Tavern, Eli truly understood Sara's dilemma. She'd been dealing with an impossible quandary: her sister's future happiness or her father's solvency. Did she disappoint her father and discourage this marriage that would save the family business? Or did she risk her sister's heart?

And Eli knew in that moment, despite Sara's half-truths and fabrications, despite her disapproval and distrust of him, that he loved her.

The emotion swamped him like a ten-foot wave crashing across his bow. He reached to steady himself against the mantel. But there was no question he loved her. He loved her for her gentle lies, her stubborn propriety and for struggling to give her loved ones the happiness they desired in the face of impossible odds. Eli took a deep fortifying breath. "Mrs. Larkfield, you and I have things to discuss."

"Yes, I understand, Captain," Sara admitted, just a hint of anxiety in her voice. The appeal in Sara's eyes took the wind out of his angry sails. "You have every right to be outraged. I will do everything I can to fulfil the agreement to your satisfaction."

"Might you be saying that Abigail is free?" Bascom asked in a small voice, as if he hardly believed the possibility himself. Eagerness shone in his pale gray eyes.

Eli studied the young schoolmaster more closely this time. He saw a courageous soul who had presented himself to his lady's intended bridegroom prepared to fight for her hand. Eli admired Bascom.

"I am saying Abigail is free," Eli said, looking at Sara who refused to meet his gaze. "If Mrs. Larkfield and I can come to an agreement about the marriage contract."

Still Abigail hesitated, glancing in the direction of her half sister.

When Sara nodded her consent, Abigail ran toward Jerome. He met her in the center of the parlor, clasping her in his arms and lifting her off the floor. Abigail giggled, the sound of her delight pure and buoyant.

Eli had to smile at the exuberance of their joy. He turned to Sara, who also watched the young couple with a wistful smile playing across her lips. When she caught him observing her, the smile disappeared.

"Abigail, Mr. Bascom, Mrs. Larkfield and I still have matters to discuss."

Eli caught Bascom's eye and gestured toward the door. Without further delay, Bascom led Abigail from the small parlor.

With only the cozy popping of the fire breaking the silence of the room, Sara and Eli faced each other.

Chapter Nine

Sara watched Eli cross the room to the table and snap closed the dueling-pistol box.

"So there will be no need for these," he said without looking at her.

"No," Sara agreed, much relieved. "I suspect the guns appealed to Mr. Bascom's sense of the dramatic."

"Indeed," Eli said. "I suspect as much also, however, he was willing to do what he thought he had to do."

"You are angry, of course?" she said, moving on to the window. She gazed at the winter scene beyond, chilled and fearful of what would come next. She was about to lose what she had just discovered. "You have a right to be."

"I would like an explanation."

"Abby was honest, Eli. Papa had thrown Jerome out of the house and we had heard nothing from him for over three months," Sara said, staring out at the forested snowy hills behind the inn without seeing. "I'm embarrassed to admit I never considered the possibility that Papa might waylay letters to Abigail. But, yes, he would have, especially if they arrived after you had made your offer."

"So he is not going to be pleased about Abigail and Jerome being reunited," Eli said. "Will he be angry with you?"

Sara looked at him, surprised by his concern. Papa would be angry, but she had weathered that storm before. What she feared most now was losing Eli. He would never be part of the Conway family. He had no reason to linger at Freedom Tavern. Soon he would walk out of the parlor and out of the inn and out of her life. She would never see him again.

Sara shook her head, trying to clear it of the panic that set her heart thumping. "Naturally, I will not allow Abby to travel to Albany with Jerome unless they are man and wife. They will be married tomorrow. Thanks to you, a wedding is already arranged, is it not? Since Papa sent me in his stead, there is nothing he can do."

She turned back to the window. "I have some resources of my own. I'm certain Mr. Stark and I can work out the details of the expenses."

"Let's not be too hasty about working out the details of this marriage agreement."

Sara closed her eyes trying to calm herself. "The default is ours. What is there to be settled?"

She could hear his footsteps on the carpet as he moved closer, talking over her shoulder, but never touching her. Yet, he stood so close his breath tickled her ear. "If you and I were wed, I'd still become a member of the respectable Boston Conways and thereby fulfill the agreement. Your father's business would be saved."

Sara caught her breath. He was willing to keep her as part of the bargain. All she had to do was agree, and she could marry the man she loved—bought and sold—just like her first marriage. His offer was so tempting.

Yet Eli had changed something inside of her. In a few short days, he had shown her she had a right to expect more out of life. She wanted the best for herself now. Selfish as it made her feel, she knew second-best solutions were no longer good enough for her. With a shaft of pain slicing through her, she realized that she could never accept Eli's proposal. She wanted Eli to ask her to marry him out of love, not for the respectability the Conway family could bring him. She would accept nothing less.

Sara released a slow, painful sigh. "Your offer is generous, but I must refuse."

"I assure you, generosity has nothing to do with it." Eli paced across the room toward the door, and Sara expected to hear it open and close behind him, but it didn't. Curious, she glanced around to find him facing her across the parlor.

"Let's just forget the damned marriage agreement between your father and me. I'll invest whatever sum he needs to keep his business afloat. Will you accept my word on that?"

"Of course, but—"

"I want you to understand that the agreement is set aside."

"For what purpose?"

"So I can ask you to marry me without pressuring you to give any answer other than your own."

Sara hesitated, trying to make sense of what he'd just said. "Sir, declaring the marriage agreement null and void is a kind gesture. Offering to invest in Papa's business is more than generous; still, that fact changes nothing between you and me. I must—"

Hastily, Eli strode across the room and put his finger to her lips. "You needn't say yes now, Sara. I want you to know that I have learned much from all of this. For one thing, your father and I had no right to make the agreement about Abigail's future. I've learned the heart signs no contracts."

Sara tried to speak, but he continued to silence her with his finger. Then he said, "Most important, I made the mistake of letting business and reputation make me lose sight of my goal."

"I'm glad you understand all that for Abby's sake," Sara said when Eli took his finger away from her lips. "However, the fact remains—"

"Don't say anything more. I want to show you something." He suddenly seemed excited by a new thought that had occurred to him. He gestured to the spot where she stood. "Don't move. Promise me you'll wait here."

Sara stared at him, wondering where on earth he thought she would go to. "Of course, I'll wait."

She waited. Her head swam with all the strange developments that had occurred in the past few hours. Abby had been reunited with the love of her life, and she herself had fallen into a sea captain's arms and into love.

Maybe she was being foolish in denying him. All she had to do was say yes and she could be the wife of the man she loved. She could have a home and children with Eli and live closer to happiness than she'd ever dared hope. Few women had the luxury of choosing to spend their lives with the men they loved. She'd never expected to have it, yet she also knew Eli did not love her. She would not have him without true love. In a matter of hours, he would sail out of her life and be gone forever, and she would swallow her tears and wish him well.

There was a commotion outside the parlor door and Eli entered, a blue velvet bag resting in his hand. He closed the door. "Now I have a story to tell you."

"A story?" Sara repeated, curious and surprised.

Taking Sara's hand, Eli drew her away from the window and down on the settle by the fire. "Once there was a raja in India who was wed to a beautiful princess. They loved each other very much. The raja, as part of his office, always wore a many-stranded belt of pearls. When it happened that their kingdom was attacked and he had to go to war, his rani, the princess, asked him to give her a token of his love that she could wear always. He gave her this."

Eli looked down at the blue velvet bag cupped in his hand. "Before I open this, I want you to know that I bought them for you two years ago in Amsterdam."

Sara gawked at him. "We'd never met then."

Eli smiled a soft knowing smile. "Hear me out. I'm not mad. I asked an old Dutch merchant for just the right gift for my bride, whom I'd never met. When he asked me what she was like, I told him about you. You see, I've always known you, Sara. A woman of selfless generosity, loving courage and true loyalty. I've always loved you. I've just been waiting to find you. Now that I have, please accept this token of my love."

He loosened the drawstring of the blue velvet bag. "Hold out your hands."

Too inquisitive to argue, Sara did as told. Eli turned the bag upside down over her palms. A rope of lustrous pearls spiraled from the bag, dropping in radiant white loops between her fingers. Their warmth, taken from Eli's hand, seeped into Sara and melted her heart.

"Be my bride, Sara Larkfield," Eli whispered.

Sara stared at the pearls, then up at Eli. She could hardly believe the riches being offered to her. "I don't know."

Eli took the necklace from her hands and slipped it around her neck. It fell below her waist. He looped it around her neck again and again, his fingers brushing gently against her cheek. The gentle warmth of his touch tingled against Sara's cheek and radiated throughout her body.

"They are the most beautiful things I have ever seen," Sara murmured, putting her fingers on the pearls at her throat. "They are warm, almost as if they are alive with beauty."

Eli nodded. "They are the gems of the sea. Pearls are the symbol of perfect love and beauty. The only suitable gift for the woman I would trust my heart to."

Sara opened her mouth to protest that she couldn't possibly accept such an expensive gift, but Eli put his finger to her lips once more. "Listen to me. The pearls are yours no matter what you choose to do. I'm not giving them to you to buy your acceptance. I'm giving them to you because I want you to have them.

"You are free to agree to be my wife or to deny me. All I ask is that in making your decision you don't make your choice based on Abigail's happiness. Nor is there any reason to let your father's business affairs decide for you. I love you, Sara. I ask only that you choose your own happiness."

Sara stared up at him, astonished by his words. Her throat tightened and she felt hot tears roll down her cheeks.

"Sweet heaven," Eli moaned. "What have I done now?"

Sara shook her head and muffled a sob before she could speak. "Nothing. Everything. Don't you know you already gave me the greatest gift you could give. You gave me the knowledge that I can expect more out of life than I have had the sense to demand."

Sara shook her head, yet the tears continued to fall. She took his hands, hoping he did not mistake her weeping for anything less than joy. "Eli, I don't need your pearls. I need your love."

A slow smile spread across his face. "You have that." He kissed her lightly on the lips. "Let's make tomorrow a double wedding then? No reason to waste the preparations."

"Yes, oh, yes." Sara laughed. Eli pulled her into his arms and silenced her laughter with a kiss.

Chapter Ten

Sara's wedding day, Christmas morning, dawned bright and with the peal of church bells piercing the clear morning air. The aroma of roasting meat and cinnamon-spiced apple pies filled Freedom Tavern.

Try as Sara might to tell herself that she wasn't excited about her wedding day—it was her second marriage after all—she was elated in a way that she'd never been in her entire life. She was going to stand before the preacher with Eli, the man she loved, the man whose touch thrilled her. And she would be united with him before the Almighty, her sister, the Starks and the good citizens of Port Freedom. He was her choice, and she was his. Her fingers shook so, she could hardly manage the tapes of her petticoat. Abby's fingers weren't any steadier.

When Medora Stark poked her head into the girls' room to see if they needed help in dressing, she understood immediately and sent someone up. Sara needed help to pack her bags. Eli had asked her if they might spend their first night together on the *Victoire* and she had agreed. They would leave as soon as the dancing and wedding supper were over.

As she slipped on her plum-colored party gown with the lace collar, she felt as giddy and light-headed as Abby acted. There had been no time to make or find a more suitable wedding dress. The plum gown flattered her coloring and its neckline worked perfectly with the pearls, allowing the loops to lie smooth and radiant against her throat. The dress would do nicely, she decided. Sara nestled white paper roses on her hair like those used to decorate the pine garland of the inn.

Abby pulled on her own new blue wedding gown, the one luxury Papa had permitted for her marriage to the captain. Abby wore matching blue ribbons in her hair.

"You look wonderful," Sara said, helping her sister fit the dress in place.

"Wouldn't Papa thunder if he knew I'm marrying Jerome in this fine gown?" Abby said, and the sisters giggled.

"In time, when Papa sees how happy you are and how successful Jerome is, he will bless your marriage," Sara said, eager to reassure her sister.

Eli and Jerome awaited them at the foot of the stairs. Jerome wore a dark blue frock coat and striped waistcoat. His sandy-brown hair was as mussed as it had been the day before. Sara was beginning to believe he'd been born with his hair like that.

Eli was unbelievably handsome in a dark gray cutaway jacket over an oyster satin waistcoat. He smiled at her, the pride of love and ownership gleaming in his rich dark eyes. Butterflies fluttered in Sara's belly and she went soft and warm inside. No one had to tell her that what happened between Eli and her from this day forward would be unlike anything she'd ever experienced before.

The double ceremony was attended by some of the inn guests, a few citizens from Port Freedom, and the crew from the *Victoire.* As Medora Stark sniffled and unashamedly wiped away the tears with the corner of her apron, Alex Stark gave her an ardent hug.

All went smoothly until the minister asked for a ring. Jerome looked so surprised and astonished that Sara almost panicked. Surely he'd had enough sense to think of the wedding ring. After much pocket searching and fumbling, he produced a gold band from his waistcoat and slipped it on Abigail's finger. The wedding guests' collective sigh of relief filled the room.

In another moment, Eli had slipped a golden band on Sara's finger, too. It went on as a perfect fit.

"A good omen," Eli whispered with a smile of satisfaction. Then he added with a grin, "You know, we seamen are very superstitious."

"I'll remember to bring you only *good* luck," Sara whispered back before he kissed her.

The guests applauded. The musicians struck up a dance. Medora dried her eyes and shared a sound kiss with her husband before she and Alex began serving the rum punch.

The celebration was a blur of proffered best wishes and kisses of congratulations from strangers and new acquaintances alike. Food and drink flowed freely. Abigail and Jerome held the center of the dance floor. Jerome was proving to be as tireless a dancer as his new wife.

Finally, Eli drew Sara into a corner. "Say your farewells, sweetheart. The carriage is waiting to take us to the dock."

A duchess with a duke. Or more exciting, a lady with a pirate.

Sara laced her fingers through Eli's hair, tugging at him until he ceased torturing her with heated kisses to her thighs and returned to her breasts.

He smiled at her and reached for the pearls. Tenderly he rolled a loop of pearls across her nipple and back again. The sensation made Sara suck in her breath and moan with pleasure.

The sensitive bud swelled before her eyes until Eli took it in his mouth and began a new kind of torture. He teased and suckled her until the heat of his lips on her became the center of all existence. Her body grew damp and dewy for him, and his fingers found the dew between her legs. She knew he was pleased from the low satisfied sound he made.

Sara gave herself up to the enchantment of each stroke of his fingers. She tried to explore him, though she was not nearly so expert in the art as he was. But her awkwardness did not trouble him. He took her hand in his and encouraged her to touch him in ways she would never had dared on her own. She discovered he was much larger than she had anticipated. And he was hard and smooth and he, too, offered her a pearl of dew.

"See. I've needed and wanted you all my life," he whispered in her ear as he used her fingers to spread the pearl up and down his shaft. The needful ache inside Sara grew insistent.

When he gently pushed her down and covered her, she offered herself for his entrance. Taking him inside was painless, thrilling and fulfilling. This lovemaking was new and wondrous and strange, and she didn't want it to end. She wanted to accept his passion, to treasure it and to give it back doubled and redoubled if she could. She wanted to please Eli as much as he pleased her.

As pleasurable as holding him was, the ache deep inside her would not relent. She wondered if something was wrong.

"Sweetheart, it's all right." Eli whispered words of love and encouragement in her ear as he moved inside her, building the pressure, nurturing her desire, inflaming her need.

She was too weak with desire to do more than surrender to the need to hold him there, to pull him in even deeper. Her hand played down the valley of his back until she was lost once again in the deep ache that was swelled into glow of exquisite pleasure. With Eli's urging, she offered herself up to it. When the sweet incredible shattering ecstasy came, she hardly heard her own cry of release or Eli's own groan of gratification.

Safe in Eli's arms, Sara floated back to earth like a leaf drifting on the breeze, a gentle lulling settling. She felt him kiss her ear, roll onto his side and pull her close.

Smiling, Sara took the long rope of pearls and looped it over Eli's head. "There. We are as bound together in our love as the raja and his rani."

Eli chuckled. "I want six," he whispered in the darkness.

"Six?"

"Children," he supplied. "The raja and his rani went on to have twelve children. I only want six."

The thought of babies made Sara smile. She'd never really thought of babies in her marriage before meeting Eli, but she liked the idea. "You are ambitious enough, sir."

"Three sons and three daughters."

"I promise to do my part," she said, still smiling. "But *my sons* will not go to sea when they are ten as their father did."

Sara could hear the smile in his voice. "And *my daughters* will choose their own husbands."

"What if you don't agree with your daughters' choices?" Sara baited.

Eli kissed her, a slow, loving kiss. "I will bite my tongue and remember what a good choice their mother made."

A knock on the cabin door awoke Sara. Before she could sit up, Eli stuck his head into the cabin. "Sweetheart, we're clearing port. Get dressed. We'll be sailing by Freedom Tavern in a few minutes."

Sara hastily pulled on her clothes, and still wearing the pearls beneath her cloak, she joined Eli at the *Victoire's* helm. The day was clear and the breeze fresh. The ship clipped along nicely over the sea-green water, sailing close to the wind.

"There." Eli pointed to the many-gabled profile of the inn as they neared the shore.

"Oh, where are they?" Sara cried.

"Here." Eli handed her the spyglass, but she had already spotted Abigail in her green fur-trimmed coat and Jerome in his brown suit coat and hat. They waved. Sara waved in return and Eli joined her.

"Oh, I hope I've done the right thing," Sara murmured.

"Do they look happy?"

"Yes," Sara admitted, eyeing her sister and brother-in-law through the spyglass.

"Are you happy?" Eli asked, his lips close to her ear. Her body suddenly grew warm, responding to the pleasure his nearness brought.

"Oh, yes," she said, unable to resist smiling up at him.

"Then you've done the right thing."

He kissed her lightly and smiled. Both turned to wave farewell to Abigail and Jerome and Freedom Tavern.

Rachel's Hero

DEBRA DIER

For my aunts, the sisters McTigue: Mary, Hope, Frances, Helen.

Chapter One

Port Freedom, New Hampshire—1889

It hurt when a hero fell from grace. Rachel Stark didn't want to believe it. For the past ten years, she had tried to find excuses for the apparent neglect and general lack of interest T.S. Beauchamp had for his young sister. Yet tonight, as she listened to Marianne Beauchamp's tearful rendition of her brother's latest atrocity, Rachel had acknowledged the truth: T.S. was no longer the same charming young man she had known. Her hero had turned into a callous stranger.

"T.S. wants to sell me." Marianne rocked back and forth, hugging her arms to her chest like a little girl lost in the woods. "I'm no better than a slave if I stay in that house."

Priscilla, Rachel's youngest sister, sat next to Marianne on the Empire sofa beside the carved oak fireplace, trying to comfort her dear friend. "We'll protect you from that monster. Won't we, Rachel?"

"Marianne is welcome to stay as long as she wants." *Monster.* How could T.S. have changed so drastically? Rachel wondered. She had known T.S. most of her life. Her eldest brother, Josh, and T.S. had been best friends from the time they were children, inseparable until the day Josh went off to college in Boston. Instead of college, T.S. had gone to work, trying to save his father's faltering business empire. He had succeeded. Splendidly. Unfortunately, according to his sister, the price of success had been every shred of his compassion.

Rachel lifted her cup. A wisp of steam touched her face, carrying the rich fragrance of hot chocolate. She sipped the sweet liquid, trying to keep her own emotions under check. Yet doing so was impossible. Regret and disappointment gathered in her chest, rolling into a tight knot pressed against her heart. Deep inside, she cradled the wounded remains of the love she had cherished for the young man who had once saved her life.

T.S. had been her hero since she was ten years old. Through the years, her youthful admiration had altered into infatuation and finally a love that wouldn't let go of her—no matter how hard she tried to forget him.

Both Priscilla and Marianne jumped at the jingle of the doorbell. Rachel's heart bumped into the wall of her chest at the thought that T.S. might be standing at her front door.

Her eyes wide and rimmed with red, Marianne looked at Rachel. With huge blue eyes, delicate features and luxurious black hair, Marianne had always been a pretty little girl. But this past year, the little girl had blossomed into a beautiful young woman. "You mustn't answer it."

"There's no reason to hide." Rachel set her cup and saucer on the pedestal table beside her chair, appalled at the sudden shaking of her hands. She stood and reminded herself of all the reasons she couldn't possibly still harbor an infatuation for T.S. Beauchamp.

Her brown eyes wide with fear, Priscilla stared at Rachel. "You can't let him in."

"It will be all right." Rachel smiled at the girls, hoping to lessen their fears. Marianne had turned seventeen the first week of December. Although Priscilla was actually a few months older than her friend, she looked no more than fifteen, with her copper-colored hair and a sprinkling of freckles across her upturned nose. Still, both girls were at an age when romance and drama ruled each day. "It might be someone looking for a room for tonight."

Priscilla rolled her eyes. "Rachel, you know very well we seldom get people looking for rooms in December."

It was true. Freedom Tavern seldom had guests during the winter. Summer and fall were the busy seasons. "The town meeting is probably over by now. Perhaps father forgot his key," Rachel said.

Marianne shook her head. "It's my brother. I know it is. He probably tortured the servants to find out where I went."

"Perhaps it is your brother," Rachel said softly. "If it is, it will save us the trouble of sending him a message letting him know you're safe."

"He doesn't care if I'm safe. He hates me. He has always hated me." Marianne dabbed at her cheeks with her lace-trimmed handkerchief. "He blames me for mother's death."

"I'm certain he doesn't blame you," Rachel said, hoping she sounded more confident than she felt. The truth was, she hadn't even glimpsed T.S. Beauchamp in twelve years. She had no idea what the man thought.

"You mustn't tell him I'm here!" Marianne said. "He'll drag me back home to that . . . that . . . little toad."

"No, he won't." Rachel patted Marianne's shoulder. "You're safe here. I promise."

Marianne cringed at the impatient ring of the bell. "If you must speak with him, please tell him I shall not be bullied into marrying Darwin Whitteck."

"I shall make certain he knows how you feel." Now if only she could make certain of how she would feel seeing T.S. again after so many years, Rachel thought as she left the back parlor, the one reserved for the family.

Gas jets burned behind frosted-glass globes in a brass fixture suspended from the ceiling near the entrance to the inn. The hissing flames cast a golden glow against the oak-paneled walls of the wide hall, which ran the entire length of the big house.

Rachel's heart thudded against her ribs as she approached the front door. The bell near the entrance jingled with an impatient tug from the person on the other side of the door. The bright chime pounded against her heightened senses. It was silly becoming so agitated over the mere thought of seeing a man. The time for foolish infatuations was past, she assured herself. She was no longer an impressionable fourteen-year-old girl. She was a twenty-six-year-old woman, quite capable of dealing with a man like T.S. Beauchamp.

She gripped the cold brass handle, took a deep breath and pulled open the door. Golden light spilled through the doorway, carving a wedge of light in the darkness, capturing the tall, broad-shouldered man standing on the landing. He stared down at her, frowning, as though she weren't at all what he had expected to see when the door opened. He, on the other hand, was precisely what she had expected.

His eyes were every bit as dark as she remembered, as black and mysterious as a midnight sky. However, his handsome face—with its sharply carved cheekbones, slim nose and full lips—was not quite as she remembered. He looked harder now, as though life had forged all the softness in him to steel. Rachel forced air past her tight throat, fighting against the horrible attraction this man still held for her. "I must say, Mr. Beauchamp, you don't look like a monster."

T.S. swept her from head to toe with a glance designed to take her measure. She resisted the urge to smooth her hand over her hair, regretting the fact that this man's opinion meant so much to her. "I see you've spoken to my sister, Miss Stark."

Rachel shivered as the wind whipped around him and pierced the burgundy wool of her gown. Fine flakes of snow swirled with the wind, brushing her face with the crisp scent of winter tinged with a thread of burning wood. "Marianne had a great deal to say."

"I can only imagine." His lips flattened into a tight line. "I would appreciate it if you would tell my sister I've come to collect her."

The man might have been speaking of a bag of laundry. "I don't believe Marianne wishes to be *collected,* Mr. Beauchamp."

T.S. hunched his shoulders against the brisk December wind. "I suggest you tell her I'm here."

Rachel rubbed her hands over her arms, trying to quell the shaking that came from more than the cold air. "I suggest you come back in the morning. Marianne might be in a better mood to speak with you."

Thick black lashes lowered as he narrowed his eyes. "She will see me. Now."

Rachel refused to flinch under a glare she suspected T.S. used to menace his business rivals. Or anyone else who got in his way. "I realize you're accustomed to giving orders. However, if you think for one moment I shall allow you to abuse that dear young woman while she is under my protection, you're very much mistaken."

"Abuse?" T.S. stared at her a moment, the anger in his expression disintegrating into shock. "I don't know what my sister has told you, but I've certainly never abused her."

"That, sir, is a matter of opinion. Good night."

He held the door when she tried to close it. "Miss Stark, I intend to speak with my sister this evening."

Rachel pinned him in a look she hoped was as cold as the wind swirling around her skirts. "You have done quite enough to upset her for one evening."

With one hand on the brass handle, he held the door steady when she tried once more to close it. He leaned toward her until his face was level with hers. He was so close she could smell the subtle, spicy fragrance of his expensive cologne. "I shall not leave until I have spoken with my sister."

"She doesn't wish to speak with you."

"This is ridiculous," he said, his breath brushing her face in a warm cloud of steam. "First she runs out of the house as though it were on fire, leaving our guests to wonder if she had suddenly gone insane. Now she refuses to speak with me. What the devil does she think I'm going to do?"

"Drag her home by her hair, I believe."

His lips parted, but not a word escaped for a full three beats of her heart. "Very amusing, Miss Stark."

"I'm afraid I don't find it amusing at all." She shivered in a cold gust of wind.

"Neither do I." He frowned at her. "I suggest we continue this discussion inside before you catch cold."

"There isn't anything more to—" She gasped as he grasped her arm and ushered her into the hall, his long fingers curving snugly around her upper arm.

He released her and closed the door, the solid oak thudding softly. "Now, Miss Stark—"

"Mr. Beauchamp, I don't appreciate being hauled about as though I were a wayward child."

His full lips tipped into an arrogant grin. "Perhaps you should stop behaving like a child."

Her back stiffened. "Perhaps you should stop behaving as though you own the world and everyone in it. If you think I shall allow you to bully Marianne into returning to your house, think again."

"Bully?" He fixed her in a steady glare. "Miss Stark, in the last three minutes, you've accused me of being an abusive lout and a bully."

She nodded. "So it would seem."

He studied her a moment as though trying to piece together the clues to a riddle. "How long has it been since someone threatened to box your ears?"

She lifted her chin. "Not since I was twelve."

T.S. brushed snow from his hair, the thick mane spilling over the collar of his dark gray coat in ebony waves. Gaslight flickered behind glass overhead, shimmering against his thick, wind-tossed waves, finding sapphire-blue highlights deep in the damp black depths. His cheeks were ruddy from the cold. Still, she had to admit, the seventeen-year-old boy she had last glimpsed twelve years ago had grown even more handsome than her memory of him. Countless times she had imagined this man standing here. Only, in her imagination, he had come to see her on matters far more pleasant than his present motive.

"Which one of Josh's little sisters are you?"

The rogue didn't even have the decency to remember her. When she thought of all the years she had dreamed of this man, all the times she had hoped to catch a glimpse of him again, all the wasted hopes, she wanted to scream. She pressed her lips into a tight line, hoping she looked aloof and disapproving, in spite of the fact her legs were shaking like aspic. "I'm Rachel."

"That's what I thought." A hint of a smile touched his lips. "You've changed. You used to like me."

She had little doubt the man knew just how infatuated she had been with him. She had followed T.S. around like a besotted puppy. "I was fourteen the last time I saw you. You were a likable young man then. Unfortunately, it would seem you also have changed."

He frowned, his black brows drawing together over the narrow line of his nose. "What exactly has Marianne told you?"

She folded her hands at her waist. "Enough to make me believe you haven't the slightest idea of how to care for a spirited, terribly romantic young woman."

He gave her a hard look. "This isn't your concern."

"Marianne has come here for protection, and I intend to give it to her."

"Protection?" He shook his head as though he couldn't believe her words. "My sister is hardly in need of protection."

"Yes, I am. And I'm staying here," Marianne said, her voice taut with emotion. "So you might as well leave."

Rachel turned to find Marianne and Priscilla standing near the staircase at the far end of the hall. Both girls were staring at T.S. as if he were a monster who might strike at any moment. Still, there was a steel edge of defiance beneath Marianne's fear, a stubborn streak stiffening her spine.

T.S. marched toward his sister. "I've come to escort you home."

"Don't come near me." Marianne held her hand up to keep him at bay. "You only want me to come back so you can sell me to that little toad. Well, you needn't worry about being rid of me. I shall never again set foot in your house."

T.S. paused in the center of the hall. A muscle flashed in his lean cheek with the clenching of his jaw. "I regret to say I find your behavior quite unacceptable."

"I don't care what you think of my behavior. I hate you!" Marianne turned and ran up the stairs, white lace petticoats flashing with the swirl of her dark blue skirt.

"You ought to be ashamed of yourself." Priscilla turned and followed in the wake of her friend.

T.S. felt as though he had been slapped hard across the face. Heat prickled his cheeks. He wasn't accustomed to insults. Especially in the presence of an audience. He had known his sister was a spoiled child, but he had never suspected she would do something this outrageous. The fact his sister had poured out her heart, and his business, to anyone was galling enough. To have his reputation tarnished in the eyes of this strangely disturbing woman certainly didn't help his mood.

Taking time to smother his emotions before he addressed Rachel Stark, he stared at the staircase long after his sister and her friend had disappeared. "I suppose you found that little drama amusing," he finally said without looking at her. He didn't care to see the triumph in her eyes.

"I'm afraid I found it terribly sad."

He glanced at her, surprised by the soft tone in her voice. In place of triumph he saw something far more disturbing in the startling green depths of her eyes: disappointment. The woman was looking at him as though he had just smashed all her dearest hopes. A strange feeling of regret turned over in his chest.

He hadn't thought of Josh's little sister in years. Yet he could still remember Rachel darting about his heels—a skinny little girl with huge green eyes and light chestnut hair, which had hung to her waist in thick braids. He recalled the way she had always looked at him as though he could pluck every star from the sky. It would seem the lady had outgrown the hero she had once worshiped.

Of course, it didn't make any difference to him. He certainly didn't have the time or inclination to care what any woman thought of him. With his looks and his wealth, T.S. was accustomed to dallying with women of rare beauty. He chose only worldly women—actresses, wealthy widows. Women who might hope to coax him to the altar, but wouldn't expect it. He didn't have time for demanding commitments. And he had no wish for anything more than a casual affair. He had seen how easily love could destroy a man. Only a fool would tangle with that dangerous emotion.

Still, for some inexplicable reason, the disappointment in Rachel Stark's eyes disturbed him. "I assure you, Miss Stark, the only reason for sadness is the deplorable state of my sister's manners."

She fixed him in a disapproving stare. "You're the only family Marianne has. And you're a stranger to her."

Gaslight fell full upon her upturned face, stroking the blush December had painted upon her smooth cheeks. He caught himself wondering why he hadn't remembered the small bewitching mole above the right corner of her upper lip. "I'm hardly a stranger. I'm her brother."

"When was the last time you shared a day with her?"

He clenched his jaw at her accusing tone. "I have a business to run, Miss Stark. I can hardly be expected to spend all of my time with Marianne."

"From what I can see, you spend as little time with her as possible."

He stared into Rachel Stark's disapproving green eyes and acknowledged the fact she had grown from a gawkish little girl into a reasonably pretty woman. Still, he doubted he would have noticed her in a crowded room. She didn't possess the sparkling beauty he preferred. Although slightly taller than average, she had a figure that was hardly exceptional. But he had to admit, for a woman as slender as she was, she filled out that burgundy gown with an adequate amount of curves in the right places.

Her hair was hardly remarkable. Yet the light slipped golden threads into the light chestnut curls piled high at the back of her head. Although oval in shape, her face wasn't perfection. All the same, with her slim upturned nose, sharply defined cheekbones and huge green eyes, she was, perhaps, something more than pretty. And she did have a most interesting quality about her.

Most of the women he knew were so busy trying to trap him, and his sizable fortune, they nearly broke their necks attempting to please him. Not Rachel Stark. He had to admit that he found her impertinence intriguing. "Do you make a practice of meddling into other people's business? Or am I just lucky?"

She smiled, and a swift jab of heat hit his belly. The warmth of her smile managed to elevate her looks to something far more potent than he had imagined possible. Perhaps he would have noticed this woman in a crowd.

"I'm afraid it's a family flaw," she said. "My family fought for independence from the Crown. We fought to free the slaves. We Starks tend to rush in when we see oppression."

"Oppression?" This was nonsense. Complete and utter nonsense. "Marianne has been coddled since the day she was born. How on earth could you imagine she was somehow oppressed?"

"You want to force her into marriage with a man who thinks more of a nugget of malachite than he does of the lady he intends to marry."

T.S. dismissed her words with an impatient wave of his hand. "It's an excellent match. The girl is simply too headstrong to see it."

"Marianne would rather work as a maid cleaning floors and changing beds than marry the man you have chosen for her."

He stared at her, not quite believing her words. "A maid?"

She nodded. "For four years. Just until she is no longer under your oppressive thumb."

His sister wanted to work as a maid rather than marry the heir to one of the richest men in Boston. He had thought Marianne simply high-strung. Now he realized she was insane. "The girl has been spoiled out of her mind. She obviously has no idea of what is best for her."

Rachel tilted her head, fixing him in a chilly stare. "It's obvious you have no idea what is best for Marianne."

T.S. had never in his life lifted a hand against a woman. He would never sanction such cowardly behavior in any man. Still, there was something about this woman that stretched the control he prided himself on to the breaking point. What was even more shocking was the realization that striking her was the last thing he wanted to do. And the alternatives were every bit as disturbing. "How long have you been an expert on how I should conduct my affairs?"

"I've known Marianne since she was a little girl. I might not have any idea how you should conduct your business affairs, but I do know your high-handed tactics will only serve to chase Marianne away. If I were you, I would take some time to get acquainted with my sister, to learn her hopes, her dreams, all she wants from life."

T.S. fought the ridiculous urge to snatch Rachel up off the floor and slam his mouth over her impertinent little mouth. To shut her up, he assured himself. Certainly not because the strange female had captured his interest. "I don't recall asking your advice."

"No." She lifted one finely arched brow. "I suspect you seldom ask anyone for advice. But in this case you need some."

He narrowed his eyes into a glare that had made more than a few men who had dared to question his judgment cower. Rachel Stark didn't flinch. "I'm amazed it's been so long since anyone has threatened to box your ears."

"It might be annoying to hear, Mr. Beauchamp, but I can't stand by and watch you try to ruin your sister's life."

"Marriages have been arranged for centuries. Believe me, Miss Stark. Love is a highly overrated emotion."

She leaned toward him, the little mole at the corner of her lips tipping with the conspiratorial curve of her smile. "Tell me something."

The delicate scent of roses wafted with the heat of

her skin, tempting him to draw closer. "What?"

Her eyes glittered. "Shall you remove the manacles from her wrists before you lead her to the altar?"

He curled his hands into fists at his sides, guarding against the shocking urge to shake her. "There will be no need for manacles."

"If you try to force Marianne to marry a man she doesn't love, she will find some way to escape you."

"I'm certain I can make Marianne see the potential in this match."

"You really have no grasp of the feminine mind if you believe that bit of nonsense."

"How can a man expect to grasp something that keeps flitting off in a hundred different directions at once? It isn't our role in life to understand women. Men can merely hope to guide them."

Rachel's pretty lips flattened into a tight line. "May I suggest, in this case, Mr. Beauchamp, your rudder is turned in the wrong direction."

Damn irritating female. T.S. thought of one place he would like to lead her at the moment: straight to his bed, where he would take particular pleasure in showing the bossy little female her proper place. "I know what is best for my sister."

"You know what is best for you and your business. Not for Marianne."

"You're mistaken."

She sighed, regarding him with that irritating look of disappointment. "I wish I were."

"I have no intention of allowing that girl to go running around with her delusions of romance and love, casting about for a husband on her own."

"Marianne has every right to choose her own husband."

T.S. stared into Rachel's wide, furious eyes and realized he wanted very much for this woman to understand his motives. At the moment, the reason he wanted her to understand what might appear callous behavior eluded him. In fact, he felt certain he didn't really want to know. Still, he insisted she understand he was entirely in the right.

"Being an heiress," T.S. said, "the girl would have half the fortune hunters in the world after her. With her willful, terribly romantic disposition, she wouldn't be able to see past the handsome face and winning charm of the first scoundrel who decided to pounce. In time, Marianne will see I have her best interests in mind."

"Mr. Beauchamp, you don't have the slightest idea what her best interests might be."

He clenched his jaw, fighting against the anger simmering inside him. He prided himself on his ability to maintain his calm through the most difficult circumstances. But this woman had the uncanny ability to push him to the brink.

No one challenged him and walked away unscathed. He intended to make certain his sister married Darwin Whitteck, and he would just have to teach Miss Rachel Stark a few lessons in the process. "We shall see who is right, Miss Stark."

Rachel smiled, her eyes glittering as though she knew the answer to a secret he needed very much to know. "Yes, Mr. Beauchamp, I believe we shall come to see who is right."

A half hour later, T.S. was sitting in his study with Granville and Darwin Whitteck. He sipped his brandy, hoping the mellow liquor would ease some of the tension lingering from his encounter with Rachel Stark. Never in his life had he met a more infuriating young woman. According to his butler, Marianne spent most of her time with Rachel's sister.

No doubt both girls were worse for their exposure to that tempestuous green-eyed witch.

Still, he had learned early how to spot and exploit an opponent's weakness. If Rachel Stark exerted half the influence he suspected she did, he could use her. All he had to do was gain her confidence.

T.S. glanced at Darwin, wondering how the young man was taking the fact Marianne had run away rather than accept his proposal of marriage. Darwin stood staring intently into the glass case housing the mineral collection T.S. had gathered when he was a boy. A fraction below medium height, slender with brown hair and brown eyes, Darwin perhaps wasn't the stuff of a young woman's dreams. But he was certainly stable.

"I hope you aren't disappointed, Darwin," T.S. said.

"Not at all." Darwin glanced at his host, gaslight glittering on the round lenses of his wire-rimmed glasses. "It's a small collection, but really quite interesting. If you should ever take a notion to selling that piece of malachite, I would very much like to have it."

"The malachite." Had the young man even noticed his future bride's tearful escape from the house this evening? T.S. swirled the brandy in his snifter, staring at the ripples in the amber liquid. An uncomfortable feeling jabbed at his belly, one he quickly banished. Perhaps Darwin was a little dull. But Marianne needed a calming influence in her life. "Consider it yours."

"Really? Oh, that's wonderful." Darwin pushed against the nosepiece of his glasses. "Thank you."

T.S. nodded. "I'm sure you'll get much more enjoyment out of it than I will."

"I have to say I'm disappointed." Sitting in a leather wing-back chair near the white marble hearth, Granville Whitteck tugged the lobe of his right ear. "I had hoped to announce the engagement at the ball I'm giving to celebrate the New Year."

T.S. regarded the gray-haired man sitting across from him. "There is no reason why you can't."

Granville frowned, thick gray brows tugging together over his prominent Roman nose. "Except, of course, the bride-to-be has run off."

"A temporary setback. My sister is currently under the influence of a woman by the name of Rachel Stark. She has filled Marianne's head with ridiculous notions of independence."

Granville grimaced. "One of those militant types."

"Yes." T.S. stared down into his brandy, where gaslight threaded gold through amber, reminding him of Rachel's hair. "I'm quite confident I can gain Miss Stark's confidence. Once she is firmly entrenched in my camp, I'm certain I shall have no trouble at all making Marianne see the advantages of marrying your son."

Granville rose from the chair, drawing every inch of his five feet nine inches into a stiff line that accentuated the paunch pushing against his green-and-yellow-striped waistcoat. "How long do you suppose it shall take to straighten out the girl?"

T.S. smiled, thinking of the challenge ahead of him. He was going to enjoy putting Rachel Stark in her place. "By Christmas Eve, my sister will be anxious to pick out her trousseau."

Granville's gray brows lifted a degree. "That's a little less than two weeks."

"Time enough." T.S. was certain there wasn't a female born who could match him in a game of wits. Including Miss Rachel Stark.

Chapter Two

Rachel smiled as she pulled two pans of cinnamon rolls from the oven. The dough in one pan had risen high above the dark rim; cinnamon and butter bubbled in a neat spiral through the golden dough. The dough in the other pan hadn't quite made it to the rim. The cinnamon and butter was thin in some places, thick in others. Perhaps they weren't the prettiest rolls she had ever seen, but they were the first Marianne had ever made. More importantly, Marianne had actually enjoyed herself this morning.

"Oh, they smell wonderful," Marianne said, smiling at Rachel.

"Yes, they do." Rachel set the pans on a cooling rack on the counter by the stove. She had thought baking might prove a nice diversion for Marianne—something to take her mind off of her troubles. Although cooking wasn't exactly Marianne's strong suit, what she lacked in talent she made up for in enthusiasm.

Rachel joined Marianne and Priscilla at the long oak table, which dominated the center of the big room. Morning sunlight streamed through the windows of the kitchen, spilling bright winter light across the flour-strewn table. Flour streaked one side of Marianne's face, coated her arms all the way up to her elbows and dusted her rose-colored gown every place her apron wasn't.

"Rachel, do you think a man expects his wife to know how to cook?" Marianne plunged her hands into the pile of bread dough on the table in front of her with all the enthusiasm of a child making mud pies. Puffy plumes of flour shot upward from the dough.

Rachel glanced at Marianne's lumpy pile of dough. "Not all men."

Priscilla grinned at her friend from across the table. "If you marry someone rich, like Darwin Whitteck, then you won't have to cook."

Marianne crinkled her nose at her friend. "You can have him."

Priscilla's face puckered as though she had bitten into a lemon. "No, thank you. I'm going to wait for my one true love, just like Rachel. And I don't care if I have to wait just as long."

One true love. Rachel had believed in that fairy tale all her life. Now she wondered if she wasn't simply a fool.

Her expression growing serious, Marianne looked at Rachel. "Do you think there is one special man for each of us?"

Rachel pushed the heels of her palms into her own pile of dough, stretching the elastic mound, the rich yeasty smell flooding her senses. She was hardly an expert in the field of men. She had spent most of her life in love with a man who had turned out to be an infuriating rogue. She hated to think she would spend the rest of her life in love with the man. "I like to think there is more than one man who could make each of us happy."

"What if you've already met a man you think is very special?" Marianne asked, her voice growing soft and dreamy. "Someone you've known most of your life. And what if he likes you, but he never thinks of you in a romantic way?"

Keeping her eyes averted from both girls, Rachel stretched the dough. Had she been so obvious? Heat rose in her cheeks when she wondered if everyone could see how horribly infatuated she had always been with T.S. Beauchamp.

Priscilla laughed. "You better learn to cook if you're hoping to marry my brother Alex."

Rachel glanced at Marianne, noting the color rise in the girl's cheeks. "Alex?"

Marianne's lips curved into a shy smile. "Do you think he'll ever notice me?"

Rachel doubted even her brother Alex, who had been immersed in his medical studies the past few years, would have trouble not noticing how Marianne had changed this past year. "I suspect he will definitely notice."

Marianne frowned down at her dough. "If he doesn't, I don't know what I'll do."

Rachel felt Marianne's despair. She recognized the same feeling of hopelessness that had haunted her far too often over the years. She patted Marianne's sticky hand. "You're far too young to give up hope."

"And far too gloomy." Priscilla tossed a ball of dough at her friend, hitting the top of Marianne's apron. Before Marianne could react, she tossed another missile, hitting Marianne's shoulder. That started the war.

T.S. was relieved to discover Rachel Stark's low opinion of his character did not extend to her father's opinion of him. Henry Stark greeted T.S. warmly when he came to the Freedom Tavern. Aside from a few streaks of gray in his dark brown mane, Mr. Stark had changed little since the time when T.S. had spent most of his days and nights with Josh's family.

Strange, T.S. had forgotten how much he had always enjoyed being here. In many ways, after T.S.'s mother had died when he was twelve, the Stark's big house had become his home. Since the Stark family had three daughters and two sons, the inn had always been filled with the same kind of warmth and laughter his own home had lost.

After a few moments of polite conversation, during which T.S. learned about Henry's new granddaughter and the fact that his wife was spending a few weeks in Boston with their eldest daughter and the new addition to the family, Henry directed T.S. to the kitchen.

"Rachel has the girls baking this morning." Henry chuckled under his breath. "And from the sound of it, they're having a good time at it."

"It certainly does."

Laughter, along with the rich aroma of warm cinnamon and freshly baked bread, spilled through the open door near the far end of the hall. As T.S. followed that intriguing thread of laughter, his mouth grew moist from the rich fragrance. He froze on the threshold of the big room, stunned by the sight that greeted him.

A battle raged in the kitchen. Giggles filled the air.

Rachel, Marianne and Priscilla darted around a big oak table, which stood in the center of the brick-lined floor. They were flinging bits of dough at each other. As he took a step into the room, Priscilla threw a ball of dough at her sister. Rachel ducked, and the missile flew over her head.

T.S. barely had time to register what was happening before the dough smacked his chin. A thick yeasty smell flooded his nostrils. The sticky dough clung to his skin a moment before it oozed from his chin and fell with a soft plop on the tip of his champagne-polished black boot. All the giggles stopped, caught in the throats of the women who now stood staring at him.

Marianne and Priscilla both looked as though they expected him to spit fire at them. Rachel, however, didn't exhibit a single twinge of fear. A challenge glittered in the emerald depths of her eyes. She looked as though she expected him to explode with rage and thought herself prepared to deal with it.

Never underestimate an opponent, he thought. He bent and plucked the dough from his boot. "I believe this was meant for you," he said, offering Rachel the glob of sticky dough.

Rachel hesitated a moment before lifting the dough from his hand. "You've taken us quite by surprise, Mr. Beauchamp."

"In more ways than one, I would wager," he said.

Rachel's answering smile was no more than a slight curve of her lips. Yet it was enough to start a slow simmer of heat deep inside him. "Perhaps."

T.S. stood looking at her, his mission momentarily forgotten. Last night, he had thought the woman pretty. This morning, with the sunlight in her hair, and the color high on her cheeks, she rivaled the most beautiful women he had ever known.

"What are you doing here?" Marianne demanded.

He looked at his sister, all the warmth Rachel had conjured inside him freezing in Marianne's frosty glare. "I brought you a peace offering."

Like a fawn frightened by the sudden movement of a hunter, Marianne stepped back as he approached her. "I don't want it."

T.S. pulled a slim black velvet case from his coat pocket. "Don't you even want to take a look?"

Marianne shook her head. "I don't want anything you have to give. You can't buy me."

The look in Marianne's eyes shocked him. It was true he had never been close to his sister, but he had certainly never done anything to warrant her fear and hatred. As he watched her leave the kitchen, his chest tightened with emotions so long buried he hardly recognized them: regret, yes, along with humiliation and a nibble of pain. The spoiled child had managed to spear him with her sharp words and her even sharper hatred. Priscilla followed Marianne, leaving T.S. alone with Rachel Stark.

"I'd say that went particularly well, wouldn't you?" Rachel asked.

T.S. cringed inwardly at the sarcasm in her voice. Once again he tried to assure himself that the opinion of this woman didn't matter. He should turn around and walk away from her without so much as a nod of his head. He certainly shouldn't stand here and allow the impertinent little shrew to snap at him. Her footsteps tapped the brick-lined floor as she approached him.

Intending to cut the green-eyed witch into ribbons with the sharp edge of his tongue, T.S. looked straight into her eyes. Heat speared through him, swift and hot. All the moisture in his mouth, along with every sharp word he had wanted to say, turned to dust.

Rachel offered him a towel. He stared at the white cotton a moment, confused by more than the gesture.

"You have dough on your chin," Rachel said.

Dough on his chin. And mush in his brain. T.S. slipped the towel from her hand and scrubbed his chin, wiping away the sticky traces of dough.

Last night, he had convinced himself the attraction he felt for this strange female was nothing more than a momentary aberration. This morning, after awakening from a disturbingly erotic dream in which Miss Stark had played a major role, he had assured himself there would be no other such instances. Now, as the heat she ignited in his blood settled in a smoldering pool in his nether regions, he admitted getting the lady out of his dreams might be a more difficult task than he had originally thought.

"It would seem my sister is not only headstrong, but stubborn as well," T.S. said.

Rachel crossed her arms at her waist and glared at him like a governess disappointed with her charge. "It seems to run in the family."

"Nonsense." Obviously this woman had no ability to judge character. "I'm not at all stubborn."

She rolled her eyes toward heaven. "I wonder what you would do if someone tried to force you to do something you found repulsive."

T.S. set his jaw. "Marrying one of the wealthiest young men in Boston should hardly be repulsive to the girl."

Rachel frowned. "No one but Marianne has the right to determine what she finds repulsive and what she doesn't."

He drew in a deep breath, filling his senses with the rich scent of cinnamon rolls. Yet he caught a trace of roses threading through the warm scent, a whisper of fragrance that tempted him to draw closer to this strange woman. "I happen to be her guardian as well as her brother."

"A guardian should look after the welfare of his ward."

"That's precisely what I'm doing." He offered her the towel. "If left to her own devices, that girl would make a complete mess of her life."

Rachel snatched the white cotton from his hand. "You don't know her at all if you honestly believe she is incapable of making one of the most important decisions of her life."

Rachel's words pricked T.S. with something far too close to guilt. He glanced away from the anger in her beautiful eyes. He stared down at the slim black case he still held clenched in his right hand. He had thought an expensive strand of pearls would coax Marianne out of her dark mood. Now he realized the problem with Marianne was deeper than a child's spoiled whim. "Perhaps I don't know her very well. I never suspected she actually hated me," he said, keeping his voice light, as though unconcerned with the foolish sentiments of one spoiled child.

"Strange," Rachel said softly. "Marianne believes you hate her."

T.S. glanced at her. "What the devil has put that ridiculous idea into her confused little brain?"

"I don't know. What could it be?" She pressed her fingertip to her chin as though taking a moment of serious consideration. "The fact that you insist she marry a man she cannot abide? Or perhaps the fact that you haven't spent a single birthday with her in twelve years?"

Heat prickled T.S.'s neck as he held her disapproving look. He had reasons for avoiding his sister's birthday. None of which he intended to share with this beautiful, infuriating, green-eyed temptress. "I have a business to run, Miss Stark. The very business that has built Marianne's inheritance into a sizable fortune. I certainly don't have time to hold the girl's hand every hour of the day."

Rachel was quiet a moment. She seemed to be choosing her words carefully before she spoke. "Marianne is under the impression you avoid her birthday because you blame her for your mother's death."

His chest tightened. "That's nonsense."

She didn't look convinced. "Is it?"

"Of course it is." Against his will, memories flooded him, bringing with them an icy chill. His mother's voice whispered in his memory, taking him back to that horrible day.

"Take care of your father and little Marianne. They need you."

She was lying in the bed where his sister had been born hours before, and she was smiling at him. Somehow even then, at the age of twelve, he had known it would be the last time he would ever see her smile.

T.S. gripped her slim hand. Words congealed in his throat. Words her smile kept at bay: "Don't go away, mama. I need you."

Instead of begging his mother for something she couldn't give, he had promised her he would look after his father and the baby she had brought into this world on the day she had left it. He had held her hand and watched the life drain from her beautiful blue eyes. He had looked across the bed and watched his father dissolve into heart-wrenching sobs. But T.S. hadn't cried. Not that day. Not any day since. He had promised his mother he would be strong.

It was much later when T.S. had realized his father had also died that day. Oh, Malcom Beauchamp had kept breathing for six more years. But all the life inside him was buried with his wife. The man T.S. had known and loved and respected had dwindled into a man who couldn't face life unless he did so through the bottom of a liquor bottle.

T.S. stared at the slim black case he held. He had tried to keep his promise. He had tried to keep his father safe. But nothing he had done had altered his father's journey straight to the grave. He had failed his mother once. He didn't intend to fail her again.

T.S. would protect Marianne. Even if she didn't see the wisdom of his choice now, she would—eventually. He would make certain she was married to a nice, stable man. In time, when she was older, she would realize respect and comfort were far more desirable than love and passion. "I know what is best for her."

"You're little more than a stranger to her. How could you even begin to know what is best for her?"

"That's absurd."

Rachel crossed her arms at her waist. "She doesn't even know what your initials stand for. She is your sister, and she doesn't even know your real name."

T.S. stuffed the slim case into his coat pocket. "My initials stand for the first names of two of my great-grandfathers."

She waited a moment, expecting him to continue. "Which are?"

"Better forgotten."

She sighed. "You certainly don't care to share much of yourself, Mr. Beauchamp."

Impertinent little female. "My name is hardly the issue."

"The fact you and your sister are strangers is."

Rachel might have been one of the most infuriating women T.S. had ever known, but she did have a point. "What would you suggest?"

"Take some time to get to know your sister, Mr.

Beauchamp," Rachel said, her voice touching him with the gentleness of a caress. "We're planning to cut a Christmas tree after lunch. Come with us. Spend some time with her."

"I have a meeting this afternoon."

Rachel pursed her lips. "Of course. You're a busy man."

It was there again, that chilling disappointment in her eyes. "I suppose I could take an hour or so to hunt for a Christmas tree. If you don't mind waiting a few hours, I could arrange to return here by two."

The little mole at the corner of her upper lip tipped with the warm curve of her smile. "I'm certain Marianne will be pleased."

T.S. frowned, stunned by the warmth unfurling inside of him. "I hope you can convince her to go along once she knows I'll be accompanying the expedition."

"You'll see. Marianne isn't nearly as stubborn as you think she is."

Chapter Three

"I'm not going if he is." Marianne sank to a wing-back chair near the fireplace in the family parlor. "He's plotting something. I know it."

Rachel ignored the accusing look Priscilla sent her. "Marianne, I think you should give your brother a chance. He may very well be interested in getting better acquainted with you."

Marianne shook her head. "I wouldn't be surprised if he is planning to kidnap me."

Rachel pulled her shawl closer around her shoulders, trying to ignore the doubts whispering like frost across her hopes. "I don't believe that for a moment."

Marianne lifted her chin. "You don't know him."

Rachel jabbed at the logs on the hearth with the tip of a brass poker, sending sparks scattering across the blackened andirons. Did the boy she had known still exist inside of that hard facade? "I'm afraid you don't know him either. And that's the problem."

"I don't trust him," Marianne said, her tone leaving no room for doubts.

"Because he is a stranger." Rachel glanced over her shoulder at Marianne and saw the fear behind the girl's defiant mask. "T.S. is the only family you have. Don't you think it's time you and your brother become acquainted?"

Marianne hugged her arms to her waist. "T.S. never wanted to become acquainted with me."

"It isn't too late," Rachel said. "All he needs is a chance to understand how you really feel. He has been so busy with his business dealings that he has lost all sense of what it means to enjoy the closeness of family. We need to show him what he has been missing. You need to give him a chance."

Marianne glanced at Priscilla, who sat on the sofa across from her. "I suppose he wouldn't try anything, as long as you and Rachel were there."

Priscilla smiled. "If he tries to kidnap you, he'll have to take me, too."

"And me." Rachel slipped the poker back into the brass stand beside the fireplace. "So you see, you're perfectly safe. He certainly isn't insane. And only an insane man would kidnap three angry women."

Marianne nodded. "Very well. If he wishes to come, I shall not object."

Rachel had hoped for a little more enthusiasm. Still, it was a beginning. She stared into the hearth, where flames of red and gold licked at the sides of two plump logs. Once T.S. understood Marianne, he would stop trying to control her life. It would simply take a little time—that was all. He was a good man, just a little misguided, she assured herself. It might be foolish, but she intended to do everything she could to redeem her fallen hero.

* * *

Rachel Stark was the most impertinent, infuriating . . . intriguing woman he had ever met. T.S. sat behind the desk in his study, rolling a gold fountain pen between his fingers, trying to concentrate on work. Yet his mind kept drifting, his thoughts drawn to a green-eyed temptress.

"Your Salem facility is on schedule with the machinery. Everything should be ready to ship when the new mill opens." Anson Kimball pulled a stack of papers from his brown leather satchel and placed them on the desk in front of T.S. He stood beside the desk, shifting papers as he spoke. "So far everything is going according to plan."

It was good to hear something was going according to plan, T.S. thought.

"The mill should be up and running at full capacity by July. Although you could cut two months from the schedule if you didn't insist on using local tradesmen."

"It's good for the town."

Anson nodded. "That's true. But the facility will cost approximately twelve percent more to build using local men."

"I'm aware of the figures." T.S. stared at the jade-green band adorning the center of the pen. Emeralds were closer to the shade of Rachel's eyes. But he doubted he could find emeralds that would capture the right shade. And he knew there wasn't a gem on earth that could match the spark of fire in those emerald eyes. She was a tigress in her misguided attempt to protect his sister. "There are some things that can't be measured in terms of money, Anson."

Anson smiled, deep lines flaring from his brown eyes. "That's true. The town can use the employment. It's something your father would have done in the old days."

His father had been a fine businessman, always concerned for the economy of the town his family had helped to establish. Of course, that had been before he had lost all interest in his business. In his family. In his life.

"Since it appears as though the merger with Whitteck Shipping is in jeopardy, we should—"

"It isn't in jeopardy." T.S. twisted the pen in his fingers. "Simply postponed for a short while."

Anson lifted his white brows. "I thought Marianne had refused young Whitteck's proposal."

"The girl needs a little time to come to her senses." T.S. needed a little time to alter Rachel Stark's thinking. Once he had her on his side, Marianne would soon see the advantages of marrying a nice, stable man like Darwin Whitteck.

Anson rested his fingertips on the green leather desk pad. "Would you like a little advice from an old friend?"

T.S. glanced up at him. Anson had been his father's attorney, as well as his closest friend. T.S. had known the man all his life. "Over the years I've discovered you shall give it whether I want it or not."

Anson grinned. "Talk to Whitteck. Tell him Marianne isn't ready for marriage. Allow the girl some time to find a more appropriate husband."

T.S. frowned. "There is nothing wrong with Darwin."

"I'm certain he will make some nice, boring young lady a fine husband. But Marianne has too much spirit for the young man. She is a great deal like your mother."

T.S. squeezed the pen. "I don't recall my mother ever allowing her temper to control her."

Anson glanced up at the portrait of Julia Beauchamp hanging above the gray marble mantel. "She led your father on a merry chase. Refused to marry him until he could convince her he was madly in love with her."

T.S. stared up at the portrait of his mother. She smiled down at him from the confines of a gilt-trimmed frame. Her blue eyes were filled with mischief; her hair tumbled around her shoulders in blue-black waves. Marianne did resemble her in perhaps more than looks. "If I allow my sister to choose her own husband, she will end up swept off her feet by some fortune-hunting scoundrel. I intend to protect her from that unhappy occurrence."

"Will you also protect her from finding real happiness?" Anson asked.

T.S. tapped the end of the pen against the desk pad. "I know what is best for Marianne. She needs proper guidance, a firm hand on the reins."

Anson released his breath in a sigh. "You're one of the most shrewd businessmen around. But I have to say, I believe you might be in a little over your head with this one."

"Nonsense. I know precisely what I'm doing." T.S. stood, his burgundy leather chair rolling back from the desk. "Now you'll have to excuse me. I have an appointment to keep with my sister."

A fresh dusting of snow covered the countryside. Snow coated every branch of the sugar maples on the west side of the inn, turning the sprawling stand of trees into glorious sculptures that glittered like diamonds in the sunlight. Bells attached to the harnesses of a team of bays jingled on the crisp air as the horses pulled a sleigh through the powdery snow.

Rachel sat on the black leather seat beside T.S. in the front of the sleigh, while Priscilla and Rachel sat in the seat behind them. Both girls had scarcely uttered more than a handful of words since T.S. had arrived at the inn a half hour ago. T.S. had abandoned his attempts to engage his sister in conversation. He seemed content to guide the horses and ignore everyone, including Rachel. Although the man was a wizard at business, she suspected he felt completely out of his element with a temperamental seventeen-year-old girl. Well, they certainly wouldn't make any progress if she left it up to the Beauchamps to end this war.

Rachel glanced over her shoulder and smiled at Marianne, who sat huddled beside Priscilla beneath a red-and-white plaid carriage rug. "Did I ever tell you about the day your brother saved my life?"

Marianne frowned, her eyes filling with curiosity. "T.S. saved your life?"

"Yes, I wouldn't be here today if not for him." Rachel grinned when T.S. tilted his head to look at her. "He was quite the hero."

"T.S.?" Marianne stared at her brother, her expression revealing the same disbelief that filled her voice. "A hero?"

A muscle flashed in T.S.'s cheek as he clenched his jaw. Although he made no response, it was clear Marianne's shocked response had pricked him.

"What happened?" Priscilla asked.

Rachel pointed toward the covered bridge that spanned the river and connected her father's property with the road leading into town. "It happened near the bridge the first week of May about sixteen years ago. A nasty little boy tossed my doll into the river. So naturally I jumped in to save her. Well, I hadn't counted on the current being so strong or the water being so bitterly cold. I managed to rescue my doll, but I had a much more difficult time making it to shore."

T.S. glanced at her. The narrow brim of his dark gray hat cast a shadow across his eyes. Yet she caught a glimmer of amusement in those dark eyes. A whisper of a smile tipped one corner of his lips, and that tiny smile kindled warmth deep inside of her.

Perhaps he hadn't changed so completely, Rachel assured herself. Deep inside, she had to believe he was still the same young man who had risked his life to save a foolish little girl from drowning. "Your brother came to my rescue. If not for him, I would have drowned."

Marianne's eyes were wide as she stared at her brother's sharp profile. "Did you really save her life?" she asked, her voice betraying her astonishment.

T.S. frowned, keeping his gaze fixed on the horses. "Someone had to pull the little nitwit out of the river."

Marianne shook her head. "I never would have suspected you to ever have jumped into a freezing river to save anyone."

His lips pulled into a tight line. "Careful, Marianne. All that flattery is likely to go straight to my head."

Marianne sat back against the leather padded seat, staring at her brother as though she weren't quite certain what to make of him. Did she have some doubts about the blackness of her brother's character? Rachel hoped it was a beginning, one wobbly step toward a possible reconciliation.

A few minutes later, T.S. halted the team near a stand of pine trees growing on the bluffs overlooking the ocean. He came around the sleigh to help Rachel alight. Instead of offering his hand, he grasped her waist and lifted her out of the sleigh as though she were as light as a maple leaf. He held her a moment, her feet dangling above the snow, her face level with his. His shoulders were broad and hard beneath her palms. His dark eyes searched hers for a moment as though he were looking for answers to questions he was surprised to have. When he finally set her lightly on the ground, she was appalled to discover her legs were shaking like leaves in a summer storm.

Marianne and Priscilla didn't wait for his help in leaving the sleigh. They set out through the ankle-high snow in search of the perfect tree. Rachel and T.S. followed at a more leisurely pace.

The scent of pine threaded through the cold air and mingled with the salty tang of the sea. Rachel's footsteps crunched a lazy rhythm against the snow, harmonizing with each step T.S. took. She couldn't recall all the times she had dreamed of spending a few moments in his company. And here he was, walking beside her. It was difficult to believe this was real.

"What happened to the little boy who tossed your doll into the river?" he asked.

She glanced up at him, startled by the question. "He married my older sister, Lydia. They live in Boston."

He nodded. "With a new daughter."

She smiled, thinking of Lydia and her beautiful new daughter. "They're coming for Christmas. All the family is."

He was quiet a moment, staring ahead to where the girls were flitting from one tree to another. "You surprise me. I thought you didn't approve of me. Yet you turn around and try to elevate me in Marianne's eyes."

She pulled her green-plaid wool scarf closer around her neck. "I didn't say I disapproved of you, Mr. Beauchamp. How could I when I scarcely know you?"

He frowned. "I've known you since you were a child. Do you really feel I'm a stranger to you?"

She paused to examine a tall spruce, each long

branch frosted with a thick white icing of snow. He paused beside her, improperly close, so close he shielded her from the chilly breeze. Inside, a familiar heat rippled through her, the same warmth that kindled whenever he was near. "I'm hardly the same as I was when I was fourteen, Mr. Beauchamp. And you certainly aren't the same as when you were seventeen."

"I don't see where I've altered so drastically," he said, his deep voice filled with agitation.

Rachel glanced up at him, smiling into his serious-as-a-judge expression. The man radiated power. One look into those blacker-than-sin eyes revealed a will cast from solid iron. He carried himself with all the dignity and authority of a prince. The reason people jumped at his command was obvious. But she intended to show his imperial highness that she was not impressed with his lord-of-the-manor attitude.

"The young man I knew," she said, "would never have tried to force his sister to marry against her will."

He lifted his chin. "It's an excellent match."

She rolled her eyes. "It's a life sentence in a loveless prison."

"It's obvious you and I don't see marriage in the same light." T.S. dismissed her by turning away and walking toward the bluffs.

Rachel glared at him, wishing she could grab those broad shoulders and shake him until some of the ice cracked. Were they really so far apart in what they wanted from life? Could they find a way to bridge the chasm? She caught up with him, refusing to allow the discussion to end.

"I believe marriage should be a union between two people who share an uncommon affection for one another. A man and a woman who feel more alive when they are together than when they are apart."

T.S. paused near the edge of the bluffs, his thoughts plunging into the gray water churning against the rocks sixty feet below them. "It would seem you're as painfully romantic as my sister."

"I suppose I am. I'm told we Starks always have been. . . ." Rachel lifted her face to the wind, wishing she weren't such a hopeful romantic. The odds of winning a small portion of this man's guarded heart certainly weren't in her favor. Still, hope led her down a path that might very well lead to heartache. "Tell me, Mr. Beauchamp. What do you look for in marriage?"

"I don't look for anything in marriage." He slanted her a glance. "I don't plan to marry."

His words settled like lead pebbles against her heart, where hope was struggling to survive. Since the time she was a little girl, he was the only man she had ever thought of in terms of living happily ever after. "You mean to say you intend to live your life alone."

T.S. looked at her as though she were a naive little girl. "I'm not always without feminine companionship, Miss Stark."

Images of this man with a score of beautiful women flickered in Rachel's mind. He was ridiculously wealthy as well as sinfully handsome. She had little doubt the combination afforded him ample company with women far more worldly and much more beautiful than one besotted female from Port Freedom. "You're content with mere . . . acquaintances."

He shrugged. "To be quite frank, I see no benefits in marriage."

The man had locked away his heart, hidden it in a place safe from the yearnings of a romantic who had foolishly fallen in love with him. She should definitely bury her feelings for this man. "I see. You don't want affection cluttering up your nice, orderly life."

One corner of his mouth tightened—the only sign of his growing annoyance with the conversation. "Love is an overrated commodity. It robs the intellect."

"It feeds the soul."

T.S. clenched his jaw. "Or destroys it."

"Mr. Beauchamp, my parents have been married for over thirty years. I can assure you, they have not suffered from loss of intellect. Nor have they been robbed of their souls. And I've never seen any two people more in love."

"My parents were also in love." T.S. stared out across the roiling gray water, his jaw clenched, his lips drawn into a tight line. "When my mother died, my father lost his will to survive. His daughter didn't mean anything to him; nor did his son or his business. Nothing mattered. He destroyed himself, all in the name of love."

Rachel wished she could slip her arms around T.S. and hold him. He needed someone's arms around him, even if he refused to admit he did. Instead she settled for the simple pleasure of touching his arm. He glanced down at her; his eyes were filled with a wariness that came from the emotional isolation he seemed to cherish. "What happened with your father was a tragedy. But to allow his weakness to dictate the course of your life is even more tragic."

T.S. smiled, a cynical twisting of his full lips. Tiny lines flared out from his blacker-than-midnight eyes. "I believe I'm the best judge of how to run my life."

Rachel stared up into his handsome face, trying to find a way to reach past the barriers he had erected around himself. "What about children? Will you deny yourself the pleasure of looking into your son's face and seeing a trace of yourself there? Will you never miss your daughter's smile?"

T.S. glanced away from her, staring down at the waves smashing against the ice encrusted rocks. "I have no desire for children."

Beneath his hard mask, Rachel sensed a sadness within him, pain from wounds carved long ago across his soul. She felt certain—without really understanding the reason—that he needed the warmth of affection. The same warmth he insisted he didn't want. She felt with even more certainty that he would reject any attempt she made to touch him.

A wise woman would back away from this difficult man. Yet Rachel could no more turn her back on him than she could rip his image from her heart. She had to find a way to make him see the value of affection. For Marianne's sake. For his. For her own.

"Perhaps you don't want affection in a marriage," Rachel said, "but not everyone shares your opinion. Marianne wants more from marriage than security. She wants to wake up each morning filled with the anticipation of seeing the man she loves."

T.S. looked at her, fixing her in a hard, penetrating gaze. "And is that the reason you haven't married? Are you still looking for the man who can fill your heart with anticipation? How many more years do you expect to throw away on this elusive search for love, *Miss* Stark?"

Spinster. Poor misguided romantic. Fool chasing moonbeams. T.S. said all of these things with his sharp words. He meant to humiliate, to demonstrate the foolishness of a romantic heart. Rachel glanced away from him before he could see the hurt his words had inflicted.

Staring down at the restless waves, she ignored the

pain in her heart. "I realize you think I'm foolish to wait for my one true love like some misplaced fairy-tale princess. But I won't settle for anything less than a deep, abiding affection when I marry."

Chapter Four

T.S. stared at this strange female. *A fairy-tale princess.* Somehow that suited her. Beautiful and regal one moment, soft and dreamy the next. Taunting. Tempestuous. Tempting. She was all these things and more. She had a certain quality about her, as though she carried all the light and warmth of the sun inside of her. In the light of her innocent dreams of romance, his own ideas on the subject looked sordid. Cold. Harsh. Unyielding. His were the thoughts of a man doomed to spend the rest of his life alone. Which is exactly what he had decided suited him. Love was for fools. Wasn't it?

Yet lately T.S. had admitted to having a few doubts. There were moments when he wondered if the pleasure he found in closing a crucial business deal would be enough to sustain him the rest of his life.

T.S. couldn't deny this woman intrigued him. And he couldn't deny he had hurt her with words designed to keep her firmly behind the wall he had erected to keep the world at a distance. What he wanted to deny was the guilt sinking claws into his gut. He searched for words that would soften his careless blow, but apologies didn't come easily to him. In the world of business, the only world he felt comfortable in these days, men were expected to be harsh, cold and calculating.

A single lock of hair had escaped the curls piled snugly beneath Rachel's green velvet bonnet. The long coil fluttered in the breeze, brushing the back of her dark green coat, shimmering red and gold in the sunlight. A fire in winter. Before he fully realized what he was doing, he had lifted that wayward curl in his gloved hand, wishing he could feel the silky strands against his bare hand.

Rachel glanced up at him, her eyes wide and filled with questions that had no answers. At least none he wanted to contemplate. For a moment, T.S. caught himself staring into the emerald depths of her eyes, captured by the emotion shimmering there.

Rachel looked so sad. Heartbroken over a few careless words spoken by a man who had forgotten all the softness that had once filled his life. Odd little female. Certainly not a woman with whom T.S. wanted to become entangled. Still, for some unforgivable reason, he wanted to chase away all the sadness he sensed inside of her.

"I didn't mean to insult you," he said, the words sounding stiff to his own ears.

"And here I thought you wanted to put me firmly in my place," Rachel said, her soft voice carried on the crisp air.

T.S. thought of a few places he would like to put her, as well as a few positions. All of which were every bit as disturbing as the heat she managed to ignite in his blood whenever he was near her. T.S. stared down at the curl lying across the palm of his black leather glove, and he thought of how much he wanted to pull all the pins from her hair and feel the slow tumble of her hair across his bare chest. "I'm accustomed to putting people in their places. Usually only when it's warranted. In this case, it wasn't."

"I only want you to understand how Marianne feels," Rachel said softly.

He allowed the silky strands to fall through his gloved fingers. The breeze lifted the shiny tresses and spun them into shimmering flames. "I know."

"If you try to force her to marry Mr. Whitteck, I'm afraid you will only manage to destroy any chance you might have for ever establishing a relationship with her."

T.S. looked at Rachel, uncomfortable with the way she seemed to look straight through the walls he lived behind. "Marianne and I have never been close."

Rachel sighed, her breath turning to steam on the cold air. "I cherish the time I spend with my family. There is no reason why you and Marianne can't find that sense of closeness."

T.S. didn't really know how to be a part of a family. He wasn't certain he wanted the closeness that came with opening himself to another human being, even his sister. Still, it was unsettling to realize he was more alone than he had ever really imagined. No one cherished time spent with him, including the women who drifted in and out of his life. "I wonder if Marianne and I could ever be close."

Rachel smiled up at T.S. "I have a feeling you can accomplish anything you put your mind to."

That smile. Lord, she smiled at him and an odd sensation coiled in his chest, something altogether too close to need, which was a close cousin to longing. Both of which he could do without.

T.S. stepped away from Rachel, hoping the added distance would ease the ridiculous attraction the woman held for him. If he didn't curb it, he would do something shocking—such as take the infuriating woman in his arms and touch that tiny mole above her upper lip with the tip of his tongue. "We better find the girls and that perfect tree. I don't have all day to spend on frivolities," he said, sounding harsher than he'd intended.

Rachel frowned. "The young man I knew was quite accomplished at having fun."

"I assure you, Miss Stark, I know how to enjoy myself."

Rachel considered T.S. for a moment, as though she were trying to see something more in him than what he allowed the world to see. "It doesn't show," she said and drifted away from the bluffs.

T.S. followed her, his footsteps crunching indignantly against the snow. "And what exactly do you mean by that?"

She shrugged. "You never smile."

"You're mistaken."

"You can't mean to call that tight grin you favor people with a smile? Why, at times I can't be certain if you're smiling or if you've experienced a sudden pain."

One corner of his lips twitched with his growing agitation. "I didn't realize you found my smile so displeasing."

"I always thought you had a most engaging smile. It was warm and easily given." She slanted him a look. "It's really a pity you've lost it."

"I haven't." He forced his lips into a smile.

She lifted her brows. "Have you a headache?"

"No, Miss Stark. But I suspect you quite capable of

giving me one." He marched away from her before he lost the fragile control over his emotions. Before he grabbed the infuriating female and slammed his mouth over her impertinent little mouth. To teach her a lesson, he assured himself. To show her . . .

Something struck his back, straight between his shoulder blades. T.S. halted, then pivoted. Staring at Rachel for a moment, he noted the impish grin on her face and the snow she was packing in her hands. "Miss Stark, did you hit me with a snowball?"

T.S. looked stiff enough to snap in a strong gust of wind, Rachel thought. She smoothed her hands around her tightly packed ball of snow. "As a matter of fact, I did."

He narrowed his eyes into that cower-in-your-tracks glare. "If you have any intention of tossing—"

She smacked his shoulder with the tightly packed snow ball. Snow sprayed across the dark cashmere and struck his stiff cheek.

T.S. stared at her. "What the devil do you think you're doing?"

"Starting a war. The young man I knew loved to play in the snow." Rachel bent and snatched a handful of snow from a drift between a pair of spruce trees. The arrogant, stiff-necked, dictatorial monster needed a little lesson in being human, she thought, packing the snow tightly in her hands. "But I suppose you don't remember how to enjoy a good, old-fashioned snowball fight. Or do you?"

T.S. scrubbed at the snow on his coat. "I certainly don't care to—"

"Defend yourself, Mr. Beauchamp." Rachel tossed the ball from one hand to the other, grinning at him, challenging him.

"Miss Stark, I insist you—"

She tossed the ball. It smacked his chest and splashed snow down the front of his dark gray coat. T.S. stood frozen, staring at her, his eyes wide and black as coal.

"You look like a snowman." Rachel grinned as she scooped up a big handful of snow. "Is that what you are, Mr. Beauchamp? A snowman? All icy inside?"

"I really must insist you stop this nonsense."

Rachel nailed him in the chin with the lightly packed ball. T.S. blinked, his long black lashes glittering with snow. For a moment, he didn't move. He just stood staring at her as snowflakes clung to his cheeks. But she sensed that her last hit had cracked something inside him—his icy control.

Rachel held her breath and waited for an explosion. She prayed he would pick up a handful of snow and toss it at her. Slowly his lips tipped upward; his eyes smoldered with something more than rage. In that grin, she caught a glimpse of the young man she had known.

T.S. grabbed a handful of snow. "Prepare to be boarded!"

"Maybe you haven't changed so drastically."

Rachel snatched a handful of snow, but his missile hit her shoulder before she could throw. Her laughter sparkled on the cold air, like bells proclaiming a joyous occasion. When she tossed her snow ball, he ducked, and the ball whizzed past his ear.

"Nice try," T.S. shouted. Then he slung a firmly packed ball at her.

Rachel jumped to the side, but the perfectly aimed ball hit her hip. Snow splashed against her dark green coat. "Villain!"

T.S. laughed, the dark sounds rumbling from deep in his chest. "Give up?"

"Never!" Rachel threw a well-packed ball.

T.S. dodged the shot. "You never could hit a moving target."

"Oooo!" She scooped up two big handfuls of snow and packed them into a weapon the size of a cannonball. "We'll see what I can hit with this."

T.S.'s dark laughter filled the cold air as Rachel rushed toward him. He didn't try to duck or dodge or retreat. As she drew back her arm to sling her missile, he lunged at her. She squealed with the sudden impact of his arms around her waist. He tackled her, taking her back into a plump snowdrift.

T.S.'s hat flew from his head. White plumes of snow flew all around them and sparkled like silver in the sunlight. As he rolled with her down the gentle slope dipping away from the bluffs, their laughter mingled in joyful harmony. When they stopped, he pinned her to the ground, trapping her beneath his big body.

"Now, Miss Stark, are you ready to surrender?" he asked, his deep voice filled with humor.

Rachel's green velvet hat had slid over her eyes; a single black ostrich feather brushed the tip of her nose. She struggled to free her arms, which were pinned against his chest. "You don't . . . play fair," she said between giggles.

"That depends."

Rachel blew at the black ostrich feather tickling her nose. "Depends on what?"

T.S. eased the hat back on her brow. "On who makes the rules."

Rachel stared up into his black eyes, and all the breath evaporated from her lungs. Snow dusted his tousled hair and his smiling face as though nature had showered him in diamond dust. Her skin tingled with the sudden acknowledgment of his body pressed against hers. All doubts about this man being made of ice vanished as his heat radiated against her. The layers of clothes between them couldn't suppress a heat as potent and unexpected as a breath of summer in the depths of winter.

"I get the impression you like to make the rules," Rachel said.

"When I can." He brushed the snow from the curve of her cheek with the back of his fingers. The cold black leather was a poor substitute for the warmth of his skin. He studied her features as though he had never really looked at her before and he was surprised by what he saw. Her senses were filled by the warm scent of his skin—tantalizing spice of cologne and an even more intriguing spice that was his alone.

T.S. lowered his eyes, his gaze touching her lips. "In my rules, the winner can demand a forfeit from the loser of any war."

Rachel's heart pounded so hard against the wall of her chest that she was certain he could feel it. "What forfeit?"

His breath touched her cheek in a warm brush of steam. "This."

A groan lodged low in Rachel's throat at the first touch of his lips against hers. She shouldn't allow this; it was really quite improper. But she couldn't find a word of protest in the muddle that had once been a fully functioning brain. She had dreamed of a moment like this far too many times to ever really believe it would come true. Yet here he was, kissing her, and the reality of the moment sang in her veins. His lips, firm and soft, glided over her lips. The weight of his body pressed her down into the snow. She should be cold, cushioned as she was by icy snow. Yet his warmth chased away the chill.

Heat spilled into Rachel's blood and gathered like liquid sunlight low in her belly. T.S. parted his lips over hers and deepened the kiss. She flexed her fingers against his chest, wishing she could slide her arms around his neck and hold him. Dear heaven, she wanted to hold him until she drew her last breath.

A growl rumbled from within T.S.'s chest, the dark primitive sound whispering to a need hidden deep inside Rachel. When he touched her lips with the tip of his tongue, she opened to him, welcoming the slow slide of his tongue into her mouth. All the while, pleasure shimmered along every nerve in her body.

Rachel had never imagined a kiss could be more than a brush of lips against lips. This kiss, with the slow teasing of his tongue against hers, was a revelation. The flutter of a pulse in the tips of her breasts surprised her. The awakening of a pulse low in the most private region of her body shocked her. Yet she didn't want the sensations to end. She wanted more. And somehow she knew what she craved was well in his power to give.

Rachel felt T.S. stiffen, and then he was pulling away from her, ending the kiss. Staring up at him, she resisted the urge to beg him to continue. As he stared down at her, his breath escaped his parted lips in warm puffs of steam that touched her lips. Confusion—and something more—filled the black depths of his eyes. Even in her innocence, she recognized the desire burning in this man.

T.S. cleared his throat. "I better let you up before you catch a cold."

Rachel touched his shoulder. "Strange, I don't feel cold."

He frowned. "You will."

She resisted the urge to pull him back down when he drew away from her. This wouldn't do. She couldn't go about throwing herself at this man. She really had to regain some control over her emotions. Before she did something foolish.

T.S. stood and helped Rachel to her feet. He stepped away so quickly she stumbled. But he grabbed her arm and imposed balance in a world suddenly knocked off its axis.

"Thank you," Rachel said, smiling up at him.

T.S. held her a moment, looking at her as though she were a mystery he could not solve. Then he backed away from her. "We had better find the girls and that perfect tree. I have a great deal of work to do this afternoon."

Realizing that T.S. was safe again behind the walls that kept him isolated from the world, Rachel said, "I had hoped you might stay and help us decorate it this afternoon."

"Impossible." He looked away from her, staring toward the ocean that rolled in gray waves beyond the bluffs.

"I understand," she said softly. "You're a busy man. Your days are filled with important meetings."

T.S. set his jaw. "I have a business to run."

Rachel nodded. "You couldn't possibly take a few hours to do anything as frivolous as decorate a Christmas tree."

He brushed at the snow clinging to the front of his dark gray cashmere coat. "I'm certain you shall have more than enough people to accomplish the chore."

Rachel studied him a moment, suspecting he was more uncomfortable than what he wanted her to see. "Strange, I've always regarded decorating a Christmas tree as a pleasure, not a chore. I suppose it's all a matter of attitude."

T.S. frowned. "Miss Stark, the boy you knew didn't have as much responsibility as I do."

"Perhaps you have too much."

T.S. glanced away from Rachel as though he were afraid she would see something in his eyes. Without another word, he marched away from her, stiff and far too proud.

Rachel watched him, aching for the vibrant boy lost inside the icy sculpture of the man T.S. Beauchamp had become. She was certain there had been a time when he had looked forward to decorating for Christmas. But that was a long time ago. Somehow she had to find a way to remind him just how important it was to enjoy this wonderful season. As well as all the seasons of his life.

Chapter Five

This was foolish. He had work to do. He shouldn't be here. Yet T.S. couldn't find the will to leave. He tried to assure himself he was here simply because it fit into his plans concerning Marianne. But he suspected the reasons were much more closely related to a different lady.

He fastened a glass bell to a branch of the tall spruce tree he had lugged into the family parlor of Freedom Tavern an hour ago. The bell rang sweetly as it settled into place, conjuring a memory within him of his mother's voice whispering softly: *Every time a bell rings, an angel gets his wings.*

Regret tightened around his chest with the memory. Christmas had always been Julia Beauchamp's favorite time of the year. She had always made certain her house was filled with garlands of fragrant evergreen branches, flowers and candles as well as cookies and cakes and candy. After she died, T.S.'s father had not celebrated Christmas or any other holiday.

The only Christmas celebrations T.S. had known since he was twelve had been right here, surrounded by Josh Stark's big family. Strange, he hadn't realized how much he had missed it, until this moment. Three fat logs crackled on the hearth, sighing under the fiery caress of red-and-gold flames, chasing the chill from the air, filling the parlor with a cozy warmth. The scent of pine mingled with the fragrance of the gingerbread Rachel had baked while he and Henry had arranged the tree in a corner near the windows.

As T.S. stepped back from the tree, he watched Rachel as she and the girls placed the last ornaments on the graceful green branches. Tilting her head this way and that, Rachel searched for the ideal place to hang the glass star she held. While T.S. looked at her, an odd sensation coiled in his chest, an emotion he couldn't identify, and with it came a sense of uneasiness. He could easily grow accustomed to being near this woman. In fact, he had an uncomfortable feeling that the woman could infect his blood like a plague.

Kissing Rachel had been a mistake because now T.S. knew exactly how soft her lips were. How sweet she tasted. How right she felt lying beneath him.

"You do the honor, T.S.," Henry said, offering him a porcelain angel. It was the same angel that had graced the top of the tree in the Starks's parlor for as long as T.S. could remember, a pretty, fair-haired lady in a white silk gown. "Put her in her place."

"I'm certain you'll be very good at it." Rachel's voice betrayed a trace of amusement.

T.S. glanced from the porcelain angel to the woman standing a few feet away. She was grinning at him, and her beautiful eyes were filled with the same humor he had heard in her voice. He knew exactly where he wanted to put Rachel—on her back, in his bed. And that knowledge didn't relieve him from the uneasiness coiling inside him.

Once the angel was in her proper place, he would leave. He had spent more than enough time with the far-too-disturbing Miss Rachel Stark. He lifted the angel to her place on the top of the tree and stepped back to admire her. Rachel touched his sleeve, and he was appalled to feel his chest tighten.

"Thank you," she said, smiling up at him.

Heat sizzled though his belly. He swallowed against the knot in his suddenly tight throat. "My pleasure. Now if you'll excuse me, I—"

"Have work to do," Rachel said.

He felt a smile tugging his lips and quickly crushed it. "I'm glad you understand."

Rachel glanced to the piano standing in one corner of the room. "We were just about to sing a few carols. Marianne is going to play the piano for us. Do you think you might stay a little while?"

T.S. wanted to stay. There was something about this woman that drew him to her like a starving beggar to the promise of a feast. "I really should be leaving. I have a report I have to review."

"I understand." Still, she looked disappointed. "We're going to attend a charity bazaar in town tomorrow morning. Will you join us?"

T.S. did need time with Marianne. He needed time to persuade Rachel to join his cause. He couldn't do that from a distance. It would suit his purpose to spend time with Rachel. That was the only reason he intended to spend time in this woman's company, he assured himself. He would get what he needed from the woman—her support with Marianne—and then he would say farewell to the odd female.

"What time shall I meet you?" he asked.

Rachel smiled. "Around ten."

"I'll see you tomorrow then."

"I'm certain Marianne will be pleased."

T.S. glanced to where his sister had taken her place on the piano bench. She was staring at him as though she expected him to take a bite out of Rachel. She certainly didn't look anxious to spend any time with her brother. That realization left a hollow feeling in the middle of his chest. "There's no need to see me to the door. I can find my way out."

He stood near the tree, watching as Rachel and the others gathered around the piano. There were plans for the new mill to finalize, reports to review, business to conduct. And still he stood watching Rachel like a lonely mongrel begging for a scrap of affection. Even as his head enumerated every reason why he should leave, his heart begged to stay.

T.S. turned his back on the little gathering and left the room. The joyful sound of voices lifted in harmony with the soft notes of a piano followed him with every step he took. How long had it been since he had listened to carols? A lifetime.

T.S. opened the door of the closet beneath the stairs and stared at his coat. Hesitating, he listened to the carol and tried to find Rachel's voice in the joyful chorus. She was the type of woman who could inspire a man to believe he could pluck every star from the sky. She could wiggle her way under his skin and make a home for herself in his heart. That was the last thing he wanted. Or was it? He thought of the evening stretching out ahead of him, an evening filled with nothing more than the papers scattered across his desk. It was how he filled most of his evenings.

The music and voices wrapped around him like a tether drawing him back to the parlor. As if he were a man lost in a dream, he moved toward the piano and paused when he reached Rachel's side. When she looked up at him, her eyes filled with a warmth as tangible as the brush of her shoulder against his arm. He drew in his breath and added his rusty baritone to the assembled voices.

Sitting on the window seat in the parlor, Rachel stared out at the moon. The silver crescent amid a scattering of stars smiled at her from a black sky. In her mind, she relived every moment of the day, lingering on the startling few moments when T.S. had kissed her.

Could a woman place any meaning on a kiss? Could she suppose the man cared for her—or at the very least found her attractive?

Hope stirred in her heart, arching upward like a tender vine. Hope could be dangerous. Hope could lead a poor unsuspecting fool straight down the road to ruin. Still all she had at the moment was the sweet, tender hope that T.S. would one day care for her as much as she cared for him.

"Making wishes?" Henry asked as he came up behind her.

Rachel tilted her head and smiled up at her father. "Just admiring the moon."

He sat beside her on the jade-green cushion. "I do believe you have an admirer, my girl."

"Oh?" Rachel hoped she didn't look as excited as she felt. "And just who do you mean?"

Henry leaned back against the casement. "The same young man you were in love with when you were fourteen. The man I suspect has kept you from marrying any of the suitable young men who have tried to coax you to the altar. The man who couldn't keep his eyes off you this evening."

Rachel glanced across the room to where Priscilla

and Marianne were playing chess and hoped they couldn't hear the conversation. "I didn't realize I had been so obvious."

"A father notices these things." Henry kept his voice low; his words were for Rachel alone.

When Rachel met her father's steady gaze, his green eyes revealed his concern for her. "Well, I might have been in love with the T.S. I knew, but I scarcely know the man he has become."

Henry lifted his dark brows. "I fell in love with your mother in two days."

Rachel grinned. "Mother has always told me you fell in love with her the first time you saw her."

Henry winked at her. "It took that extra day to be sure. Always remember to take that extra day."

With her fingertip, Rachel scraped at the lacy pattern of frost etched in the corner of one square windowpane. "I'm certain T.S. would take more than a day to be certain. In fact, I doubt he has any intention at all of falling in love with anyone."

"Perhaps not. But there are some things in this life that we can't control."

"I have a feeling he takes pleasure in controlling more than most."

"From what I've heard, and a man like T.S. generates a great deal of gossip in a town this size, he is a real demon in the business world. Ingenious at making money."

Rachel smiled. "I believe that is obvious."

"For all that's obvious, there remains a great deal of the man that remains a puzzle. From all accounts, in spite of his hard business deals, he remains an honest man. He rescued the Beauchamp textile mills and managed to expand the business to include shipping and railroads and who knows what else. He is dedicated to his work with no time for friends. Still, he donates generously to charity. And it's hardly a secret his money was responsible for building a new wing to the hospital, even if he did try to keep it quiet."

Rachel carved a heart in the frost against the windowpane. The wing was donated in the memory of his mother. It didn't take long for people to realize who had donated the money to build it. "He has a good heart. I know it."

"Yes, but for all of his qualities"—Henry pursed his lips and studied Rachel a moment before he continued—"I wonder if he has room in his life for a wife."

Rachel glanced away from her father and stared at the pattern the warmth of her fingertip had painted against the glass. "Perhaps not."

Henry touched her arm. "I don't want to see you hurt."

Rachel managed a smile despite the weight pressing against her heart. "Don't worry. I know exactly how remote the possibility is that T.S. Beauchamp will fall in love with me."

Henry cupped her cheek in his warm palm. "You're a beautiful, intelligent, warmhearted woman. You have a great deal to offer any man. I just wonder if T.S. has his eyes open enough to see what's standing in front of him."

There had to be a chance, Rachel assured herself. She refused to give up hope. She had glimpsed the man beneath the stern mask. She had felt the heat shimmering beneath the ice. And she intended to rescue that man from his self-imposed prison of loneliness.

T.S. sat in a leather wing-back chair in his study, staring down into his glass of brandy. Anson had left hours ago after dumping on the desk a report concerning a mining investment in Colorado. That report, along with a stack of correspondence, sat on the big mahogany desk, waiting for T.S. Yet he couldn't find the concentration he needed for work.

No matter how much he wanted to deny it, his plans for manipulating Rachel Stark weren't working as well as he had anticipated. Strange, he could deal with the most hardened businessmen, but he lost his footing when he was around her.

He twisted his glass, swirling the brandy, watching gaslight twist and ripple through the amber liquid. There was nothing wrong with the way he lived his life, he assured himself. He was successful. Other men envied him. Yet tonight, sitting here, his life seemed strangely unsatisfying. For the first time in a very long time, he was aware of how large this house was. How empty. As empty as he felt inside.

You don't want affection cluttering up your nice, orderly life, Rachel's voice whispered in his memory. The woman certainly could cut a man to the bone. Yet there was no malice in Rachel. She honestly believed in her romantic notions of love and devotion.

He glanced up at his mother's portrait and wondered what she would think of her son. Family had meant everything to her, and here he was, without so much as a dog to keep him company on this cold winter's night. What would she think of the man he had become?

He sipped his brandy, and the aged liquor warmed his throat. Yet it couldn't touch the ice lurking in that deep, empty part of his soul. He wondered if anything or anyone could. As the thought formed, Rachel Stark's image blossomed in his mind. She was smiling at him in that soft way that sent heat sizzling along his every nerve.

Odd little female, he thought, smiling into his

brandy. As much as he wanted to deny it, he was looking forward to that charity bazaar tomorrow morning—and the chance to see Miss Rachel Stark once again.

Chapter Six

"I don't trust him." Marianne paced the length of Rachel's bedroom. She pivoted when she reached the windows, the white eyelet curtains fluttering in her wake. "T.S. has never gone out of his way to spend any time with me. And now, all of a sudden, he is spending every day with us. Going to a charity bazaar, of all things. Not to mention taking us to see the lighting of the Christmas tree in the town square. I've never known him to go out of his way to even glimpse that tree. Now skating! Why in the world would he invite us to go skating with him tomorrow?"

Rachel plunged a hairpin into a sagging curl at the back of her head. "We used to go skating quite often."

Marianne marched across the room, then paused beside Rachel's chair. "You and T.S.?"

"We all did. T.S., Josh, Lydia, me. Even Alex." Rachel resisted the urge to smooth fresh rose water behind her ears. She wasn't going to a ball, she reminded herself. Only to collect a few things for Marianne. She might not even see T.S. again today. After a short visit this morning, he had left, intent on accomplishing some of the work that had piled up over the past few days.

Marianne frowned. "Well, T.S. is only doing it now because he wants to catch me off guard. He thinks he can strike when I least expect it."

Rachel turned on the seat of her vanity chair and looked up into Marianne's suspicious expression. "Perhaps he has remembered how much he always enjoyed skating and he wants to share that enjoyment with you."

"You're too trusting," Marianne said with a huff.

"People can change, Marianne." Over the past few days, Rachel had glimpsed a subtle change in T.S. She was quite certain it wasn't merely her hopeful imagination. On several occasions, she had actually caught him smiling. A genuine, warm-your-heart kind of smile.

"T.S. only wants me to think he has changed."

Rachel stood and smoothed the wrinkles from her dark green velvet riding habit. "Why not come with me? That way you will see for yourself T.S. is not about to lock you up in your room."

Marianne stepped back from Rachel. "I'm not setting foot in that house again."

Sighing, Rachel realized Marianne was no closer to trusting her brother than she had been days ago. Unfortunately, every day with T.S. only served to fuel the horrible attraction Rachel had for him. She stared at the dark-haired doll sitting against the lace-trimmed pillows piled against the carved headboard of her bed. She had nearly drowned trying to save that doll. And she refused to give up on the man who had saved her life.

"Is there anything else you want besides your skates and your blue velvet skating dress?"

"My rose silk gown. The one with the ivory lace, not the one with the black velvet trim." Marianne toyed with the pale blue satin ribbon at her waist. "I would like to wear it Christmas Eve."

Rachel smiled. "I'm sure Alex will like it very much."

Marianne crinkled her nose. "I hope he does."

"I'm certain he will find you all grown up and so beautiful he won't be able to take his eyes off of you." Rachel only wished she could be half as certain another gentlemen would take notice of the lady who adored him. She opened her bottle of rose water and smoothed a few drops behind each ear. She needed every advantage to win this battle for that man's heart.

It had been years since T.S. had strapped on a pair of ice skates. Thirteen years to be precise. Still, he was certain he would have little trouble becoming proficient in short order. He had to perfect his skill. He didn't have any intention of falling in front of Rachel.

T.S. glided across the frozen surface of the lake near his stables, managing to keep his skates steady. There wasn't anything to this, he assured himself. He pushed off with his right skate, then his left, gaining a little momentum. In no time at all, he would be skating as well as he—

"Practicing?"

The sound of Rachel's voice startled him. His skates slipped in entirely different directions. Trying to catch his balance, he windmilled his arms. He skidded straight into the snow packed along the sides of the lake. His skates stopped, but he didn't. Instead, he pitched forward headfirst into a snowbank.

A soft giggle rippled on the cold breeze. T.S. pulled up on his hands and knees, turned his head and frowned at the woman standing on the opposite side of the lake. Early afternoon sunlight touched her smiling face with gold, a tribute to the beauty in its midst. In spite of the sting of the frigid snow, he felt a smile curving his lips.

"Are you all right?" Rachel asked, giving him a wide smile.

T.S. turned and planted his bottom in the snow. "The only thing damaged is my pride," he said, wiping his hand across his face.

Rachel pulled her features into a serious expression, which was spoiled by the glitter of humor in her eyes. "For a man like you, that can be a very serious injury."

He grimaced. "Now that hurt."

"Let me help," she said, stepping onto the ice.

T.S. frowned when he saw her skates. "Do you always come prepared to join a skating party, Miss Stark?"

Rachel glided toward him as graceful as a swan skimming across a lake in summer. "I came to collect a few of Marianne's things, such as her skates. Hedley told me you were back here."

T.S. rested his arms on his raised knees and stared up at her. "So you decided to join me."

"I had a feeling you might need a little help." She bent so close toward him that he caught a thread of roses curling around him on the cold winter air. She used one end of the emerald-and-blue-plaid scarf looped around her neck to wipe the chilly remains of snow from his cheeks.

Sunlight touched the curls framing her face, spinning chestnut strands to gold. She looked like an angel sent to rescue some poor mortal in distress. "It seems when you're around I always manage to take one on the chin, Miss Stark."

"It's a very stubborn chin." Rachel offered him her gloved hands.

T.S. glanced at her hands, long fingers within black leather reaching for him. It had been a long time since he had asked for help from anyone. For the past twelve years, he had learned to hide any weakness that might betray him to the wolves that prowled his world. There was no room for weakness in the competitive world of finance. No room for emotion. Yet this was hardly a negotiation with a shipping magnate. This was a beautiful woman generously offering her help to a man sorely in need of it.

"Take my hands, Mr. Beauchamp," she said, her voice warm with her smile. "I promise I won't let you fall."

T.S. grasped her slender hands and found the balance he needed in this slippery realm. As he stood there, clasping her hands firmly in his, looking down into her emerald-green eyes, he wondered if he had found something more.

"Let me help you get the feel of it again." Rachel released his right hand and slipped her arm lightly around his waist. "Just follow along with me until you feel comfortable on your own."

Slipping his arm around her shoulders, he took his balance from her. Relying on someone else felt odd. He hadn't done it for a long time. Yet in spite of his best resolve, he had to admit he was strangely comforted to feel he wasn't entirely alone.

Since the time when he was a boy, T.S. had acknowledged an emptiness inside him, a void waiting to be filled. Trying to fill that hollow place with business, he had taken pleasure from the deals he made, the money he accumulated. Yet the emptiness remained.

T.S. had told himself there was security in that emptiness. No one could take something away from him if he never had it. If he never experienced love, he would never miss it. His logic had always seemed sound enough. Until now.

Time after time in the past few days, T.S. had caught himself searching for ways to make Rachel smile. He couldn't deny he desired her warmth and light like a man trapped underground craves the sun. He had started looking forward to each new day and the opportunity it brought to be in her company. At first, he had found ways to dismiss the attraction. Now he realized he wanted something from her he had never sought before in his life.

They glided around the frozen lake, her strides smooth and sure, his as wobbly as a child taking his first steps. In time, his balance altered, adapting to the skates and the slick surface beneath. Still, he didn't break away from her.

The cold air stroked his face as they increased their pace. The delicate fragrance of roses in winter teased his senses, beckoning him to brush his lips against her neck. She looked up at him, her smile as innocent as an unsuspecting angel. The lady had no idea how much he wanted to take her in his arms and make love to her.

"You're doing very well," Rachel said. "In no time at all, you'll be skating as powerfully as you always did."

T.S. tightened his hand against her shoulder, afraid suddenly she might draw away from him. "Thanks to you."

Rachel stayed close against his side, looking shy

suddenly. "As I recall, you picked me up off the ice more than once."

"That was a very long time ago."

It seemed a lifetime since he had enjoyed anything as simple as skating. Oh, he worked at finding enjoyment. When he was in New York or Boston, he often took ladies to the theater or the opera or some other expensive outing. Yet somehow the memory of all those nights in the company of one beautiful woman after another dissolved in the light of this woman's smile.

T.S. kept his arm around Rachel's shoulders when she paused near the edge of the lake. He didn't want to let her get away from him.

"It doesn't seem you need my help anymore," she said. But she made no move to pull away from him.

He wasn't ready for his time with her to end. "Would you join me for some refreshment before you leave? A little hot chocolate to warm you?"

Rachel hesitated a moment. "That would be lovely."

T.S. released the breath he hadn't realized he had been holding. He nodded, because at that moment he was afraid his voice might betray more than he wanted to reveal.

Certainly no one would call this elegant room a parlor, Rachel decided. Not with that thick Savonnerie carpet stretching an intricate pattern in rose and ivory to all four corners of the huge room. A parlor would not have those white panels trimmed delicately in gold covering the walls. And the rose silk-brocade drapes perfectly matched the shade of rose in the carpet and the tapestry upholstery covering chairs and sofas that would be at home in a palace. In fact, she suspected a few of them had once graced a palace or two. No, she was quite certain this room must be called a drawing room.

While sitting on an elegant Sheraton sofa near the white marble fireplace, Rachel stared up at a landscape hanging above the mantel. Every floor of the three-storied mansion was filled with fine paintings and exquisite furniture, as well as expensive—and in some cases priceless—porcelain and objects of art. It was beautiful. It was also as cold and flawless as a museum dedicated to opulence. Was there any wonder why Marianne had spent most of her time since she was a child in the comfortable surroundings of the Freedom Tavern?

"You're frowning," T.S. said. "Are you thinking you shouldn't be alone with me without a chaperon?"

Rachel glanced to where T.S. stood beside the fireplace. "Mr. Beauchamp, I'm far past the age of needing a chaperon."

T.S. rested his arm against the mantel, a smile tipping one corner of his lips. "I see. You're too old to spark the interest of a man."

"I would hope that isn't true."

"Ah." He cocked one black brow. "You still have some hope of meeting your one true love."

Uncomfortable with his teasing, Rachel glanced down into the cup of hot chocolate she held. "You needn't be so cynical. There are still people in the world who believe in romance, even if you don't."

"I'm sorry," T.S. said. His voice was gruff in spite of the apology as though the words were difficult for him to form. "Some habits are difficult to break."

Rachel glanced up at T.S. and found him watching her as though he were trying to decide what species she might be. She had the feeling he liked to place the people he met in carefully defined categories. And he still hadn't decided where she fit. "You weren't always so cynical."

T.S. glanced toward the fire. "I suppose it takes a while for anyone to have his eyes fully opened."

Rachel sipped her hot chocolate, the sweet fragrance of which brushed her face in a whisper of steam. She regarded T.S. a moment over the rim of her ivory porcelain cup. "And you think my eyes are still closed."

T.S. looked at her, his dark eyes filled with a need even the stern expression he used as protection couldn't hide. Fires flickered in the depths of those black eyes—desire and hunger powerful enough to brush against her like a hot July wind. "I think your eyes are beautiful just the way they are."

Afraid she might spill the hot chocolate with the sudden trembling of her hands, Rachel eased her cup and saucer to the round mahogany table beside her. She clasped those quivering hands in her lap and searched for some thread of intelligent conversation in a brain that had ceased functioning. It was true: She didn't have a great deal of experience with men. But she knew enough to recognize interest when she saw it in a man. And T.S. certainly looked interested in her.

He stared into the fire, golden light flickering upon his sharply carved features. A muscle in his cheek bunched with the clenching of his jaw. After a long while, when only the crackle of the wood filled the taut silence stretching between them, he spoke. "I'm looking forward to seeing Josh. I've never met his wife and children. It's been about ten years since I've seen him."

Rachel eased the air from her constricted lungs, grateful and at the same time disappointed in his return to safe ground. "I'm glad you've decided to spend Christmas with us."

"I'm looking forward to it. The past few days have

served to remind me just how much I always enjoyed spending time with your family. It's strange how the time goes by and we lose track of people who once meant a great deal to us." T.S. rubbed the tip of his finger against the mantel and kept his eyes averted from hers.

Rachel glanced around the room. The sight of T.S. made her restless. She sensed a sadness deep within this man, and it was all she could do to keep from doing something shocking, such as slipping her arms around him and holding him close.

"Is something wrong?" he asked.

Rachel looked at him, surprised at how well he could read her turmoil. "I was just thinking how beautiful this room would be with a few decorations for Christmas," she said, concealing her true thoughts. "A tree perhaps. A few evergreen garlands."

"Interesting you should think so." T.S. glanced at a far corner of the huge room, where gilt-trimmed armchairs were artfully arranged for conversation. "My mother always had the tree placed in this room. She would spend days decorating the house. There wasn't a room on this floor that wasn't filled with the crisp scent of pine."

"According to Marianne, she can't remember the house ever being decorated for Christmas."

T.S. turned back toward the fire as though turning away from painful memories. "It's been a long time since the house has been decorated."

Rachel studied him for a moment and weighed her words carefully. "Perhaps it's time to start."

T.S. frowned into the fire, studying the flames a long moment before he spoke. "I take it Marianne has no plans to return home in the near future."

"I'm sorry, but I'm afraid she still doesn't trust you."

T.S. tilted his head to look at Rachel. "She still

thinks I'm planning to drag her to the altar in chains."

"Are you?"

His lips flattened into a tight line. "I never planned to force Marianne into anything."

"You simply meant to persuade her," Rachel said, keeping any hint of accusation from her voice.

T.S. nodded, and an ebony lock spilled across his brow. "I thought it was best for her at the time."

"And now?"

"I can see she would drive poor Darwin straight to the asylum." His fingers brushed past the gold case of a crystal clock marking the minutes of the day. Then he flattened his hand against the mantel. "She needs more time. Perhaps to find someone better suited to her rather combustible nature."

"She'll be very glad to hear you've changed your mind."

T.S. glanced at Rachel, his expression carved with serious lines. "Do you think she'll believe me?"

Rachel smiled, hoping to lessen the impact of the truth. "Not at first."

He was quiet a moment, staring at her as though he were trying to read her thoughts. "And you? Do you believe me?"

"Of course," she said, without a moment of hesitation. "You're an honorable man. A hero in fact. And everyone knows a hero never lies."

"A hero." A gentle curving of his lips betrayed his surprise at her sentiment and the underlying pleasure it gave him. "I doubt there are many people who would share your opinion."

"I doubt you care what a great many people think."

T.S. looked straight into her eyes, and she could see the walls of his defenses crumbling around him. "I care what you think."

Rachel squeezed her hands together in a futile attempt to contain the hope surging inside of her. "Then you may rest easy, Mr. Beauchamp."

His smile came slowly, like the easy rise of the sun in an early morning sky. And it was every bit as warm. "We still have a few hours of daylight. Would you consider helping me locate the perfect tree?"

The warmth of his smile glowed deep inside of her. "It sounds like a wonderful idea."

"Perhaps you would stay and have dinner with me—and afterward help me decorate for Christmas."

Rachel molded her expression into what she hoped appeared a severe sternness. "Such frivolity, Mr. Beauchamp. I'm shocked."

T.S. drew in his breath. "Not half as shocked as I am, Miss Stark."

Joy bubbled up inside Rachel and escaped in a soft ripple of laughter. "I do believe there is hope for you yet."

He studied her a moment, smiling in spite of the serious look in his dark eyes. "I'm glad to hear you say that, Miss Stark. No one should live without hope."

No one should live without hope or affection. Yet in spite of his wealth, she suspected he had lived these past few years without many of the things that made life worth living.

"Will you stay?" T.S. asked.

In spite of the softness of his voice, she sensed a tension coiling inside of him. But she said, "Of course."

Relief flickered in his eyes. He smiled, a gentle boyish grin that stripped away all the years that had separated them. "I'll have a message sent to your father straight away."

The hope inside Rachel grew beneath his warm regard. Perhaps she could melt the ice surrounding this man's heart. Perhaps the thaw had already commenced.

Chapter Seven

Kneeling on the thick Savonnerie carpet in the drawing room, Rachel peered into one of the three trunks T.S.'s servants had delivered from the attic while she and T.S. were enjoying dinner. She lifted a glass ball from one of the wooden boxes stacked inside the trunk and hummed "Silent Night" softly as she turned the ornament in the light. Gaslight from the wall sconces glittered against the gold, spilling in delicate patterns along the sides of the glass. It was exquisite. And only one of the many treasures hidden inside each of the trunks.

"Is it straight?" T.S. asked. His voice was muffled by his position beneath the tall spruce that he and one of the footmen had carried into the drawing room after dinner.

Rachel glanced at the tree and smiled at the long legs poking out from under wide green branches. T.S. had surprised her by dismissing the servants so that the two of them could put up the tree without assistance. They were alone in the big room, with the door closed against the rest of the world.

"It leans a little to the right," she said.

The tree trembled under T.S.'s hands; long branches rustled softly as T.S. shifted the trunk in a wrought-iron stand. Then he asked for the sixth time in ten minutes, "How is it now?"

Rachel tilted her head this way and that to examine the tree, which now leaned a little to the left. T.S. poked his head out from under the branches. "Well?"

"It looks . . . nearly perfect."

He was quiet a moment, regarding her with a frown. "What's wrong with it?"

"It's a little too far to the left. But I'm sure it will be fine."

T.S. ducked back under the tree. He was, after all, a man incapable of allowing a flaw to go without tending. Breathing in the crisp fragrance of pine, Rachel continued her treasure hunt. Humming softly, she drew tissue paper back from shiny gold trumpets trimmed with red ribbons, crystal harps and small porcelain angels designed to sit on the branches of the tree.

"What do you think?" T.S. asked, poking his head out from under the tree.

For a moment, Rachel studied the tree a moment admiring the tall, stately pine. "Perfect."

T.S. flashed her a satisfied grin before slipping out from under the tree. He had removed his coat and tie and loosened the first few studs of his shirt. Rachel couldn't help thinking how domestic they seemed, like a married couple enjoying their first Christmas together. The image conjured up a warmth inside of her.

Together they decorated the tree with ornaments that hadn't been enjoyed by anyone in seventeen years. Occasionally Rachel caught T.S. lingering over one of the ornaments. But the thoughtful expression on his face disappeared each time he realized she had noticed and in its place appeared a shuttered expression designed to hide his emotions.

The ornaments for the Stark family's Christmas tree held special memories for Rachel. She could only imagine what seeing these ornaments after so many years meant to T.S. Slowly, they emptied one trunk after another and transformed plain green branches into glittering masterpieces.

"I don't believe I've ever seen more beautiful ornaments in my entire life." Rachel attached a porcelain figurine of Father Christmas to a sturdy branch. "I'm so glad you decided to bring them out of exile."

T.S. didn't respond. He didn't appear to have heard her. He was standing near one of the trunks, staring down at the small wrapped package he held.

Rachel moved to his side, but he didn't glance at her. Lost in his thoughts, he didn't seem to notice she was there until she asked, "Is something wrong?"

T.S. looked at her, his expression unguarded, his eyes filled with a pain so raw, so naked, it stole the breath from her lungs. Rachel touched his arm, knowing he needed comfort, even if he didn't think he did. Still, he didn't pull away from her. He didn't blink. He simply stood staring at her as though he were suddenly unsure of who she was.

"T.S., are you all right?"

He drew a deep breath in an obvious attempt to control the emotions she sensed whirling like a tempest inside of him. Several moments passed before he spoke. "I didn't realize this had been packed away with the ornaments."

Rachel stared at the small package—a box wrapped with white paper and trimmed with a gold velvet bow.

What horrible memories did that small box hold? "What is it?"

"It's an ornament. For me." He fingered the gold velvet ribbon, easing out a crinkle that time had pressed into the fabric. "Every year my mother would buy a special ornament for me. There are eleven of them on the tree."

And this was the twelfth. The ornament his mother had never given him, because she had died three weeks before his twelfth Christmas. "You should open it."

His hand tightened on the box. "I'm not sure that would be a good idea."

Rachel looked up at him and saw the pain he tried to hide behind an icy mask that had cracked in too many places to shield him. "She wanted you to have it."

T.S. didn't move, as though any movement might shatter the control he worshiped so dearly.

"Open it," Rachel said softly.

T.S. turned away from her and marched across the room until he reached the marble fireplace. For a moment, she feared he meant to toss the box into the flames. Perhaps he had intended to do just that, but something stopped him. Perhaps a memory. Or perhaps the need to see his mother's last gift to him.

Standing for a moment with his back to her, T.S. stared down into the flames and clenched the box in his right hand. As she watched him, she wished she could give him comfort for a wound that had never healed.

Slowly, T.S. unwrapped the gift, allowing white paper and gold ribbon to tumble to the floor. He opened the small box and stared inside. Rachel waited, watching him, until she could stand the distance between them no longer. Then she crossed the room, moving to his side.

Without looking at her, T.S. handed her the box. Inside, nestled against white satin, an ivory porcelain figurine trimmed in gold glimmered in the firelight. The artist had captured the wonder of a young boy who sat in a rocking chair and smiled down at the baby he held in his arms.

A hot sting burned Rachel's eyes, and her throat grew tight with emotion. Staring for a long time at the delicate porcelain, she gathered her composure for T.S.'s sake. "It's lovely."

"She asked me to take care of them, my father and my sister." He stared down into the fire, his jaw clenched, his hand a tight fist against the mantel. "I tried. But nothing I did seemed to matter. He just kept drinking."

With trembling fingers, Rachel eased the ornament from the box and set it on the mantel a few inches from his tightly clenched fist. "You can't blame yourself for his weakness," she said, keeping her voice level.

"I found him that day, facedown on the floor of his bedroom. I swore I would never allow that weakness to rule my life. I swore—" T.S. broke off, setting his jaw, fighting the natural flow of his emotions.

Resting her hand over the tight fist he held against the mantel, Rachel resisted the urge to slide her arms around him. "You aren't your father."

When he looked at her, firelight reflected in the fine sheen of his tears, which glittered like stars in the depths of a midnight sky. "I never wanted to need anyone the way he needed my mother."

Rachel smiled for him. "We can't always choose what we need. We can't always protect against heartbreak. But what does life become if we cut ourselves off from the warmth of affection?"

* * *

T.S. stared into her eyes and saw a warmth that had beguiled him from the first moment he had looked at this woman. That warmth tempted him, beckoned him to leave the icy realm of his safe existence. He reached for her, following a need he was only beginning to understand.

Rachel came into his arms as though she needed him as much as he needed her. He no longer tried to deny his need for her. How could he when it filled him as naturally as the elemental need to take his next breath? It was as though a part of him had been carved away long ago and he had suddenly found it. With a stunning certainty, he knew this woman filled the emptiness carved into his soul.

T.S. brushed his lips against the warm satin of Rachel's cheek; he smiled as he felt her tremble in his arms. He kissed the corner of her mouth and touched that tiny mole with the tip of his tongue. She slid her arms around his shoulders, lifting against him, turning her head in search of his kiss. He gave her what she sought, a soft brush of his lips against hers. The kiss sizzled along his nerves like fire streaking along a fuse.

T.S. tugged pins from her hair. Then he tunneled his fingers through the curls at the back of her head and released the heavy mass of chestnut waves. Firelight rippled through the soft waves like sunlight across water as he slid his hands through the silky strands. "I never realized those pigtails would feel this luxurious."

Rachel smiled up at him, a soft dreamy look in her beautiful eyes. "I always dreamed I would be standing with you like this one day."

He brushed his lips across her brow. "Did you?"

She slid her hands along his shoulders. "You were

my hero. My knight in the shiniest armor. I used to dream of the day you would take me in your arms and tell me how much you cared for me."

T.S. slipped his arms around Rachel and held her close, suddenly afraid she might leave him. And as the warmth of her seeped into his blood, he realized he wanted her to stay with him. Not just for the moment. But for the rest of his life.

He kissed her long and deep, forcing her to feel the raw aching need inside of him. She didn't draw away. She stayed in his arms, holding him, returning his fevered kisses as though her life depended upon it. Suddenly, it seemed his life depended on this moment.

T.S. craved her warmth like a frozen wanderer seeking shelter from a storm. He needed her skin against his, warming him. He slipped his hand between them and flicked open the tiny jet buttons lining the front of her riding habit.

"T.S.," Rachel whispered, pulling back in his arms. She stared up at him, bewildered by the passion he couldn't disguise. "What are you doing?"

"Let me touch you, Rachel." He eased the emerald velvet across her shoulders and down the length of her arms.

Her eyes grew wide as the bodice tumbled to the floor. "T.S., I—"

Before she could protest, he covered her lips with his and sealed in the words that would keep him from taking what he wanted. It was too late for denials. Too late to alter the path that might very well lead to ruin. At the first touch of her lips beneath his, he had abandoned all hope of denying his need.

With an experience born in countless cold affairs, he lured her into his sensual realm, stripping away her clothes, drugging her with kisses, inflaming her with his hands, his lips, his tongue. She trembled in his arms, soft sounds spilling from her lips, each pleasured whisper a trickle of brandy tossed upon the fire in his blood.

In spite of the lust pumping hard and fast through his blood, T.S. recognized his own reaction to this woman. His hands had never shaken like this as he had undressed another woman. He had never wanted any other woman with this craving that sank like a lion's claws into his soul. He wanted her as he had never wanted another woman—completely, irrevocably. He wanted to possess her. Now and forever.

He stripped away his clothes, touching her, kissing her, never giving her a chance to deny him. When he was as bare as she was, he lifted her in his arms. She slipped her arms around his neck and looked up at him, and he could see his own need mirrored in her gaze.

T.S. laid Rachel upon the soft white linen of her petticoat. Her hair spilled in a glimmering nimbus around her beautiful face. The golden firelight flickered across her smooth skin, stroking her, caressing her, beckoning him.

He drank the firelight from her skin, tasting the smooth curves of her breasts, flicking his tongue against the taut tips, suckling like a babe in her arms. She whimpered softly and clutched at his shoulders. He followed the flickering firelight, learning every curve, every line, every secret of her woman's body.

Soft feminine curls brushed his cheek. Sweet feminine need flowed like honey against his lips. He felt her desire rising with the trembling of her body. She slid her hands through his hair and tugged him closer. She clutched at his shoulders. His name escaped her lips as the pleasure built and crested within her.

T.S. flowed upward along her body, kissing her, touching her. He cupped the lush mound between her thighs and watched the bewilderment turn to wonder in her eyes. Tears sparkled in the emerald depths, tears born of passion.

"T.S.," Rachel whispered, gripping his shoulders, arching into his hand. "I need—"

"I know." He eased between her thighs, groaning at the erotic brush of damp curls against his arousal. He kissed her and slid into her feminine passage. He felt the moment her innocence surrendered to his need, knowing in that instant that his life was altering as surely as his body altered hers—forever.

Rachel stiffened beneath him, gasping against his lips. He pulled back to look at her. Tears slid from the corners of her tightly clenched eyes and fell like acid upon his heart.

"Give me a chance to make it better." T.S. smoothed the hair back from her brow. "Don't give up on me, Rachel."

She opened her eyes, a brave smile curving her lips as she looked up at him. "I've never given up on you."

"Rachel, my beautiful, sweet Rachel." As he lowered his lips to hers, he slid his hand downward across her belly. He stroked the secret little nub hidden beneath sleek feminine petals, coaxing passion to rise and chase away pain. He dipped his tongue into her mouth, tasting her, withdrawing and thrusting time and time again. All the while, he held his body still inside of her and allowed her time to adjust to the length and breadth of him inside her.

Soon he felt her passion stir. When she arched her hips against him, he moved inside of her. Before long, she met his thrusts, learning the rhythm, seeking instinctively for what her body craved.

T.S. felt her pleasure rise; he heard it in the soft

cries that rose from deep in her throat and sank straight into his heart. He moved inside her, denying his own hunger for release, the need to lift her to the summit driving him.

They moved one into the other, seeking more than could be found in their separate existences. T.S. felt the pleasure rise in Rachel, but he controlled his own, needing to reach the summit with her. He moved faster inside her. She lifted to meet him until they were both striving for the elusive gift that could only come when two are fused into one. In one sudden instant of divine pleasure, it was theirs—a passion so powerful it swept them both from the anchor of earthly cares.

Rachel shuddered and cried out his name as he poured the essence of himself into her. They held tight, one to the other, man and woman lost in the wonder. T.S. pressed his lips against her neck. He was joined with this woman, fused so tightly he didn't know his breath from hers, his heartbeat from hers. Never in his life had anything felt more right than holding Rachel this way.

Perhaps it had been wrong to seduce her, to seal her fate with his. Yet he couldn't risk losing her. Not when he had finally found his heart.

T.S. smoothed his hand across Rachel's cheek, slipped his fingers into her soft hair and smiled down into her drowsy eyes. She looked up at him, as though he had plucked every star from the sky and placed them at her feet. He had never meant to become entangled with any woman. Yet he couldn't deny this woman was in his blood. In his heart. He also couldn't deny how much he wanted her in his life.

"You do realize," he said, "I shall expect you to make an honest man of me after this."

She smiled shyly with soft lips lush from his kisses.

"Just what exactly are you saying, Mr. Beauchamp?"

T.S. drew in his breath, filling his senses with the exotic scent of roses threaded with the musk of their lovemaking. "Marry me, Rachel. Remind me every day how good it feels to be alive."

She touched his cheek, her fingers trembling softly against his skin. "I've been waiting a very long time for you to say those words."

T.S. turned his head and pressed his lips against her palm. "Thank God, you waited for me to find my way back to you."

"I've never wanted anyone. Except you. Only you. Always you."

He brushed his lips softly across hers, but his kiss left him hungry for more. "As much as I want you in my bed tonight, I don't think your father would understand."

Rachel lifted her brows in mock horror. "No, I don't believe he would."

"I hope you don't believe in long engagements."

She traced the curve of his lower lip with her fingertips. "A month? My mother will want some time to prepare for the wedding."

A month. It seemed a lifetime. He slipped his hand around hers and kissed her fingertips. "I doubt I shall be able to keep my hands off of you for a month."

Rachel grinned. "In that case, I have a feeling our first child might come a little early, as they say."

T.S. gathered Rachel close and rested his cheek against her hair. He was more content than he had been at any time in his life. He glanced up, and his gaze snagged on the porcelain ornament. Memories flickered inside him. An icy breath whispered across his skin and threatened all the warmth he had found in Rachel's embrace. What would he do if she were ever taken away from him? he wondered.

Rachel snuggled against him, brushing her lips against his neck. "Are you cold?"

T.S. held her close, refusing to surrender to the weakness. "Not when I'm with you."

Rachel tilted her head and smiled up at him. "I shall make certain you're never cold again, my love."

He cupped her cheek in his hand, fighting the weakness, the fear. He was not his father, he assured himself. And Rachel was not his mother. He wasn't going to lose her. Still, he couldn't shake the sense of disaster settling over him like a shroud.

Chapter Eight

Rachel sipped warm milk, hoping to calm her excitement enough to get some sleep. It was after midnight. Yet each time she closed her eyes, T.S. taunted her in the most beguiling fashion. She kept seeing his face as he had looked leaning over her, his chest brushing her bare breasts. Her skin tingled with memory. Squeezing her mug between her hands, she looked out a kitchen window and smiled up at the stars. All those wishes hadn't been wasted after all. She was actually going to marry the man of her dreams. Her very own hero.

"It seems I'm not the only one who can't sleep."

Rachel glanced toward the door, smiling when she saw Marianne. "Too much excitement."

Marianne stayed on the threshold of the room, looking at Rachel like a friend standing a deathbed vigil. She started to say something, then thought better of it.

Rachel gripped her mug. This evening everyone had been stunned by the news of her engagement. Marianne was so stunned she hadn't offered a word of congratulations. "I was just having some warm milk. Would you like a cup?"

Marianne shook her head. "No, I think I'll just go back to bed."

"Marianne," Rachel said as the younger woman turned to leave.

Marianne turned in the doorway. "What?"

"You haven't said a word about my engagement. Are you disappointed in your brother's choice?"

"No." Marianne pressed her hand to her heart, her face reflecting her horror of the thought. "How can you imagine I would think you weren't worthy of that man? You're more of a sister to me than T.S. has ever been a brother."

Rachel slid her thumb over the rim of her mug. "Something is wrong."

"I hope there isn't. I just keep thinking he is up to something. I can't get it out of my mind that he is—" Marianne hesitated and shook her head as though she wanted to dismiss the words she hadn't been able to speak.

Rachel squeezed her mug. Absorbing the warmth radiating through the thick porcelain, she tried to chase away the chill Marianne had brought into the room. "He is what?"

Marianne glanced away from Rachel. For a moment she stared at a line of moonlight slanting across the brick-lined floor. "A merger with Whitteck Shipping would mean a great deal of money. Millions."

"That has nothing to do with me. I'm hardly an heiress."

"He knows how much I depend on your judgment." Marianne glanced at her. "Your engagement happened so quickly. I keep wondering if he isn't trying to use you to get to me."

The words stunned Rachel like a hard slap across the cheek. T.S. would never do anything so underhanded, she assured herself. It was ridiculous to imagine that a man like T.S. would for any reason offer marriage to a woman he didn't want. Wasn't it?

"Oh, I didn't mean to upset you." Marianne rushed across the room, her blue velvet robe fluttering around her legs. "I shouldn't have said anything."

Rachel managed a smile despite the nasty doubts Marianne's words had conjured up in her mind. "Marianne, I seriously doubt your brother would marry me simply to close a lucrative business deal. That is a rather large sacrifice."

"It would be a sacrifice to a man who has a heart. But T.S. never believed in love. The only thing that ever mattered to him was making money. I just keep—" Marianne looked at Rachel with wide eyes. "I'm simply being foolish—that's all. I just want you to be happy. Are you happy?"

"Of course." But Rachel had to admit she had been a great deal happier before this conversation.

"You do love him?" Marianne asked.

"I've loved him for as long as I can remember."

Marianne looked amazed by the idea. "But I thought you would want a passionate man."

Rachel glanced down at the moonlight spilling across the wooden counter, and heat spread across her breasts at the memory of his mouth tugging against her nipples. "Oh, I suspect there is a bit of passion inside of your brother. I'm certain, however, I shall have to work at provoking him."

Marianne squeezed Rachel's arm. "I hope he will make you happy."

"There is no one I want more as my husband than

T.S. Beauchamp." Rachel patted Marianne's hand. "Now don't you worry. Everything is going to be just fine."

T.S. stood in one corner of the Starks's parlor, watching his fiancee cuddle the newest addition to the Stark family circle. He wondered when he had ever seen anything quite so beautiful. *His fiancee.* They had been engaged for three days, and he still had trouble believing this lovely woman was really going to spend the rest of her life with him.

Dressed in sapphire-blue velvet, Rachel sat in a rocking chair near the hearth. She was holding her youngest niece and chatting with her sisters, her mother and Josh's wife. Josh's two sons and daughter sat with Lydia's son in one corner of the room, playing with a wooden train set. Thomas Taylor, Lydia's husband, sat on the window seat with Henry, discussing Boston politics.

It was the first time in many years that T.S. had spent Christmas Eve with anyone. And he realized there was nowhere else he would rather be than here with Rachel. The warmth in this room came from more than the fire crackling on the hearth. It radiated from these people, so snug and secure in the circle of family affection. And he was a part of it all, a thread in this glittering tapestry of life.

"I have to say, the news left me stunned." Josh handed T.S. a cup of mulled cider. "You and Rachel. What a surprise."

"I have to say I'm a little stunned as well." T.S. was also uneasy. He couldn't remember the last time he had been this happy. And he couldn't shake the feeling it was all going to be taken away from him. "Your sister knocked me off my feet."

Josh lifted his cup in salute, his blue eyes filled with

humor. "Here's to you and my sister. May you find as much joy in your union as I've found with my Brianna."

T.S. sipped his warm cider and silently fought his anxiety. He was worrying needlessly. He supposed it was to be expected. He had guarded his heart for a long time. It was going to take a while to get accustomed to sharing his life with someone.

"It looks as though we might have another alliance between our families in the making." Josh nodded toward the sofa, where his brother sat with Marianne.

T.S. studied his sister and Alex, amazed at how happy Marianne looked. He couldn't remember the last time he had seen her smile as though someone had given her the most delightful present in the world. It didn't take a mind reader to see his sister was infatuated with Josh's dark-haired young brother. And from the grin on his handsome face, Alex had apparently noticed how beautiful Marianne looked in her rose-colored gown.

Alex was hardly one of the wealthiest men in Boston. But he would do well as a doctor. Perhaps Marianne could choose her own husband without catastrophic consequences. T.S. smiled, feeling the uneasiness fade inside of him. Everything was going to be fine.

Shortly after nine that evening, the front doorbell jingled. Henry left the parlor and returned a few moments later. He wasn't alone.

T.S. was standing with Rachel and the others near the piano, listening to the debate raging between Josh and Lydia concerning which Christmas carol they should sing first. T.S. noticed their visitor at the same time as Marianne. She stared up at him, her eyes filled with fury.

"What is Whitteck doing here?" Marianne demanded.

"Whitteck?" Rachel touched his arm. "T.S., did you invite Mr. Whitteck to join us?"

There was no fury in Rachel's eyes, only concern and a flicker of doubt that whispered like frost across the base of his spine. "No, I didn't invite him."

"Really?" Marianne glared at him. "I suppose he is simply looking for a room for the night."

T.S. had a very good idea what Whitteck was looking for and why. The last thing he needed tonight was Whitteck stirring up things that should have remained forgotten. The quicker he got rid of the gentleman, the better. "I'll take care of this."

T.S. crossed the room. He greeted a frowning Granville Whitteck, then drew him out into the hall. "I wasn't expecting you."

"You said everything would be taken care of by Christmas Eve."

"I should have wired you and informed you of the situation. I didn't expect you to come without hearing from me."

Granville rubbed his chin. "I take it all has not gone according to your plan. The girl is still reluctant to marry my son."

His plan. Lord, it seemed a lifetime since he had planned Marianne's future as coolly and dispassionately as he would negotiate the merger of two companies. "Marianne has a mind of her own. With very definite views regarding marriage."

Granville pursed his lips. "What about this Stark woman? I thought you were convinced you could manipulate her to your own purpose. Haven't you been able to convince her to help you with Marianne?"

"I'm afraid I also have a mind of my own, Mr. Whitteck," Rachel said from behind T.S.

T.S. froze at the icy sound of Rachel's voice. He turned and found her standing a few feet away, staring at him as though he had just slithered out from beneath the nearest rock. "Rachel, I—"

"I don't wish to be unpleasant, but I believe it would be best if you and Mr. Whitteck left." Rachel folded her hands at her waist, fixing T.S. with a look that bore no hope for negotiation. "Now."

Music floated into the hall. The joyous sound of voices raised in celebration mocked the fear crowding his chest. T.S. turned to Whitteck. "Granville, if you wouldn't mind returning to the house. Miss Stark and I have a few things to discuss."

Whitteck nodded, looking confused and more than a little uncomfortable by the turn of events. A cold wind swept the length of the hall as he opened the front door and left, but the December wind was a hot August breeze compared to the look in Rachel's eyes.

"I believe I asked you to leave, Mr. Beauchamp."

He stepped toward her. "Rachel, give me a chance to explain."

"There is no need. I think I can piece together the situation without your assistance." She stared at the polished oak planks beneath her feet. "You thought I would help you in your quest to see Marianne married to a man she doesn't love. Your plan failed. Now I think it would be best for everyone if you left."

She turned away from him. But he gripped her arm, holding her when she tried to break free. "Please don't turn away from me. Let me explain."

Rachel stood like an ice statue and stared straight ahead at the light from the parlor spilling across the floor. "Are you going to tell me you never meant to use me?"

"I won't lie to you. In the beginning I thought I could convince you I knew what was best for Marianne." He held her tighter than he should. Yet he still felt her slipping away from him. "I never realized you would convince me how important it was to marry only for love."

"There is no need to continue this farce, Mr. Beauchamp," she said, her voice as cold and dispassionate as a judge passing sentence. Still, a small tremor betrayed her barely restrained emotions. "I don't know how far you intended to go to ensure my cooperation, but your effort was in vain. I never would have helped you convince Marianne to marry a man she didn't love. Even if you had gone through with our marriage."

Slivers of ice pierced T.S. with each finely honed word. "You can't deny you're in love with me."

Rachel looked up at him with tears shimmering in her eyes. "How dare you! How dare you flout my feelings for you!"

He cupped her face in his hands. "You love me. And I'm not going to let you leave me."

"Go away!" Rachel broke free from T.S. and ran toward the stairs.

T.S. watched her run up the stairs, a hard hand squeezing his heart when he realized he might lose her forever. He couldn't let that happen. He wasn't going to let her get away from him.

Rachel had never really understood what people meant when they spoke of a broken heart. But now she could feel that horrible ache centered in her chest. A wrenching realization that her entire life had ended. From this moment until that final moment when she drew her last breath, nothing would ever matter again.

"Rachel, wait!" T.S. shouted, following her up the stairs.

She ran until she reached her room on the third floor, but she couldn't outrun the pain. Through a sheen of tears, she found the lock and bolted her door against the man chasing her. She wouldn't allow him to see her tears. She wouldn't allow him to know how easily he had destroyed every hope and dream she had ever possessed.

"Rachel." T.S. jiggled the handle, trying to open the door. "I have to talk to you."

Rachel swallowed hard and cleared the tightness from her throat. Lifting her doll from the bed, she stared through her tears at the sweet porcelain face. "There is nothing left to say."

His fist thudded against the door. "Has anyone ever told you how damn stubborn you can be?"

She lifted her chin. "Go away, Mr. Beauchamp."

"I'm not going anywhere until you give me a chance to make you understand the truth."

"I don't want to hear any more of your lies." Standing by her canopied bed, Rachel stared at the door and waited for a response. Moonlight spilled through her windows, casting the door in a pale glow. She held her breath, waiting, wondering if he had given up on her. And in that moment, as her broken heart pounded against her ribs, she realized how desperately she was hoping he could convince her every lie had been the truth.

"Open this door," T.S. said, his voice low and deadly serious. "Or I swear I'll knock it down."

Rachel clutched her doll to her chest and stared at the door. "You wouldn't dare."

"You know better."

Rachel crept toward the door. "You're acting like a barbarian."

T.S. tugged on the handle. "I told you love robs the intellect."

She rested her hand on the handle, hope struggling to rise from a murky pool of pain deep inside of her. "I don't want your lies."

"Damn stubborn female." He released his breath in a frustrated sigh. "Stand clear, Rachel. I'm coming in."

"Go away!"

"Get out of the way."

The stubborn oaf would hurt himself. She threw the bolt and pulled open the door. "If you—"

T.S. lunged forward, one foot raised like a battering ram. Rachel jumped aside. He hit moonlight instead of solid oak. Then he whizzed past her, his eyes wide with shock. She reached for him, but her fingers gripped thin air. When his foot hit the floor, he pitched headfirst, then smacked the carpet with enough force to rattle the glass chimney of the table lamp beside her bed.

Rachel ran to his side and sank to her knees beside him. "Are you all right?"

A low groan rattled past his lips. Gaslight from the hall spilled through the doorway and embraced the man lying in a crumpled heap on the blue-and-white carpet. He lay on his side, his face turned toward the windows. He was far too still.

"Stubborn oaf." Rachel stroked the back of his head, her fingers sliding through thick ebony waves. "It would serve you right if you hurt yourself terribly. You aren't hurt terribly, are you?"

T.S. turned his head, frowning as he looked up at her. "It's all right. My chin broke the fall."

Relief bubbled up inside her, escaping in a nervous giggle.

He pulled himself into a sitting position, grimacing as he settled against the carpet. "I can only imagine how entertaining you would find a hanging."

"Only if it were yours."

He studied her a moment, then a smile curved his lips as she valiantly tried to quell her giggles. "I love the sound of your laughter."

His soft words, spoken in that deep husky voice, snatched the laughter from her. He looked so sincere. His eyes held such need and longing she could almost believe him. "I think you should leave."

Touching the doll Rachel still held, T.S. smoothed his fingers over the dark curls. "Is this the doll you rescued from drowning?"

She rose to her feet with all the dignity she could manage. "If you think you can manipulate me by using the past, you're mistaken."

He rose with a fluid grace born of power. "Rachel, I intend to tell Whitteck to forget any thoughts of a marriage between Marianne and Darwin."

"I seem to recall you saying that three days ago. I suppose it takes more than three days to send a wire to Boston these days."

"It isn't something I wanted to say in a telegram."

Rachel could understand his thinking. She only hoped it was the truth. "Why did you invite him here?"

"I didn't. He came on his own."

"Because you had assured him you could convince one foolish romantic to betray an innocent young girl in need of protection." She turned away from him and fought against the tears burning her eyes. "And I was a fool. I actually believed you had fallen in love with me."

T.S. rested his hands on her shoulders, and the warmth of his palms penetrated the velvet of her gown. "You said you had never given up on me. Don't give up on me now."

Rachel curled her shoulders, trying to escape the

betraying warmth of his hands. "You used me."

T.S. held her as if he were a drowning man clinging to a lifeline. "I wanted to. For a while, I even convinced myself I was seeking your company simply because it suited my plans. But you managed to spoil all of my worst intentions."

She felt herself weakening. "You're very good at manipulating people."

"Not you. Never you. From the first moment I met you, you've kept me off balance." T.S. brushed his lips against the sensitive skin beneath her ear. The soft touch whispered across her skin. "Before I even knew what was happening, I found myself hopelessly in love with you."

His words breathed life into her hopes, "Please don't lie to me."

T.S. turned Rachel. When she tried to look away, he gripped her chin gently and forced her to look up into his eyes. "I've never lied to you. I never will."

"I want to believe you." She touched his face and brushed her fingertips over the red marks the carpet had scraped upon his chin. "But how can I? You won't even share your real name with me, and you expect me to trust you."

He set his jaw. "Tristram Sylvester."

Rachel frowned. "Tristram Sylvester?"

"That should prove something."

It proved he was willing to bend, even if he did look as though he might break from the strain. "You love me?" she asked, her voice scraped raw by her emotions.

T.S. released his breath in a long sigh. "Unfortunately, I do. So much it scares me."

He had been secluded behind his icy walls a long time. She suspected it would take a long time to melt all the ice.

"If you think this is easy for me, you're wrong. I never wanted to fall in love. I never wanted to need anyone the way my father needed my mother." T.S. smiled, a man appreciating the joke destiny had played on him. "I never realized I wouldn't be given a choice. But when you came back into my life, I didn't have a choice. Love has a way of sneaking up when you least expect it."

Rachel studied T.S. a moment, and all the doubts that held hopes and dreams beneath a clouded pool of pain dissolved into mist. The sincerity in his dark eyes left no room for doubts. "I've been meaning to marry you for the past twelve years. I suppose it would be foolish to allow you to get away now."

"Rachel," he whispered, taking her into his arms. "Stay with me, my love. Marry me. Give me a reason to face each morning. And every night."

The warm spicy scent of his skin curled around her. He held her close against his chest, so close she could feel his heart beating strong and sure against her cheek, so close she could feel the fear inside him. It would take a while before T.S. was comfortable sharing his life with her. Still, she intended to give him a lifetime to realize she would always be here for him.

Rachel tilted her head and smiled up into his handsome face. "You know Tristram Sylvester, I do believe there is some hope for you yet."

T.S. kissed the tip of her nose. "A man should never live without hope. You are my hope, Rachel. My warmth. My light."

"I love you, T.S." She smoothed her hand over his rough cheek. If she lived to be one hundred, she would always love this man. "You are, and always will be, my very own hero."

Epilogue

Port Freedom, New Hampshire—1899

T.S. sat in a rocking chair near the hearth in the family parlor at the Freedom Tavern, cradling his six-month-old niece, Sarah, in his arms. He smiled up at his sister when she touched his shoulder.

"Do you want me to take her so you can join in the singing?" Marianne asked, drawing her fingertip over the pink ribbon at the top of her daughter's gown.

T.S. shook his head. "She's sleeping."

"In all this commotion? It must have something to do with feeling secure in her uncle's arms." Marianne leaned forward and kissed his cheek before joining her husband at the piano.

T.S. smiled at his wife, who stood with their two sons and daughter near the piano. Nine-year-old Matthew was shuffling sheets of music, searching for the carols Lydia and Josh were telling him to find. Seven-year-old Julia sat beside her uncle Alex on the piano seat picking out "Silent Night" on the black and white keys. A few feet away, five-year-old Peter sat on the floor between Alex and Marianne's five-year-old son and three-year-old daughter, along with Priscilla's four-year-old daughter, and two other cousins, playing with a wooden train that had served to entertain Stark grandchildren for the last fifteen years.

Although the room was filled with the chatter and laughter of family, all of T.S.'s attention was riveted on the woman who had captured his heart ten years ago. The look in Rachel's beautiful green eyes as she smiled at him warmed T.S. in a way the fire burning in the hearth never could. They spent every Christmas Eve here, with Henry and Eleanor Stark, surrounded by the ever increasing circle of their family. However, since his marriage to Rachel, they had established a few traditions of their own.

Every Christmas, they added to their own tree a special ornament celebrating the most recent year of their life together. Christmas morning, amid the crisp scent of pine, T.S., Rachel and their children plowed through all the presents piled under a stately spruce standing in the drawing room of their home. Each year, he and Rachel made certain every room in their big house glowed with the sparkle and fragrance of Christmas.

In Rachel, T.S. had found his hope. With each passing year, their love grew stronger. Together they had created a place of warmth and light, a home filled with laughter, where each season of the year was a brilliant celebration of life and love.

Author's Note

I hope you enjoyed spending the holidays with T.S. and Rachel. I had a wonderful time bringing their story to life.

I enjoy putting twists into my stories involving plot as well as character. For my next book, *Lord Savage,* I wondered what would happen if a young man was raised in a culture completely contrary to the one in which his family belonged.

Ash MacGregor doesn't remember his childhood before the time he came to live with the Cheyenne at the age of five. When an English duke claims Ash is his long-lost grandson, the young bounty hunter has difficulty believing the truth. The rugged Westerner has even more difficulty trying to adjust to the role of English gentleman, especially with a teacher as distracting as Lady Elizabeth Barrington. Added to his troubles is someone who would like to see the new heir of the Duke of Marlow dead.

Lord Savage contrasts Victorian England with the Old West. It throws together a savage bounty hunter and a proper English lady in a story filled with adventure, romance and mystery. *Lord Savage* will be available mid-November of this year.

I love to hear from readers. Please enclose a self-addressed, stamped envelope with your letter.

Debra Dier
P.O. Box 584
Glen Carbon, Illinois 62034-0584

Home for Christmas

RUTH RYAN LANGAN

To Tom, for so many Christmas memories.

Chapter One

Malibu, California—1996

"Adam, where is your mind today?" Olivia Martin peered over the rim of her half-glasses. She'd been Adam Holt's literary agent for the past seven years, and she had learned to gauge the writer's moods. Something was troubling him. And when something was troubling Adam Holt, it was wise to take cover. "You've been pacing like a caged lion."

"Have I?" Adam stopped his pacing to stand at the floor-to-ceiling windows overlooking his Malibu beachfront. With his hands jammed in his pockets, he watched a golden retriever fetching a ball from the surf. A bikini-clad blonde chased the dog until both disappeared from view. He turned toward the glass-topped table, where Olivia had spread the latest contracts for his signature. "Did you know that in just three days it will be Christmas Eve?"

Olivia lifted one elegant hand to remove her glasses. "I'd have to live on Mars not to know that. In fact, I thought this contract would be a very welcome Christmas present. Apparently you were expecting something more generous. Would you like me to go back to them and—"

Adam held up his hand, then ran it restlessly through his hair. "No, that's not what I mean. It's just—" He shrugged and began to pace once more, his voice low with feeling. "I can't stop thinking about Christmas in New England, with snow and kids on toboggans and skaters on real ponds."

Not a lion, Olivia thought as she watched him. *A panther. A very dark, very restless panther.* She sighed. She'd come to care very much about this man, who was such a paradox. His literary success had bought the usual trappings: this house, once owned by one of Hollywood's most famous directors; a garage filled with sports cars; and beautiful women on his arm at publicity and charity events. But despite the fact that he could be absolutely charming in public, there was a dark, private side to Adam Holt. In the years she'd known him, Olivia had never heard him mention his childhood. And as far as she knew, Adam had no family, at least none that he talked about.

His moods always seemed darker at this time of the year. And every year, after a few days on the East Coast, he returned ready to settle down and produce another blockbuster.

It was time to soothe the beast.

"Tell you what. Why don't you sign these contracts and then take some time in New York. If you like, I'll ask my assistant to book you a flight and a room at the Plaza. You can walk through the snow in Central Park, watch the skaters at Rockefeller Plaza."

Instead of seeing the expected smile, she watched

Adam's frown deepen. He turned to stare out the window again, lost in thought. Then he suddenly nodded. "Yes, it's been too long." He crossed the room and picked up the pen, scratching his name on a dozen different documents. That done, he said, "Tell Mary I want to stay at the old Freedom Tavern. It's a bed-and-breakfast in Port Freedom, New Hampshire."

If Olivia was surprised by Adam's choice, she gave no indication. She'd send him to Timbuktu to keep him happy and productive. "Consider it done."

Port Freedom, New Hampshire

"Where've you been?" The gray-haired woman removed a mop and rags from a cupboard as the back door opened. "I expected you back hours ago."

"Sorry, Maggie. The van wouldn't start." Caroline Stark nudged the door shut with her hip and deposited two bags of groceries on the table. "I had to get Jerry Simpson's boy to give me a hand since Jerry was out on a call."

Caroline opened the door and weathered another blast of winter wind as she trudged back to the car. She returned minutes later with two more bags. As soon as Caroline pried off her boots and stepped into a pair of scuffed slippers, Maggie began mopping up the puddles.

"One of these days that old van's going to break down in the middle of nowhere, and you'll find yourself walking," Maggie muttered. "And with your luck, you'll be transporting your best customers, who'll then cancel their reservations and leave you high and dry."

Caroline laughed, though she knew there was some truth in the older woman's statement. "I think the van's safe for a little while longer. When Jerry got back with the tow truck, he and his son checked everything, from battery to transmission fluid."

"Good. By the way, it looks as if your holidays won't be as lazy as you'd hoped."

"Why?" Caroline hung the keys on a hook and slipped off her coat as she headed across the room to unpack the groceries.

"Got a call while you were out from a woman in California. Booked a room for the whole week."

"California? When is she arriving?"

Maggie shrugged. "Some time tomorrow. But the reservation isn't for her. It's for some man. I figure he's probably her boss."

"Did you get a name and credit card number?"

Maggie nodded. "I wrote everything down, just the way you like it. It's in your office." She nodded toward a pile of fresh linen still warm from the dryer. "Want me to start on one of the guest rooms?"

Caroline thought a minute. "Since our guest is a man, let's give him the Elias Room. It always feels like a man's room to me."

Maggie picked up an armload of linen and left the room. When Caroline finished storing the groceries, she hurried upstairs to lend a hand.

"Nice work." Caroline studied the elegant four-poster, freshly made up with clean sheets and blankets and covered with a heavy quilt of dark burnished plaid. She folded an afghan and tossed it on the foot of the bed.

"We'll need more logs," Maggie called as she began arranging logs and kindling in the fireplace.

"I'll get them." Caroline made several trips from the back porch to the guest room until the basket beside the hearth was filled.

"This robe?" Maggie held up a thick terry robe for Caroline's inspection.

"That'll be fine. I just stowed some fresh soaps and toiletries in the hall closet."

While Maggie finished with the bathroom, Caroline vacuumed and dusted, then stood back to study the room with a critical eye. The room earned its name from the portrait of Caroline's ancestor, Elias Stark. Two comfortable high-back chairs were pulled in front of the fireplace. Between them was a table with a reading lamp. One wall was lined with shelves of books, while another wall was hung with pictures dating back to the early part of the century. In front of the window was an antique desk and an assortment of stationery and pens.

Maggie paused in the doorway. "Thinking about the extra work you'll have to take on during the holiday season?"

Caroline shook her head. "You won't hear me complaining. Not when I think about the check I just wrote to cover the work on my van. Right now I'd welcome a dozen guests."

At the crunch of tires in the driveway, Maggie walked to the window. "Here's Will. He said the newscasters are calling for another snowstorm. He decided to come for me early, before the roads get closed." When her husband looked up, she waved to let him know she'd spotted him. "Do you need anything else?"

"Not a thing, Maggie." Caroline followed her out of the room and down the stairs.

"All right. See you in the morning."

"You might have to dig your way out of your driveway first," Caroline said with a laugh.

Maggie hesitated. "I hadn't thought of that. With a guest coming, I'd better get an early start."

"Don't worry about it. I can handle it. Just be careful."

The older woman pulled on her coat and took her leave.

When the door closed, Caroline climbed the stairs to her own room and kicked off her slippers. She hadn't eaten since early morning, but despite her hunger, what she really craved was a long hot bath.

She filled the tub and added her favorite bath oil, then stripped and pinned her hair into a knot on top of her head. When she settled herself into the warm scented water, she gave a sigh of pure pleasure. After the day she'd put in, this was heaven. Caroline lingered until the water began to cool, then dried herself quickly and slipped into a cheery red velvet lounging robe.

Though it was late, and her bed looked inviting, Caroline had no intention of sleeping until after she'd satisfied her hunger. Padding down the stairs, she paused in the doorway of the main parlor. Maggie had built a fire earlier, and the embers were still glowing. Caroline poked at the coals and added a log. Within minutes, the fire was blazing. This, she decided, was where she wanted to eat her late supper. In front of the fire.

She was just starting toward the kitchen when she heard the sound of a snowplow heading up her driveway.

"Bless you, Hal," she said aloud as she ran to the front window to wave.

Hal Winslow ran a service for lawn maintenance and snow removal in the city of Port Freedom. Knowing that she lived alone, he often took a swing up the long private driveway leading to her place to assure that she wasn't snowbound. She was always grateful for his kindness.

Just as Caroline started to turn away, she saw the truck come to a stop. The passenger door opened, and the figure of a man was caught in the headlights as he climbed down and walked toward her front door. Before he could knock, she hurried to open it and was greeted by a swirl of wind and snow.

"Tell Hal I—" She stopped in midsentence.

It wasn't Hal Winslow's assistant who stood facing her. It was a tall imposing figure hunched in a denim jacket. She tilted her head to see his face. For a moment she forgot to breathe. Her heart forgot to beat. She was staring at a face from her past. A face she had carried in her mind for more than a decade.

"Hello, Caro."

No one else had ever called her that. No one except Adam Holt. The man she had once loved more than life itself. The man who had left Port Freedom without a word or a letter. The man who had broken her heart.

Chapter Two

"Mind if I come in?"

Adam's voice was the same. Low and deep. Touching a nerve that Caroline had thought dead. Or at least buried so deeply it could never be uncovered. Numbly, she stood aside as he stepped past her into the foyer. It took a moment to realize that he was carrying a leather garment bag over one arm.

"What—" She was struggling to make sense of this. But her mind seemed incapable of functioning. "What are you doing here, Adam?"

"You're expecting me," he said simply.

"I don't under—"

"My agent assured me that she'd called and made the reservation."

The call from California. It occurred to Caroline that she hadn't even taken time to check her office. Oh, how could she have overlooked such an important detail? If she had seen his name, at least she would have been prepared. Instead, she was standing here feeling like the worst sort of fool, with her heart pounding and her trembling legs threatening to fail her at any moment.

Somehow she managed to find her voice. She was relieved to note that it sounded almost normal. "Maggie said someone was coming tomorrow. How did you happen to be here now, riding with Hal?"

"When I heard about the snowstorm, I grabbed an earlier flight. At the airport, I found out the roads were closed, so I hitched a ride with Hal. He and I are old school chums."

"I see." With considerable effort, Caroline was beginning to pull herself together. Her tone hardened. Just a fraction, but enough to signal that she was in control. "What brings you back to Port Freedom?"

"Just a whim."

Adam was studying her so closely she had to turn away. "If you'll follow me, I'll show you to your room."

Caroline climbed the stairs, achingly aware of the man trailing behind her. Leading the way along a hall, she opened the door and stood aside to allow him to precede her.

She studied his profile as he looked around. There was a sculpted leanness to his face. High cheeks, straight, even nose, firm chin. And lips that could be called pretty if it weren't for the danger always lurking behind that smile.

Had he always been that tall? Had his shoulders always been that wide? She'd thought, hoped, that she had magnified everything about him. But now she was forced to admit that the years had been kind to him. He had acquired a polish, a sophistication, that he wore with the same ease with which he wore his clothes.

Oh, why did he come here? And why now?

"This is nice," Adam said. "Mind if I use the fireplace while I'm here?"

"That's what it's for." Caroline remained near the door, feeling entirely too uncomfortable being in the same room with him. Her nerves were strung so tightly she feared that at any moment they would snap. She needed to escape. "Have you eaten?"

"Not since this morning."

"I was just going to fix myself something." Caroline started out of the room and realized Adam was following. "Wouldn't you like to unpack first?" She wanted . . . needed to put some distance between them. At least for a few minutes, until she had herself more in control.

"I'll unpack later." Adam pulled the door shut and matched his steps to hers.

Very well. Caroline would treat him like any other paying guest. "Would you like to eat in the dining room or the parlor?"

He grinned at her formal tone, reading her mind. "Wherever you like."

"All right." She wanted to run. But she forced herself to walk beside him down the stairs. At the kitchen, he held the door and she led the way inside, switching on lights as she did.

"Sorry to make more work for you," Adam said.

"It doesn't matter. I don't mind." But she did. She minded everything about him. Especially the ease with which he invaded her home and disrupted her comfortable routine.

Caroline could feel him watching her. It made her movements stiff and awkward.

Adam leaned casually against the counter and studied her as she rummaged through the refrigerator and brought out eggs and vegetables.

"Will an omelette be all right?" she asked.

"Sounds great. Am I the only guest?"

"Yes. It's Christmas and most people—" Caroline stopped and felt her cheeks flame. It had been Christmas when he'd left. A Christmas she would never forget.

The silence stretched between them before Adam said, "I read about your mother's death this past summer. I'm sorry."

Caroline began to crack eggs into a bowl. "She was never well after Dad passed on. But these last five years were the worst."

"Did you care for her alone?"

"Most of that time. The last year I had Maggie Monroe. She and her husband, Will, are retired teachers. When they settled here in Port Freedom, I thought I'd found gold. Maggie helps around the house, and Will helps with odd jobs."

Adam glanced around, noting the discolored ceiling tiles in one corner, which signaled a leaking roof, and the rug stuffed under the door to keep out the cold. Obviously Will Monroe was a better teacher than handyman.

"What about your brother? Doesn't he help?"

She flushed. "It's not his fault. Graham's caught up in a whole new way of life these days."

Adam arched a brow. "I suppose it's pretty heady stuff moving in Washington's inner circle, wheeling and dealing with the big boys. Is he coming for the holidays?"

"He said he'd try. I've been looking forward to seeing him and his family. They haven't been here since last Christmas." Her voice lowered, and Adam could hear the underlying pain. "He's hoping to clear his desk in time."

"I think even politicians make time to celebrate Christmas."

Caroline glanced up at the disapproving tone of his voice, then looked away when she realized he was still studying her. "Would you like tea or coffee?"

"Coffee. If you'll show me where it is, I'll make it."

Adam's offer caught her off guard. Most of her guests never came near the kitchen. None offered to help. "The beans are in that canister. The grinder is on the shelf above it."

He filled the pot with water from the tap and spooned coffee beans into an electric grinder. Soon the kitchen was filled with the wonderful aroma of fresh coffee. For her part, Caroline put a large skillet on the stove to heat, then began to chop vegetables.

"I'll make the toast." Adam uncovered a loaf of freshly baked bread and rummaged through a drawer until he located a sharp knife for slicing. "Looks homemade. Did you bake this?"

She nodded and he said, "Smells good." He sliced off a small piece and ate it. "Tastes good, too."

Caroline cautioned herself not to be flattered by such a simple comment. Then they fell silent while Adam fed bread into a toaster and Caroline poured the egg mixture into the skillet. The silence lengthened as she divided the omelette onto two plates and set them on a tray, along with cups and saucers and silverware.

As she started to pick it up, he took it from her hands with a terse, "Lead the way."

Caroline preceded him along the hallway, feeling a prickling along her scalp. In the parlor, she moved aside a small sculpture on the coffee table to make room for the tray.

"You can set it here."

A pair of love seats flanked the fireplace. When Caroline sat on one of them, Adam sat on the other facing her, with the table between them. His gaze was drawn to the bundle of fur curled up in front of the fire. "Don't tell me that's McPherson."

She nodded. "The same."

"But that cat must be"—he calculated—"eleven or twelve years old."

"Twelve. But don't let him hear that. He thinks he's still a kitten."

As if sensing their interest, the big gray-and-white tabby yawned, stretched, then ambled over and made figure eights around Adam's legs. When Adam leaned down and scratched behind the cat's ears, he was rewarded with a loud purring before the cat leapt to the back of the sofa to curl up into a ball.

Adam bit into the omelette. "This is a whole lot better than the ones I make."

"You cook?"

"I had to learn. It was either cook or live on takeouts."

So. Adam lived alone. Caroline didn't know why that fact should make her heart skip several beats.

"As I recall," he said, breaking a piece of toast, "your mother hated to cook. How did you get so good?"

Caroline couldn't help laughing. "You're right. My mother was an . . . uninspired cook."

"You're being kind. When the cook took a day off, your family practically starved."

Her smile grew. "That's true. And Mother never even attempted to keep house. Maybe that's why I was so drawn to it. I can remember following the maids around, imitating them. I could never understand why anyone who lived in a house with so much history took so little interest in preserving it. But

Mother had her social issues. And Father had his political issues."

As if regretting her lapse, Caroline said quickly, "And you have your literary success. You must be proud."

Adam set his empty plate on the tray and stretched out his long legs. "It's satisfying."

When he said nothing more, she said, "Not to mention exciting. I've seen your picture in the papers and magazines at the opening of your movies."

"They aren't my movies," he said almost gruffly. "The books are mine. The ideas. The rest—" He waved a hand absently. "I go because I'm expected to."

"Are you saying you don't enjoy it?"

"The glamorous life of Hollywood is fun. For about five minutes."

"What happens after five minutes?"

"You start to see past the smiles and the rented tuxedos."

Adam leaned forward and poured two cups of coffee, then handed one to her. As their fingers brushed, she felt the heat. At once, she wrapped both hands around the cup to hold it steady.

"I've loved all your books." The words were out before she could stop them.

It was his turn to look surprised. "You've read them?"

Caroline nodded. "Your characters are complex. And the plots very dark."

Adam was studying her again. "I don't claim to write love stories."

"No, you could never make that claim. But the endings are always . . . satisfying, if not always happy."

"I don't believe in happy endings." Adam stood suddenly and began to prowl the room, stopping occasionally to study a painting or touch a finger to a pewter candlestick. "I like what you've done with this room. It's warmer than I remembered."

"I changed the wallpaper—and lightened the ceiling to show off the hand-carved moldings."

Adam remembered it as dark and cold, like the people who'd lived here. "You seem to have a knack for making this old place feel like home."

Caroline blushed. "It's easy when you love it the way I do. Would you care for more coffee?"

He shook his head. "I've had enough."

"Then I'll take these things back to the kitchen." She lifted the tray and walked from the room, leaving him alone.

When Caroline returned, Adam was standing at the bookshelf, studying the titles. The cat was nestled in one of his arms, purring contentedly.

"You weren't joking," he said without turning. "You have every one of my books."

Caroline kept her tone brisk, businesslike. "I want to offer my guests an opportunity to read while they're here relaxing. I hope, before you leave, you'll autograph them."

She saw the annoyance. Brief. Fleeting. And then, in the blink of an eye, it was gone and Adam managed a smile. "Of course. It would be my pleasure."

While she was in the kitchen she'd had a chance to think of a polite escape. She lifted her head a fraction. "I'll say good night now. Feel free to stay and enjoy the fire. In that cabinet to your left is a video library. You can use the VCR here or the one in your room."

If she thought to be rid of him so easily, she was mistaken. He crossed the room in easy strides. "It's been a long day. I was thinking of turning in, too."

Without a word she banked the fire. He set the cat

on the rug, then walked up the stairs beside her. At the head of the stairs she paused.

"Good night, Adam."

"Is that your room?" He nodded toward the closed door.

"Yes. Why?"

His lazy smile sent her heart spinning. She'd seen that smile a hundred times when he was about to tease her. "Just like to get my bearings, Caro. I'd hate to walk into the wrong room by mistake some night."

Adam lifted a hand to a little tendril of her hair that had pried loose from the knot on her head. His smile disappeared. In its place was a strange, haunted look. "Hal told me that you never married."

Caroline absorbed the jolt and struggled to show no emotion. But her eyes narrowed with sudden anger. "You discussed me with Hal Winslow?"

"We discussed a lot of old friends. And he asked me why I'd come back to Port Freedom."

"What did you tell him?"

Adam watched as the strands sifted through his fingers. Then his gaze locked on hers. "I told him I had some . . . unfinished business. Good night, Caro."

She waited until he was gone before walking into her room and closing the door. Leaning against the door, she felt breathless, as though she'd just climbed a mountain.

Chapter Three

Shirtless and barefoot, Adam leaned a hip against the windowsill and watched the falling snow. He'd managed to unpack and grab a few hours of sleep. But now, with dawn just coloring the horizon, he was wide awake. Across the room, his laptop computer hummed on the desk.

Coming back to Port Freedom had been tougher than he'd expected. Especially when that front door opened and he'd had his first glimpse of Caroline's face.

She should have gotten older. Instead, she was even lovelier than he'd remembered. And he remembered everything about her. A voice like a blues singer. Low, husky, whispering over his senses. Hair like autumn leaves, more red than brown. Eyes that changed color with her moods. Gold like a cat's when she was angry. Green when she was aroused. And a fire in those eyes. A fire that spoke of a fierce independence.

There had been a moment, outside her bedroom door, when he'd been tempted to throw caution to the wind. To unpin her hair and watch it cascade down her back in a curtain of silk. To draw her close and feel the press of her body against his. To watch those eyes darken like the storm-tossed Atlantic. To touch her mouth with his and feel it soften and open. But it was too soon.

Adam pressed his forehead to the cold windowpane. God, even now he wanted her. All the years and all the miles hadn't changed a thing. If anything, they'd only deepened the yearning. Still, he resolved to move slowly. The chasm between them was wide and deep. It would take a whole lot more than a kiss. Or a tumble in bed. Though he'd settle for either right now.

He pulled a sweater from the drawer and shrugged into it, then headed for the door. What he needed was coffee. Hot and strong.

Caroline awoke to the wonderful fragrance of coffee and bacon. Thank heaven for Maggie.

Knowing the kitchen was in capable hands, Caroline took her time washing and dressing. Ordinarily she'd wear jeans and a sweatshirt. Instead, she pulled on warm woolen charcoal slacks and a green turtleneck, then brushed her hair until it fell in waves to her shoulders. She added a touch of color to her cheeks and lips. And though she hated to admit it, she knew why she was taking such pains with her appearance this morning: Adam.

It was pure vanity. And why not? He'd walked out of her life. Now he was back. And for the few days that he was here, she'd make him regret the choice he'd made.

Caroline padded lightly down the stairs and rushed

into the kitchen. " 'Morning, Mag—" She skidded to a halt.

Adam poured pancake batter into a skillet. "You're just in time. Another five minutes and I'd have had to eat all this by myself."

Caroline looked around. The table had been set for two. Coffee dripped into a pot. Bacon sizzled on the stove. McPherson was curled up on the windowsill. And the man flipping pancakes looked even more in control this morning than he had last night.

"Why are you doing this?" Caroline asked.

"Why? Because I woke up hungry. Some innkeeper you are, Caro. Your guest has to fend for himself."

Adam held her chair and she had no choice but to sit at the table.

"Juice or milk?" he asked.

"Orange juice." She'd play it his way. For now.

He poured juice into two glasses and handed one to her. While she sipped, he filled a platter with bacon and a stack of pancakes. When he'd located syrup and filled two cups with coffee, he took his seat across from her.

Seeing her plate empty he held out the platter. "You'd better help yourself before I get started. I've worked up a mean appetite."

Caroline took pancakes and a strip of bacon and watched as he filled his plate.

After the first bite, she gave him a look of surprise. "You weren't kidding. You really can cook. This is good." She took her time, enjoying every morsel. "It isn't often I get to be pampered."

Adam heard the weariness in her tone and decided to keep the conversation light. "Better watch out. I might be after your job."

"I'm sure writing pays better."

"Yeah, but the hours are lousy. I'd already written half a chapter by four this morning."

Caroline couldn't hide her shock. "You write at night?"

"Nights. Days. Even holidays."

"Why?" she asked simply.

Adam looked at her a moment in silence, then picked up his cup and drank. "It takes me away."

"From what?"

He shrugged. "I don't know. My life maybe. Why do you run a bed-and-breakfast?"

"To survive." Caroline realized he'd just evaded her question by asking one himself. No matter. She'd give him an honest answer. "No, that's not true. It isn't just a matter of survival. I love this place. And the only way I can afford to live here is to make it turn a profit."

Adam's eyes narrowed. "Your parents were wealthy. Didn't they leave you anything?"

She flushed and fiddled with her spoon. "You know how . . . careful my father was."

Caroline saw Adam's frown and knew he would have labeled her father much more than careful. Joshua Tyler Stark had been a hard, unyielding, narrow man who saw himself as a moral, upright pillar of the community. A man not unlike her brother, Graham. Neither man had approved of Adam Holt, the fatherless youth who always seemed just one step away from trouble. Trouble with school authorities. Trouble with everybody in Port Freedom. And trouble with the law.

"He left the house to me because he knew I'd never let it pass out of family hands into the hands of strangers. And he left a trust. But what he hadn't counted on was my mother's long illness."

"Is there any money left in the trust?"

Caroline was reluctant to talk about something so

personal. "A little," she said evasively. "But it means I have to be careful."

"Is the bed-and-breakfast making a profit?"

Caroline smiled. "Thank heaven, all my weekends aren't like this. But the truth is, people aren't standing in line to spend their nights at the Freedom Tavern. We're a little off the beaten track."

Uncomfortable beneath Adam's scrutiny, she stood and retrieved the coffeepot. When she paused beside him to fill his cup, he breathed in the delicate floral scent that would always be Caro and thought about the child of wealth and privilege she had once been. Strange, how quickly the fates could alter the course of lives. But nothing would change her. She would always be strong, determined. And fiercely independent.

"Since you made breakfast," she said firmly, "I'll clean up the dishes."

Adam glanced at the sink and stove, overflowing with bowls and skillets. "I think I got the best of the bargain."

Caroline managed a soft laugh. "I think you're right."

Caroline cut chunks of meat on a board and dredged them through flour. The back door opened and Maggie dashed in on a whirl of snowflakes.

"I see you finally dug your way out," Caroline called over her shoulder.

"If it hadn't been for Hal, we'd still be digging." Maggie shook snow from her coat. "Who's the stranger out there on the ladder?"

Caroline glanced out the window to see Adam just moving past her line of vision, followed by a reluctant Will. "The California reservation."

"Your Christmas guest is climbing up to the roof?"

"I know it sounds odd. But Adam Holt grew up here

in Port Freedom. He . . . used to spend a lot of time here."

Maggie gave her a long look. "That's the name I wrote down. Adam Holt. But until this minute I didn't make the connection. *The* Adam Holt? The writer? He's the one staying here for Christmas?"

Amused by Maggie's reaction, Caroline merely nodded and went back to her cooking, placing the meat in an oversize stew pot.

When she'd recovered from her shock, Maggie said dryly, "That's an awful lot of food for two."

"I want to be prepared in case my brother and his family make it in from Washington."

"Maybe I'd better start on the other guest rooms," Maggie said, though she had her doubts about this phantom brother. In the year she'd been helping Caroline, she had yet to meet him. Or to field a phone call from him.

When Maggie made her way upstairs, Caroline listened to the tramp of feet on the roof, followed by the sound of hammering, as Adam and Will worked side by side. For some strange reason, the thought of it made her want to weep. Instead, she plunged into even more work, as she kneaded dough for bread and started a batch of cinnamon biscuits.

Maggie lifted a basket of linens from the dryer and carried it to the kitchen table. She stopped in midstride at the sight of the handsome stranger lifting the back door from its hinges. He lay it across a pair of sawhorses and began planing.

Across the room, Caroline removed a pan of steaming biscuits from the oven. She didn't blame Maggie for staring. In faded denims and plaid shirt, Adam looked like a character from one of his books. Rugged. Slightly dangerous. The sleeves of his shirt, rolled to the elbows, strained against a ripple of muscles. A lock of unruly dark hair fell over his forehead. A forehead furrowed in concentration.

"Hi," he called as he worked. "You must be Maggie Monroe."

"And you're Adam Holt. I've seen your picture on the back of your books. Caroline told me you were staying here. How does a writer get to be a roofer and carpenter?"

"I did a lot of things on my way to becoming a writer," he said simply.

Maggie glanced at Caroline, who was busy spooning fresh batter into muffin tins. Was it just her imagination, or did her young friend seem a bit tense? Could it be that there was . . . something going on here?

As Maggie folded, she said conversationally, "Caroline said you grew up here in Port Freedom."

"That's right." Adam ran his hand over the smooth wood, then continued planing. "Caro and I went to the same school. In fact, her brother, Graham, and I were friends."

Caro. Maggie's antenna went up another notch. "Did you ever help out here at the tavern?"

"Plenty of times." He leaned into his work, running careful strokes along the bottom of the door.

Maggie shot another glance at Caroline, who had paused in her work to watch Adam's long, almost graceful fingers move over the wood. When Caroline saw Maggie looking at her, she flushed and returned her attention to the muffins.

When the phone rang, Caroline turned to Maggie. "Do you mind getting that? I'm almost through here."

The older woman walked to the front hall. A minute later she returned. "Looks as if you'll get your Christmas wish, Caroline. That was your sister-in-law. She said they're waiting for you at the airport."

Caroline looked up in surprise. "Oh, that's wonderful. I wish they'd phoned before they left home. I would have been waiting." She set down the bowl of batter, looking flustered. "Maggie, do you mind finishing here while I go for them?"

"Of course not. Are you sure the van will get you there and back?"

Seeing Adam's head come up, Caroline's flush deepened. "Stop worrying. I'll be fine."

She left the room in search of her purse. When she returned, Adam had set the back door on its hinges.

Swinging it open and shut, he gave a satisfied nod. "You won't have to force it anymore. And that weather stripping should keep out the cold."

"Thanks," she muttered distractedly as she pulled on her coat. When Adam took a jacket from a nearby peg and slipped it on, she asked, "Where are you going?"

"With you."

Caroline glanced across the room at Maggie. "This is your doing, isn't it?"

Maggie gave her a smug smile. "I may have mentioned the problems you've been having lately with your van. But the decision to go with you is Adam's."

"I don't have time to argue with either of you right now," Caroline muttered, taking the keys from their usual hook.

"That's what we were counting on." Adam gave a wink in Maggie's direction.

When they were gone, Maggie decided to test the skill of their new guest. After opening and closing the door several times, she was forced to admit that it hadn't operated that smoothly in years.

She smiled. The man who'd fixed it was a pretty smooth operator himself.

Chapter Four

"Aunt Caroline!"

A russet-haired bundle of energy dressed in a Redskins jacket and cap was the first to spot Caroline and Adam. Caroline's eight-year-old nephew Tyler, her brother's firstborn, had to be first at everything. First son. First grandson. And first Stark child to attend elementary school outside of New Hampshire. He launched himself into her arms, nearly throwing her offbalance.

"Ty." Caroline gave him a warm hug, then held him away a little to study him more closely. His usual sunny smile was gone, replaced by a definite pout. She blamed it on the long, difficult day of travel. "I think you've grown a foot since I last saw you."

"Two-and-a-half inches. Mom measures me every birthday." He stared past her to the tall man who stood just behind her. "Who's this?"

"Ty, I'd like you to meet Adam Holt."

"Hi," Tyler said. "Do you live here in Port Freedom?"

"I used to."

"So did I. Do you miss it a lot?"

"Sometimes. How about you?"

Tyler nodded. "Especially at Christmas. I was afraid we weren't coming this year. It wouldn't be Christmas if we couldn't come to Aunt Caroline's."

She ruffled his hair affectionately and said over his head, "I pay him to say that."

They looked up as Tyler's mother and little sister came toward them.

"Amy didn't want to come," Tyler whispered. "She's afraid Santa won't know where to find her."

"Caroline." Paige Stark, tall, blond, with fresh-scrubbed good looks, embraced her sister-in-law warmly.

"Paige, I'm so glad you came. I'd like you to meet Adam Holt."

"Hello, Adam. I don't believe we've met before. Are you from around here?"

"I used to live here."

"How nice that you came back for Christmas. Are you here visiting family, too?" Paige asked.

"I'm staying at the Freedom Tavern," he said.

Caroline turned to the solemn little five-year-old girl who stood a little apart, looking as though at any moment she might burst into tears. Catching Amy up in a warm hug, Caroline murmured, "Hello, Amy darling. I've missed you."

Chubby arms wrapped around Caroline's neck, and a small face pressed itself to her cheek. "I've missed you, too, Aunt Caroline."

"Amy, say hello to Adam."

The little girl chanced a quick peek at the tall

stranger, offered a muffled greeting, then buried her face once more in Caroline's neck.

Adam felt a jolt of recognition at the sight of Caroline holding a red-haired little moppet with stormy eyes and a parade of freckles across her nose. For the space of a second, he thought he'd stepped back in time.

Caroline smoothed the little girl's hair. "Tyler tells me you're worried about Santa finding you on Christmas Eve." When Amy nodded, Caroline said, "Well, don't you worry, darling. Santa knows these things. He'll find you. And I just know he'll leave you all sorts of wonderful presents." Caroline glanced around. "Where's Graham? Don't tell me he's still searching for the luggage."

Paige avoided looking at her children as she said, "At the last minute he decided not to come. Too much business."

Caroline hoped her disappointment wasn't obvious. No wonder her niece and nephew had lost their smiles. "Has he booked a later flight?"

Paige shrugged. "He said he'd see."

Caroline was instantly aware of the underlying pain in those words. There was a strained silence.

Adam finally said, "Tyler and I will take care of the luggage."

Caroline, still holding Amy, linked arms with Paige. "Good idea. We'll get the car and meet you at the curb."

A short time later, the van, with Adam at the wheel, headed through the snow-covered countryside.

Paige leaned back with a sigh. "I can't believe how easily you get through all this snow. You should have seen the Beltway this morning after only an inch of slush."

"Out here we're used to it," Caroline commented. "Besides, we don't have all that traffic to deal with.

Still, it's coming down harder than I'd expected. On the way here, Adam made me promise to let him drive home. He doesn't like the way I plow through drifts."

"Drifts?" Paige asked.

"It's drifting along the roads. The newscasters have been telling us to prepare for a blizzard."

"A blizzard," Amy said with a wail. "That means Daddy won't be here for Christmas."

"Now, honey, you don't know that," Caroline said soothingly.

Tyler sat up straighter and peered out the side window. "My friend B.J. is going to Disney World this year for his Christmas vacation. He was bragging to everybody. Wait till I tell him we had a blizzard."

"Maybe even Santa and his reindeer won't get through if it's a blizzard," Amy said, pressing her nose to the glass.

"Are you kidding?" Caroline was determined to keep all gloomy thoughts from the children's minds. "Santa and his reindeer love blizzards. In fact, maybe I should use this in my new brochure. Freedom Tavern Bed-and-Breakfast is rated over Disney World by one out of every three of our patrons who love blizzards. Especially Santa."

She and Adam were still laughing as they passed across a covered bridge, then moved more slowly along an unplowed, tree-lined road. The van turned up a curving driveway, past snow-laden trees, toward the sprawling New England farmhouse.

"Funny," Paige remarked, "but every time I come here, I feel as if I've come home."

"What's so funny about that? This is your home," Caroline said emphatically. "And don't you forget it."

"Thanks." Paige reached a hand to Caroline's. "But you know what I mean. It's Graham's home, yet I think I've always loved it more than he." She peered through the falling snow. "I can't wait to see what you've done to the old place since my last visit."

"Not much, I'm afraid. I'll give you a tour before dinner."

Adam brought the van to a stop, and he and Tyler unloaded the luggage. When Caroline reached for a suitcase, he took it firmly from her hand. "Take Paige and Amy inside. Tyler and I can see to this, can't we, partner?"

"I guess so." The boy turned worried eyes to Adam. "Do you think all this snow might keep my dad away for Christmas?"

Caroline heard Adam's reassuring words before she trailed Paige and Amy up the steps.

When they opened the door, Paige breathed deeply. "Something smells wonderful. Is that stew?"

"Um-hmm. Thought you'd appreciate a hot and hearty meal after a day of traveling."

As they stepped into the kitchen, Maggie dried her hands on her apron before greeting Paige and her daughter. "I'm so glad you folks made it for Christmas," she murmured. Seeing Tyler and Adam, she arched a brow. "Caroline, I thought I'd get to meet your brother."

"Graham didn't come," Caroline said.

"Didn't come for Christmas?" The older woman glanced at the sad faces of the children. "Is he coming on a later flight?"

Caroline shrugged. "We're hoping he'll make it."

Maggie sniffed, her only sign of disapproval, then said briskly, "I've put the kettle on for tea. Why don't you children follow me, and I'll show you to your rooms."

Adam trailed behind, handling the luggage.

When they were alone in the kitchen, Caroline busied herself making tea. Over her shoulder, she said,

"I'm so glad you were able to come, Paige. It wouldn't have seemed like Christmas if I hadn't had this chance to see you."

"I was beginning to think it wouldn't feel like Christmas at all this year," Paige admitted.

Caroline chanced a quick look at the worried frown. "That bad?" She filled two cups and carried them to the table. "Want to talk?"

Paige shook her head. "Not now. It'll just put me in a sad mood. Maybe another time."

Caroline nodded. "Whenever you want to talk, I'll be here to listen."

Paige sipped her tea. "There's something soothing about this place. I'd been hoping . . ." She lapsed into silence, then said, "I know it sounds silly, but I thought, if only Graham would come back here for a few days, he'd realize how fast-paced our lives have become, and maybe he'd pull back and"—she shrugged—"maybe he'd agree to slow down a bit and enjoy what he has."

"He's a lucky man. With you and the children, he has something very special. But Graham"—Caroline chose her words carefully, sensing how raw Paige's emotions appeared to be—"never seemed satisfied with all that he had. Graham always seemed to want more."

Paige nodded. "It's sad that some people just can't appreciate what they have until they lose it." She got wearily to her feet. "If you don't mind, I'll go up and help the kids unpack."

"There's plenty of time, if you'd like to soak in a tub or take a nap. I'll have dinner ready around six-thirty."

Paige bent and kissed her cheek. "Thanks. I'll see you then."

When she was alone, Caroline remained at the table, sipping her tea, her mind in turmoil. Four words continued to play in her mind. *Until they lose it.* Was her brother about to lose his greatest treasures?

"It can't be that bad," Adam said suddenly.

Caroline turned to see Adam leaning against the kitchen door, watching her. "I didn't hear you come in."

"That's obvious." He remained where he was, afraid that if he got too close he'd need to touch her. And if he touched her, he wasn't sure he'd be able to stop. This house, this woman, this season—they all evoked too many memories.

Caroline stared into her cup. "Did you see how unhappy they are?"

"I'd have to be blind not to see it."

Her voice lowered. "Then what's wrong with Graham? Can't he see what he's doing to them?"

Adam did go to her then. And allowed himself to touch a hand to her shoulder. "Poor Caro, you always wanted to make everything right. But you can't fix the whole world. You can't make your brother unselfish after all these years. And you can't spare those two sweet kids from the heartache that's coming."

Caroline got to her feet and faced Adam. "I have to try. I have to do something."

It occurred to Adam that this was one of the things he'd always loved about Caroline Stark. She'd never calculated the odds. She'd always just plowed ahead, determined to face things head-on.

"Okay. Tell you what." He lifted a finger to her cheek to brush away a strand of hair. At once, he realized his mistake. Her skin was incredibly soft, like the underside of a rose petal. And she smelled sinful, not at all like a sedate innkeeper. "We'll make this their best Christmas ever."

"How?"

Adam knew he was playing with fire. But then, he'd always enjoyed that sharp, narrow edge of danger. That was one of the things the Stark family had disliked about him. That and the fact that Caroline had always been a willing partner in his escapades.

Adam brushed his lips over hers. At once, the sexual jolt was so strong, he nearly reeled. He caught her by the shoulders and stared down into her eyes. It was with a sense of satisfaction that he realized her eyes had turned a deep shade of green. So. She wasn't immune to his charms.

He wanted to kiss her again. A real kiss. But he could hear Maggie's footsteps heading toward the kitchen. He gave her a wolfish smile that had her heart doing somersaults. "Leave it to me."

Chapter Five

"You've done enough in the kitchen, Caroline." Maggie filled the sink with hot water. "I'll tidy up here. Why don't you go upstairs and change."

"Change?" Caroline glanced down at her rumpled slacks and sweater. "What's wrong with what I have on?"

"Nothing. If you were spending the night alone. But it's a festive season, and you have company."

"You're as transparent as glass, Maggie Monroe. I know what you're thinking. And for your information, I'm not interested in parading myself in front of Adam Holt."

"Why not? He's handsome, charming and successful. And from the way he watches you, he's interested."

Caroline felt a quick dart of pleasure. And just as quickly rejected it. "Well, I'm not."

Maggie shot her a look that had the rest of her vehement denial dying on her lips. "Tell that to someone who doesn't know you so well. Go on with you now," Maggie said, shooing her out of the kitchen. "I'll finish up here."

In her room, Caroline slipped into a pale pink cashmere dress that skimmed her body and fell in graceful folds to just above her ankles. She wasn't doing this because of Adam, she told herself sternly. The dress had been Paige's extravagant present last year, and Caroline wanted her sister-in-law to know how much she appreciated it. She was doing this for Paige and the children. To keep the mood—what had Maggie said?—festive.

Caroline freshened her makeup and touched her favorite perfume to her throat and wrists; then she studied her reflection in the mirror with a critical eye. "Liar," she said aloud.

Just as Caroline stepped from her room, the door to Adam's room opened. She knew, by the sudden darkening of his eyes, that she'd made the right choice.

"You look beautiful, Caro." So much for the glib writer. The words certainly didn't do her justice. She was so lovely she took his breath away.

"Thank you. And you look—" She wanted to say handsome, but finished lamely, "you look very nice, Adam."

He'd changed into gray pants and a simple gray sweater. His dark hair still glistened with little drops of water from his shower. He placed a hand beneath her elbow as he walked beside her down the stairs.

When they entered the parlor, she said, "If you'll toss another log on the coals, I'll sort through my supply of music."

Within minutes, the strains of a familiar Christmas carol began to play softly while a fire blazed on the grate. They looked up as Paige and the children paused in the doorway.

"Oh." Paige gave an appreciative look around. "Caroline, this is wonderful."

The coffee table between the love seats was adorned with Christmas angels in a nest of candlesticks and evergreens. The mantel had been decked with more greens and angels, surrounded by gleaming candles in antique holders. Adding the perfect touch was McPherson, stretched out on a rug in front of the fire. Both children ran to the cat, who allowed them to hug and pet him and lavish him with affection.

"Look, Mom," Amy called excitedly. "McPherson remembers us. He's licking us."

"Of course, he remembers you," Caroline said with a laugh. "You fed him so many scraps the last time you were here I had to put him on a diet."

The little girl lifted the cat in her arms and he yawned and closed his eyes.

Suddenly Tyler looked around in dismay. "Aunt Caroline, where's the tree?"

"Your aunt was saving that for your arrival." Adam caught the look of surprise in Caroline's eyes. "We thought we'd take you two into the woods tomorrow morning and cut down whatever tree you choose. And then you and Amy can decorate it."

The children's eyes lit with excitement. "We can cut our own? Any one we want?" They ran to the window to stare out into the darkness. "Any tree we want," they repeated as they studied the darkened outlines of a whole forest of trees.

"I want the biggest tree in the woods," Tyler said.

"Me, too." Amy nodded in agreement.

"That was absolutely brilliant," Caroline whispered

in an aside. "How did you ever come up with the idea?"

Adam shrugged, enjoying the moment. "I just asked myself what I would have wanted when I was their age. Are you sure you don't mind if we cut down a tree?"

"Adam." She touched a hand to his arm. "You could cut down a dozen trees if it would keep the smiles on those two faces."

He closed a hand over hers, and the look in his eyes had her heart tripping over itself. She stepped back, feeling a little too overwhelmed by him.

"I promised you a tour, Paige, to show you what I've done. If you children would rather skip this, Maggie has a treat for you in the kitchen."

They needed no coaxing as they happily skipped away, the cat still held firmly in Amy's grasp.

Caroline linked arms with her sister-in-law, then paused on the stair. "Adam, would you like to join us?"

"No, thanks. I'll wait down here. And maybe open a bottle of wine. Any preference?"

Caroline glanced at Paige, then shook her head. "Surprise us."

When they reached the head of the stairs, Caroline took Paige through five of the six bedroom suites. They had been decorated in a variety of periods, showing the growth of the house from its humble beginnings as a simple eighteenth-century tavern to the elegance of a prosperous twentieth-century New England showplace.

"We'll have to skip the suite Adam is occupying," she said. "I don't think he'd appreciate having us invade his privacy."

"You gave him Elias's room?"

Caroline nodded. "It's the biggest of the suites, and

it's filled with history. Not only are the bed and desk part of the original furnishings, but the chairs and table are early nineteenth century. It's a thrill to know they've survived all these years."

A short time later, as they headed downstairs, Paige rested a hand on Caroline's arm. "I know all this takes a lot of money. Are you doing all right?"

Caroline had no intention of adding to her sister-in-law's worries. "I'm doing fine. I do most of the work myself. The contractors around Port Freedom know me, and when I have to hire them, they're willing to allow me to pay them a little at a time." She squeezed Paige's hand. "Come on. Let's see what wine Adam chose for us."

Adam was standing in front of the fire, absorbed in the music. He stared into the flames as though they held the answers to all life's secrets. He looked up as the women entered, then pulled himself out of his dark thoughts and offered each of them a glass of red wine.

"Did you enjoy the tour?" he asked.

Paige nodded. "I love what Caroline's done with this place. I envy her."

"You envy me?" Caroline gave a short laugh. "With my debts, my work and this sleepy little town?"

"You seem . . . serene," Paige said. "This town and this house suit you."

"It's true." Adam returned the bottle to a silver tray. "But then, I've always believed Caro could be at home anywhere in the world."

"How long have you two known each other?" Paige asked.

"All our lives." Adam's gaze was fixed on Caroline. "I remember when she was no bigger than Amy."

"Adam was so sure of himself. So . . . tough. Always challenging the establishment." Caroline wasn't aware of the subtle change in her tone. "Even when we were kids, you were comfortable with yourself, Adam. You always knew who and what you were. I'm not at all surprised by your success."

After a moment of silence, Adam turned to Paige and effectively changed the subject. "How did you and Graham meet?"

"We met in law school. After graduation, we set up a practice here in Port Freedom." Paige sipped her wine a moment before saying, "For a girl born and raised in Manhattan, this was pure heaven. After Tyler and Amy were born, I thought our lives were just about perfect. But then one day Graham announced that he'd been invited to Washington to join the White House staff."

"Don't you like being in the political inner circle?" Adam asked.

Paige shrugged. "I try to. At first, I threw myself into Washington with the same enthusiasm I'd had for Port Freedom. But there are so many demands on Graham's time. And the funny thing is, he doesn't seem to mind. I think he's flattered by all the attention. But he doesn't see what it's doing to us. To our marriage. To the children."

How could her brother not see? Caroline wondered. It had become obvious to her almost from the beginning. He was willing to sacrifice everything, including the love and respect of his family, for his own ambitions. Still, it would be hard to escape the allure of all that power. Caroline glanced at Adam and knew in her heart that he was a man who wouldn't succumb to such a temptation.

Determined to lighten the mood, Adam picked up the bottle of wine. "Come on. Let's see what Tyler and Amy are up to."

They followed the sound of the children's laughter

to the dining room, where McPherson was entertaining them.

"Watch what Maggie showed us," Tyler called. "McPherson never misses."

The boy tossed a cotton ball and the cat reached out a paw, batting it to the floor and pouncing on it, much to the delight of the children.

"That's the most exercise that old cat's had in a year," Maggie said as she carried in a steaming tureen of stew. She returned a minute later with a basket of homemade bread and rolls and glasses of milk for the children.

"There's coffee in the kitchen," she called, "and Caroline's cherry cobbler warming by the stove."

"You're not joining us?" Adam asked.

Maggie shook her head. "Will came early to pick me up. He said some of the roads are already closed."

Almost at once, the children's moods were shattered. They raced to the window.

"How will Dad get here?" Amy asked, and Tyler shrugged, clearly distressed.

They pressed their faces to the window and looked out at the curtain of snow. When they finally walked to the table, their smiles were gone.

Caroline saw the worry etched in their mother's eyes. Thinking quickly, she said, "Tyler, why don't you lead the blessing?"

She stretched out her hand to Tyler and felt her other hand engulfed in Adam's big palm. She would have sworn that a current of electricity passed between them. A betraying blush warmed her cheeks. A glance at Adam's face told her that he had felt it, too.

When the others had clasped hands around the table, the little boy bowed his head slightly and said, "Bless this food—and please find a way to get Dad here for Christmas."

"Amen," the others intoned.

There was a strained silence as Caroline ladled stew into bowls and passed them around the table.

"Oh, Caroline." Paige bit into a freshly baked roll. "This is heavenly. It's exactly what I needed."

"I'm glad. I wanted to keep it simple on your first night here."

"Simple." Paige laughed. "Simple is carryout. Or pizza delivered. This is a feast."

Adam nodded in agreement. "I don't know what you put in this, but stew never tasted so good."

Caroline basked in the glow of their compliments.

A short time later she got to her feet. "I'll bring in the coffee and dessert."

"Why don't we take it in the parlor?" Adam suggested.

She nodded. "Good idea."

She was surprised when he followed her to the kitchen and helped her assemble everything on a tray. In no time, they were seated in front of the fire in the parlor.

"What a wonderful meal." Paige sighed and stifled a yawn. "And what a perfect evening. But I'm afraid the day is catching up with me. I think I'll have to go up to bed soon." She got to her feet. "Before I do, I'll help you clean up."

"Not tonight." Caroline shook her head firmly. "It'll only take me a few minutes. Right now, you need your rest."

Paige didn't have the strength to argue. She turned to her children, who were lying on a rug in front of the fire. Between them, the cat purred so loudly he sounded like an engine. "Come on. Time for bed."

"Can I take McPherson up with me?" Amy asked.

Caroline nodded. "I think he'd love to sleep on your

bed for a while. Just be sure to leave the door opened a little so he can get out later."

"Are we still going to chop down a Christmas tree in the morning?" Tyler asked.

Adam nodded. "Right after breakfast."

The brother and sister needed no coaxing as they got to their feet and headed for the stairs while their mother was still saying her good nights.

"I wish," Paige muttered, "they could get themselves together this fast on school nights."

"Come on, Mom," Amy called impatiently. "McPherson's yawning."

Paige brushed a kiss over Caroline's cheek and then Adam's. "See what I mean? We'll see you in the morning."

When they were alone, Caroline walked to the window and stared out at the falling snow. The only sound was the hiss and snap of the fire.

"I've missed this." Adam's deep voice alerted her to the fact that he had crossed the room to stand directly behind her. "Every year at Christmas time, I found myself thinking about Port Freedom. About you."

"Really?" She struggled to keep the anger from her voice, but it managed to slip in, laced with pain. "If you missed it so much, why didn't you come back sooner?"

"I thought about it." He lifted a hand to her hair, then seemed to think better of doing so and lowered his hand to his side, where he clenched it into a fist.

"Why now?" She did turn then, but the minute she saw his eyes, she wished she hadn't. They were dark, fathomless. Drawing her in against her will to a place she didn't want to go. "What brought you back to Port Freedom now, Adam?"

"You."

The word hung between them.

He saw her blink once, as though denying his answer. "I thought that's what drove you away." Her voice betrayed her pain.

"If you thought that, you're dead wrong."

"It's what—" She heard the tremble in her voice and hated it, but forced herself to go on. "It's what Graham told me the night you left."

"Graham's a liar."

Caroline tried to back away from the fury she could read in Adam's eyes. But there was nowhere to go. She was already backed against the window.

Seeing her reaction, he caught her roughly by the shoulder. The softness of cashmere and the skin beneath forced him to loosen his grip. "I'm sorry, Caro. I know he's your brother. I didn't come here to fight with you."

"Then why did you come?"

"I told you. But I guess words aren't enough." He dragged her close, all the while watching her eyes. His lips nuzzled hers and he heard her little intake of breath. Then, almost against his will, his mouth closed over hers. Now there was no gentleness. Not in the hands that held her. Nor in the kiss that drained her. A kiss that spoke of hunger, of loneliness, of need.

Caroline hadn't intended to respond to Adam's touch, his kiss. But she couldn't make her body behave. His mouth, so potently male, was avid, eager. And when his tongue flicked over her lips, then darted inside her mouth, hers met it. The taste of him was dark, mysterious. Tempting.

In some small part of her mind, she realized that he knew exactly what he was doing. He knew her so well. Knew just how to slip past her defenses. But her body didn't care. She could feel her skin heat, her bones begin to melt as he took the kiss deeper.

Adam lifted his head and kept his eyes open as he brushed soft butterfly kisses over Caroline's temple, her lids, the tip of her nose. She was exciting to watch. His heartbeat accelerated at the whisper of her lashes, the flush that stole over her cheeks. He felt her breath hitch, her body tremble, when he skimmed his thumbs over the tips of her breasts.

This time, when he took her mouth, it was with a savageness that caught them both by surprise. He took. He devoured. And she did the same, giving herself up to the pleasure of the moment.

How could he have lived so long without this? Without her?

With an effort, Adam lifted his head and filled his lungs on a long, deep draft of air. He'd miscalculated. He'd expected the rush of adrenaline, the heat of passion. What he hadn't anticipated was the hard, driving need. A need that threatened to break loose at any moment and shatter all his cool control.

Struggling for a lightness he didn't feel, he nibbled his way to her ear. "Would you like to continue this upstairs?"

"No." Caroline was surprised at how much effort that simple word cost her. Especially when she wasn't sure she meant it. "You can go up to bed. Alone. I'm going to tidy up the dishes."

Adam's eyes darkened with a deadly light. "You don't mean that."

"Yes, I do. This was a nice . . . diversion, Adam. But I have work to do."

His quick, dangerous smile was back. "You'd better be careful picking up those dishes, Caro." He lifted her hands to his lips and brushed a kiss to each palm. "You hands are trembling." Then he surprised her, and himself, by adding, "I think I'd better help you. Just so you don't break anything."

With a casualness he didn't feel, he strode across the room, leaving her leaning weakly against the windowsill. Her hands were still shaking. And her heartbeat was still unsteady.

Chapter Six

Caroline awoke to the sound of pounding across the hall. She sat up and shoved hair from her eyes. Was Adam hammering something? Making more repairs?

"Wake up, Adam," came Tyler's voice. "You promised we could cut down a tree right after breakfast."

Not hammering. Knocking.

Caroline glanced at the clock on her nightstand. It was five-thirty. Not even dawn. With a groan she rolled over. But a few minutes later, she heard the sounds of a door being opened and closed and whispered voices trailing down the stairs.

With a sigh of resignation, she slipped from bed and padded to the shower. Fifteen minutes later, she headed toward the kitchen and the muffled sounds of voices. When she stepped inside, she found Adam and the children whispering like conspirators.

"Didn't anybody tell you it's still nighttime?" She inhaled the fragrance of coffee and sausage.

"It's morning, Aunt Caroline." Tyler finished his juice and reached for the pitcher of milk. "And Adam didn't say what time we could cut the tree. He just said after breakfast."

"Makes perfect sense to me." Adam was standing at the stove, stacking sausages and slices of French toast on a platter. Behind him the windowpanes were frosted with snow. The fading moonlight reflected off snowdrifts.

"You're just in time," he called. "Amy wants powdered sugar on her French toast, and I can't find it."

After Caroline opened a cupboard and located the sugar, she filled a small crystal bowl to the brim.

"Save some for me," she muttered as she set it in front of her niece and took the seat beside her.

"How'd you know we were up?" Tyler asked.

"You weren't exactly as quiet as mice."

"We were trying to be."

Adam handed Caroline a cup of coffee, and she shot him a grateful smile before taking a long drink. "I guess I don't really mind the early hour. In fact, I'm eager to see which tree you and Amy choose."

"It'll be a big one," the boy assured her.

"Can McPherson come with us?" Amy asked.

"He doesn't care much for snow. He prefers to sit indoors and watch silly humans freeze." Caroline sipped her coffee. "How long did he stay in your bed?"

"The whole night. He was still there this morning on my pillow. He had his motor running." The little girl spoke around a mouthful of French toast slathered with syrup.

Caroline glanced at the thin morning light just beginning to creep across the sky. "Did either of you think to wake your mom?"

"I did." Tyler drained his glass and wiped away a

milky mustache. "She said she needed a couple more hours."

"Smart woman." Adam took the chair beside Tyler and began to fill his plate. "Why didn't I think of that?"

" 'Cause you were already up," Tyler said.

"You were up before dawn?" Caroline shot Adam a glance, but he pretended not to notice as he poured syrup.

"And his computer was on," Tyler added. "Adam let me read what he'd written."

"What did it say?"

The little boy shrugged. "I don't remember. Something about a man's thoughts being as dark as the sky outside his window."

"Another mystery," Caroline remarked.

Adam gave her a quick smile. "Maybe I've decided to write a romance."

"Want my advice? Stick to mysteries."

"Just for that," he said, getting to his feet, "I think you should clean up this mess while we get ready to tackle the great outdoors."

He speared a last bite of sausage and set his plate in the sink. With a trill of laughter, Tyler and Amy followed him from the kitchen and went in search of snowsuits, boots and mittens.

"I think this is the best tree in the whole forest," Tyler pronounced.

He and Amy rode on the front of a toboggan pulled by Adam and Caroline. Behind them, secured by ropes, was the tree they had finally selected.

"If you ask me," Caroline muttered, dropping down to rest on a fallen log, "we looked at every tree in the whole forest."

"But we had to be sure," Tyler said. "And how could

we be sure unless we looked at all of them?"

"Very wise." Adam winked. "And your choice was far superior to the one your aunt had picked out."

Caroline got to her feet. "Are you saying I have no taste in Christmas trees?"

"That's what I'm saying. Unless you were choosing it for its comic value."

Seconds later, a snowball grazed the side of Adam's head. The children broke into a fit of giggles when he turned just in time to get a second snowball down his neck.

"And a lousy aim, too." He scooped up a handful of snow and hit her squarely in the face. "That's how it should be done."

"You just declared war." Caroline dropped to her knees to replenish her ammunition. "Who's with me?"

"I am," little Amy called, rushing to her aunt's side.

"Come on, Tyler." Adam handed him a snowball. "We guys have to stick together."

"That's right. I'm with Adam." Tyler proudly fired his first shot.

"Traitor." Caroline sent a barrage of snowballs their way.

"Well, don't just stand there," Adam told the little boy. "I need all the help I can get."

"Aw, they're just girls." Tyler formed an arsenal of snowballs, then began throwing them.

"Just girls, are we?" When Amy took cover, Caroline hauled her to her feet. "You can't win that way, darling. Come on. You have to charge right in. Like this."

Armed with a handful of snowballs, she began running forward and tossed them as she ran. Tyler was forced to duck. But Adam stood his ground until Caroline was close enough to catch. Reaching out a hand, he pulled her close and scattered the remains of her snowballs. Then he said, "Now that I've disarmed you, what are you going to do, Caro?"

She lifted her gloved hand to smear snow over his face. Her action made the children shriek with laughter.

"Oh, you never should have done that." Adam scooped up snow and did the same to Caroline.

Again the children howled with laughter. Adam and Caroline joined in, laughing so hard they dropped to their knees in the snow. When the laughter finally faded, Adam removed his glove and began to wipe the snow from Caroline's face. Her cheeks were bright pink, her eyes warm with laughter. Without a thought to what he was doing, Adam lowered his head and kissed her.

Despite the cold, Caroline felt the rush of heat and twined her arms around Adam's neck to kiss him back. It seemed the most natural thing in the world.

Beside them, the two children began to laugh and tease.

"Adam and Aunt Caroline are kissing," they chanted.

Adam caught Caroline's hand and helped her to her feet, then turned to Tyler and Amy. "As a matter of fact, that was so nice I think I'll do it again."

And he gave her a long, slow, leisurely kiss that had her blood heating and her heart racing.

"I think that's how all good fights should end," Adam declared, much to the delight of the children.

A few minutes later, Adam and Caroline caught up the toboggan rope and, side by side, hauled both tree and children back to the house.

"These look so old."

After a hearty supper of Maggie's homemade vegetable soup and roast beef, Tyler and Amy gathered around the box of ornaments that Caroline had brought from the attic.

"They are old, Tyler." Caroline began unwrapping them. "Some of these belonged to my father and grandfather. The rest were new when your dad and I were no older than you are now."

"Can we put them on the tree?" Amy asked.

Adam sat back on his heels and surveyed his work. He'd spent the afternoon pruning branches and setting the tree in its stand before adding strands of twinkling lights. "I've done my part. The rest is up to you."

"Oh, boy." The two children began feverishly unwrapping the ornaments and hanging them on the branches.

Maggie entered, carrying a tray of gingerbread cookies and mugs of eggnog. From the kitchen wafted the wonderful fragrance of cinnamon and spice.

"Will's here, so I'll be leaving now," she announced. "I can't wait for morning to see how your tree looks. And remember, you two are going to help me decorate sugar cookies."

"Can we eat some, too?" Tyler asked.

"Of course. It wouldn't be any fun baking them if we couldn't eat our fill. Especially on Christmas Eve."

" 'Night, Maggie," the children called in unison. "See you in the morning."

From her position on the love seat, Paige watched as her son and daughter stifled yawns. Despite their eagerness to decorate the tree, they'd been fighting sleep for the past hour.

"I think," she said, "that early wake-up call has finally caught up with you. What do you say we go up to bed and finish this in the morning?"

"Can we leave the ornaments right here?" Amy asked.

Caroline nodded. "They'll be here waiting for you tomorrow." She bent and hugged her niece and nephew.

"Good night, Aunt Caroline," Amy said. "Can I take McPherson to bed with me again tonight?"

"I think he'd be insulted if you didn't invite him along."

The little girl picked up the cat, then paused in front of Adam to say shyly. "Good night, Adam. Thanks for our tree. I really love it. And . . . I love you, too."

Before Adam could do more than offer a surprised grin, Amy followed her mother from the room.

"Good night, Aunt Caroline." Tyler hugged her, then turned to Adam. "Thanks, Adam. This was the best day I've ever had."

"Me, too, partner." Adam watched him leave, a little dazed by the outpouring of affection.

When they were alone, Caroline turned to stare at the lights of the tree. "I agree with Amy and Tyler. I can't remember when I've had a better day." She turned and held out her hand. "Thank you, Adam. You've given those two children something they'll never forget. And I'll never forget it either."

Adam went to her almost reluctantly, as though afraid to get too close. He took her hand between both of his and stared down at it. "Such a small hand, Caro. And so soft. It's hard to believe all the work it's capable of." He lifted it to his lips and she caught her breath at the rush of feelings his touch evoked.

Instead of pulling her hand away, she pressed it to his cheek. He stood very still, absorbing the jolt.

"You're so good with children. You should have half a dozen of your own."

"Maybe I will. One day." He didn't make any moves. Couldn't. He was walking a tightrope and about to fall. This time, it had to be her call.

Caroline lifted herself on tiptoe to touch her mouth to his. Heat flared at the first contact. He kept his eyes on hers, watching the way they darkened. Still, he didn't touch her until she sighed and brought her hands around his waist, pressing her lips to his throat.

That was Adam's undoing. Dragging her against him, he tangled his hands in her hair and covered her mouth with his.

The thought of all that passion, all that power, held so firmly in check had her pulse pounding, her blood heating. "Is that offer still open, Adam?"

He thought for a moment he hadn't heard her. Had only dreamed her words because he wanted her so badly. But then he looked down at her and saw the invitation in her eyes.

"Do you know what you're saying?"

Her eyes remained level on his. "I know, Adam. I want you to make love with me."

"I won't settle for a quick tumble, Caro. I'll want more. I'll want everything you have to give."

She didn't look away. "I understand."

"No, you don't. Not yet anyway. But you will. Oh, God, Caro, you will." He scooped her into his arms and headed for the stairs.

She wrapped her arms around his neck and pressed her lips to his throat. And thrilled to the fact that his pulsebeat was as erratic as her own.

Chapter Seven

Adam barely made it to his room. He stopped just inside and nudged the door closed. After setting Caroline on her feet, he cupped her face with his hands and studied her by the glow of lamplight.

"Adam."

"Shhh." With a sort of reverence, he kissed her long and slow and deep. As though he had all the time in the world. And all the while his blood was pulsing, and the need was building.

"There's no need for words, Caro."

She knew he was right. Instead, she poured all her feelings into the kiss. He did the same. Though the passion was still there, simmering between them, there was a softness, a gentleness as well.

Adam tasted the sweetness, the goodness in her and marveled that it had survived. Through all the years, all the disappointments, it was still there, easing, soothing. Waiting. And now he was back to claim it.

And he wouldn't be rushed. He wanted to taste it all, savor it all. He wanted to touch her everywhere. All the places he'd only dreamed of. And to take his time kissing her. He wanted long, slow kisses that clouded his mind like a drug.

His lips moved over Caroline's face, touching, tasting, tempting. He loved the smell of her hair, the flavor of her skin, the softness just here, at the base of her throat. He heard her quick intake of breath and nibbled until her sigh became a moan of pleasure.

Adam's first inclination was to tear her clothes from her and take her right away. But he forced himself to go slowly as he drew her sweater off and slid her slacks over her hips. Beneath them he found silk and lace. As he'd expected. Caro was a woman who would wear silk and lace even beneath denim. It pleased him, even as it aroused.

She wondered how much longer her legs could hold her.

As if reading her mind, he took her hand, and together they dropped to their knees.

After Caroline unbuttoned his shirt, she slid it from his shoulders. Her hands lingered on his chest, then slid upward to twine around his neck. When he was naked, he drew her down until she lay over him, her body cushioned by his, her hair spilling over both of them like a veil.

She floated on a cloud of sensations while his hands and lips moved over her, stroking, soothing. Arousing.

"How long I've waited. To touch you. To taste you." Adam ran openmouthed kisses across her shoulder to the delicate hollow of her throat. "To have you." He took her breast, nibbling, suckling, until she moaned and writhed and whispered his name.

Outside, the wind picked up, sending a spray of

snow and sleet against the windows. But neither one heard as they lost themselves in the pleasure. The room was chilled, the fire on the hearth long ago burned to embers. But neither one noticed as heat rose up between them, filling their lungs, making their bodies slick with sheen.

Adam moved to Caroline's other breast and feasted until pleasure became need. Hard, driving need that threatened to devour them both. Now all gentleness, all tenderness was stripped aside, revealing a hunger that demanded to be fed.

This darker side of Adam had always excited Caroline. Knowing that it was her touch and her taste that unleashed it made her bold. Exulting in her power, she brought her lips and fingertips across his chest, and lower, to the flat planes of his stomach, and then lower still.

On a growl of pleasure, they rolled over the floor. Caroline shuddered and strained against Adam as he slid over her, damp flesh to damp flesh, and took her to dark, new places where she'd never gone before.

Adam felt her stiffen as he brought her to the first peak of pleasure. He gave her no time to recover as he moved upward until his lips found hers.

"Adam." Her eyes were wide, reflecting the storm that raged within. She didn't think it possible to want more, but she did.

He levered himself above her. "Say it." He kept his eyes steady on hers. "Tell me you want me."

"I do. Only you, Adam. I love you."

Love. It was more than he could have hoped for. All that he'd ever wanted. He felt his control shattering as he stood on the very edge of a precipice. And then there was only need clawing for release. As he entered her, she wrapped herself around him, moving with him, wanting to hold him like this forever.

Adam filled himself with Caroline. Her taste, her scent. And he knew that he would carry this moment in his heart forever. He whispered her name as his lips covered hers.

Together they began to move, climbing higher, then higher still, until they teetered on the very summit. Without hesitation they stepped over the edge. And experienced the most incredible flight of their lives.

"Am I heavy?"

"Um-hmm."

Still they lay unmoving, wrapped around each other, feeling as fragile as glass. Afraid that if either of them moved, it would all be shattered. The mood. The moment. This tenuous bond they had shared. And so they lay on the hard floor until their breathing finally returned to normal and their heartbeats settled down to a steady rhythm.

Adam rolled to one side and drew Caroline into his arms, then cradled her against his chest. "I want you to know I didn't plan this."

"I believe it was my idea," she said with a laugh.

"No, I mean all of this. Coming here. Getting caught up in the past." He brushed hair from her eyes, then allowed his hand to linger on her face. "I didn't mean for any of this to happen."

"Then why did you come, Adam?"

"I couldn't stay away any longer. I tried." He ran a hand through her hair, loving the silkiness of it, the softness. "God knows I tried. For so many years I managed to hold the demons at bay. But this year, I just had to come back. I had to see you, even if it meant having the door slammed in my face."

Caroline chuckled. "That thought crossed my mind."

"Why didn't you?"

"I needed the money."

At his little frown, she couldn't help laughing. "Sorry. I couldn't resist. But the truth is, I was curious. And intrigued, I suppose. And if we're going to be honest now, I was attracted."

"You were?" Adam arched a brow and his lips curved into a smile.

"Don't flatter yourself." Caroline lifted a finger to trace his lips. "I've been told I have very strange taste in men."

"How strange?"

Her smile grew. "I'm lying on the cold hard floor with you, when there's a perfectly soft bed just across the room. That ought to tell you something."

He threw back his head and laughed. "Would you like me to carry you to bed?"

"That would be nice."

As he stood and lifted her in his arms, his eyes took on a dangerous light. "Seems a shame to waste the whole night sleeping. I mean, as long as I'm taking you to my bed, maybe we could try a rewrite of that scene."

Caroline brushed her lips lightly over his. "I guess that's what I get for being with a writer."

"Research," Adam said, setting her gently among the sheets. He lay beside her and drew her firmly into his arms. As his lips found hers, he muttered against them, "So much damned research."

"What are you doing?" Caroline awoke to find Adam sitting up in bed beside her, staring at her. On his face was a look of intense concentration.

"Just looking."

"At what?" She sat up, shoving a tangle of hair from her eyes.

"At you. I'm memorizing you." Adam traced a finger across her shoulder. "Every line." He moved his finger lower. "Every delicious curve." He smiled at her shivering response.

"I thought you did that all night."

They both laughed. It had been a glorious night. Though they'd managed to doze, neither had spent much time asleep. At times, their lovemaking had mirrored the frenzy of the storm raging beyond their walls. Frantic, demanding. At other times, they'd been as gentle, as comfortable as old lovers, wrapped in each other's arms, whispering secrets of the heart.

Caroline glanced across the room to where a log burned on the grate. "I see you've been busy."

"It was that or have you freeze when you got out of bed."

"Very thoughtful, Mr. Holt."

"Always willing to oblige, Miss Stark."

"What time is it?"

He studied the clock on the nightstand. "Almost six."

"I'd better get going. It's Christmas Eve. And I have a mountain of food to prepare."

As she started to slide out of bed, he dragged her back and kissed her.

"Adam"—she pushed a little away—"you're going to make me late."

He gave her a grin that had her heart tumbling; then he kissed her again, with a thoroughness that had her head spinning. "I'm about to make you even later."

The press of his mouth to hers swallowed whatever she'd been about to say. And then they were lost once more in that private place where only lovers can go.

* * *

"Remember my promise." In the parlor, Maggie deposited a tray filled with mugs of hot chocolate and a plate of cinnamon toast. "When you children have finished decorating the tree, you can help me decorate my special sugar cookies."

"We'll be finished in a little while," Tyler assured her, unwrapping another wad of tissue.

When Amy unwrapped a glittering star, her eyes rounded with excitement. "Look, Tyler!"

The boy solemnly took the ornament from her hand and examined it before handing it back. "Aunt Caroline used to tell me that was a magic star," he declared.

The little girl turned to her aunt. "Is it really magic?"

Caroline gave her a gentle smile. "I always thought it was when I was your age. I remember my father lifting me up to place it at the very top of the tree and telling me to make a wish. And whatever I wished for, I would find on Christmas morning."

Amy walked to Adam and held up her arms. "Would you lift me up?" she asked. "All the way to the top of the tree?"

He picked her up and crossed to the tree, holding her very still while she set the star in place. For a moment, she squeezed her eyes tightly shut. Then she smiled.

Paige, seated on one of the love seats, sighed as she watched.

Hearing the sound, Caroline turned and whispered, "Have you heard from Graham?"

Paige nodded. "I called home early this morning, but he'd already left for the office. His assistant assured me that no one was working past noon today. But when Graham finally called, just a little while ago, he told me not to expect him. After hearing about how the snow has closed some roads and airports, he said it wasn't worth the effort."

"Not worth the effort?" Caroline looked horrified. "But it's Christmas Eve. It's supposed to be . . . special. Besides, we both know what Amy just wished for." She brightened. "I know. He plans to surprise us."

Paige gave her a gentle, strained smile. "You know Graham better than that. He's not fond of surprises. If he planned on coming, he'd say so."

"I don't believe that," Caroline said fiercely. "I just refuse to believe that Graham would disappoint his family."

Across the room, Adam stood by the window and heard the tone of desperation in Caroline's voice. He knew her so well. It wasn't Paige she was trying to convince; it was herself.

He turned for a moment to watch the children. Then he stalked from the room, calling over his shoulder, "I'd like to borrow the van for a while."

"Now? Why?"

Caroline started after him, but he stopped her with a look.

He softened the blow by winking. "It's Christmas Eve, Caro. You know. A time for shopping. A time for secrets. Not a time to be asking questions. I'll be back in an hour or so."

How could she argue with that? She bit back whatever else she was going to say. Minutes later, she heard the purr of the engine and the crunch of tires in the snow.

Chapter Eight

Caroline basted the goose, then closed the oven and crossed the room to stare out the window. Daylight was just beginning to fade. Dusk was settling over the land. Snow was still falling, turning the landscape into a glittering Christmas card.

As he'd promised, Adam had returned within an hour. After sequestering himself in his room for a short time, he'd rejoined the others without a word.

This should have been the most perfect Christmas Eve of her life. In the other room, the children could be heard, their voices high with excitement as they basked in the glow of the tree. Their presence added just the right note to this old home, which had heard so many children's voices throughout the years. But there was a wistful note as well, due to the absence of their father.

Caroline's disappointment in her brother left an ache that wouldn't easily heal. There was a selfish, willful streak in Graham that she could no longer deny. Had he always been this careless of the affections of others?

Her head came up as she heard Adam's deep voice teasing the children. His mere presence warmed her. After all these years of wondering and wishing, he was actually here. And what they had shared last night had been the most wonderful gift of all. Why then was she feeling so sad?

Despite their feelings for each other, there had been no promises made. And there were still so many unanswered questions. Why had Adam left her all those years ago without a word of explanation? It was so unlike him to act the coward. Yet everyone had said that the town of Port Freedom was too small for a rebel like Adam Holt. That sooner or later he'd leave or be forced out. And they'd been right, of course. Adam never could have achieved such success here. He'd needed to grow and learn. To spread his wings and fly to cities like London, Paris, New York.

In the years since he'd left, Caroline had learned, as well. Learned that life could go on even though a heart was shattered beyond repair.

But during their long night of lovemaking, Adam hadn't spoken a word of explanation. And when Caroline had finally asked him, he had said that he couldn't speak of it. Or wouldn't.

Now, for the sake of Tyler and Amy, she was determined to shake off this mood. She intended to see to it that this was the most memorable Christmas Eve of their young lives.

She turned up the Christmas music. And plunged herself into satisfying work.

"Oh, Caroline." Paige took another sip of Dom Perignon. "You do know how to celebrate."

The feast could have been out of another century. Roast goose with a rich cherry glaze. Potatoes swimming in gravy, and tiny spears of asparagus nestled on beds of spinach. There were homemade breads and rolls dotted with nuts and currants and baked to perfection.

"Leave room for her apple spice cake and plum pudding," Maggie warned.

Caroline had insisted that Maggie and Will enjoy Christmas Eve supper with them since they had no family in Port Freedom.

Will patted his stomach. "I might need to take a couple of turns around the yard for a half hour or so if I'm going to eat another thing."

"I might join you, Will." Adam watched Tyler slip a scrap of meat to the cat, who crouched under his chair. When the little boy looked up, Adam winked.

Watching them, Caroline recognized the look of affection exchanged between Adam and her nephew, and she felt her heart turn over. How sad that her brother didn't know what he was missing.

She pushed back her chair and retrieved a cart containing a silver coffee service. Her long black velvet hostess gown rustled around her ankles. "We could always take our coffee and dessert in the parlor."

"Sounds fine to me." Adam, in suit and tie, set the champagne on the trolley and began to roll it toward the other room. "It'll give us all a chance to get up and move."

The others followed at a leisurely pace.

In the parlor, Caroline left the lights off so that the room was warmed only by the glow of the fire and the winking lights of the tree. On the stereo, Bing crooned an old favorite. Outside the window, snow fell like a curtain.

The adults sipped coffee and tasted Caroline's exquisite desserts. The children, wearing party finery, sat cross-legged on the rug in front of the fire. McPherson lay between them, and they pampered him like a potentate. On a footstool, Caroline placed glasses of milk and a plate of pastries. Every other minute, Amy or Tyler would rush to the window to peer into the darkness, then, subdued, return to play with the cat.

Maggie studied the children. "Do you remember, Will, the way our children used to fuss and fidget on Christmas Eve? Like puppets on a string. So excited they were ready to pop."

The old man nodded. "And you along with them." He turned to Adam. "I never knew anyone who enjoyed Christmas more than Maggie."

"The years fly by," she mused aloud. "And one day you wake up and everyone's gone."

Adam saw the look of pain that Caroline couldn't conceal before she ducked her head. A glance at the clock on the mantel showed the late hour. He asked casually, "Does old Reverend Symes still hold a Christmas Eve service with the reenactment of the first Christmas and a children's choir?"

"Oh, Mom." Tyler jumped up with an eagerness that surprised everyone. "We went last Christmas. Could we go again?"

Paige considered. "I doubt Amy would last through it. I'm not even sure about you, Tyler."

The boy and girl watched their mother with pleading looks.

She gave a shrug. "It's a very special night. Why not?"

Adam turned to Will. "How about it? Are you and Maggie up for it?"

The older man shot a glance at his wife's beaming face and nodded. "We'd love it."

"I'll get the van." Adam replaced his coffee cup and strode from the room while Caroline banked the fire and switched off the lights of the tree. The others began a scramble for coats, boots, hats and gloves.

In the hall, Adam stopped a moment to touch a hand to Caroline's face. Seeing his caress, Maggie went very still. A slow smile touched her lips. In the years she had come to know Caroline, she had wondered if this fine young woman would ever find a man to touch her heart. Adam Holt was such a man. Did they know yet? Maggie wondered. Were they aware just how much love was revealed in their eyes?

The only traffic moving on the dark, lonely stretch of road was their van. And far ahead, clearing mountains of snow from their path, glowed the headlights of Hal Winslow's snowplow.

"I can't remember when I was so moved." In the darkness of the van, Maggie's voice was hushed out of deference to Amy, asleep in Caroline's arms.

"The best part was the angel." Tyler's lids drooped, then closed. At least he'd managed to stay awake through the service. But the motion of the van was too soothing for him to resist any longer.

"I thought the best part was the shepherd." Adam's voice was warm with laughter. "The one who lost his flip-flop—I mean sandal—and, as he bent over to pick it up, hit one of the Magi with his cane, knocking him off his plastic camel."

"I don't know," Caroline said when she had recovered from a bout of laughter. "The children's choir was hard to top. Especially the girl in the back row who managed to sing off-key and louder than everyone else."

They were all chuckling as Adam brought the van smoothly up to the back porch.

"Sure you two don't want to spend the night?" Caroline asked. "It's awfully late to be out. And you'll just have to turn around in a few hours if you're going to join us for Christmas breakfast."

"It's only a couple of miles. We'll be fine. Especially since Hal's out plowing." Will helped his wife from the van. "We'll see you in the morning."

In the silence that followed, Paige gave a long deep sigh. "All through the service I kept hoping . . ." She couldn't stem the tears that she'd been holding in for such a long time.

Caroline caught her sister-in-law's hand and squeezed.

"Hey, partner." Adam nudged Tyler, and the little boy opened his eyes. "Think you can walk inside while I carry your sister?"

"Yes, sir." Tyler climbed from the van and walked between his mother and aunt.

Adam lifted Amy and snuggled her to his chest. As he did, she wrapped her chubby arms around his neck and murmured, "Is it Christmas morning yet?"

"I guess it is." Adam's voice was muffled against her temple. "Since it's past midnight."

"Then let's go inside and say hello to Daddy."

Caroline and Paige stopped in their tracks.

"What did you say?" Caroline asked.

"You remember, Aunt Caroline." The little girl clung to Adam as he climbed the steps and walked into the kitchen. "I made a wish on your magic star."

Caroline crossed the room, struggling for the proper words to prepare her little niece for the disappointment she would have to face. Slowly she trailed the others into the parlor, which was illuminated by the lights of the tree and the blazing fire on the grate.

The realization caused her to stop in midstride. She

distinctly remembered turning off the lights. And surely the fire would have died to embers by now. She gasped as a shadowy figure half rose from a chair in the corner.

"Daddy!" Amy said.

As soon as Adam set her down, Amy flew into her father's arms. He lifted her high, then, still holding her, bent to embrace his son.

"I knew you'd come, Daddy." Amy's voice was high-pitched with excitement. "I made a wish on Aunt Caroline's magic star. And I just knew you'd come."

"Aunt Caroline's still got that star?" Graham glanced at his sister, who was staring at him as if seeing a ghost.

"Uh-huh. And Adam lifted me up so I could hang it on the tree and make my wish. And I knew you'd come. I just knew it."

"You knew more than I did, honey." Graham studied his wife, who remained in the doorway. The tears were still wet on her cheeks and lashes.

"How'd you get through the snow, Dad?" Tyler tugged on his father's pant leg.

Before Graham could speak, Adam said, "I'll bet I can guess. I thought I saw a sleigh flying across the trees just before we got home."

Tyler's jaw dropped. Amy's eyes looked as big as saucers.

"You came with . . . Santa?" Amy's voice was little more than a whisper.

There was a moment of silence as her father studied Adam. Then he returned his attention to his children. "I was lucky he was headed this way and willing to let me hitch a ride. Otherwise, I'd still be stuck in Washington."

"Did he bring us presents?" Amy asked, glancing at the tree.

Graham stroked a hand across his daughter's cheek, then stared down at his son. "The sleigh was filled to the brim. But he had some other stops to make first. You understand."

The little girl nodded. "I guess he'll have to come back while we're asleep."

"That's right. Which reminds me. What are you two doing up so late?"

"We went to church," Tyler said.

"And we saw angels and shepherds and a baby in a manger," Amy said, stifling a yawn.

"Sounds wonderful." Again he looked toward his wife, and his tone softened. "I'm sorry I missed it. You'll never know how sorry. But I'll make you a promise. I'll never miss anything so important again."

"Will you tuck us in, Daddy?" Amy burrowed her face against his throat and closed her eyes. The late hour, coupled with the excitement of her father's arrival, defeated her.

"How about if your mother and I both hear your prayers and tuck you in?"

Amy's voice was muffled. "I'd like that, Daddy."

Paige did come to him then. Openly weeping, she stood on tiptoe to brush her lips over his. Then, with one arm around his waist, and the other holding firmly to Tyler, she walked beside him to the stairs.

At the foot of the stairs, Graham turned to Adam and Caroline. "If you don't mind waiting until after the children are in bed, I have some things I'd like to say."

Caroline and Adam watched in silence as the happy family disappeared up the stairs.

Chapter Nine

Adam lifted a bottle from a silver tray. "There's still champagne left. Would you like some?"

Caroline nodded, afraid to trust her voice. Her emotions were still too close to the surface.

He filled two champagne flutes and handed one to her. They sipped in silence, both lost in thought.

At the sound of footsteps on the stairs, they turned to watch Graham and Paige enter the parlor hand in hand.

"Champagne?" Adam asked.

They both refused.

"That was fast." Caroline smiled. "Are the children already asleep?"

"Almost as soon as their heads hit the pillow," Paige said softly. "I don't think I've ever seen them so happy." She squeezed Graham's hand. "And all because their father came to his senses."

"Yes." He flushed, obviously uncomfortable. "Well,

I'm afraid I can't take the credit." He led his wife to a love seat, then crossed the room to stand in front of the fireplace. For a moment, he stood quietly, his hands behind his back, his head bowed. Then he turned.

"There are some things I need to say." He grimaced. "Actually I've needed to say them for a long time."

He met his sister's eye. "Ten years ago, after you and Adam argued, I let you think he left town without a word to you. Actually, he'd left you a letter. But I gave it to Father. And after reading it, he decided to destroy it."

Caroline felt as if all the air had been squeezed from her lungs. "Father . . . destroyed a letter to me? He . . . decided? Without telling me?"

"You were only eighteen," Graham said quickly, "and crazy about a guy who, in Father's opinion, would probably end up in jail. Or worse."

Caroline felt a white-hot flash of anger. "And that's it? He just trampled my dreams, took away my hope and said it was all for the best?"

"Wait, Caro. Your father was right to be concerned. I certainly didn't show much promise." Adam touched a hand to her shoulder, but she shook it off.

"And what about you, Graham? Were you pledged to preserve my honor, too? Is that why you never bothered to tell me?"

Her brother shoved his hands in his pockets and hunched his shoulders as he faced her. "I'd like to say it was your honor that concerned me. But that would be a lie. It was much more than that. You see, your argument with Adam and his leaving were my fault. A week earlier, I'd . . . gotten myself into some trouble."

"Trouble?" Caroline tensed.

"I got drunk with some friends and on a dare

smashed the window of Murphy's Market."

"You smashed that window?" Caroline's face registered her shock. "But I thought Adam—"

Graham interrupted. "The theft itself was petty stuff. A pack of cigarettes, a six-pack of beer. But it would have gone on my record."

"Your record," Caroline said dryly. "And Father's dream of his son at Harvard Law School might have gone down the drain."

Graham nodded. "Exactly. So . . . I asked Adam to take the rap for me."

"You asked—" She turned to Adam. "You mean, you weren't responsible?"

"Adam wasn't even there," Graham said.

Caroline studied Adam's face and was assaulted by the truth. "Oh, Adam. I was so angry at you for doing something so stupid. I hated the fact that everyone was saying it's what they expected from Adam Holt."

She turned on her brother. "And you! How could you? How could you ask a friend to take the blame for your mistake?"

"Because I told myself that with Adam's record another minor scrape with the law didn't matter." His voice suddenly lowered. "That's what I told myself then. But the truth is, I was a coward."

"Now there's something you could never say about Adam." Caroline's eyes narrowed. "And this is how you thanked him for saving your miserable hide. By allowing Father to think the worst of him." Her voice wavered. "And by allowing me to think it as well."

Graham nodded his head.

"And what," she demanded, her voice trembling with feeling, "brought on this sudden bout of honesty? How did you finally develop enough backbone to admit the truth?"

Graham's glance darted to Adam, then back to his

sister. "I got a phone call today from an old friend. A true friend. He told me he'd kick my hide just the way he did when we were kids if I didn't wake up and realize what I was doing to my wife and children. He said he'd even arranged transportation through the snow so I'd have no excuse."

Caroline's brow furrowed as she turned to Adam. "So that's why you needed to go to town. I thought you said you were shopping."

He grinned, and she felt the familiar jolt to her heart. "I did a little of that, too. But I needed to talk to Hal Winslow about hiring his . . . sleigh and reindeer."

"Sleigh and reindeer?" And then the truth dawned. "The snowplow. That's how you got Graham here."

"Since the airport was closed, it was . . . quite a ride from the train station," Graham admitted with a wry smile. "We had time for a long conversation. Hal told me that the town of Port Freedom really needs a good lawyer. And since I'm soon going to be looking for a new place to work, I thought I'd talk it over with my wife and see if she'd mind relocating."

"Mind? Oh, Graham, are you serious?" Tears shimmered in Paige's eyes. Eyes that were focused on her husband with a look of so much love it was almost blinding.

Graham crossed the room to take her in his arms. Then, holding her close, he offered his hand to Adam.

"I know it's awfully late for this, but I hope you can find it in your heart to forgive me," he said solemnly. "And to accept my thanks for waking me up to my foolishness."

Adam accepted his handshake. "After that confession, how could I not forgive? I think you've finally found your courage, Graham. And judging by the looks of things, I'd say you've more than earned a second chance to make things right."

"Thanks, Adam." Graham turned to Caroline. "I'm really ashamed of my behavior. I'd like to make things right between us."

She glanced at Adam, then at her brother. "If Adam can forgive you, I don't see how I can do less."

Stiffly, Caroline offered her cheek. But when her brother kissed her, she felt a sudden rush of tears. Taking his face between both her hands, she pulled him close and whispered fiercely, "You're all the family I have, Graham. And the love I saw tonight in the eyes of your wife and children made my heart happier than it's been in a very long time."

Graham kissed Caroline again, then wrapped his arm around his wife's shoulders. "If you two don't mind, Paige and I have a lot to talk about. And an awful lot of loving to catch up on."

When they were alone, Caroline walked to the window and looked out at the falling snow glittering in the moonlight. With her back to Adam, she asked, "What did the letter say?"

"It doesn't matter now, Caro."

She shook her head. "I need to know."

"It said that you'd been right. I'd been spinning my wheels here and earning myself nothing but trouble. That I was going away to make my fortune. That I had no right to ask you to wait for me. But that I knew, without a doubt, that you were the only one I'd ever love. And that if you ever wanted to see me you could reach me through Hal Winslow."

"Oh, Adam." She went to him and touched a hand to his cheek. "I feel . . ." A long, deep sigh escaped her lips. "I feel so ashamed. You were so noble, taking the blame for my brother's mistake, just months after your mother's death. And on top of all that heartache, I blamed you. We argued. And you—"

He touched a finger to her lips to silence her. "Don't

you see? You were right. I never would have found myself if all of this hadn't happened."

They stood and listened to the silence of the old house settling around them. "But even though you never tried to reach me, I couldn't stop thinking about you. About this house, this town." He reached into his pocket. "And now that you know everything, I have something to ask you." He removed a small plastic bag. Inside it, something glittered and gleamed. "Most of the stores in Port Freedom were already closed. I found this in the five-and-dime." He held up a gaudy ring. "But I thought, if you accepted, I'd replace it later."

Caroline slipped it on her finger and studied it through a blur of tears. "Oh, no, you won't. I intend to wear it forever."

"Even if it turns your finger green?"

She thought about it, and Adam said, "We could go shopping on Rodeo Drive."

She shot him a quick smile. "I might be bribed by a few expensive baubles. Now what did you want to ask? Are you going to say the words? Or is this all the eloquence I can expect?"

Adam took hold of both her hands and stared down into her eyes. "Caro, I've loved you for such a long, long time. I want to marry you and live with you right here where it all began."

"You'd give up all those glamorous places and live here in Port Freedom?"

Adam brushed his lips over hers. "It's where my heart has always been." He lifted his head. There was a gleam of humor in his eyes. "Of course, once in a while, if you don't object, we could visit the house in Malibu or the flat outside London or the apartment in Paris."

"I suppose I could force myself."

"Is that a yes?"

"Oh, Adam. I feel as though my heart is too full. I feel bursting with happiness." Caroline could no longer contain the laughter that bubbled up in her throat despite the haze of tears. Throwing her arms around his neck, she cried, "Yes. Yes, I love you. Yes, I'll marry you. And, yes, I want to be with you for the rest of my life."

Adam lifted her in his arms and started for the stairs.

"What are you doing?" she asked.

"We have a lot of years to make up for," he muttered against her lips.

As he carried her, she began chuckling against his throat. "Hal Winslow. Santa and his sleigh. That was absolutely brilliant."

"Thank you. I'm glad you like it. He's bringing Amy and Tyler a kitten."

She looked at him in astonishment.

"I told you," he muttered. "Most of the stores were already closed. I was forced to do all my shopping in the five-and-dime and the animal shelter."

"Who says you can't have everything you want in a small town?"

"Who indeed?" Adam nudged open the door to his room and carried Caroline to the bed. With his lips on hers, he murmured, "I know I've found everything. And more. You've even made me believe in happy endings. Merry Christmas, Caro."

She had no chance to respond before his lips claimed hers. But as the kiss deepened, and the familiar rush of heat began, she knew that all her Christmas wishes had been granted. She had her family around her, the love of the only man who had ever owned her heart and a lifetime of dreams to share. This was truly the best Christmas ever.

"Welcome home," she whispered.

Enchanted Christmas

Emma Craig

Noah Partridge has a cold, cold heart. Honey-haired Grace Richardson has heart to spare. Despite her husband's death, she and her young daughter have hung on to life in the Southwestern desert, as well as to a piece of land just outside the settlement of Rio Hondo. Although she does not live on it, Grace clings to that land like a memory, unwilling to give it up even to Noah Partridge, who is determined to buy it out from under her. But something like magic is at work in this desert land: a magic that makes Noah wonder if it is Grace's land he lusts after, or the sweetness of her body and soul. For he longs to believe that her touch holds the warmth that will melt his icy heart.

___52287-X $5.99 US/$6.99 CAN

Dorchester Publishing Co., Inc.
P.O. Box 6640
Wayne, PA 19087-8640

Please add $1.75 for shipping and handling for the first book and $.50 for each book thereafter. NY, NYC, and PA residents, please add appropriate sales tax. No cash, stamps, or C.O.D.s. All orders shipped within 6 weeks via postal service book rate.
Canadian orders require $2.00 extra postage and must be paid in U.S. dollars through a U.S. banking facility.

Name____
Address____
City_________________________State________Zip____________
I have enclosed $ __________ in payment for the checked book(s).
Payment must accompany all orders. ❑ Please send a free catalog.